TWO PERFECT COUPLES

BOOKS BY RENITA D'SILVA

TWO PERFECT COUPLES

RENITA D'SILVA

bookouture

Published by Bookouture in 2025

An imprint of Storyfire Ltd.
Carmelite House
50 Victoria Embankment
London EC4Y 0DZ

www.bookouture.com

The authorised representative in the EEA is Hachette Ireland
8 Castlecourt Centre
Dublin 15 D15 XTP3
Ireland
(email: info@hbgi.ie)

ISBN: 978-1-83525-900-9
eBook ISBN: 978-1-83525-899-6

This book is a work of fiction. Names, characters, businesses, organizations,
places and events other than those clearly in the public domain, are either the
product of the author's imagination or are used fictitiously. Any resemblance to
actual persons, living or dead, events or locales is entirely coincidental.

For my mother, Perdita Hilda D'Silva

The best person I know, and the most generous and gracious.
Who looks for the best in people always.
Who is joyous, celebrating every moment, even those that
test her.
Who lives life by her principles, forgiving those who hurt her,
being kind always, looking beyond grievance to love. Doing good.
Sharing everything she has. Spreading happiness.
A brilliant orator, storyteller, writer, educator, human.
Mumms, you have suffered so much and could have been bitter
about it. But instead you smile, dispensing joy and love and
happiness. You have touched, informed and transformed
innumerable lives, both as a teacher and as a human being. You
are amazing.
I am SO proud that you are my mother.

Everyone is a moon and has a dark side, which he never shows to anybody.

Mark Twain

ONE

GALGIBAGA BEACH, GOA

12:15 a.m.

I gulp down the dregs of the wine in my glass and close my eyes. A gentle breeze soothes my face, fragrant with exotic spices. The relaxed murmur of my husband and friends echoes beside me – banter, laughter and loosened tongues from the drink we've been consuming all evening.

'Isn't it time we checked on them?' Paul asks, stretching languidly, his chair scraping and dislodging mounds of sand, sending tiny crabs scuttling in its wake. 'Whose turn is it?'

'I'll go. I haven't done mine yet.' I am loath to open my eyes.

'I'm sure they're OK.' Lydia's voice made hoarse and throaty by wine. 'All was quiet when I last looked. Rachel said there hadn't been a peep from any of them.'

'I'd better go anyway. It's been, what... an hour since we looked in on them?' I open my eyes and stand, the sand warm beneath my feet, undulating like silk, spun gold, now rife with shadows.

The only lights alleviating the darkness come from the bar shack beside us, the candles at our table, and our cottage a few paces away. The other cottages, spotted along the beach but far enough away so we do not feel crowded, are dark, their inhabitants fast asleep, I imagine.

'Anyone for a top-up?' Paul asks, a slight slur to his voice, swaying on his feet as he stands.

'I'm good, thanks,' Yash and Lydia say at the same time.

'Snap,' Lydia says and they both giggle like teenagers.

Grow up, I think sourly, suddenly feeling extremely weary, wanting, despite the beauty of this quiet, tropical beach, to be anywhere but here, even back home in cold, rainy England.

The hair at the back of my neck rises and I shiver – I'm being watched.

Out of the corner of my eye, I see that it's Paul. I release the breath I was inadvertently holding. Paul waves at me, giving me a thumbs up as he stumbles the few paces to the bar shack.

The barman, who is slumped behind the counter, snoozing with his head in his hands, snaps to attention when Paul approaches. He smiles, his forehead scrunched in concentration as he reads Paul's lips to make sense of his accent. He nods vigorously and holds up two bottles of wine, one red, one white, Paul pointing to the red, which in the dark glows viscous and rich like blood.

The barman's wife – the cook – and their daughter have long since gone home, packing up for the day, after checking that we did not want any more of their spicy fried sardines, their fiery chicken kebabs. Their little girl, bringing plates to our table, had smiled shyly at us.

This afternoon, or, a quick glance at my phone to check the time – *only* the time, determinedly ignoring the flashing message icon – *yesterday* afternoon actually, as it is after midnight, the barman's little one had teamed up with my Mia in the sandcastle competition Yash organised versus Team Zoe & Bella and Team Ajit & Paul (Ajit insisting when his sisters complained of unfairness that since he was the youngest and the only boy, he needed a grown-up to help but he would do most of the work). The barman's daughter was diffident at first but soon she and Mia were at it with gusto, somehow overcoming the language barrier in the manner of kids, and when they won, she had beamed as wide as Mia, displaying wonky teeth. Rachel had not joined in the activities, of course, glued to her phone with that peculiar, focused intensity of teenagers. ('Bring her to paradise and what does she do but stare at that little screen like her life depends upon it,' Paul had joked fondly, Rachel rolling her eyes briefly before her gaze was dragged back to the offending device.)

I shake my woozy head, not wanting to be reminded of the other events of the day, focusing instead on thinking about the children. They are in our cottage, just beyond, fast asleep, dreaming happy dreams, I hope.

The barbecue where the barman's wife was cooking the fish and the chicken has been tidied away, only the scent of smoke, charred meat and grilled chillies perfuming the night air.

My gaze shifts to Paul, as he lurches his way back to the table, holding the bottle triumphantly aloft. I recoil from the malevolent frown distorting his face – he doesn't know I'm watching him.

I look away, down at the sand shifting beneath my feet, pondering what I just saw, my heart thudding in my chest as fear squeezes it in a stranglehold. That alien expression on Paul's face, transforming the man I've known for years into someone I do not recognise.

I look back again at my friends and husband, the candles flickering upon the tabletop dappling shadows onto their faces. Paul is sitting at the table now, topping his glass to the very brim and taking a big sip. His face is set in its usual benign, slightly goofy expression.

It was just my mind, muddy with alcohol, making up things that aren't there, imagining strange expressions on friends' faces. Yet, why does my heart not settle, persisting in beating too fast?

My husband. The planes of Yash's face – familiar, known and yet curiously strange in this murky, shadow-sprinkled light.

Mosquitoes buzz and flies hover around my husband and friends, despite the anti-bug lamps dotting the bar shack and the mosquito-repellent cream we have slathered upon ourselves, all of us experts, in just a couple of days, at periodically slapping them away.

Quarter past midnight. The few other families who had been on this secluded stretch of beach – mostly holidaymakers like us – have left long since.

It is still pleasantly warm – the perfect denouement to what should have been an amazing day. In the UK, the temperature is in the single digits, frost and icy winds predicted, but here, it is lovely, just right.

I walk towards the cottage, stumbling slightly from being suddenly bereft of the illuminating pools of turmeric light from the bar shack. The lights are on in the front room of the cottage; the wire mesh screen that accompanies all the doors and windows here – to dissuade mosquitoes and flies from getting in – is shut, and so is the front door, well, insofar as it can be shut; it sticks, we discovered when we moved into the cottage. From here, through the pixelated haze of the screen, and the glass pane of the door, I can just about make Rachel out. She is lounging on the sofa, headphones on, attention fixed on her phone.

I turn back, briefly – the shack with the barman nodding drowsily at the counter, the table on the sand with its pirouetting candlelight, the murmurs of friends, Yash's bark of a laugh, loud in the susurrating dark.

Yash. My husband. Relaxing with our friends, making the most of our longed-for holiday. Our children sleeping peacefully in the cottage. I should be happy.

I blink to clear my head. I am weaving through the sand. I drank too much after the stresses of the day and I can't seem to remember much after that third glass. Did we have an argument? Yash and I? Lydia, my best friend, and I? I vaguely recall shouting. My accusatory finger in someone's face. Whose? It is all hazy. God, how much did I drink? I don't usually – I tend to get either argumentative or melancholy, or worse, both, when drunk and I don't like it. I think I fell asleep for a bit. Right there on my chair in the sand. When I woke, my throat hoarse, feeling unsettled, as if I was forgetting something, I tried to read what had happened in the others' eyes. But they seemed normal – or as normal as very drunk people can be: Lydia giggly, Paul monotone, Yash over-the-top.

I climb up the steps to the veranda and breeze through the front door, albeit slightly unsteadily, plastering a smile on my face, pushing my unease away.

There's a strange smell in the cottage, pungent, smoky sweet. I shut the wire mesh screen behind me, stand just inside the open front door and sniff, trying to place it.

'Oh, hi, Jo.' Rachel smiles up at me, briefly dragging her eyes away from her phone.

Such a pretty girl, I think. Shame she hides her beauty under that hideous mask of make-up.

I am overcome by the need to gather my three close to me, breathe them in: their scent of innocence and guilelessness. I want them to ground me, to shake off the melancholy that has gripped me despite us holidaying in paradise.

Lizards scuttle in the wooden beams of the cottage overhead and I am once again struck by how different this place is from home. So warm and tropical even past midnight, the breeze drifting in from outside carrying a hint of salt and secrets, the flavour of night and something fruity marred by the peculiar tart odour in the room.

'Can you smell that, Rachel?'

'What?' She scrunches up her nose.

'It stinks in here, don't you think, of... rotting pears. That's it.'

She sniffs. 'I can't smell anything.' She ducks her head, staring intently at her phone but... Is that a blush colouring her face under all that make-up?

From the beach, laughter drifts up to us. I turn, squinting into the darkness. I can just make out our table by the bar shack, lit by the fluctuating glimmer of candles. Two figures have stood up and are running into the water, sending up spray as they splash each other. I can see there are two, but I cannot make out which two. The person left at the table is drinking steadily and watching the others, like I am doing.

The water must be cold now and we are all barely dressed and yet the two figures don't seem to mind.

I shiver, shake my head, clear my throat.

'Everything OK, Rachel?' I ask.

'Yes, it's been very quiet over here.' She yawns widely.

'You tired?'

'I can stay up for another hour, I think, and then I'll go to bed.'

I nod. 'I'll tell the others that we need to call it a day soon.'

She smiles. Her phone beeps and she goes back to tapping it, her fingers jiggling over the keys.

I walk past her, to the door from the living room that emerges into the hallway with corridors coming off either side. The corridor on my left leads to the kitchen on one side and bathroom and toilet on the other, while the one on my right, which I turn into, takes me to the bedrooms.

The cottage has five bedrooms. The first door off the corridor to my left is Rachel's bedroom. Next to it is the room my girls are sharing with Bella, Lydia and Paul's youngest. The adults' bedrooms are opposite – first on the right is Lydia and Paul's and next to it is mine and Yash's. The room farthest along the corridor on the left is Ajit's bedroom. He insisted on having one all to himself, despite my reservations.

'Why don't you share with Zoe?' I'd suggested on our first afternoon here when the kids were excitedly choosing rooms.

'Mum, I'm nearly six!'

'You're not nearly six, cheeky. You've just turned five.'

'Months ago!' Ajit's eyes wide and offended. 'And I sleep on my own at home.'

'Yes, but this is a new place and—'

'Please, Mum.'

Yash had come up to me then, throwing an arm around my shoulders, kissing my cheek, expansive in holiday exuberance, breath smelling of the beer he'd already indulged in. 'What's the harm, if he wants to? We're opposite and the girls are next door.'

'All right.' I'd given in. 'But, Ajit, if you wake in the night, you know where we are. And the girls have a spare bunk – you can always share with them.'

'Wow, Mum, thank you.' Ajit had beamed that smile that seemed to involve his entire body, draping his arms around me – my son is warm and expressive, very open and affectionate. I make the most of his bubbly regard, knowing that far too soon he will not want to be seen with me, that he will shy away from touching me – having watched friends' loving sons morph with little warning into moody and distant teens.

Already he's asserting his independence – he's only recently begun calling me Mum and a little part of me shattered when I first heard it. 'Aren't I your mummy any more?' I asked and he scrunched up his nose and said, 'Only *babies* call their mothers Mummy.'

As I walk down the corridor leading to the bedrooms, a blast of air smacks my face. It is not coming from the front door, the way I came in. Nor from the window adjoining the kitchen at the opposite end to where I am standing. I peer into the gloom in the direction of the bedrooms and see that the window at the far end is open. The wire mesh screen that covers all the windows here is also open and rattling in the salt-stained breeze.

This particular window, unlike the others, is long and low, glass-paned, with a view of the stretch of sand bisected by the road and the coconut plantation beyond.

'Look,' Rachel had said when we were first scoping out the cottage, opening the window wide and climbing through it with scant effort. 'I can walk right through.'

'I can too,' Ajit had said and although he'd needed to stretch a bit, using both hands to hold onto the window ledge, he was able to follow suit.

My boy and Rachel had stood on the strip of sand outside the window, the humid breeze making their hair dance around their faces, and grinned at us. I had shivered then, despite the warmth, and ushered the children – although if I called her that to her face Rachel would be sure to take offence – inside, making sure to shut the window behind them, and the mesh screen too.

And now it's wide open and flapping in the warm night air. I shudder, hugging myself, gripped by fear, my mouth dry suddenly. Didn't Paul shut and secure all the windows when we went down to the beach? Or was it Yash? In any case, one of the men was responsible for locking the windows.

I recall Lydia saying, 'Guys, could you make sure the windows are locked? I don't want any bugs coming in and hounding me in the night.'

'Besides Paul, you mean,' Yash had said, winking suggestively, and Lydia had giggled.

I had walked away then, out onto the veranda, and so I didn't really notice who secured the windows – *if* they did.

Did Lydia open the window when she came to check on the kids before me, because it was getting too warm, perhaps? I remember that we had switched on the ceiling fans in the kids' rooms and adjusted the air conditioning as well so the children wouldn't be too hot.

So why open the window? Especially when Lydia was the one who didn't want to be pestered by flies and bugs.

The room nearest to the open window is Ajit's bedroom. He chose the room because he liked the sheets on the bunks – they were pale yellow and patterned with squares as opposed to plain white. 'White is boring, Mum. The girls have got the boring bedroom. Hee hee.' Ajit had giggled, his eyes sparkling mischievously.

I put my hand on the knob and turn. The door opens soundlessly and I squint, my eyes gradually adjusting to the gloom which is pricked every so often by the blinking red light of the mosquito repellent electric coil.

It is quiet and cool, the ceiling fan whirring tiredly. Two bunk-beds. Sheets bunched on the bottom bunk of the left one, neatly folded and seemingly untouched on the one on my right.

But they are empty. No child in either one.

I blink, once, then again.

No Ajit.

I tell my thumping heart to still. There must be some mistake.

I search the top bunks – perhaps Ajit decided to climb and sleep on the upper bunk, for the novelty factor.

They are empty.

I look under the beds.

Empty.

I open the wardrobe in the corner.

Empty.

I run into the corridor, trying to contain my nerves, which are screaming that something is very wrong.

He'll be in one of the other bedrooms, I tell myself, even as I pray, *Please*.

I open the door to Rachel's bedroom. It is dark. And still. No monotonously rotating ceiling fan. No mosquito coil. I switch on the light, opening the wardrobe, looking under the bed.

There is nobody in here.

Sometimes, Ajit wakes and climbs into bed with us – he has a vivid imagination and is often hounded by nightmares. But that's usually in the early hours of morning. This was why I didn't mind leaving him in Rachel's care, knowing we'd be back before he woke – if he did. He'd slept soundly our first night here, tired out from his holiday adventures, and I'd assumed he'd do so again. But where is he?

Stop panicking, I command myself. He'll be in the girls' room. Won't he?

The fortune teller's crazy eyes loom in my panicked mind, her matted hair a black-grey shield as she held a cowering Ajit to her: 'I'm saving him from a fate worse than death.'

Honestly, Jo, get a grip, I chide myself. But my hand is shaking as I open the door to the girls' bedroom, blinking rapidly as my eyes adjust to the darkness.

Here too, like in Ajit's room – which doesn't contain my boy – the red mosquito repellent coil light pulses periodically. The ceiling fan whirs; the air is cool and smells sugary.

Bella is spread-eagled on her bunk, the blanket tangled with her limbs. Mia has the blanket pulled up to her cheeks and around her ears, only her nose and mouth poking through, as is her way. She lies on her back, mouth slightly open, soft sweet breaths escaping her lips. Zoe is face-down on her bunk, blanket kicked off. Wrestling even in her sleep. My middle child. Fiercely individual, always wanting to carve out a place for herself. Shouting to be heard above the gentle nudging of our eldest and the sweet cajoling of our youngest.

Ajit.

He's not in here.

I check again, just in case. But no. Three bunks occupied. Fourth empty. Wardrobe empty.

Where could he be?

My baby. My Ajit. His little-boy smell: mud and mischief and adventure. His beaming smile that takes over his whole face. The way he throws his arms around me in a hug.

I run out of the girls' room, my fuzzy, alcohol-deadened mind suddenly, scarily sober. The open window.

No. Can't be.

Rachel would have heard something.

Think, Jo.

Another memory of our first afternoon in this cottage, when the kids had run around, excited, exploring, choosing their bedrooms and their roommates, arrives in my spinning, terrified head.

'And which one is your bedroom, Mum?' Ajit had asked, coming up to me, slipping his little hand inside mine.

'This one, darling, opposite you.'

I fling open the door, agitatedly switching on the light.

Nothing. Empty bed, wardrobe with clothes chucked in anyhow, our suitcases beside it, half unpacked. No child.

My boy is here somewhere. He's safe. He *has* to be.

I look under the bed, in the wardrobe, even *inside* the suitcases.

No Ajit.

I return to the living room, panic coursing through my body, my mouth bilious with it. Rachel hasn't moved from the sofa and she does not look up from her phone, oblivious to what's going on and supremely unconcerned in the way of teenagers.

'Rachel, did you open the window at the end of the corridor near the bedrooms?' I ask, as I scan the living room for spaces where a little boy might hide.

'No. I haven't touched anything,' she says, looking away from her phone and at me at last, in that blank way teenagers do, as if she is not really listening, her mind on the conversation she is having with her friends via her phone. 'But that might explain why I've been feeling a draught in here and it's gone cold this past hour.' And, smiling, 'Not like at home, of course. It's been cold for *here*, I meant.' Then, reading the fear I'm trying and failing to hold in, perhaps, 'Wasn't the window always open?'

'I don't think so.' It doesn't look like Ajit's in the cottage. Where could he *be*? 'Have you moved from here at all?' I ask as I check under the sofa. No Ajit.

Rachel finally gives me her full attention. 'I went to the loo a couple of times.' She nods towards the door off the living room, which emerges into the hallway branching into two corridors, the one on the left leading to the kitchen, bathroom and toilet and the one on the right to the bedrooms. 'What are you doing, Jo?' she asks as I look behind the sofa.

No Ajit.

I ignore Rachel's question, ask another of my own, heart thudding in my chest. 'Did you check on the children?'

She nods. 'Once since Mum came. I looked in on them on my way back from the loo. They were fast asleep.'

The loo. Of course, I think, relief flooding my mouth, nectar-sweet. Ajit will be in there. I've been silly, panicking for nothing when I should have checked first. I chide myself for my paranoia as I make my way to the loo. It's been a long day, that fortune teller's ominous prediction – I shudder involuntarily – and those graves – *don't think about that* – have thrown me, left me feeling nervy.

I fling open the door, calling, 'Ajit, love?' convinced I will see my boy. But... Ajit is not in the loo. Oh dear God, where on earth is he then? I bend over double, trying to catch my breath that is stuck somewhere in my choked-up chest.

He's here somewhere, hiding, waiting for you to find him, my conscience soothes. Somehow, I gather my breath and stand back up, resume my search for my son.

I look in Lydia and Paul's room, the bathroom, the kitchen, switching on lights willy-nilly.

'What's the matter, Jo?' Rachel asks as I rush back into the living room, scour the veranda. She actually sets down her phone, which I have never seen her do – she is glued to that thing. Even in the midst of my panic, I notice this.

And just like that, everything else flies from my mind except what I cannot comprehend, can't get my head around. 'Ajit. I... I can't find Ajit.'

And it is when I say those horrible words out loud, when I see the shock on Rachel's face, followed by the incredulity, the disbelief, the distress as what I'm saying sinks in, that I crumple.

TWO

12:30 a.m.

Rachel is flying out into the darkness to get the others, a little girl again, all traces of sullen teen gone.

I look everywhere I can think of. Under the sink in the kitchen. Even in the fridge. I run back to the bedrooms, check them again. I run to the open window – why, how, is it open? – look outside. The sand is silky velvet, the road quiet. Cicadas screech and coconut palms wave and the sea purrs and growls as it ebbs and surges.

My son is nowhere to be seen. How can he be just... gone?

The front door slams open, and Yash is beside me, throwing his arms around me, speaking too loudly, his voice throbbing with the barely reined-in panic I'm experiencing. 'Is it true what Rachel said about Ajit?'

My husband is wet. Cold droplets clinging to his body, oozing salt and misgiving, the acid tang of drink and befuddlement, the algae and brine flavour of the sea.

I cannot stop shivering and I cannot find my voice. I nod, my desperate gaze meeting Yash's.

He lets go of me, his face haggard, blanched of colour. Then he is running, sprinting down the corridor, not bothering to be quiet. His voice, raised in a shrill pitch that I haven't heard before, coloured by anxiety. 'Ajit, sweetheart, where are you?'

I hear Mia call, 'Dad?'

He likes to play hide-and-seek, I think, my heart rising in hope despite knowing that I've checked every corner of this cottage to no avail. Perhaps I missed something – a small space only Ajit can squeeze into and he's waiting there for one of us to find him. After a bit, he will tire of hiding, pop out and say, 'Fooled you, Mum! That's the best hiding place ever!' Let this be what he is doing. *Please.*

I am aware of Lydia and Paul also running into the kids' bedrooms, opening doors, checking every room, calling for Ajit.

I search the living room. Again. Behind the sofa. Underneath the dining table. My heart thudding in fear and hope. He's hiding somewhere, surely? He'll be found just now, either by myself or one of the others.

Rachel looks at me, her gaze huge and worried, looking for reassurance that I cannot give.

Both the front door and the mosquito mesh screen are wide open – nobody having bothered to close them when they rushed in. The beach shimmers before me, shadowy and secretive. The silky-sweet call of waves, so tantalising to a child, unaware of their duplicitous nature, the dangers they conceal beneath their mischievous white-capped froth.

I shudder, wrapping my arms around myself, wishing it was my son I was holding.

I turn away from the open door, the gleaming swell of seductive ocean. Could Ajit have slipped out, walked to the beach? He is such an adventurous little boy and he has always loved the sea. He was amazed by how warm the water was when we first went in. He had turned to me, eyes sparkling, as he danced among the waves. 'Mum! This is amazing! The best holiday ever!' So easily pleased. Such a happy child.

He cannot swim. Not properly. Not without his armbands or one of us beside him, keeping a vigilant eye. I picture his little body tossed about on the waves, dashing against the rocks.

No.

'Who opened the window?' I hear Lydia ask. 'Was it always open?'

So Lydia didn't open it when she came to check on them. Then who did?

And here I was thinking the children were safe in their beds, and the only way out of the cottage was past Rachel and through the front door, which we *could* (just about) see from where we were sitting on the beach.

'Ajit,' Paul calls in his blustery, florid voice. 'Where are you?'

'He couldn't have climbed out, could he?' Yash's voice splashed yellow with alarm.

My nimble five-year-old. I recall when he first learned to crawl. I knew he was capable of turning over onto his tummy when I laid him down on his back, but I wasn't aware he could move yet. He was beside me on his play mat on the living-room floor. I turned around to tidy up some toys and when I looked back, he was halfway across the room. He had stopped at the other end and grinned at me, his toothless, charming, irresistible grin.

He is always climbing, running, jumping, skipping; active, never still. How did I assume he would sleep quietly, in one place, on the second night of our holiday, when, in his own words, he was, 'so excited I could burst, Mum'?

Please God.

As if prayer was insurance against bad things happening to you.

I double over, holding my stomach.

'Mum, do you have a tummy ache?' It is Zoe, her voice insistent, her sleep-tinted eyes huge with concern. 'Are you ill? Why're all the lights on?'

Then Mia, rubbing her eyes, clutching Lamby, the soft toy she needs to fall asleep. 'What happened? Why is everyone calling for Ajit? Is he hiding?'

My two girls, looking fragile, so very young in their pyjamas – flowery pink for Mia, black stars against a grey background for Zoe, who eschews everything pink just because Mia likes it – their tired, confused faces, drowsy limbs.

Ajit had insisted on wearing his favourite SpongeBob pyjamas last night even though I couldn't find them initially. They weren't in the wardrobe – I had to upturn all of our suitcases. There was a moment of anxiety, when I thought I'd forgotten to pack them. His face was scrunched up all ready to cry, when I found them tucked among Mia's T-shirts.

'Thank you, Mum.' He'd grinned, tears forgotten, flinging his arms around me. My impulsive, affectionate boy. 'You're the best mum in the world.'

No, I'm not, Ajit. I abandon you when you are at your most vulnerable, fast asleep in a strange bed in an unfamiliar place. I'm sorry, son. So sorry.

'Don't you think...' Paul's voice is uncharacteristically hesitant. 'We... Shouldn't we call the police?'

The police.

Yash and I stare at each other as the words slip between us, sitting squat upon my heart, weighing it down even further.

The police.

That will make it official. It means... It means there is a possibility...

In our shared gaze, we see all the things that could happen to our baby, that might already have happened.

No, I want to scream.

'Yes.' Yash's voice stumbles on the word.

No.

Why didn't I check on the kids earlier? Why did we wait so long after Lydia looked in on them? Why did I leave my children at all and go to the beach with the others?

THREE

12:45 a.m.

'But how do we go about calling the police here?' Lydia asks.

'The barman will know,' Paul says. 'He volunteered to search the cottage surrounds for Ajit when Rachel came to fetch us. I'll ask him.'

He sounds relieved to have something to do. Then he's gone.

'I'm just popping outside to look around the cottage,' Yash calls, wild-eyed as he rushes past us and out the front door, into the night.

My son is not in his bed, peacefully sleeping. He's not anywhere in this cottage. Where is he?

My stomach dips and I feel sick.

It is a nightmare. It has to be. I will wake any moment and it will be over. Ajit will be in my arms. I will be breathing in his soft, clean scent. The mint shampoo in his hair which I scrubbed just a few hours ago to rid it of the sand that had accumulated in just a short time on the beach.

'Stay here with Lydia and Rachel a minute, darlings,' I tell my girls and follow Yash outside.

The beach is dark, secluded, quiet. So very vast. I feel despair judder through my body, rooting it to the spot. How can we find Ajit here?

But, my mind rationalises, refusing to entertain the possibility that he's lost, *he's only small*. Even if he came out here, during that short window of time between when Rachel checked on the children and he was safely in bed and when I did, he wouldn't have got far.

The only light comes from the barman's shack, a single lantern casting a liquid yellow glow. I can just make out Paul standing next to the barman, his phone glued to his ear. Calling the police.

I shudder.

The sea beguiles and whispers with gentle murmurs as it flows and recedes, the white caps just visible in the darkness, the violet sky above pierced here and there with pearl drops of stars. Ajit couldn't have come towards where we were sitting, beside the shack – one of us would have seen him.

Yash is running along the beach to the left of the cottage, so I turn to the right.

I circle our cottage, calling for my boy, softly. There's the odd coconut tree beside the road, but otherwise the beach is wide open. No hiding places.

I come to the back of the cottage, stand outside the open window. I can look into the cottage from here – the corridor, lit up but empty, bedroom doors open. Everyone must be in the living room.

Did someone else stand here, watching? Waiting for the right time to grab my son?

I shiver, hugging myself. *No, please, no.*

I thought my children were safe, in a cottage in a quiet holiday resort, mere metres away from where we sat, but they were incredibly vulnerable. So defenceless. How could I have left them?

Yash, circling the cottage from the other side, joins me. He is panting.

My eyes have adjusted to the dark now and I see the same expression of terror and despair on his face that I'm sure is on mine. We look at each other and at the road behind us, so close to the open window. We read the thought in each other's terrified eyes that we cannot voice.

Someone could have waited out here in a car until the coast was clear, climbed in through the window, snatched Ajit and driven off and we would be none the wiser.

No. I cannot entertain the possibility. I cannot.

We *will* find him. And if not us, then the police will. He's not taken. He's hiding.

'I'm going to look in the coconut grove,' Yash says and disappears across the road and into the copse of trees beyond, which loom shadowy and forbidding.

The very same coconut grove where I found the graves... I shudder. Were they a premonition? A warning?

Don't think like that.

Ajit wouldn't have gone there of his own accord, I am thinking. He's afraid of the dark.

So many places for him to have disappeared to, and we... we thought he was safe.

I will never forgive myself, when we find him – and we *will* – for leaving my children alone, under the protection of a fourteen-year-old. What was I thinking?

'He doesn't appear to be in there.' Yash is back, eyes gleaming wild in the sinister darkness.

'What do you mean, *appear* to be in there?'

'I couldn't see much. We need to search in daylight.'

Daylight. I shiver. Ajit will be found before then, surely?

'He wouldn't have gone in there by himself. It's too dark,' I say.

'I know.' Yash's eyes meet mine, haunted with the endless possibilities we are shying away from.

'Where is he, Yash?' I whisper. 'Where is our boy?'

My husband gathers me in his arms as I sob my uncomprehending grief into the night.

FOUR

'Mum? Is Ajit outside? In the dark?' Mia's lower lip wobbles. Although, at nine, she is the oldest of my three, she's also the most sensitive. She has been waiting by the door for Yash and myself to return, Paul arriving at the same time, having called the police.

In my husband's embrace, which reeked of fear, I had briefly indulged my anguish, then wiped my eyes fiercely. I had no right to cry. I was to blame, having allowed this to happen. I had sniffed, swallowed my sobs, said to Yash, 'We should go back.' A huge part of me hoping, *wishing*, Ajit would have been found when we returned.

But he's not here.

'I'm going to look for him while we wait for the police,' Paul says and runs outside.

The snarl and roar of the sea – so very close. How easily it can trap human beings, their bodies folding, yielding, puppet-slack...

I shudder inwardly, even as I open my arms and my girls

tumble into them, although they have recently begun resisting hugs, especially at the school gates, in front of their friends.

Lydia is on the sofa, her skin, the gleaming alabaster of polished marble, dotted with salt where droplets of seawater have dried, her arms around her girls, one on either side, Rachel, usually not seen dead hugging her mum, subjecting herself to her embrace.

Lydia catches my eye, her blue eyes bright with anxiety, her blonde hair wet but sleek despite it, a swaying curtain framing her heart-shaped face, which is pale and drawn now. We are so different – her svelte figure that belies her age, defies having given birth to two kids, so unlike mine; she, cool and calm while I am nervous and anxious about the smallest thing; she, a confident go-getter, me, insecure, always worrying – and yet, we are best friends.

Of course we've had our ups and downs. But Lydia has been there for me at my worst. She is the keeper of my secrets, knows me warts and all and loves me despite it. She and Paul are our oldest friends and given the lack of family on both Yash's side and mine, they *are* family. I have not been envious of her before – well, not *really*. I have wished for her body, her looks, her self-belief and positive attitude every so often, but I've never been truly jealous of her. Now, however, I am. Deeply, furiously, desperately envious. For she has both of her children. While I have lost one of mine.

No. No. We *will* find him.

Won't we?

The front door opens and I wish, fiercely, that it is Ajit.

It is Paul. Empty-handed.

Nevertheless, I ask, unable to quell the tremor in my voice, 'He wasn't outside?'

Paul shakes his head, his gaze raw, agonised. 'Not in the immediate surrounds. But the barman is searching just in case.'

There *must* be some mistake. Somewhere we haven't looked.

Where could he be? He's only little. He couldn't have got far.

So why didn't we find him?

And then, a thought. Could that crazy fortune teller have taken him?

Get a grip. She didn't know where we were staying.

But she could have followed...

No. No. There hadn't been anyone following us. I had checked, repeatedly, my whole being on hyper alert.

But you've been worried someone has been stalk—

Stop this. Concentrate on finding Ajit, I tell myself as firmly as I can in the midst of my terror.

Everyone seems to have congregated in the living room suddenly and it feels too small and claustrophobic, smelling acrid, of distress and upset.

'Ow, Mum, you're holding too tight,' Zoe, fiercely independent even at eight, complains, wriggling in my arms.

In my panicked anguish, I've been crushing my girls to me.

Bella is sitting on the sofa beside Lydia, Rachel on Lydia's other side, both girls looking flabbergasted, apprehensive. Pale as wisps of fog caught in the headlights of a car.

'Do you think he... might have climbed out of the window?' Lydia asks, wringing her hands.

My heart clenches in fresh terror as my friend voices the possibility I've tried to shy away from. I think of the road, how someone could have been waiting there, unseen by us. So close to my beloved children. I think of the coconut grove beyond...

'We were sitting right there. We would have seen him if he walked onto the beach?' Paul says, but the last part of his sentence is raised in question, asking us for confirmation.

Would we? Myself and Lydia were the only ones facing the cottage; Yash and Paul were turned away from it and facing us.

We were all drunk. I was keeping my eyes closed much of the time, trying not to dwell on the events of the day. I even fell asleep for a while, I think, after the confrontation that may or may not have happened. Why can't I remember?

Oh, oh, oh. I thought my children were safe in here, with Rachel, and us just outside. How could I have been so naive, so *careless* about my children's safety?

'Why is the window open? You locked it, didn't you, Yash, mate?' Paul says.

'Perhaps it doesn't shut properly, like the front door,' Lydia says, her voice small and cowed.

'Did you see anything, Jo, when you went around the cottage this evening after Lydia had checked on the kids?' Paul asks. 'Was the window open then?'

What is he talking about?

'I didn't come back into the cottage tonight, before now,' I snap.

'Not *to* the cottage. Behind it,' Paul says.

'I haven't been near the cottage since we went down to the beach after putting the kids to bed, except just now when I discovered that Ajit...' I shiver as the reality of the empty bed, my missing child, slams me afresh.

'Um, actually, Jo...' It's Rachel. Hesitant. Eyes wide and worried. 'I did see you. I thought you were coming up to the cottage. I waved. But you ignored me, went off the path and around the cottage. I assumed you were just stretching your legs.'

'What? When was this?' Why don't I remember?

I look to Lydia and Yash for confirmation.

'We went for a swim. It must have been then,' Lydia says.

I think of the time I cannot recall or account for. I fell asleep. Didn't I? I woke with a hoarse throat; the soreness you get after a bout of yelling. The fierce, throbbing desire to get away, run. Had I acted upon it? Why did I go around the cottage? Did I notice the window? Was it open? Did *I* open it? My head aches from trying to grab at facts that elude me.

'I *cannot* remember,' I say, my voice desperate, frustrated.

'It's all right.' Yash puts his arm around me.

I cannot take comfort from it. We both know it's not all right. *Nothing* is.

'How can he be missing?' Yash asks, sounding both perplexed and petrified.

Missing. One small word encompassing infinite dread.

I don't know where he is. This child who can't fall asleep unless I read him a bedtime story.

'Mum, I'm scared,' Mia whispers into my chest.

I'm scared too, terrified.

'Shh, it's OK,' I say, automatically offering comfort. Although, of course, it will be OK only when my boy comes back, fits into my arms in the space that is bereft without him, waiting for him.

'But where is Ajit?' Mia asks.

How to answer Mia? What do I say?

'We've searched the cottage. I... We... don't think he's in here, right?' Yash looks round at each of us, his voice is tight with fear.

I clasp my girls to me. If he isn't here, then where is my boy?

'He must be outside. We might have missed something when we looked around just now. He... he'll be frightened.'

And at Yash's words, my whole being is gripped afresh by raw, burning fear.

My baby. He's afraid of the dark, although he doesn't like to admit it. 'I'm not!' he always says when the girls accuse him of being a scaredy-cat. His voice aiming for indignant but sounding tremulous.

'We'll search again. Paul, you go in that direction all the way down to the beach. I'll look by the bar and beyond. Lydia, would you look behind the cottage, please?' Yash turns to me.

'Jo, stay here with the kids, will you? One of us should be here in any case. If... when he comes back.'

'But...' *I want to come too*, I want to say. I'll search for my boy, not give up until I find him and he's safe in my arms. I will never let him out of my sight again.

But one of us needs to be here with the kids. We left them with Rachel and...

I read all of this in Yash's gaze. I nod and he nods back – everything conveyed without words, the hallmark of a long marriage.

He rushes outside, Paul and Lydia following, swallowed up by the night now the bar shack is in darkness.

I look at the waves tossing against the rocks, the dark beach. The sand with its scuttling crabs that so fascinated my boy. If I close my eyes, I can see him in his swimming trunks, his compact little body glistening with droplets, bent double on the sand, teasing the crabs with a twig he'd found on the beach. 'These crabs are cute, Mum, not like mean Mr. Krabs at all.' Shaking his head and grinning at me. 'Do you know, Mum, that SpongeBob and Patrick and Sandy and Mr. Krabs and Plankton all live under here?' He had laughed as he gambolled among the waves.

'Yes, but you and I can't live in the ocean, as we can't breathe underwater,' I had warned.

'Sandy can't either. That's why she has to wear a helmet and an astronaut suit.'

'Well, we don't have that, so don't you go trying.'

'I know, Mum!' Rolling his eyes and shaking his head, affording me a glimpse into the teenager he would one day become.

He will get a chance to become a teenager, won't he?

Don't think that way. Don't go there. They'll find him.

Did he wake up and, finding the window open – why didn't I double-check that it was locked? – climb out of it and set off on an adventure? Was the pull of the sea strong enough that he was able to brave the scary dark?

'Where is Ajit, Mum?' Mia asks again, speaking out loud the thought that is ricocheting in my head.

What do I tell her?

'My mum and dad and your dad are out looking for him. They'll find him, won't they, Jo?' Bella speaks up from the sofa, her voice small and lost-sounding. She has curled herself into a ball, as if trying to disappear into the sofa, her face bleached of colour, the washed-out cream of sky in the wake of a snowstorm.

'Bella, Mia, Zoe?' I say.

They look at me, three small, worried faces.

'Did you hear anything, see anything?' I ask.

'No,' Zoe and Bella say in unison, while Mia shakes her head, no.

'We were fast asleep,' Zoe adds.

I turn to Rachel. 'Did he come to you, Rach?'

'No,' Rachel says. 'None of them did. And I didn't hear anything either.'

'Are you sure?' There's something in Rachel's eyes – a shadow, the bruised purple wash of guilt.

'Yes.' But she won't meet my eye, worrying her top instead.

There's something she's not telling me, I'm sure of it. It might not be important, but, equally, it might be crucial in finding my boy. I *want* to know what she knows. But Rachel appears really scared, like the child she is, despite the Goth get-up. I can't push her – this is traumatic for her, for all the girls. I'll ask Lydia to talk to her. Perhaps she'll tell her mother, whatever it is, and *soon*.

How is it fair that Lydia and Paul have all their children safe while I don't?

It's an uncharitable thought and I try to push it away as soon as I think it, my overwrought mind centring on Ajit again.

A sudden thought pushes to the forefront, nudging everything else away — something that has been nagging at me since I discovered my boy missing from his bed. Ajit's SpongeBob soft toy that Yash won for him at Chessington World of Adventures last year.

I close my eyes as the memory of that day assaults me. Yash taking time off during half-term to accompany us, the children excited and talking nineteen to the dozen. The toffee and caramel scent of popcorn and doughnuts, the whirr and drone of rollercoasters mingling with the delighted screams of Zoe and Yash, the only ones among us brave enough to ride on them. Feeding the animals at the zoo, the slimy slither of eager animal tongues, the contented natter and high-pitched laughter of our happy children. The highlight of the day was Yash winning the toy for Ajit, by netting the ball in the basket three times in a row.

That SpongeBob is something Ajit is never without.

It wasn't on the bed, I'm sure. Ajit's sheet was bunched but he wasn't on his bed and neither was SpongeBob. He must have taken it with him. But where?

He's only wearing short-sleeved pyjamas. He will be cold at this time of night. And his feet... His feet.

'Just a minute, my darlings.' I dislodge my girls gently from my lap. Once bereft of their warmth, I start to shiver uncontrollably. But I'm on a mission.

Hugging my arms around myself, I run down the corridor and into his room. Ajit's room which does not contain my son. I search under the bed, on the bunks, like I did just a few minutes previously when I discovered my son's absence and my world imploded. His favourite teddy bear is here but his slippers are not and neither is SpongeBob.

A sliver of relief pierces the panic in my heart. He is wearing slippers. So he got up, took his SpongeBob, wore his slippers and climbed out the window. He left of his own accord — perhaps he wanted to find Yash and me. It's a scenario better than any of the gruesome others I've been picturing. Any minute now one of the others will find him.

They *will*.

Paul says I walked past the cottage earlier. Rachel confirms it. I rack my brains, but much of the evening is a frustrating blank. Why can't I remember? And what else might I have done that I also cannot recall? Did I see anything then? Did Ajit see me and come to me? Did *I* open the window? I'm so angry with myself, hot tears stabbing my eyes. Why did I drink so much?

I walk into the living room and my girls immediately climb back onto my lap. Mia is sucking her thumb, a habit she has long outgrown. Zoe is biting her lower lip and looking at me with huge, anxious eyes. I gather them both to me, kiss the tops of their heads.

Outside, I notice wavering bursts of light – Yash, Lydia, Paul, the barman, searching for Ajit using the torch apps on their phones.

To a little boy enamoured with SpongeBob, how would the beach look? A little boy unable to sleep, climbing out the open window and setting off on an adventure. Fireflies, pinpricks of light, guiding the way, penetrating the darkness he is afraid of. Ajit would have thought them magical.

My baby. In slippers. They won't work on the sand. He won't have got far. Hopefully soon, one of the others will come running inside, holding him, grinning from ear to ear, saying, 'Look who I found wandering on the beach!'

The thought does not still my frantic heart. I will only relax when Ajit is here, beside my girls, snug within the protection of my arms.

Did someone take him?

And then an even more dreadful, if possible, worry seizes my heart, causing me to hug my girls tighter. Will whoever took Ajit come back for my girls?

No. Not if I have anything to do with it.

I should have been here all along. With my children. Watching over them.

But I went along with the others and spent the evening down at the beach, leaving my precious babes in the care of a fourteen-year-old. I had too much to drink and went for a wander around the cottage that I cannot for the life of me remember.

I hold my girls, gleaning comfort from their innocent trust, their sweet warmth. And I wait, dread keeping time with my thundering heart.

FIVE

DAY 1

2:00 a.m.

Police everywhere, shouting orders, bagging evidence, riding roughshod over the holiday cottage into which we arrived with such excitement just the day before yesterday.

I recall Ajit running up the steps, his mouth an O of delight as he took in the veranda, the many rooms, the sand, the sea. 'Mum, can we go to the beach, can we, can we...?' he had begged, skipping from foot to foot in excitement, almost as soon as he and his sisters had claimed their bedrooms and I had deposited our bags in the room that was to be mine and Yash's.

I had nodded and he had jumped, clapping his hands, before rummaging through the bags for his swimming shorts. He had even found his sisters' swimsuits for them, so as not to waste a precious minute – and he had run round the living room unable to sit still as he waited for the girls to emerge from the bathroom.

'They take so long to change,' he had huffed and Lydia and I had laughed.

Then we had taken the kids to the beach, the sun beating

down on our heads, a welcome change from the freezing grey skies we had left behind – Ajit's hand in mine, urging me to run with him all the way, stopping every once in a while to marvel at something or pick something up: the crabs, a seashell, a perfectly shaped pebble.

We had paddled in the sea, the warm water lapping at our feet in a welcoming caress. Did I warn him then of how dangerous the sea could be, how temperamental?

I can't remember.

He refused to wear the armbands he needs to swim, not wanting to appear babyish in front of Rachel, whom he adores. They've always shared a special bond, those two, Rachel so patient with him, more kind to him than she is to her sister.

Ajit did not even want me to pack the armbands, but I did anyway. They are in our bedroom, with all of our suitcases. Is my boy out there in the sea without them? I shiver, hugging myself, but it is no comfort.

Once the police arrived, we were all, Lydia, Paul and their girls included, shepherded, kindly but firmly, by a few of the policemen to a holiday cottage a few paces down the beach, which is empty and which the police had already checked to make sure Ajit wasn't in there. Hiding or hidden by someone? I wondered, shivering. I can't stop shivering.

'We will let you back into your cottage once we've completed our investigation,' the policemen promised.

Mia and Zoe are asleep in one of the bedrooms, tired out after their broken and eventful night. I'm grateful for it, for I don't know how to answer their increasingly worried queries about their brother, the police and why they have had to move from *their* cottage to another.

Yash had returned from outdoors after searching for Ajit, defeated, to find the cottage full of police and the girls' heads drooping against my chest. He had carried first Mia and then Zoe to the cottage we had been moved into, making sure one of the policemen kept watch on Mia while he came back for Zoe.

We had stood side by side, Yash and I, watching our daughters, their even breaths, their perfect eyelashes fanning pink-tipped rounded cheeks, and I could have stood there forever, or at least until Ajit was found.

But terrible reality intervened and Yash had been called away first and myself almost immediately after, by a different policeman, to be questioned – separately – about what had happened and to provide information about Ajit to help the police with their search.

'Mrs Kumar,' a kind voice says. 'May I have a word?'

A policeman I vaguely recognise interrupts my melancholy musing.

'I've already talked to one of your colleagues.'

'I know, but I'd like to go over everything again in more detail, if you don't mind.' His English is very good, better than that of his colleague whom I spoke with earlier, each word carefully enunciated. 'Can we talk in private?'

Too spent to argue, I follow him into one of the empty bedrooms in this cottage. As I do, I recall an article I read recently about crime in India – I had been reading anything and everything that mentioned India in the lead-up to our holiday. I had been alarmed when the article claimed that much of the time, policemen in India were in cahoots with criminals, taking bribes and turning a blind eye.

I had brought it up with Yash, a tad hesitantly. Yash's parents were first-generation immigrants from Gujarat; they'd moved to the UK for better prospects before Yash was born. They had worked hard and expected the same from their only son.

'Which was fair enough,' Yash told me, 'but they were also very strict, rigid and uncompromising, punishing me if I fell short of their exacting standards. Whatever I achieved, it was never enough, I could always do better.' A muscle in his jaw twitching, eyes stark with pain.

The result was that as soon as he was old enough, Yash had rebelled against his parents and Indian culture, because 'they kept shoving it in my face. Their excuse when I got ninety-eight instead of the expected one hundred: "Not good enough for an Indian."' Yash's voice bitter.

When Yash was younger and more pliable, his parents couldn't afford to visit India. When they finally earned enough to spend on tickets, Yash refused to go. So this holiday was, like mine, his first visit to the land his parents hailed from.

While Yash had eschewed his Indian heritage when his parents were alive, now he embraced it. He was also, understandably, very protective of the country his parents were from and its people. That is why I had been tentative when I'd discussed with him the article I'd read about the police here taking bribes.

He had said, gently enough, 'Jo, that article sounds very biased. And, in any case, love, we are going on *holiday*. A once-in-a-lifetime break. We'll be spending all our time on a luxurious, secluded beach. I don't think we'll have any encounters with the police; at least, I hope not. Try not to worry, please?'

He'd opened his arms and I'd gone into them but, even as he'd kissed me and I'd kissed him back, I couldn't help feeling a wee bit patronised, treated like he would one of the kids: 'Here, a hug and a kiss, that'll make it better.' And at the back of my mind, the anonymous texts I'd been receiving, their insinuations about my husband festering, eating away at me, making me doubt, wonder, question everything.

This was why I had been looking forward to this holiday. A break from the constant creepy feeling of being followed, spied upon, the hairs at the back of my neck always standing on alert; the chance to recharge with my family, away from prying eyes and probing, horrible, accusatory, lying messages.

I haven't told Yash about the stalking, how I've felt as if someone has been watching me, clocking my every move. He'd only ask if I was taking my medication, I've reasoned. He'd urge me to see my counsellor again. I don't want to see her – the medication she prescribed made me groggy, as if I was not quite all there when I wanted to be present for my children, savour every minute with them.

But I didn't, did I? I left my kids in a holiday cottage in an unfamiliar country in the care of a fourteen-year-old and sat on the beach drowning my woes in drink, so much so that I cannot recall going for an amble around the cottage about the time Ajit went missing. Did I see anything? Why can't I remember? How could I have been so irresponsible?

As if sensing my angst, the policeman questioning me says firmly, 'We have men searching the surrounding area. We will find Ajit.'

He sounds so confident that, despite my misgivings about Indian police, I experience a kindling of hope. *We will find Ajit.* I imagine gathering my son in my arms, breathing in his familiar little-boy warmth. Once he is safely with me, I will never again let him out of my sight.

'Do you mind if I close the door?' the policeman asks.

I shake my head, no.

The policeman is short – shorter than me, even, and I'm only five foot five. He is balding, his oiled, sparse hair combed sideways to cover the bald spot, and moustachioed. His moustache is impressive, contrasting magnificently with the meagre hair on his head. Ajit would have liked that. Ajit...

'I... I'm sorry, I've forgotten your name.'

When they came into the cottage from where Ajit went missing, a khaki-clad bustling mass making my son's disappearance – his *disappearance*; surely that means he will reappear soon? – official, they had all introduced themselves, but everything was a blur as I digested the fact that this was truly happening. The police were involved.

'I'm Inspector Sharma and I am in charge of this investigation. I understand you've already supplied information about Ajit to one of my colleagues – his height, weight, age, what he was wearing, distinguishing features, any health issues?'

'Yes.'

'And a recent picture of Ajit?'

'My husband texted the pictures to one of your colleagues.' My voice catches as I realise, afresh, that they were taken just a few hours ago. Oh, what I wouldn't give to go back to those blissful hours! I swallow down bile and regret and ache. 'There were a couple of close-ups of Ajit.' Ajit grinning, showing off the gaps in his mouth – the milk teeth he's lost. The adult versions are yet to grow back.

'Ma'am,' the inspector says, 'Mr and Mrs King both mentioned you going for a walk around the cottage after Mrs King had checked on the kids. Did you notice anything out of the ordinary?'

I twist my hands together in my lap, even as I try, once again, to urge my memory to give me *something*. Anything. But it's a blank. Tears of frustration and upset sting my eyes. 'I don't remember. My memory of the whole evening is patchy.'

The inspector nods impassively. No judgement in his gaze as he asks, 'Can you recall if the window was open by any cha—'

'No. It's all a blank.' My voice is shrill with annoyance at myself for my actions. Why did I drink so much? How can I not remember when it is *crucial* to my son's well-being?

'If and when you do remember, please let myself or one of my men know,' he says calmly.

'Yes,' I say, willing my memory to cooperate. *Come on.* But all I remember is waking up with a hoarse throat at the table by the bar shack beside my husband and friends, and weaving my way to the cottage and into the nightmare of my son missing from his bed...

'Ma'am, in the lead-up to Ajit going missing, did anything unusual happen, anything that might have given you cause for worry?' the inspector is saying.

'Well...' I pause.

Do I tell him about the fortune teller? The graves? The texts I've been getting, even here? I have tried to dismiss them, although they are seared in my mind. What if they were actually threats? What if they are connected to Ajit going missing?

Too late I understand that I shouldn't have deleted them. But the kids sometimes borrow my phone to play games and I did not want them to inadvertently read those horrible words.

The kids... Ajit...

I might not trust this man, but he is, for now, our main hope of finding my son. I read somewhere that the first few hours are crucial when children go missing. If this man doesn't deliver upon his promise to do everything in his power to find Ajit, I'll go to the UK police, but right now, I will believe him. I have to.

And if the text messages have anything to do with this...

'I've been receiving text messages from a withheld number,' I say.

The inspector leans forward, pen poised over his notebook. 'Oh?'

'The first one arrived three weeks ago...'

SIX

THREE WEEKS PREVIOUSLY

The text comes as I'm about to do the school run.

Ajit only started school in September and needs help getting ready. But this morning, the girls are playing up as well.

'Hurry up, girls, we're running late. Zoe, have you brushed your hair? You'll have to tie it back, love, they sent that letter about nits, remember? You don't want them in your hair, do you?'

Zoe makes a face at the mention of nits and starts hunting for a scrunchie.

'Mum, I can't find my shoes,' Mia calls from upstairs.

'I spilled cereal on my book bag.' Ajit's voice and eyes are wet with tears.

Aargh. I want to scream, to pull my hair out. At this rate we'll *never* get to school on time. I will, once again, be pulled up by a disapproving Mrs B (who personally welcomes each and every one of the pupils into 'her' school), in front of all the other bang-on-time mums gossiping in their huddles after seeing their treasures safely in.

I could really do with an extra pair of hands. Where is Yash when I need him? Working. Always working. And when I complain: 'I'm doing it for you and the kids, Jo.' Looking at me with wounded eyes.

The exact same look Ajit is giving me right now.

I gather him close, breathing in his milk and chocolate scent, while shouting instructions to my other two. I wipe his sticky fingers and his dear little face. 'Chin up, sweetheart. I'll make sure your book bag is good as new.'

The clock in the hall chimes half past. We really should leave *now*. The school is a good ten-minute walk – run – away.

I scrub off the congealing lumps of soggy crunchy-nut from the book bag, which feels suspiciously light. 'Ajit, where's your reading diary? Shouldn't it be in here?'

'Can't find it, Mum. I looked *everywhere*.'

'Oh dear. Too late now. I'll bring it in later, love.'

'But, Mum...' His lower lip trembling, preparatory to fresh tears.

'I promise I'll drop you off and come right back for it. But we really must set off now, sweetheart, you don't want another late tick in the register, do you?'

Ajit shakes his head, eyes brimming. My heart goes out to him, my boy who loves school and wants to do everything right.

'Give your nose a blow, there's a good boy. Zoe, Mia, come on now or we're leaving without you.' I run a hand through my hair without thinking.

'Mum, you've got cereal in your hair!' Ajit cries.

'Oops. No time to do anything about it, love. Zoe, Mia, downstairs now.'

'But, Mum.' Mia's voice a whine. 'I *still* can't find my shoes.'

'Have you looked under the bed?'

Zoe skips downstairs, her red-gold hair a waterfall cascading from the scrunchie at the top of her head, her school bag thumping on the stairs behind her. She takes one look at me and bursts out laughing. 'Mum, what have you *done*?'

In the hallway mirror, as I wrestle Ajit into his shoes, I catch a glimpse of myself. Wild-eyed, wan-faced, hair clumped together with the milky wet cereal.

'Mum,' Zoe says, hands on hips, 'you can't go out like that.'

My little girl sounds very much like a stern judgemental aunt.

'Mia, we're late,' I yell as I try to get rid of the cereal. But it's stuck tight. I try hiding it behind my other hair. A lost battle as the lank strands, in dire need of care, straggle listlessly. There's nothing for it but to cut off the offending strands. My hair is thin as it is and this will make it even more so, and uneven to boot. I'll need to book a hair appointment, ideally before we go on 'the holiday of a lifetime' that we've been looking forward to forever, it seems, and now it's nearly here! I can't recall when I last had the luxury of free time to spend at a hair salon rather than just cutting it myself over the bathroom sink. Before the kids probably.

A scream builds inside me.

And that's when my phone pings.

I know I shouldn't. I don't have time. But I need just one moment to myself. One moment away from it all.

Pushing away my misgivings, I pull my phone out of my pocket. A text just come in. From a withheld number.

And immediately all thoughts of sticky cereal-encrusted, lank hair, self-styled bad haircuts, being late again on the school run fade in the face of fresh, terrifying madness.

My dear, did you know...

Your husband is having an affair.

All the way to drop-off I feel eyes on me. The hair at the back of my neck standing to attention. The sensation of being watched.

My phone keeps beeping, but I ignore it.

I've deleted the offending text, but I can't erase it from my mind, where it is stubbornly doing loops.

I hurry the children along, ignoring the looks from mums walking back in their tight little cliques; the ones who don't know me pretending they're not taking note of my every transgression to dissect in minute detail later, the ones who know me doing the same while calling, 'Hiya, Jo,' with careful smiles.

I know for a fact that once we walk past, I will be the subject of frenzied gossip: my dishevelled appearance, Mia in her mufti shoes (she couldn't find her school shoes, another job for me when I get home), Ajit dragging his feet the closer we get to school, worried about his missing reading diary, me hurrying him along none too gently, Zoe marching ahead pretending not to hear my hissed instructions to stay close.

'Look at the state of her,' they'll nudge, smug in their steady-as-clockwork lives, their perfectly turned-out kids, their handy husbands who stick to nine-to-five office hours, hurrying home at the end of the working day early enough to help with their children's bath and bedtime. 'Always late. How she has let herself go! No wonder her husband is looking elsewhere...'

Is he?

Do they know? Are they in on it?

Is it one of these yummy mummies who's having it off with *my* husband? Did one of them send that text?

Don't go there. Don't start that again. You've been doing so well.

But Yash has been coming home later and later recently. He's blamed it on work and I've been too tired and zonked out to worry about him as well as the kids.

Stop.

I must see the counsellor again. Not that she's much help considering how much she charges...

Perhaps I need to start taking my pills. Yash thinks I'm still taking them. But they make me groggy, and I don't like it, that sensation of wading through water, of being not quite all there. Even Lydia noticed that I wasn't myself when I was on them, that I was not as focused on the kids. This was what made me finally stop. But now... Should I start taking them again?

That text... It *was* real. I didn't imagine it.

'Mum. *Mum.*'

I come back to earth with a snap. Shake my head. My hair sticky. My baggy jumper and tracks, spattered and worn. I feel dirty, ugly, a million years old.

I will never measure up. Lori was always the beautiful one.

No. Stop.

Count the positives.

I have three gorgeous children. A – faithful? – husband. A family very different from my own.

Really?

'Mum, Mrs B wants a word.'

Of course she does.

But even the head teacher's politely worded, politically correct dressing-down doesn't affect me. I can't stop myself from looking over my shoulder. Goosebumps erupting on my skin. The hairs at the nape of my neck on high alert. 'Mrs Kumar, this can't continue. The children are consistently late and it is our duty to report—'

'Yes, thank you,' I say, unable to listen a minute longer, cutting the head teacher short.

The woman stares at me in amazed shock, her eyes nearly popping out from behind her glasses. I'm willing to bet nobody has ever dared interrupt this severe woman in mid-sentence before. If I was in the right frame of mind, I'd actually find it funny, squirrel it away to laugh about with Yash later.

Yash...

That text. Uncompromising. Matter of fact. *Your husband is having an affair.*

No.

I must have said it out loud for the head teacher's lips disappear, her expression even more grim as she leans forward, hands joined, voice aiming for concerned but falling short. 'Mrs Kumar, is everything OK?'

'I... I need to go.'

I run all the way home, the sensation of being watched dogging my every step.

That evening, Yash is late. Again.

This time – instead of collapsing in Ajit's bed while reading him his bedtime story, waking up in the middle of the night to stumble into our bedroom, Yash sleepily spooning me, his hot, dream-infused breath in my ear: 'You were fast asleep when I came in; didn't want to wake you' – I stay up.

I used to make an effort, have dinner waiting for Yash when he came home. But lately he's been working all hours, and I have had to throw away his dinner more than once, so now I don't bother. He and Paul lost a few key clients after Brexit and with economic uncertainties, they've struggled to recoup, build their business back to how it was. 'We're keeping afloat. Just. But it means we have to work all hours,' Yash has said, when I've complained.

And recently, he's confided that there's been money going missing from the business, which he's trying to get to the bottom of in his own time. 'I haven't told Paul about it,' Yash said.

'Why not?' I asked.

'I'm not sure. I've a bad feeling about this. I'd rather confirm how and why it's happening and then I'll tell him.'

When Yash comes home at half eleven, a cold draught in his wake, I jerk awake. I've been nodding off on the sofa, television blaring, a late-night drama.

I shudder as much from an uneasy feeling of déjà vu as from the chill. I've been here before.

'You're up.' Yash beams. Drawing me into a hug.

He is drunk. Smelling sour. The tang of alcohol mingling with smoke and the nippy bite of outdoors. Other people's sweat.

All through the long evening, I've been debating with myself. One finger on my phone. Wanting to call Yash. Check on him. There have been no more insinuating texts. But the thought is now well and truly in my head.

I've been so caught up with the kids. I've trusted Yash. Have I been wrong to do so?

I wanted to call so badly. But I thought, *no*. I trust him. I do.

I won't regress. I'll count my blessings. I am lucky. My husband and children are my world. My family is not like my childhood one.

Yash loves *me*.

Doesn't he?

'Where were you?' I ask.

Is that guilt colouring his face?

Stop imagining things.

'I told you, love, potential client meeting.'

'So late?'

'Well, this is the wooing stage. We had to take them out to drinks.' He is fiddling with his tie, loosening it, not looking at me. Is he uncomfortable or am I imagining it?

'We?'

'Paul was there as well.'

'You said he hates these things.'

'I do too.' He stretches. Sighs. 'I'm shattered, love. Shall we go to bed?'

He's his usual self, I decide. He's not lying, as far as I can tell.

Or perhaps he's just become better at it...

Stop.

In bed, me spooning him, I say, 'I got a text.'

I hear the smile in his voice as he says: 'I got loads. It's a competition now?'

'It said you're having an affair.'

He stills in my arms. Turns around so he's meeting my eye.

'Who sent it?' Voice harsh. Smile quite gone from it.

'The number was withheld.'

'They're crazy. Playing games.' Yash is angry, the muscle in his jaw jumping, eyes flashing sparks. 'How dare they? Where is the text? Show me?'

'I deleted it in case the children...'

He's looking at me, sharply. 'You believed this... prankster?'

'I—'

'How could you, Jo?' he says tightly, his mouth a thin line. 'Whoever it is is taking the piss,' he hisses, drawing me even closer into the circle of his arms.

We are eye to eye. Our hearts beating in sync. Our lips touching, breath mingling.

'I love you.' His gaze holding mine, steady, sincere. 'Only you. Here, I'll show you.'

He does.

I believe him.

Yash leaves before the kids wake up, kissing me thoroughly. 'You are the only one for me, Jo.'

It is only after he's gone and I'm getting the lunchboxes

ready before rousing the kids that I think to check my phone – I left it downstairs the previous night.

Another text, once again from the withheld number:

Do you really believe your husband's lies no matter how he delivers them?

I shiver, the hairs at the back of my neck standing up. Has someone been spying on us in our bedroom?

NINE

DAY 1

2:15 a.m.

The inspector's voice jolts me from my ruminations. 'You've received these texts here?'

'Yes.' I shudder. 'I thought they'd stop once we left the country. But I received one in the taxi on the way here...'

India. Glaring gold sun, dazzle bright. Sweltering heat, glorious. Noise, chaos, crowds, bustle. The tang of dirt and spices. Gritty, humid air stroking our faces. The kids, although worn out from the flight, avidly take it all in, tugging at my hand and pointing out anything they find exciting, different.

Yash goes up to a counter with Paul, negotiating for a taxi.

'Just get the first one available,' I call to him, not wanting to waste time bargaining for the best deal as Yash is wont to do, with tired children in tow.

The taxis pull up, one for each family. The drivers expertly load our luggage onto the top of the cars, tying them with rope, while we watch, fascinated.

'Don't worry, no falling,' our driver says with a grin, displaying a few rotting teeth, lonely soldiers poking out from a cavity-shot battlefield.

The kids and I get in the back, Yash in front beside the driver.

Ajit falls asleep as soon as the taxi starts up, despite it bumping over innumerable potholes, having watched cartoons for several of the long hours of flight. Men in dust-gilded turbans pull rickshaws and others in multi-hued loincloths cycle alongside our taxi. Quaint shops with bright awnings advertise their wares alongside vendors hawking kaleidoscopic spices and pyramids of exotic fruit spread out on newspapers by the side of the street. Others fry food and brew tea regardless of the crowding flies, the women with their vibrant saris, bangles catching the light. Mia and Zoe gaze out the window, mesmerised at the landscape, dust rising up in an orange cloud, smothering the colourful people in a saffron haze. And, looking at this country so different from our own, I relax, overcome by well-being, finally, for the first time since those offending text messages started arriving.

I trust Yash, and I want to believe he is telling the truth, but the messages have seeded doubt, so when he's been working all hours in the run-up to the holiday, it's been hard not to wonder what he's doing, whether he's really working or up to no good.

Now, though, I feel that hard ball of tension and suspicion I didn't even know was weighing down my chest finally releasing its chokehold.

My girls, like myself, marvel at the cows and dogs claiming the road, completely unfazed by the overcrowded hustle of vehicles. We are simultaneously awed and terrified by the haphazard driving, the cacophony of horns. Then, the taxi turns a corner and there it is. The sea. Like a scarf twisting in the breeze, arching towards the horizon. The girls are so excited that they squeal. Ajit wakes up, rubs his eyes and claps his hands in delight. Yash turns around in his seat beside the driver and his eyes meet mine. He is glowing as he takes in his children's joy. I smile at him, in this moment, entirely, absolutely happy.

My phone pings. The roaming feature kicking in, I think, welcoming me to India.

India! We are actually here!

Absent-mindedly, I look at the screen and my smile disappears.

You are a fool to believe your husband.

I gasp.

Yash turns from the front seat, his gaze flitting between my phone and my face, asking sharply, eyebrows raised, 'Everything OK, Jo?'

'Mum, what's the matter?' Zoe, my ever-perceptive middle child, queries.

For a few days after I'd questioned Yash when I received the first of these horrid texts, he'd asked, when he got home, very late, from work, 'Received any more?'

'No,' I lied each time, having decided that I trusted my husband over the anonymous prankster who was trying to cause trouble in my marriage.

Yash would gather me in his arms, kissing me. 'I was working, you know.'

And although I chose to believe him, there was still that small niggle...

Now, both Yash and our middle child are continuing to look quizzically at me, identical creases at the centre of their foreheads.

I conjure a smile for their benefit. 'Just amazed at how different it all is,' I manage. But the words from the text fester in my head, seeping their poison into what was supposed to be a joyous, freeing holiday, uncomplicated time with my family, so I cannot quite meet my husband's eye.

Ajit tugs at his sister's hand. 'Zo, look, monkeys beside the road!' His voice a thrilled shriek.

Zoe turns her attention back to the exotic surroundings. So does Yash. I don't know if he believed me.

My hand shakes as I delete the text, turn off my phone and drop it in my bag.

We are driving beside the sea, the road winding and scenic, the breeze tasting of heat and salt, the smell of seaweed and spices, the roar of the ocean loud in our ears, but not as loud as the clamour in my heart.

Who is doing this? Why?

Whoever it is is playing with me, hell-bent on destroying my happiness, peace of mind, for some reason. This mean, spiteful coward of a sender wants to ruin the holiday I've been so looking forward to. A chance to recharge, rejuvenate away from the daily grind of school drop-offs and pick-ups and home life. I won't let them. I am wiping the message from my mind, there, gone. I'm revelling in my children's joy, their laughter.

We come to a stop beside a copse of coconut trees, beyond which sand sparkles gold and leads onto the shimmering, surging expanse of cream-capped turquoise. The other taxi is not here yet, our driver having made good time. To our left, a cottage, set in the sand. Snug and pretty, a fairy-tale tropical haven, complete with thatched roof and veranda.

The kids tumble out of the taxi, so very excited. All three tugging at my hands. 'Can we have a dip in the sea? Please, Mum, *pleeeease*?'

'We will as soon as the others turn up. Play in the sand for now, right there where I can see you.'

They skip into the sand and begin digging in it.

'Bury me, Zo.'

'Let's build a giant castle.'

'This sand is *so* warm.'

Yash gets out, stretches as he stands beside me, watching our beautiful kids frolic in the sand, framed by the sea, haloed by sun, golden innocence, a huge grin on his face. He slips an arm around my waist, pulls me close. 'Paradise, eh?'

I tuck my head in the hollow of my husband's neck, breathe

in his familiar lemony scent, and say, without consciously meaning to, 'I got another text message about you. That withheld number again.' My voice raised in question.

Yash takes a deep breath, a muscle in his jaw working. 'Ah, I guessed as much. In the taxi, right, when you gasped?'

I nod.

His voice tight as he says, 'Jo, I haven't cheated. Someone is messing with you, I don't know why. Show me your phone.'

'I deleted it in case the kids...' It is gone from my phone, but how I wish I could delete its poisonous implications from my mind.

The drone of an approaching car – Lydia, Paul and their girls arriving.

Yash tips my head up, looks into my eyes. 'Jo, love, we've blown the last of our savings not tied to the company on this holiday of a lifetime. Let's enjoy it, eh?'

I nod.

'I haven't cheated on you,' he says again, emphatically. 'I love you. You believe me?'

I look at this man whose every expression I know by heart, his handsome face now creased and weary from the journey, his eyes upon mine, earnest, loving.

Who is doing this, trying to come between us?

Yash reads my thoughts before I can voice them. He smiles, planting a kiss on my lips just as the Kings' taxi pulls up.

Paul guffaws, 'Look at you, lovebirds, at it before the holiday has even begun.'

Yash lets go of me to join Paul to see to the luggage and pay the taxi drivers.

Bella enthusiastically kicks off her shoes and joins Mia, Zoe and Ajit in sandcastle-making. Rachel squats on the sand and poses for selfies.

'Wow, isn't this something?' Lydia breathes. In her aquamarine sundress, her honey-coloured hair gilded by sunshine, she manages to look sultry and cool despite the fact that it's over thirty-five degrees centigrade and we've just endured a nine-hour flight. In contrast, I'm sweaty, my hair frizzy, perspiration beading on my face and making my baggy T-shirt and worn leggings stick to my body. I used to make more of an effort, wearing clothes that showed off my curves, artful make-up that highlighted my features to their best advantage, but with Yash working so much and me having to manage three children and housework, I've been too tired and stressed to bother.

I usually tell Lydia everything. She's my best friend, my oldest friend, she's been there through all my ups and downs. But I haven't told her about these texts. I haven't had the time – we've both been busy getting ready for the holiday. I thought I'd tell her once we were here, once I had gained some distance from them.

But now, I find my mouth is dry. I can't tell her. I don't want to bring them up, ruin this holiday before it's even begun. I will be giving the text writer the advantage, playing right into their hands.

No. I'm going to enjoy this holiday, every beautiful moment, starting now, standing here with my friend, watching our children play, the sand warm and silky-soft beneath my feet. The sea green-blue, roaring and tumbling playfully against the sand, the sun bright gold above.

A shout from our taxi driver: 'One hundred rupee tip. Everyone give.'

'When we booked the taxis, they said fixed price,' Yash says firmly.

Our driver's dark eyes flash amber sparks. 'I wait here. I take time. Give hundred rupees.'

'No.' Yash folds his arms across his chest. For him it is a matter of principle.

I want to intervene, *Yash, it's a hundred rupees. One pound, give or take. What does it matter?* But I don't want to undermine my husband in front of the taxi drivers.

Lydia is with me on this, for she shakes her head, clicks her tongue.

The drivers both move forward as one, scowls on their faces, eyes shooting daggers, fingers pointed at Yash. 'You...'

The children have stopped work on their sandcastle and are watching the altercation. Even Rachel is looking up from her phone. I feel my heart beat very loudly in my chest.

Paul intervenes, all six foot four of him, getting between Yash and the men. 'We paid at the airport. Leave now.' He doesn't raise his voice, but the threat is implicit.

Paul wouldn't harm a fly – he's a gentle giant. *We* know it. The taxi drivers don't. They see a big man standing up to them and retreat, looking disgusted, mumbling among themselves. One of them spits vehemently in the sand.

Just before they get into their cars, our driver yells, 'You pay. We make sure of it.'

Paul turns away from them, picking up most of the bags. 'Let the holiday begin.' He grins, cheerily. Unpleasantness wiped out. Gentle giant again. 'Who's up for a race to the cottage?'

The cottage looks beautiful, red bricks glowing honey amber in the sunshine. Surrounded by golden sand leading to the sea that gleams a brilliant silvery blue, capped by playful wavelets. But... there it is, the unpleasantly familiar prickle at the nape of my neck. The feeling of being watched that had stalked me in England, that, like the texts, I assumed would stop here, in this tropical paradise halfway across the world.

I look around. Nothing but sand. Blue sky. Rippling turquoise expanse of sea stretching to infinity. The indolent breeze scented with dust and exotic fruit ruffling the palms of the coconut grove across the road. Paul nearly at the cottage, kids and Yash keeping pace. Lydia beside me, Rachel behind us. Nobody else that I can see.

And yet I feel watched. In my bag, my phone. Switched off. I'm afraid to switch it back on in case there's another message. Just like back home.

Holiday of a lifetime. Open space all around and yet... I feel trapped.

Lydia is looking quizzically at me. 'You OK?'

The children are up ahead with Yash and Paul. I'm tempted to come clean to Lydia that I fear I'm being followed, but I don't want to ruin the holiday mood. It's her holiday too – she's been looking forward to it as much as I have and I don't want to badger her with my problems, make it all about me. That is also partly why I haven't told her about the texts, although usually she'd be the first person I'd turn to. She has been enthusiastically counting down to the holiday and I didn't want to spoil the fun by banging on about my worries. As it is, it feels like I'm always doing so, our friendship one-sided, with her placating me all the time, although she staunchly maintains otherwise. Lydia has never judged me, even at my worst. She's just been there, helping pick up the pieces. She knows things about me that I don't – *can't* – tell Yash.

I have struggled with my mental health since I was a teenager, after everything that happened with my mother, father and sister, but I only really sought medical help during that terrible time when my girls were little, when I... I am unable, even now, to think of what I almost did... Yash and Lydia had staged an intervention, made sure I got the help I needed. But when Ajit was born, I suffered from postnatal depression again, worse than with the girls. Unlike Yash, busy with work, preoccupied when at home, Lydia had noticed that I was different when on the pills the counsellor prescribed, dreamy. 'And you're not quite there for the kids either, altogether more careless with them.'

When I'd looked alarmed, she'd squeezed my hand gently. 'Not to the point of putting them in danger, Jo, just less focused when you're with them.'

I shuddered, thinking of what I had done when Ajit was an infant, how my actions nearly cost one of my children...

Only Lydia knew about that – and I saw the memory reflected in her eyes. It was this that made me stop taking the pills.

When I'd confided in Lydia that I'd stopped my meds, she was concerned.

'I'm fine now, Lydia, truly,' I'd reassured her.

'Promise me you'll go back on them if you feel yourself spiralling again?' she'd asked.

'I promise.'

A lone cloud rolls across the bright dazzle of sky. It makes me shiver, even as the back of my neck prickles ominously.

What if the feeling of being stalked is because I received the text? They seem to coincide – the texts and the uncomfortable sensation of being watched.

I can't tell Lydia, even aside from the fact that I don't want to ruin her holiday with my problems. She will worry, suggest that perhaps I should start taking my meds again – the meds I've (foolishly?) left behind at home.

And so, 'I'm fine,' I lie, even as inside I'm wondering: what if my problems have started up again?

What if, like before, it's all in my head?

ELEVEN

DAY 1

2:30 a.m.

'Do you have any of these texts?' the inspector asks gently.

'No, sorry. I deleted them all – the kids sometimes use my phone to play games...'

'Ah, I see.' He makes a note in his book. 'If you receive any more, please don't delete them – we'll have a look, see if we can trace the source.'

'Yes,' I say, even as I wonder if this anonymous text sender is just someone playing a malicious game with me, or if they have taken it one step further and are somehow involved in Ajit's disappearance. I shudder. Who would hate me so much as to go to these lengths, involve an innocent child? I can think of at least one person...

Should I share my suspicions with the inspector? But that is just what they are at this point – suspicions. What if he dismisses them as paranoia? Or worse, what if he acts on them and they prove wrong and it wastes precious time in the search for my son?

I don't know what to do. I just want my boy.

'The taxi drivers. Did they seem interested in the children?' the inspector asks.

The dread in my stomach balloons. I want to retch this nightmare away, the knowledge that Ajit is missing, that he could be anywhere, with anyone. My precious little boy, whom I have failed, dreadfully. 'No. I don't... I don't... They were angry with Yash and Paul for refusing their tip. You don't think...?'

The inspector shrugs. 'People get angry for all sorts of reasons. They hold grudges. Take revenge. We're trying to cover all bases at this initial stage of the investigation.'

The investigation. My boy is, for this man, just a case to solve.

'But surely for a hundred rupees...? My Ajit...'

'It is *only* a hundred rupees to you; it is a meal for their children.' The inspector's mild voice takes on a sharp edge. 'You see, these taxi firms do not pay their drivers well, so they rely on tips from their passengers. There is a lot of misplaced rage and resentment and it takes little for it to boil over.'

'But surely you don't mean...? How were we supposed to know?' My voice a whisper of shock. I hear the taxi drivers' parting shot loud in my ear: *You pay. We make sure of it.* Is it possible...? I hold my stomach to stop myself keening. My Ajit, my beautiful boy, taken for a hundred rupees?

'Look, I didn't mean... I'm just getting a picture of the days leading up to Ajit going missing, ma'am.' The inspector's voice kinder now.

My heart is beating as if I've run a thousand miles. Somehow I manage deep breaths, attain a semblance of calm.

'The taxi drivers knew which one was your cottage?' the inspector asks.

'They must have done; they stopped almost right beside it.'

'Hmm... And the window at the end of the corridor, beside Ajit's bedroom, is just a few paces from the road. Anyone coming up to the cottage from the road will first encounter that window.'

When I left my children in Rachel's care, I only thought of the danger the sea presented. I did not think of the road.

'Ma'am, do you recall if it was open when you first arrived?'

'I...' I think back to that first day, the children skipping inside, chattering excitedly, trailing sand all over the clean floors. Ajit's wide, thrilled grin when he was allowed to have his own room while the girls had to share... 'The kids climbed out of it and afterwards I shut it behind them.' I *had* done so, hadn't I? Yes, but did I lock it? I recall Lydia saying, just after we discovered Ajit was missing, when Paul asked why the window was open, 'Perhaps it doesn't shut properly...' But it does. *I* shut it, although I cannot remember locking it.

'Even Ajit climbed out of the window?' The inspector looks up from his notebook.

'Yes, he could just about manage.'

I realise my mouth is open and I am bent double, trying to breathe.

'Are you OK?'

I'm not and will not be until my son is safe and in my arms again.

Outwardly, I manage a nod.

I did not appreciate what I had – three healthy, happy kids, a wonderful holiday – my mind instead snagging on the text I'd received, wondering who had sent it, worrying if the feeling of being watched was real or in my head. I should have held on to those magical moments instead of letting them slip through my hands like grains of sand in the supreme confidence that more similar moments would take their place.

'Some of our officers are following up on any unaccounted for or suspicious vehicles in the area. They're also trying to locate the taxi drivers as we speak.' Then, 'Apart from your husband and Mr King's altercation with the taxi drivers, did you notice anything that you weren't sure of, that made you uneasy, perhaps, anyone behaving suspiciously?'

And I am transported, once again, to that first afternoon. We had arrived in paradise and yet I was harangued by an unease I was unable to shake...

The cottage is exactly as in the photographs we were shown when booking, perfect for our needs. The fridge is equipped with milk, bread and eggs. On the table, a basket filled with tropical fruit: juicy yellow mangoes, pineapples and pawpaws, a watermelon as big as a basketball.

Once the kids have run around bagging rooms, they are eager for a swim. We change into our swim clothes, but there's a bit of a kerfuffle when we try to lock the front door.

'It doesn't shut properly,' Paul mutters, yanking it to with force. But the door refuses to shut fully.

'Aww... leave it then. Shut and lock the mesh screen, that's surely enough?' Lydia says easily. She's already down the front steps, on the beach, along with the kids, who are playing in the sand. 'Oooh it's so deliciously hot,' she exults, throwing her blonde head to the sky.

'What about our passports and money?' I ask, hating the quailing note in my voice. I don't like that I'm always the worrier in the group, the one who chews over every detail, who cannot quite relax, even in paradise.

Yash smiles, throwing his arm around me. 'It's all right.

Paul and I have locked the valuables in the safe. If anyone wants holiday clothes and racy thrillers, they're welcome to them.' And, kissing my brow, which I'm sure is bunched with concern, 'Relax, Jo. We'll only be down there.' With his other arm, he indicates the sea invitingly glimmering straight ahead. 'The cottage will be in our eyeline at all times.'

I try and do as he says, but I cannot quite ease the knot in my chest, especially now that there is activity on the previously empty beach. The prickling sensation at the back of my neck intensifies.

I look around. There are family groups dotted along the beach – mainly white, I note; tourists, like us – and the shuttered shack a few yards from our cottage is now open. There are a few customers at the bar and others sitting at the tables set beneath colourful umbrellas on the sand outside the shack. Nobody I recognise.

Of course not. I shake my head to dislodge the anxiety plaguing me. Perhaps I really should think about taking my meds again.

The barman is mixing drinks, a little girl, presumably his daughter, is serving them and a sari-clad woman is barbecuing spiced seafood and chicken on the grill.

Paul and Yash linger by the shack, debating whether to pause for a drink. Bella and Zoe attempt to converse with the little girl serving drinks, who smiles shyly at them. The salt and seaweed perfume of the sea mingling with the spicy, eye-watering aromas of frying fish and meat and the vinegar tang of alcohol shouts 'holiday!' briefly dispelling my unease.

'Come on, slowcoaches,' Lydia, who's gone on ahead with Rachel, calls, and Paul and Yash decide they'll quench their holiday thirst later.

'After all, we have the whole week, mate, and the bar is, what, five paces from our cottage.' Yash grins at Paul, who thumps him on his shoulder. 'Great booking, mate. You came up trumps.'

We nod at the families sitting at the tables outside the bar shack as we walk past.

Yash strikes up a conversation with the dad at the table nearest us. 'Have you been here long?'

'A week,' he says. He sounds European. German, at a guess.

Ajit tugs at my hands to hurry – the girls have run on and caught up with Lydia and Rachel, but Ajit wants me along; for all his gregariousness, he is a bit timid and overwhelmed when in a new setting.

The partner of the man Yash is chatting to smiles at Ajit and catches my eye. 'You have a beautiful boy.' Her two girls are around Rachel's age and glued to their phones.

'Thank you,' I say, my heart blooming with maternal pride.

As soon as we reach the water, the kids and the men take to the waves, while Lydia, Rachel and I sunbathe on the beach, Rachel a safe distance away from us oldies cramping her style.

The back of my neck prickles again and I check the beach. Nobody near us, nobody watching me. I am in paradise and I can't relax, can't shake off the feeling of being watched, can't revel in the sun like Lydia beside me, her blonde hair a shimmering halo, glimmering gold in the sunshine, impossibly long eyelashes curling seductively over her sea-blue eyes, which are closed as she snoozes, her mouth open, baby pink tongue peeking out. Even like this she is glamorous, a slumbering Barbie doll, while I swelter beside her.

My girls and Bella strike up a conversation with some other children also playing in the water, Ajit hanging back shyly.

I am just about to call to the girls to include him when one of the little boys in the group comes up to Ajit and starts chatting. Well, gesticulating with his hands. Soon, they are all jumping about, having fun.

I smile, as I watch my kids, seawater arcing froth around

them, the glorious music of their laughter. Hot, humid air caressing my face, carrying the briny tang of the ocean. My friends and family around me. And finally I start to relax.

I must fall asleep, for I jerk awake to the sound of crying. Panic clenches my heart as my eyes root out my children. They are fine, Yash and Paul swimming right next to them.

It's the boy Ajit was playing with who's sobbing his heart out while running for his mother, who is in the sea a little further along.

I look at Ajit and note that he is about to cry too. Yash opens his arms to him, but Ajit comes up to me, scattering shimmering droplets in his wake. I hold my boy, his wet, slippery body, his distressed face.

'He says I splashed him. We were only playing.' His lower lip trembling preparatory to tears.

'Shall we say sorry, anyway?' I ask and he nods.

I take his hand and we go up to the boy and his mother and apologise.

The mother can't speak any English but is very nice, smiling at us and waving off Ajit's apology, even as she chats to her boy – in Italian, I think, and even if I can't understand it, I get the gist. She's urging him to play with Ajit. He pouts for a bit, but his mother rubs his face, gives him a nudge and the next minute, he's taking Ajit's hand and they've gone back to playing together, skirmish forgotten.

I return to my spot next to Lydia, who's fast asleep, body gleaming with coconut sun lotion, breath escaping in soft sighs.

It is gloriously warm, such a change from cold and rainy England, the smell of spices and raw onions emanating from the hawker approaching us, a basket slung across his neck, peddling puffed rice flavoured with raw mango and roasted chillies in paper cones. 'Only ten rupees,' he says in heavily accented English, holding out a cone.

I shake my head, wary of eating food that might give me an upset stomach.

He hangs about for a while, beckoning to his peanut-hawking friend, who comes up and starts pestering us too; Lydia having jolted awake when the man started speaking. I can see they are hoping that their joint assault will work on us. But we don't budge and after a few more minutes of coaxing they drift away.

'I can't believe I'm saying this, but I'm too hot. Shall we move up so we are in the shade of those coconut trees?' Lydia says, and when I hesitate, she adds kindly, 'We can still watch the kids from there.'

I experience a rush of affection for my friend. She knows me so well, understands my anxieties without me having to voice them, my need to keep an eye on the kids even though Yash and Paul are right there.

It is definitely more pleasant under the coconut trees, and through the dappled sunlight filtering through the fronds, rendering dancing shapes in the sand, I watch my beautiful children frolicking in the water.

Lydia, meanwhile, is fixated by the man selling coconut water beside the road, just beyond where we are. He selects a coconut from the pyramid beside him, chops the top off expertly with a couple of swipes of his scythe and sticks a straw inside, so you drink straight from the fruit.

'Shall we?' she asks, but she's already made up her mind, standing up, dusting the sand off herself, smiling at me. 'It's fresh, so no risk of food poisoning.'

The coconut water is honey-sweet, cool and refreshing.

'This would taste heavenly with a splash of gin,' Lydia observes.

I snort, involuntary chuckles.

Sitting there, in the shade of the trees, fragranced breeze tickling my face, the coconut water syrupy in my mouth, my children playing with blissful abandon in the water, creating rainbow arcs as they splash each other, for a brief, perfect moment, I forget my worries, revelling in the here and now.

And then Lydia takes off her sarong, and something snags at the corner of my eye. The ring on the pinky finger of her left hand. Lydia wears multiple rings on every finger, so I didn't really notice this particular one before. But as she was removing her sarong, her rings were right in my face.

It can't be, can it?

'Lydia, where did you get your ring, the one on your pinky?'

It looks just like the ring I lost a couple of weeks ago. I had discovered it was missing a few days after that first anonymous text arrived.

'This?' She waves her pinky in front of my nose.

And there it is, the little scratch where I'd nicked the ring at the sharp end of the table. I'd been upset as I really liked the ring – it didn't cost much, I'd bought it at a tiny stall in the market, but the woman had assured me it was unique, that there wasn't another piece like it. Unlike Lydia, I don't wear much jewellery; I'm choosy about what I like and almost always buy pieces that are one of a kind. Yash jokes that I'm notoriously hard to buy gifts for – I'd made him return the engagement ring he gave me when he proposed and we'd chosen a replacement one and our wedding rings together.

My mind is in turmoil. Why does Lydia have *my* ring? I don't wear my pieces every day, only when I'm going out somewhere nice, and I always make sure to return them to the safe in my side of the wardrobe, tucked away from little hands. I had wanted to wear the ring to that supper with one of Yash's long-standing clients and that was when I realised it was missing. I'd looked everywhere for it, but it had well and truly disappeared.

Until now...

It is baking hot even in the shade of the coconut trees, but I feel a chill.

'Can't remember. Why?' Lydia is saying, looking quizzically at me from where she's lying, one hand flung lazily across her face, a nubile nymph. 'If you like it, you can have it.'

My mouth is bitter with befuddlement when I say, 'No, it's all right. Just caught my eye, is all.'

Am I going mad? How could Lydia's ring not only look just like mine, when the woman I bought it from assured me it was one of a kind, but also be chipped in exactly the same place? The only other explanation is that Lydia has my ring. But how? I only wore it twice, both when out with Yash. I remember putting it away in the safe both times. But when I wanted to wear it to that dinner a fortnight ago, it was missing from the safe...

'Beach too hot for you girls, then?' Yash is there suddenly, gleaming wet, our children beside him, excitedly chattering with Bella, hair slick with saltwater, droplets glittering on their cocoa skin, Paul and Rachel bringing up the rear.

'Mum.' Ajit breaks away to run up to me. He throws his wet body against mine. 'I swam in the waves. Did you watch?'

I breathe him in, my little boy, brine and innocence. 'I did, you were wonderful,' I say.

The girls have reached us now and everyone is talking all at once.

This holiday is about them, I think, taking in their excitement, shaking off my confusion about the ring.

Ajit jumps off me and as I stand up, I feel it again. My hackles rising. The prickle at the back of my neck.

Someone's watching.

THIRTEEN
TWO DAYS PREVIOUSLY

We indulge in a late lunch at the Parradis Cafe across the road from the beach, the quaint little eatery living up to its name despite Paradise being misspelled without an 'e' but with an extra 'r'. The grilled seafood platter, with ice cream for afters, is truly heavenly.

It is that weird hour between afternoon and evening, so the cafe is nearly deserted, and blessedly cool and dark after the blinding sun outside. Ajit's hair is full of sand. His eyes are sparkling. He is so happy, unable to sit still, jiggling in his seat. 'This is the best holiday ever,' he declares, face smeared with chocolate from the ice cream, and I feel the last of my unease drift away, that creepy feeling of being watched blessedly gone so I can properly relax.

When it is time to leave, I am loath to do so, afraid to break this brief contented spell. But we must and it is just as we step into the dazzling tropical sunshine, golden sand and cerulean waves shimmering before us that I feel trapped.

Physically trapped. Someone has my ankle in a vice.

I look down, and stifle a scream... A dusty, skeletal apparition is staring up at me; a pygmy, its talons wrapped around my leg, huge black eyes in a hairy face stained red with dust, stumps for legs, squats upon the sand beside my feet.

'Help.' My voice is a strangled whisper.

Yash is beside me then, his arm around me, whispering, 'Just a beggar, Jo.'

And I see then that it is. A man in desperate straits pleading for money.

'Madam, please,' the poor man cries, but he does, blessedly, release my leg from his grip and I stumble away.

'What's wrong with him? Can't we help him?' our kids plead.

'No,' Yash is firm. 'If we give to one, hundreds will follow.'

'But, Dad...' The children are upset, the happiness of before gone.

The beggar follows us for a bit, dragging himself along on the sand using his hands. When he realises we are not going to give in, his pleas change, becoming angry cries. Then, suddenly, he spits on the ground and yells, very clearly, in English, 'I curse you.'

Ajit starts crying.

I stumble and bump into Rachel, who, startled, jerks away. I crumple onto the sand and behind me the beggar laughs, his cackles loud and harsh, even as he shouts, 'I curse you. Curse you. Curse you.'

FOURTEEN

DAY 1

2:45 a.m.

'When you went down to the beach earlier this evening, was it busy?' the inspector asks.

'Not really. A couple of other families at the bar. One family down by the water.'

'Tourists or locals?'

'Tourists, I think. They were all white.'

'Anyone you recognised from before?'

'Yes, the German family we had said hello to when we first arrived were at the bar shack.'

'Did you chat to them?'

'We did. They asked after the children. We said they were asleep and that Rachel was babysitting. We must have sounded defensive because they said that they had had a wonderful holiday and it was...' – I choke on a sob – 'that it was very safe. They said that they wished they were staying for longer. Their words put us at ease.' A thought occurs to me. 'I think they said they were leaving today...'

'Don't worry,' the inspector reassures, 'nobody will be allowed to leave until we've checked them out.'

I think of the families at the beach. Tourists, like us. Would one of them take Ajit? Why am I even thinking this way? He will be found, and soon, now there's a whole team of police looking for him. Won't he?

'When you put him to bed, was Ajit OK?' the inspector asks.

I recall scrubbing Ajit in the shower before bed, trying to rid his hair of the sand and grit that seemed to be everywhere. The bubbles on his soft, yielding body...

His body... I shudder to think of someone else touching it, not out of love but out of malice, out of lust...

No. I shut my eyes tight against the image.

'Mrs Kumar?' the inspector prompts.

I take a bolstering breath. 'Ajit was happy. The thrill of having a room all to himself, like Rachel, while his sisters had to share, hadn't worn off. I asked him if I should leave the light on, but he was adamant that I switch it off. I did tell him the adults would be at the bar shack and asked if he wanted me to stay behind.'

'I'll be fine, Mum,' he had said, earnestly. 'I'm a big boy now.'

I feel light-headed with terror and exhaustion from the effort of pushing away the gruesome images supplied by my imagination. I would give anything to go back and undo what happened next, so whatever was to come, today, now, *this*, could be halted...

FIFTEEN

ONE DAY PREVIOUSLY

'Mum, I want to wear my SpongeBob and Patrick T-shirt, the new one we got in Asda, to the beach, but I can't find it *anywhere*,' Ajit cries, jumping from foot to foot impatiently, wanting to be with his sisters and Bella, who are in the sand already.

Rachel, typical teen, is still asleep, not swayed by the inviting call of the sea like the younger ones, who were up with the sun and raring to go, jet lag not in evidence.

Paul is off getting supplies. Yash and Lydia have dragged two of the chairs from the veranda down the steps and onto the sand and are stretched out on them, combining sunbathing with watching the kids.

Last night, once the kids were asleep and we were finally in our bedroom, alone, I'd meant to come clean to Yash about the constant feeling of being watched. I was going mad keeping it to myself. Usually I'd tell Lydia, but the ring – *was* it my ring on her finger or was I imagining things? – had thrown me. But just as I'd opened my mouth, Yash had gathered me to him, dark eyes soft, kissed me deeply and said, 'This is the life isn't it, love?'

And the words evaporated on my tongue. I didn't want his gaze to sour, for him to sigh, ask, when I told him I was feeling stalked, 'Have you been taking your pills?' I didn't want him to turn away from me instead of pulling me on top of him like he was doing.

'Mum, have you found it yet?' My little boy's sweet voice jolts me out of my reverie.

'Give me a minute, sweetheart.'

The T-shirt is not in the wardrobe – we haven't properly unpacked yet, we were too tired yesterday. I rummage in Ajit's suitcase. It's not in there either. I'm sure I packed it. Where can it be? It's not in the girls' bags.

'Mum?'

'Aha, here it is. Although what it's doing among Dad's things I do not know.'

'Yay! You're the best, Mum.' Ajit leaps into my arms to give me a hug. I manage to grab hold of him just in time. But Yash's bag overturns. 'Whoopsie!' Ajit pulls on the shirt and runs outside. 'Coming, Mum?'

'In a sec. Let me just stuff your dad's things into the wardrobe.'

And it is as I am doing so that I find it.

A sheer gold bikini top.

Not one of mine. I'm a size twelve, not an eight. And I definitely don't own anything in that colour as it does nothing for my complexion.

SIXTEEN

ONE DAY PREVIOUSLY

'Yash, can I speak to you for a sec?' Somehow I manage to keep my voice from betraying the torrent of emotions playing havoc inside me.

'Yes, love?' Yash says, grinning lazily at me.

'In private, please.'

'Go on, I'll keep an eye on the kids. They're playing nicely,' Lydia says expansively.

'For now.' Yash mock-groans as he gets off the lounger.

'True.' Lydia laughs. 'Don't take too long. No mischief, mind.' She winks.

I march to our bedroom, not checking to see if Yash follows.

But he does, saying, 'Jo, love, what's the hurry? Not looking for a follow-up to last night, eh?'

The laughter dies in his throat when I dangle the bikini top in his face. 'Whose is this? What is it doing among your things?'

'Jo, stop. Hang on a minute. What's got into you?'

'I foolishly believed you over the text messages. I...' I take a breath, ask, again, my voice shaking with upset, 'Whose is this?'

'I've never seen it before in my life.' He looks puzzled. Sounds convincing.

'But it was in your bag.'

'I don't know how it got in there.' Yash comes up to me, smelling of coconut sun lotion, his breath hot in my face. 'What's the matter with you? We are on holiday, for God's sake! Why...?'

His tirade is interrupted by a dishevelled, sleepy Rachel at the door to our room, her hair standing on end, eyes swollen with sleep. 'Is everything OK? I heard you guys yelling.'

I blush, even as Yash moves away from me. I'd completely forgotten about Rachel.

'Ah, you've found Mum's bikini top. She was looking all over for it. It's part of a set she bought for this holiday. Personally, I wouldn't be caught dead in it.' She smiles and holds out her hand. 'I'll give it to her, thanks, Jo.'

SEVENTEEN

DAY 1

3:00 a.m.

'Mrs Kumar,' the inspector prompts, jolting me back into the horrible present. I've forgotten his name. It is trivial information that my mind refuses to retain. 'Is there anything at all you'd like to share with me?'

Once again, I wonder if I should tell him about the fortune teller, the graves I think I saw. I don't want him to believe I'm paranoid, not to be trusted. I don't want him to focus on me when he should be out there looking for my son.

I am reminded, afresh, of that article I read before this holiday, how it condemned the Indian police, slamming them for the corruption rife among their ranks. I will talk to Yash about involving the British Consulate in the morning. But Ajit will be found by then, surely?

Please.

The policeman is looking inquiringly at me, waiting for my reply.

I am suddenly overcome with loathing for this stranger, standing here, judging us. What right does he have?

Every right, a voice in my head whispers.

The market is bustling, the busiest I've ever been in. People everywhere, packed tight. The sour smell of their sweat mingling with the sharp, festering odour of spices and drains. Food being cooked right there on the road: orange curries, bubbling rice, circles of chapatis, pepper-coated wedges of potato plopped into spitting woks with a sizzle and a squelch, slices of raw banana marinated in chilli and deep-fried fish, gutted and sliced expertly, scales winking and glimmering, staring dead eyes devoid of light, an army of scrawny cats and skeletal dogs descending on the bloody entrails.

Coming here was a bad idea, I think, even as I maniacally focus on the kids, keeping them close, their eyes wide with wonder as they take everything in.

'Keep a hold of my hands. Ajit, Zoe. Mia, you grab Zoe's.'

'Yes, Mum,' Mia and Ajit say obediently, but Zoe sighs, rolling her eyes, a preteen already, in behaviour if not in age.

My beautiful children look so out of place here, as do I, in our T-shirts and shorts, incongruent among the kaleidoscopic saris and the multicoloured kilt-like skirts worn by the men, garnering curious looks, unabashed stares. My pale skin is red and blotchy in the sun – I can never tan gold like Lydia. The kids take after Yash to varying degrees, but although they glow a beautiful bronze, they are still much lighter-skinned compared to their Indian counterparts.

I feel speared by curious gazes – in a different way to the constant creepy feeling of being stalked – but watched all the same.

I am sweaty and hot and tired from trying to navigate my children through this mob of pressing people who appear to have no regard for personal space, trying my best to ignore the sinking feeling in my stomach – I'm pretty sure we are lost. What on earth possessed me to come here on my own with the kids?

When I'd found Lydia's bikini among Yash's things, I'd felt ashamed by my overreaction, especially in front of Rachel, worrying about how much Rachel had heard of our fight.

Yash had stormed outside, straight to the lounger, before I could apologise.

I was upset that I'd ruined his good mood, our loved-up night forgotten by my paranoia. For that's what it was.

Lydia, having gauged from Yash's thunderous face that something had happened, had come to find me in the bedroom, where I was hiding, embarrassed by my outburst.

'What's the matter?' she asked.

And I finally told her about the text messages I've been getting.

'So when I saw the bikini top, I jumped to the wrong conclusion.'

'Ah, Jo, I came in here for something earlier – sun lotion, I think. I couldn't find mine. I must have picked up the sun cream but left my top behind. That's why I'm wearing my second-best bikini.' She laughed, then gently asked, 'Are you getting like before? Perhaps you should think about going back on your meds again?'

If anyone other than Lydia had suggested this, even Yash, it would raise my hackles and I would be angry and upset. But this was my friend who had seen me through my very worst and I knew she had my best interests at heart. And so, when she suggested that I should think about taking my pills, it gave me pause, secretly feeding into my worries that perhaps I was losing my handle on reality again. 'I will, when we're back,' I said.

'You've left them behind?' Her eyes were bright with concern.

'I'm fine, Lydia,' I insisted with more conviction than I felt.

'The text messages...' She took a breath. 'Are you sure you're getting them or—'

'You think I'm imagining them?' *Was* I imagining them? No. *No.* 'I saw them. I deleted them. They were there.'

'I believe you.'

But it was pretty clear she didn't. Or at the very least she doubted me. My friend who knew me better than anyone, even Yash...

It had all got too much and I'd needed to escape the claustrophobia of the holiday cottage, some space from my closest and dearest. Ironic, really, as the very reason we chose it was for the secluded beach and wide-open spaces, and yet still I felt trapped there.

When I told the kids I was going for a walk, mine wanted to come with me. It was gratifying: *They don't think I'm paranoid. They trust me, need me, want to be with me.*

But now, I wonder if their trust is misplaced. Why did I bring them here?

I told Lydia we'd be back soon, and left without telling Yash, who was asleep on the lounger. When Yash is angry, sad, worried or upset, he seeks solace in sleep. That's how he copes. I am the exact opposite, my mind whirring, too fired up to sleep.

I'd just wanted a walk along the beach to clear my mind, but when I saw the taxi drivers lounging beside their vehicles under the coconut trees by the road behind the cottage, I decided to get away, into town. Why not? The children were game, excited to be going on an adventure, and I'd be escaping the constant creepy feeling making the hairs at the back of my neck stand to attention. Then at least I'd be able to think straight.

I'd hailed one of the posse chatting languidly among themselves, tendrils of smoke from the roll-ups they shared lending a hazy sheen to the gilded air. Thankfully, the taxi drivers Yash and Paul had had an altercation with the previous day were not among them. But this lot nevertheless turned abruptly silent as I approached, as if a switch had been flipped, muting cheerful conversation, their hostile gazes flicking disdainfully over us. Perhaps word had spread among them about Paul and Yash's stinginess the previous day.

The back of my neck prickled. I wanted to leave this place, urgently.

I addressed the group, hoping at least one of them understood English. 'I'm willing to pay the fare plus a generous tip.'

One of the drivers had stubbed out his roll-up and stepped forward. 'Where to?' he asked in perfect English.

'A busy place.' Where hopefully I could lose the stalker – if there was one. Even *I* was doubting myself. The notion seemed preposterous. Why would a stalker follow me all the way to India? But there was no denying the urgent, insistent foreboding of danger.

The children had nodded along enthusiastically, Mia saying, 'Hopefully there will be shops there like we saw on the way here.'

The taxi driver had brought us to this insanely crowded market.

At first, the bustle felt freeing. In this noisy, crazy-busy place, the children and I star attractions, stared at by *everyone*, I'd finally felt the hairs at the back of my neck settle. And, funnily enough, with so many people around, the claustro-phobia that had choked me at the cottage eased.

But now... We are lost. I have tried to walk back the way we came, but instead of exiting, we only seem to have plunged deeper into the labyrinth of overcrowded alleyways that comprises this market.

The children are tired and whiny and lagging. The sun glares relentlessly. We are constantly grabbed and harangued by beggars, some of them children younger than Mia and Zoe, hefting babies on their tender hips, pleading eyes, missing limbs, sore-ridden bodies.

The scents of mouldy rubbish, fish entrails, baked earth. Too intense. The colour from the piles of spices, the vegetables set upon newspapers wilting in the sunshine, the radiant saris, the winking bangles, catching the eye, reflecting the sun, too dazzling. The noise, the pushing, shoving, perspiring crowds, the sheer incessant iridescence. All too much.

The children are drooping like the vegetables. Too hot. Their bodies limp with tiredness, slick with sweat. I must feed them, but I don't trust any of the eateries here not to upset their tummies. I need to reapply sun lotion on their sweating bodies, but I neglected to bring it with me. I need to find some shade. Ideally take them back. That is, if I manage to find my way out of this maze of cramped streets choked with people and produce. Why on earth did I think bringing them here was a good idea?

My phone has run out of charge, so I can't even call Yash to come and rescue us.

No restaurant here, only awnings under which bare-torsoed men fry freshly gutted fish coated in a lethal-looking red paste in hot oil. Rice boils and sputters in a large urn. People gather round, eating with their fingers from bowls shaped from dried leaves and held together ingeniously by twigs used as pins. They slurp tea and coffee from tumblers the size of my pinky finger, pudding-thick, bright orange with a skin of milk floating on top.

'Mum, can we go back? I want a swim in the sea,' Zoe intones.

Her voice is tired, not rife with irritation like it has been the couple of times she's asked this same question before. It worries me. The children's movements are sluggish. They seem on the verge of sunstroke.

For that matter, so am I. My throat is dry, I feel light-headed and dizzy. I can only guess how the children must be feeling.

No taxis anywhere in sight, the road here so narrow, only the occasional intrepid rickshaw dares push through, the driver's hand constantly on the horn warning people out of the way.

What have I done, dragging my precious children here just because *I* wanted to get away? How did I think I could escape my troubles here at the market when I haven't managed to despite travelling thousands of miles? If an ocean hasn't put distance between myself and the text messages insinuating horrible things, then why did I think coming here to a busy market would help?

I was not thinking – there's the problem.

I never do. I just act. Retaliate. Lash out.

Suddenly, pandemonium.

In the shocked moments after, I will understand that without warning, a car not meant to be in that part of the market had rattled down the narrow road, squashing tomatoes and fruit piles, upsetting vegetable carts, inciting a rainbow explosion of spices, people jumping out of the way willy-nilly, yelling, cursing, crying.

But right then, before I can properly register what is happening, the rogue car collides with the rickshaw just beside us, which veers almost right into us, and Ajit's hand is torn violently from mine.

My scream splinters the humid air as I gather Zoe and Mia to me.

But... Ajit... My youngest is nowhere to be seen.

'Ajit,' I call, my voice breaking, punctured by terror.

I shut my eyes tight, hoping that when I open them my son will be here with me.

But no, he is not among the rapidly multiplying host of people having, in a breathless moment, collected around the rickshaw, which has toppled into the ditch beside the road, shaking their heads and staring sadly at us.

'Ajit...' I scream and scream, holding my daughters to me.

The sun batters down, relentless. Mia is whimpering, Zoe asking in a cowed and stuttering whisper, a little child again, 'Is A-Ajit under the r-ri-rickshaw?'

No. Please no.

I've been a terrible mum, acting recklessly, dragging my children here on a whim. I wanted to get away, but why on earth did I come *here*? Will it haunt me for life, my impulsive action, just wanting, briefly, to get away from it all...?

'The c-c-c-c-car didn't s-st-stop.' Zoe's voice is uncomprehending. 'Mum, is Ajit *dead*?' A sob in my little girl's voice.

Fresh terror engulfs me, even as I try to focus on my tearful girls, scrabbling for words to set their hearts at rest. But nothing comes. My eyes are drawn to the space next to us where the car has ploughed through, leaving destruction in its wake. Rapidly filling now with a rubbernecking, gossiping crowd, eyes huge and shocked, who stare at me and my girls, nudging and pointing – they are obviously discussing what happened.

Fearfully, I crane my neck – I am taller than most, even the men. I can just about make out the rickshaw overturned onto the dirt-piled ditch by the side of the road. But there is no little boy with tousled hair and a yellow T-shirt calling for me.

Above the heads of the crowd, I see a group of men trying to right the overturned rickshaw. Is Ajit underneath? Oh God.

The back of my neck prickles. The sensation of being watched.

I'm terrified. Shying away from believing the worst. Hoping for a miracle. And now alongside the petrified thrum of fear, hot burning anger towards this unseen malevolence that's dogging me.

I swivel around, wanting to convey my fury to my aggressor: *Show yourself. Come and face me instead of hiding like a coward*, I hope my expression is saying. I've had *enough*.

All I want is my boy.

And as if I've conjured him up, I hear his voice: 'Mummy!'

Am I dreaming or...

'Mummy!'

'Mum, it's Ajit, look.' Zoe and Mia both speak at once, tugging at my hands, their voices shrill.

And then I see him – the murmuring crowd has parted to let him through. My little boy. Safe. *Safe.* Oh thank God. *Thank you, God.*

I sprint forward, keeping a firm hold on my girls, to gather Ajit in my arms, but he is pulled away and that is when I note the woman clasping my son protectively to her. Dreadlocks. Dust-spattered white sari tinted yellow at the armpits. Ash on her forehead. Wearing multiple necklaces of... eyes? Wait... Oh... Painted-on human eyes, but they appear creepily real – the effect is that of being skewered by a cacophony of unflinching, unblinking stares.

And, even as the relief of finding Ajit unscathed overwhelms, I notice that he is cowering in this strange woman's embrace, his lower lip trembling, a sure sign of tears. And I also realise that he called me 'Mummy', not 'Mum' as he has taken to doing recently, again a sign that he's distressed.

My girls hang back, afraid of the woman.

Truth be told, I am fearful too, but the need to hold my son is greater and so, I push away my misgiving and reach for my son, wanting to gather him close and never let go. But she – this woman, this absolute *stranger* – pulls him back as if she has a claim on him. The sweet relief of seeing him is made bitter by this woman's unprecedented hold on him.

She is speaking very rapidly in her language of which I don't understand a word.

I grab my son, hugging him to myself fiercely. He smells of fear and dust and as I feel his little heart beating against mine, I relax for one brief second, even as I keep a firm hold on my girls.

The woman shouts, pointing at me, her matted hair a grey-black shield.

All I want is to take my children to safety, but we are hemmed in by the crowd watching avidly, gossip hot on eager tongues, I imagine.

'Please, we'd like to get through,' I say. I can't quite keep the distress from my voice and it comes out shrill.

But the woman blocks my way, shaking her head even as she yells non-stop, her gaze fixed on me and my children cowering in my arms.

'I speak English. I translate,' a small, stout, heavily perspiring man says. He turns to the woman, asks her a question, cocks his head while he listens to her rapid-fire answer.

I don't want to listen to what this woman has to say. I am overwhelmed by the need to leave this place, ferry my children to safety. But we're boxed in by the crowd – there's seemingly no escape. A scream is trapped in my throat but I cannot lose my cool, not now. It would just upset the children even more.

Finally, the woman stops speaking and the man turns to me, wiping the sweat that is streaming down his face in rivulets with a soggy handkerchief, which only serves to lend his visage a very oily sheen.

'This woman fortune teller,' he says and the crowd angles forward even closer, forming a circle around us. I feel claustrophobic, inhaling the foetid tang of body odour and stale spices, craving the salty fresh scent and gold-frothed grumble of the sea. 'She saw accident before it happen...'

All the while the man translates, the fortune teller is staring at me and I feel judged by her and the thousand staring eyes of her necklaces. Annoyed, I shrug the feeling away – I will not be made to feel guilty by this woman; I feel guilty enough already. I will not be judged by this woman when I am judging myself more harshly than she possibly could.

'She rescue your boy, but she say he cursed for his mother bring bad luck.'

'I'm *sorry?*' I'm outraged.

But the man continues as if I haven't spoken and the woman just looks steadily at me, she and her million crazy eyes. 'She would like to keep hold of him as she is saving him from fate worse than death, she say.'

'Well, she *can't.*' I can't help the screech pincering my voice.

The people nearest to me take a step back and I can breathe again.

Gathering my children to me, I push through the rubbernecking mob, elbowing a path forward, not caring if I hit someone. I just want out.

And it is then that I feel it again. The spine-chilling sensation of being watched.

I turn, just in time to catch a fleeting glimpse of a tall head swivelling away. Familiar?

I shiver.

For a moment there, I thought I recognised...

Could it be...?

No.

Get a grip.

I really should start taking my meds again.

It can't be who I'm thinking I saw, surely? JT is firmly in my past, separated by years and oceans...

But, having said that, I could have sworn...

I shake my head to chase away my qualms, trying to find my way through the dusty market packed with people all staring unabashedly at us.

I thought my children and I would be safe in a crowd, that there was safety in numbers. I was so very wrong.

TWENTY

DAY 1

3:15 a.m.

Sudden shouts from outside. The sounds of vehicles pulling up.

My gaze meets the inspector's, hope flaring in my chest, wild and violent. *Please let them have found Ajit.*

A knock on the door. A policeman for Inspector Sharma: 'Sir.'

'Excuse me, please,' the inspector begins, but I push past him, running into the living room, almost colliding with Yash. His face is as ravaged and hopeful as mine must look.

Flashes lighting up the predawn darkness, blinding me as words stutter and die upon my tongue. Cameras catching us unawares through the open front door, questions being hurled at us, even as the police hold them back: 'Is it true that a child has been taken? A foreigner?'

Voices rising and competing with each other, inquisitive weapons tossed carelessly at us, flooring us with their barbed potency, dousing the hope that dared to bloom so briefly.

'How old is he?'

'Did he drown?'

'Run away?'

'Is he dead?'

Yash's face blanches, his skin clammy grey. I feel light-headed, as if all the air is leaving my body and I would fall, if not for Yash's arm bolstering me.

Inspector Sharma is there suddenly, and in his wake, several policemen, clad in their mud-coloured uniform. The inspector shuts the front door firmly, but the intrusive, insensitive, hurtful questions inveigle their way in regardless, echoing in my head, over and over: 'Is he dead?'

No. Please, no.

'The press has got wind of Ajit's disappearance. This is early even for them.' Inspector Sharma's face is grim. 'Someone must have tipped them off.' He raises an eyebrow at us.

I can't believe what he's suggesting. Anger, red hot, wipes away despair for a brief, blessed second.

Before I can say anything, Yash erupts, taking the words right out of my mouth. 'Can you hear them, Inspector? The questions they're asking? Why would we willingly subject ourselves to something so *cruel*?' His voice breaks, and he cradles his head in his hands.

The inspector looks intently from one to the other of us, then nods. 'This is just the beginning. They will be arriving in droves. I must ask you not to...'

The rest of his words escape me as I collapse onto the sofa, spent, devastated all over again as the last vestige of desperate hope shrivels into nothing. They haven't found him.

My son is missing. The reporter's question pounds in my head: 'Is he dead?'

'Where were you?' Yash hisses when we get back from the market, the kids and I limp with exhaustion. He is wild-eyed with anger, directed at me, even as he gathers our kids to him, showering them with kisses. 'You were not picking up your phone.'

'It ran out of charge.'

'I was out of my mind with worry. I was about to call the police.'

'I told Lydia where I was going.'

'You told her you were going for a *walk*, then you disappear, with the kids, and we cannot get hold of you. What was I to think?'

I am filled with remorse. Yash has every right to be angry. I would be too, alongside going mad with worry, if I had been in Yash's position. I've behaved terribly, first accusing Yash of cheating when I found the bikini among his things, then going AWOL with our kids.

'I'm really sorry,' I say. 'Bad judgement on my part.'

'Very,' he says, but I can see him thawing.

'I'll make it up to you,' I say.

'I'll hold you to it.' And there it is, a very small lift of his lips, the suggestion of a smile. This means we're good. Thank goodness he doesn't hold grudges, my husband. I love that about him. Once we argue and thrash our issues out, they're gone, poof, disappeared from his mind. 'Right, you lot need food and a wash and a rest,' Yash says to the kids, gently leading them inside. And to me, 'You coming?'

'In a minute.' I collapse into one of the deckchairs on the veranda and allow the salt-speckled sea air to soothe the stresses of the morning away from me.

I must fall asleep, for I jolt awake to furtive whispers.

Whoever it is is trying for quiet, but the sound carries – although I can't make out the actual words – as everything is shut at this time of the afternoon, when the sun is at its zenith, the air heavy and humid, even the sea's grumbling half-hearted and lethargic. It is siesta time for the locals, and tourists, us among them, are quick to jump on the bandwagon as nothing is open anyway and it makes sense to catch a couple of hours' shut-eye now to make the most of the balmy tropical evening later.

The shack, which is always doing brisk business when open, is boarded up. If following the same pattern as yesterday, it will reopen at around 4:00 p.m. when the deserted beach will come alive again with hawkers and sea worshippers alike. The shack will then draw a steady influx of custom, flavouring the brine air with sour hops, spiced meat and hearty chatter.

I'm hot and sweaty. My throat is parched. I need a drink.

I tiptoe indoors. The house is still. Blanketed in a drowsy hush. The only noise – if you could call it that – coming from the direction of the bedrooms, is the whispering that woke me up.

I drink two glasses of water in quick succession and grab my phone – fully charged now – thanks to Yash, I imagine, who must have put it to charge when I nodded off. The inbox is flooded with increasingly panicked messages and several missed calls from my husband from this morning; the voicemail is full. I slip it into my pocket.

I peek inside the children's rooms – they are fast asleep, their doors slightly ajar, ceiling fans working busily, mosquito coils in place, air conditioning on, windows fastened shut.

Rachel's bedroom door is shut. Presumably, she's inside either on her phone or also asleep.

I'm expecting the door to Paul and Lydia's room to be shut as well, but surprisingly it's open a tad and I can't resist a sneaky peek inside. Paul is sprawled on the double bed, taking up all the space, snoring away, mouth open. No Lydia. Why isn't she in here with Paul?

The whispers are coming from our bedroom – mine and Yash's. So Lydia must be in there with Yash. Why? And what are they conferring about when everyone else is asleep?

The door is shut. I rest my ear against it, but again, I can't make out the words, just rushed urgent whispering like the swarming rustle of bees.

I tiptoe back outside. Walk down into the sand and around the cottage, positioning myself directly underneath our bedroom window, which is wide open to let in the salt-freckled sea air.

The beach is deserted. The taxi drivers who lounge around smoking by their vehicles in the shade of the coconut grove behind the cottage have gone home for lunch, I imagine, for there are no vehicles, none at all, and thus there is, thankfully, no witness to my blatant eavesdropping.

They are by the window, my husband and my best friend, their words carrying clearly in the sun-sizzled air, which is hushed and still, as if waiting for something.

Yash: 'Did she tell you about the text messages?'

Lydia: 'Yes. I...' A pause, and when she speaks again, my friend sounds distressed. 'Did you see any of them?'

Yash: 'No. She said she'd deleted them in case the kids saw them.'

Lydia: 'I think she's... she might be making them up.'

Yash, thoughtful: 'You know, it's quite possible.'

Lydia: 'I worry she's heading for another breakdown.'

Yash: 'I do too. She's spiralling, like before. But I don't understand how, when her meds...'

Lydia: 'She's not been taking them.'

Yash: '*What?*'

Lydia: 'Yash, I...'

I cannot bear to hear any more. I stumble away, upset. My best friend and husband are worried about me, but I feel sickened by them discussing me like this, secretly, Lydia breaking my confidence, telling Yash about me not taking the pills. I tell myself it's because they care about me. But nevertheless, I can't help but feel betrayed.

TWENTY-TWO

DAY 1

3:30 a.m.

I watch the inspector issue orders to his men as my heartbeat gradually settles.

The clamour from outside is getting louder, piercing through the shut door: the grunts and groans as recording and transmitting equipment is unloaded, the squealing brakes of vehicles, dizzying flashes of light as cameras explode, shattering the darkness.

The girls, thankfully, sleep through it all.

Paul, Lydia and their girls are holed up in one of the bedrooms – Bella was upset, wanting her sister and parents with her, fearing that if she let them out of her sight they might disappear too.

Yash and I sit in the living room, drained and worried, waiting.

Waiting for our son to be found. For he *will* be, soon. Please.

Yash is slumped on the sofa, helplessness oozing out of his

pores. Yash is a doer. This sitting around waiting for Ajit must be grating on him even more than it is getting to me.

'Has he questioned you?' I ask Yash, nodding towards where the inspector is engaged in what appears to be, judging from his body language, urgent communication with the clique of subordinates grouped around him.

'Very thoroughly. Lydia and Paul too.' Yash sounds weary.

'Yash? Can we trust him to find our boy?' *Please let them find him safe and well and soon,* I think, even as that question tortures me again: 'Is Ajit dead?' My heart thuds with panic and terror.

'We have to, love. In any case, in the morning...' He flinches and I know he's thinking, hoping the same as I am: surely Ajit will be found before then? Yash swallows. 'The British embassy will send someone in the morning and they will be liaising with the inspector, keeping him on his toes. He seems competent enough.'

'Competent enough is not enough for my boy,' I bite, taking out all my frustration, my fear, my anger – at myself most of all – upon my husband.

He doesn't take offence, doesn't snap back. Instead, he puts his arm around me, and I lay my head upon his heart, hear its keening, mirroring mine, each beat a lament, a siren call for our boy.

'Jo?' Yash says softly.

'Yes?'

'During this questioning, all sorts of things will come out...'

I sit up, look at him. 'What do you mean?'

'I...' He can't find the words.

'Yash?' I ask gently enough. 'What is it?'

He's twisting his hands together on his lap, exactly like Ajit does when he's done something naughty and wants to confess. My heart clenches with longing for my boy.

Please come back, Ajit.

And then I jerk back into the here and now. 'Yash?' He won't meet my gaze.

Why won't my husband look at me? Why does he look... guilty? Caught out, like Ajit when he's sneaked two biscuits from the tin when he was allowed only one.

Please Ajit, come back to me, safe and whole, and I will allow you to eat any number of biscuits, yes, even the jammy ones you especially like which are so bad for your teeth.

'Mrs Kumar?' The inspector is there, beside us, his men having disbanded. 'Please can I clarify a few remaining points with you?'

Is it my imagination or does Yash look distinctly relieved? What is it he's hiding? I thought only I had secrets from my husband. I didn't think that my direct, open husband would be keeping things from me too. When I got those insinuating text messages, I believed *him* over the anonymous sender.

Was I wrong to do so?

And those text messages... they *are* real, aren't they, and not a product of my overwrought mind as my husband and best friend believe?

'Mrs Kumar?' the inspector nudges.

Has he sensed something between Yash and myself? He was talking to his men moments ago, but was it cover for watching us? Does he suspect *us*? What has Yash told him? What is my husband keeping from me?

I need to continue this interrupted conversation with my husband, as soon as possible. To the inspector I say, 'I can't see the point of all these questions when my son—'

'It *will* help, believe me,' the inspector interjects smoothly.

I don't know if I believe him. I don't know if I can trust him, or indeed anyone. Not even my husband who's going through the same hell as me. But for now I need the inspector – he and his team are currently my best chance at trying to find my son.

More vehicles arrive on the beach, disgorging reporters,

news anchors and journalists, the predawn no longer quiet and, with the cameras busy capturing our cottage from every angle, bright as mid-morning. It's bustling, almost carnival-like. I hate it, resent it, but am also grateful for it. At least it's no longer dark and if Ajit is out there, he'll be guided to the cottage by the light and noise. And surely, more people on the beach means more chances of finding him? *Someone* will run into him, bring him to me in the next few minutes, won't they?

I careen blindly through the coconut grove. A sudden sultry breeze fans the coconut fronds, drying the tears on my face in salty tracks. My brain whirs with thoughts, one upon the other. Lydia broke my confidence, telling Yash that I've not been taking my medication. What other secrets that I've told her but kept from my husband has she shared with Yash over the years?

Neither my husband nor my best friend believes me about the text messages. *Am* I going mad? Imagining things that aren't there?

I'm not really looking at where I'm going, so when I trip and nearly fall, righting myself just in time, it doesn't come as a surprise.

But then I register what I almost fell into, blinking once, then again.

Shock, horror, disbelief, everything else fleeing my mind.

I close my eyes, rocking on my feet. This is a nightmare. It has to be.

Yash is right. I need to take my medication. It is my mind, disturbed by the fortune teller's horrid prediction this morning, conjuring up these horrific images.

Isn't it?

It takes all of my willpower to force myself to open my eyes, look again, chanting, *Just my imagination, just my imagination,* over and over.

But it is *not* just my imagination.

They are actually here. Horrifically real.

Three small shallow graves. Child-sized. Freshly dug and waiting to be filled.

There are letters in front of each, carved into headstones shaped from sand, some of it rubbed away where I stumbled, but clear enough all the same.

Name plaques.

Mia. Zoe. Ajit.

I scream, but the beach is empty and the roar of the sea swallows my distress. The very isolation that we'd wanted when we booked this holiday is now working against me.

I want Yash. I *need* my husband.

I run back to the cottage, dread giving my legs wings, my mind shying away from what I saw.

I burst into the cottage. The kids are awake and grouped at the table eating mangoes that Lydia is peeling and chopping for them, sporting chocolate milk moustaches from the mugs they hold in their hands.

They look up at me, my beautiful children, alive and vibrantly hale. 'Mum, where have you been? Did you go for a run?'

I shudder as I think of the graves, their names etched onto sand-chiselled headstones.

No, no, no.

'Where's your dad?' I ask breathlessly.

Speaking of whom... 'Jo, where have you—?'

'Please, come with me,' I interrupt, grabbing Yash's hand, unable to conceal the urgency from my voice.

'Mum, where are you and Dad—'

'We'll be back in a tick. Stay here with Lydia, luvvies. Eat your fruit. That OK, Lydia?'

'Go on,' Lydia says, just as Paul enters the living room, yawning, tousled and bleary-eyed, asking, 'Where are you love-birds off to, eh?' and winking suggestively.

I drag my husband, protesting, 'Jo, what's going on?' back the way I've come.

When we get there, there is nothing. No graves. No names. Just pristine sand, seemingly untouched. I walk up and down, combing every inch of the coconut grove.

Nothing.

I am relieved that I don't have to see the spectacle again but also very afraid. Did I imagine the graves? I could have *sworn* they were here.

Yash sighs. But he must see something in my expression for he is gentle when he says, 'You really need to see your counsellor when we get back.'

Perhaps he's right. Perhaps I should. Perhaps after the horrific experience this morning, when I thought I'd lost Ajit and the fortune teller's terrible words, I'm making things up, the worst that could happen, my mind's way of dealing with it all...

But although, in a way, I hope I've made that gruesome image up, that's scary too. If I did, what's going on with me? I can't have another breakdown. My kids...

But I saw...

Or did I?

We walk back quietly, side by side, Yash holding my hand, squeezing it every so often.

'Over here,' Paul calls.

The kids, with the exception of Rachel, who's sitting on the veranda with her phone, are playing in the sand next to the shack with the proprietor's daughter. Lydia and Paul are sitting at a table with drinks, while keeping an eye on the kids.

'What can I get you?' Paul asks.

'Whatever you've having, mate, ta,' Yash says.

My phone beeps. A text.

Next time the graves will be filled and not only with sand and earth but with the coffins of your dead children.

'Jo? What will you have to drink?' Yash is asking. Then, as I bend over, gasping for breath, dropping the phone as if it is scalding me, his voice spikes with concern. 'Jo, love, what's the matter?'

'I... I...' I can't say it. With shaking hands, I manage to pick up the phone. 'Here, see for yourself.' Perhaps this will convince him that I'm not making up these text messages, like he and Lydia think. *Why* would I make up this horrid, horrid message?

'What is it you want me to see?' Yash is puzzled.

'Look...' But it's not there. Perhaps, in my panic, or perhaps reflexively, I've deleted it. Like all the others.

Or was it there at all?

'Here, mate.' Paul is handing Yash his drink. 'Jo, what would you like?'

I can't answer.

'Cat got your tongue?'

When I still don't reply, Paul turns to Yash. 'What's the matter with your wife? Where did you both go haring to?'

I see my husband exchange knowing looks with Paul and Lydia even as he shakes his head: *Don't ask.*

And again I feel betrayed, left out; Paul, Lydia and Yash on one side and me, with my nerves and my hysteria, on another.

They're your husband and best friends. They're on your side. They care for you, they're worried about you.

I take in my happily playing children.

Are they in danger?

Or am I losing my mind, seeing things that aren't there?

TWENTY-FOUR

DAY 1

4:00 a.m.

The inspector, once again, leads me into one of the empty bedrooms in this cottage we've been moved into.

Outside, through the small window of this room, I can see that the heavy darkness of this intolerable night has eased somewhat. This is the first dawn in Ajit's life when I don't know exactly where my little boy is. The thought is enough to set my heart racing even as my insides twist in panic and pain. Where is he? How is he? Is he all right? I can't bear it. I cannot.

'Do you have any enemies?' the inspector asks. 'Someone with reason to hate you.'

Faces rise before my eyes. I loved them, hated them. Flip sides of the same coin. But would they do this...?

I think of the texts, my suspicion – conviction? – as to who might be sending them. I think of the feeling of being watched all the time, of JT, who I thought I glimpsed at the market.

I shiver.

Are the sins of my past coming home to roost?

And in that instant, I make my decision. I don't care what

this man thinks of me, whether he decides I'm paranoid, that I'm making things up, that I'm mad, as long as he explores every avenue, finds my son.

I take a deep breath and say, 'I've been feeling stalked for a while, since the text messages started arriving.'

'Oh?' The inspector makes a note in his pad. 'Here as well?'

I nod. 'And yesterday at the market I thought I saw... someone from my past.'

'You knew them in England?'

'Yes.'

'But you think they might have followed you here?'

Do I detect a slant to the inspector's usually impassive voice? Is it curiosity? Disbelief? Suspicion? I can't tell. His face, as always, gives nothing away.

'Yes,' I say.

'Is there a reason this person might do so?'

'Yes.'

'Do you think they are capable of taking Ajit?'

I pause as memories ambush, nausea swirling in my stomach. JT outside my window when I pulled back the curtains...

'The JT I knew was unpredictable. Volatile.'

'Ah.'

I twist my hands on my lap. They ache to hold my boy.

The inspector says, 'We'll try our best to find JT. Now, please start at the beginning, how you crossed paths with this person, why you believe they might be here and might have taken Ajit.'

'I don't know if *JT* has taken my son.' I pause, my mouth roiling with salt as I think again of that glimpse of that familiar profile at the market after the horrific terror of nearly losing Ajit. 'But I can't rule it out.'

The inspector nods and waits, pencil poised over his notepad.

I take a breath, my mouth flooding with bile. 'My husband

doesn't know. Please could you keep what I'm going to tell you from him?'

The inspector looks impassively at me. No judgement in his gaze. 'I can't promise that, Mrs Kumar, especially if this person has something to do with your son's disappearance.'

I swallow. Speak through a mouthful of bile. 'I understand.'

He nods. And waits for me to begin.

TWENTY-FIVE

DAY 1

4:30 a.m.

'Sir?' One of the inspector's subordinates pops his head round the door.

'Excuse me a moment, please.' The inspector leaves the room and I perch on the edge of the bed, utterly exhausted.

I don't know how much time has passed, but word of Ajit's disappearance seems to have spread like wildfire – even more gawkers and journalists are collecting in front of the cottage, come to pick over our tragedy. Ajit's name is being bandied about. My son's name, no longer his alone, but public property.

A burst of breeze angles through the window, smelling of frenzy, noise, activity, cool but carrying the promise of heat, the smell of desperation and loss.

Why haven't they found him yet, all those people scouring the beach?

Yash comes into the bedroom, sits next to me, drops his head in his hands. 'I can't bear it, Jo. I wish there was some way we could turn the clock back.' His face haggard, blanching as he says it.

I am alight with anger, sudden and raging, directed at my husband. *If you hadn't wanted to go along with Lydia's suggestion of spending the evening at the shack, leaving the kids in Rachel's care...* It's unjustified, I know. I went too. But the urge to blame someone else is strong.

I hadn't wanted to go. I was exhausted from the stresses of the day. I wanted to read to my children, perhaps have a snooze when they fell asleep, like I used to at home. But I didn't want to be a party pooper. This was our longed-for holiday and I felt I should be making the most of it. And, I also worried that if I wasn't there, the other three would discuss my problems, my *issues*. Even if they were doing it because they cared, the thought made me queasy. And so I went along, ignoring my every instinct, leaving my children behind.

'The girls?' I ask.

'All the hoo-ha outside woke them.'

'Oh, I should—'

'They're OK. Lydia's seeing to them.'

'Why was the inspector called away, do you know?' I ask.

'Something to do with getting warrants for the search of the cottages across the road,' Yash says.

The cottages across the road. Is Ajit in one of them even now? So close and yet... lost to me.

I look at my husband and think back to what he had wanted and yet at the same time was strangely hesitant to share with me, looking relieved when the inspector interrupted us.

What secrets are you keeping from me? I think. I want to know, but I realise with a sense of something akin to detachment that whatever it is, it doesn't matter. Nothing does except holding Ajit in my arms.

Nevertheless, it is a distraction from waiting for news. From the horrid imaginings running a loop in my head of what might have happened to my boy, what he might be going through. Whatever Yash's secrets are, *nothing* can be as bad as this.

I'm just about to ask Yash what it was he wanted to tell me but was finding it so hard to when there's a firm knock on the door and the inspector enters without waiting for a response. 'Last few questions, Mrs Kumar.'

TWENTY-SIX

www.goadaily.in
13 February

Holiday Nightmare – Boy Missing
Prabhakar Tunde, Staff Reporter

Holiday of a lifetime turns into a nightmare for British couple after their child went missing late last night.

Ajit Kumar, five, was last seen sleeping in his bedroom in the holiday cottage he shared with his parents, siblings, his parents' friends and their children, when he disappeared.

Jo and Yash Kumar were holidaying in secluded Galgibaga Beach with their children and their friends, Lydia and Paul King, and their children, when their son went missing. They chose this idyllic paradise because 'they wanted to get away from it all' according to a source close to them.

Mr King and Mr Kumar run an IT services business together in Croydon, UK, and this trip with their families was to celebrate the ten-year anniversary of their joint business venture. They chose Galgibaga as it was 'private' and they wanted 'a restful holiday'. They hired the remote cottage on Galgibaga from a friend of Yash Kumar's, Ravi Chandani, who relocated to India from the UK in 2015 and started a travel company based here in Goa, selling luxury holidays to Brits.

Jo and Yash Kumar and Lydia and Paul King were on the beach at a bar shack, a few paces from the cottage, while the Kings' fourteen-year-old daughter, Rachel King, stayed behind in the cottage to babysit the little ones. She was in the living room, texting her friends, when Ajit Kumar was discovered to be missing. She claims she did not hear or see anything and that she was there the whole time. The living room was well lit and the party on the beach maintain that they could just about make Rachel King out through the glass-paned front door and mesh screen, our source states.

The Kings and Kumars took turns to check on Bella, ten, Mia, nine, Zoe, eight, and Ajit, five, who were sleeping off their jet lag. When Lydia King checked at 11:00 p.m., all the kids were present and fast asleep. But when Jo Kumar went to check at a quarter past midnight, Ajit was gone.

Interpol is liaising with Goan police to find Ajit.

Comments:

Malli, Pune 08:22 IST: Mr. Prabhakar, your 'source' close to the family is Rachel and Lydia King's social media, isn't it? How could you feed off their tragedy like this? Shame on you!

Veena, Utorda 08:28 IST: I think the source is someone else. Nowhere on Rachel or Lydia King's social media do they mention where they are going on holiday or why. I checked. Jo Kumar, on the other hand, has no privacy settings at all!

Shweta, Mumbai 08:30 IST: The little boy may have been kidnapped for ransom. I cannot begin to imagine what the parents are going through! Not good for the Indian tourism industry either if children of holidaymakers are targeted like this. #FindAjit.

Felcy, Madgaon 08:37 IST: Perhaps it isn't kidnapping but a simple case of getting lost. The child might have woken up and wandered off on his own. What were those parents thinking, leaving those young kids in the care of a fourteen-year-old – a child herself, not to mention with the sea nearby, the children sleeping in an unfamiliar place and the little boy only five years old... Neglect, that's what I call it. Pure carelessness on the part of the parents, who were thinking only of themselves. #Irresponsible #DontDeserveKids #FindAjit

Dita, Panaji 08:41 IST: I'm with you, Felcy. I feel for the fourteen-year-old, in all of this. Can you imagine the guilt that poor child must be feeling? I think we as a society should reconsider leaving children in care of other children. Fourteen is too young to foist responsibilities of looking after younger children, IMHO.

Scroll down for more comments.

TWENTY-SEVEN

DAY 1

9:00 a.m.

'Here, you need to eat something,' Lydia says, handing me a roll. One of the policemen kindly brought us some food and essentials.

I take the roll from her, look at it. Why do I need to eat something? How can I?

Outside, the picturesque beach is overrun by reporters lobbing questions to anyone unlucky enough to cross their path. So loud that I can hear even with the front door shut. Noisy enough to unearth the dead.

The dead...

Please let Ajit be safe. A prayer that doesn't make sense. The only place he is safe is here, with his parents. But we didn't keep him safe.

And yet still I pray.

In the early hours of this morning, the inspector and all but one of his subordinates finally took their leave of our replacement cottage, though there are still policemen dotted around the beach and surrounds. I know this because, after the inspector left, and with the girls asleep under the others' watchful gaze (why hadn't we done this yesterday? I couldn't help thinking), I was unable to sit still and wait for my son to turn up, and ran outside, pushing past the gangs of reporters and rubberneckers who had ambushed me, and searched for Ajit. The reporters followed at a distance, taking pictures of the mother who had abandoned her son to drink on the beach with her friends and husband, lobbing intrusive questions like so many grenades. I deserved them and the pitying looks, quickly stifled, that the policemen patrolling the beach gave me as I called for Ajit until my throat was hoarse, still holding out hope that if he was hiding, he would emerge at the sound of my voice.

I returned, defeated, to Lydia trying to feed me breakfast.

A knock on the front door. Yash's eyes meet mine, the alarm in his gaze mirroring mine. Has something happened? Have they found Ajit? Is he all right?

The policeman who is keeping us company, stationed unobtrusively in the corner of the room, stands and opens the door a crack and then wider, the pressing din from outside surging into the silent, grieving room. 'When did you find out Ajit was missing?' 'Why were you on the beach when your children…?'

Paul slips inside and the policeman shuts the door before returning to his seat, shutting out the questions that fire my guilt, make me want to bang my head against the wall and yell, 'I'm a bad mother. I should never have let my children out of my sight.'

I didn't even know Paul wasn't in here. He looks haggard, sweaty. He is panting, breathless from dodging the reporters, the mikes thrust in his mouth, the endless questions, I imagine.

The fury I feel is inky in my mouth, throbbing hot, a vial of pepper juice. How dare he trick us into thinking something had happened, that it was someone bearing news, perhaps bringing Ajit back?

'Where were you?' I ask and my voice is harsh, tipped velvet blue with anger.

'Went to get some milk.' He holds up a shopping bag. 'When they brought us supplies, they forgot the milk and I fancied some tea. He said it was OK.' Paul gestures at the policeman.

Lydia comes over from where she has been sitting at the table – like in 'our' cottage, here too there is no dining room, the table in the living room serving the purpose – with her girls and mine. The children have been confused and fractious, sporting identical anxious expressions no matter how much we try and reassure them, for they've picked up on our own angst. They've had a disturbed and bewildering few hours, having to change cottages in the middle of the night, policemen everywhere, reporters lobbing questions, noise, chaos and yet, no Ajit.

'Jo,' Lydia says in a pacifying tone. 'We're all in the same—'

'*No*, we are not all in the same situation or whatever it was you were going to say. I've had enough of being babied.' I know I'm being unfair, irrationally turning on my friends, who are only trying to help. But I'm angry, fed up, upset and, to be perfectly honest, more than a little jealous of Lydia and Paul – they haven't lost their children – and turning on them takes the onus away from my nightmarish imaginings with regards to Ajit and my guilt and anger at myself for losing my precious, beautiful boy.

'Mum,' Zoe says, coming up to me. 'Why are you shouting?'

My middle child, my fiercely independent girl, looks close to tears. Her eyes are huge and bloodshot.

I gather her in my arms, bury my face in her hair. 'I'm sorry. I'll stop now.' My voice is shaking.

'Ajit will come back, Mum. He's just run away and is hiding, is all. But the police are searching for him and they'll find him,' Zoe tells me earnestly. My eight-year-old nods like a wise old woman, repeating the words someone – Yash or Lydia or Paul – has said to her. My little girl, trying her best to comfort me and herself. *Please say this is true, Mum*, is what she is really asking.

And so... 'Yes,' I whisper into her hair, which smells of sweat and fear and is gritty with sand despite my scrubbing of the previous evening.

The previous evening – when I had all my children.

TWENTY-EIGHT

DAY 1

Noon

When morning came, I hoped that they would find Ajit.

And now it is noon.

Inspector Sharma is hopefully doing something useful, following up on the leads he spent much of the night extracting from us.

Both my girls are clingy, sitting on my lap, which suits me, for I am drawing as much comfort from them as they are from me. Mia has fallen asleep in my arms. Like Yash, she has always found solace in sleep when life overwhelms her. I envy them this ability.

Yash gently disentangles Mia from my embrace and carries her to the sofa instead of the bedroom, knowing instinctively that I don't want my girls out of my sight. Zoe snuggles closer to me and I kiss the top of her head.

'Jo.' It's Rachel. Her face, devoid of make-up, looks very young. And scared.

'Yes?'

'I haven't been honest with you.'

Ah, so I was right. She *was* hiding something.

'Go on, I'm listening,' I say, trying to sound encouraging, while inside I'm anxious, nervous, impatient. What is she going to say and how is it connected with Ajit going missing?

'Last night when babysitting, I... I drank some of the alcohol Mum and Dad had bought at the airport – the cashew liquor.'

'What?'

'And smoked one of Mum's cigarettes. I sprayed my deodorant to mask the smell – that was what you commented on when you came in.'

Ah, that explains the odd scent when I entered the cottage those few blessed moments before I discovered that my son was missing – I had thought it was rotting pears. But I'm still trying to process Rachel's words...

'Lydia doesn't smoke.' I look to Lydia for confirmation.

She is pale, her gaze slinking away from mine. 'I... I do sometimes.'

I am thrown. Lydia is my best friend. How do I not know this? Have I been so selfish, so self-absorbed, that I haven't learned this basic thing about someone whom I think of as my family, my soul sister? What else don't I know about her?

Rachel is saying, 'Ajit rumbled me and I... I was harsh with him.' She sniffs, tears swelling in her eyes, tumbling down her cheeks.

'Wait. What?' I haven't heard right, surely? But that expression on her face...

'You said Ajit didn't wake up.' I try not to sound accusatory, but, nevertheless, my voice rises involuntarily.

'I lied.' Her voice is very small. 'He came to me after Mum had left after checking on us. He said he couldn't sleep. He was shocked to see me drinking and smoking. I shouted at him but can't quite remember what I said. He... he was in tears and went back to bed.'

'You...' I can't keep the agitation I'm feeling, the hurt on

Ajit's behalf, the anger at myself for failing my son so badly, from my voice.

On the sofa, Mia stirs in her sleep, letting out a small moan.

'Jo.' Yash lays a warning hand on my shoulder. I shrug it off, thinking of my son. My beloved boy, unable to sleep, wanting comfort, in tears because this girl shouted at him. I should have been here, looking after my kids, not leaving this child experimenting at being a grown-up and wildly out of her depth in charge...

Lydia puts her arms around her daughter and Rachel lets her, even as she looks at me with tear-bright eyes. 'And then I think... in fact, I'm sure I fell asleep for a bit. I was drunk and also jet-lagged.'

No. Oh no. I didn't think I could feel any worse after Rachel's previous revelation but I do. I do. What else will I find out before this nightmare is over? I cannot bear to know how else my son was let down last night.

And yet I ask, 'For how long?'

'I woke up just before you came. I went to the loo and was just going to check on them when I saw you walking up.' She pauses, taking a breath. Lydia pats her back encouragingly. Then, taking another deep breath, Rachel says, her voice stumbling on a sob, 'I was messaging my friends and there isn't any activity recorded from me from roughly eleven twenty p.m. until around ten minutes before you came.'

I checked on the kids at a quarter past twelve. So my son was unattended for nearly an hour! And he had been awake and in tears in a strange place without anyone to offer comfort, soothe him back into slumber...

Rachel's face, worry and guilt, blurs before my eyes.

She's just a child, a voice in my head whispers.

So is my son. My baby. Completely defenceless, while we sat in a drunken stupor on the beach. Snatched away while I marinated my worries in alcohol. Too late I see that all those things I was worrying about were nothing, *nothing*, compared to this.

'Jo.' Yash's hand again on my shoulder, pressing down, urging – warning? – me to be calm. Again, I shrug his hand off with more vehemence than necessary.

Rachel looks terrified. So anxious and remorseful.

Someone else's child. Not mine.

Bile rises, overwhelms.

I stand up, gently dislodging Zoe from my lap. Yash takes her from me.

'I'm sorry, Jo.' Rachel's voice is small.

There is a scream trapped in my throat, endless, keening, and I can't reply, rushing to the bathroom, where I splash water upon my face while taking deep breaths. One. Two. Three. A lizard watches me from behind the mirror, bulbous eyes in a pale-yellow head. Rubbery body. It appears to be urging calm, patience. I take more deep breaths, counting to ten and back.

You can get through this, I tell myself. *You have to, for Ajit's sake.* The lizard watches impassively as with another deep, bolstering breath, I leave the bathroom.

I come back into the living room to a tableau of pale faces. Bella sits at the table colouring, head bent. Did the policeman who brought the supplies bring the colouring pens and drawing pad, or did Lydia have the presence of mind to get them last night, something to keep the girls occupied, as we were shepherded, panicked and uncomprehending, still coming to terms with Ajit's disappearance, into this cottage?

Why am I thinking this *now*?

Bella is drawing a picture of Ajit, her tongue poking out of her mouth in concentration – I can tell it is Ajit because of the toy in his hands. Bright yellow.

My innocent son, let down by the people closest to him, who were meant to protect him.

'I'm sorry, Jo,' Rachel says again.

My son, in his pyjamas and slippered feet, will be sweltering. *If* he is out there...

I cannot look at her. 'Have you told Inspector Sharma?'
I ask.

'I wanted to tell you first.'

And then, I cannot help it, I explode. All the fury inside me,
the anger directed at myself, erupting. 'What use is it telling
me? The inspector ought to know so they can find Ajit, for
God's sake.'

Bella stops drawing to stare at me, horror washing her face,
which looks close to crumpling. Paul goes up to her, gathers her
in his arms.

Mia wakes and starts to cry.

Zoe is sobbing in Yash's arms, covering her ears with her
palms. 'Mum, don't shout,' she pleads in between sobs.

The policeman who is watching out for us – or keeping an
eye on us? – says, 'It's OK. I tell Inspector Sahib.' He speaks
very slowly, his English not as good as Inspector Sharma's.

Rachel is weeping, huge tears silently dropping from her
eyes. Lydia, her arms around her child, glares at me, saying,
tightly, 'Jo, I cannot begin to imagine what you're going through.
But there was no need for that. She's hurting enough already.
She blames herself for Ajit's disappearance, although it wasn't
her fault. It was incredibly brave of her to tell you – it required
all of her strength. And instead of thanking her for it, you shout
at her.'

Lydia's intervention, instead of calming me, only serves to
fan the flames of my rage. 'So you knew all along?'

'She told me just before you.'

'Why didn't she tell the police earlier then, when they
talked to all of us?' Again, I can't help the harsh note that
colours my voice.

'She was *terrified*. It took all of her courage to confide in me
and then to tell you. She is just a child...'

Just a child. 'Ajit is just a child too and he's lost somewhere out there.' My voice stumbles and breaks.

'Mum, don't cry,' Mia begs.

'I'm not. It's all right.' With effort, I swallow down the salty lump that has hijacked my throat. 'I'm sorry, Rachel. It was brave of you to tell me.' And it was, I know. She is only a child out of her depth in a situation that has spiralled out of control.

'I shouldn't have shouted at him and, um, fallen asleep when I was meant to be babysitting,' she sniffles.

'It wasn't your fault. We should have been watching.' I say the words that have haunted me ever since it happened. We should have been watching. 'We didn't see anyone go into the cottage, did we?' I look at the others, wanting confirmation, redemption. Wanting someone to take away this burden of guilt dousing me.

'It was dark,' Paul says softly. 'And we were drunk. You had your eyes closed half the time, Jo.'

'Are you blaming me?' I snap, burning anger never far from the surface.

'No, just stating facts,' Paul says evenly. 'The front door was sticking and wouldn't shut fully. The wire mesh door was shut but not locked. The window was open. Anybody could have gone indoors. Anybody could have taken Ajit. No point in us blaming each other.'

'Jo, can I have a word with you, please? In private,' Yash says.

Our girls have calmed down somewhat and Lydia sits on the sofa and gathers them, and Rachel, to her.

Even in my agitation, I note that Rachel must be very upset indeed if she allowed her mother to embrace her when she was confessing to me and is now letting Lydia comfort her. I bite back the guilt of knowing that I behaved atrociously just now. But it ambushes me, bitter yellow, settling on top of the guilt I feel for not keeping an eye on Ajit last night. I feel horrible for shouting at Rachel, taking my anger at myself out on her. She didn't deserve it. Like Lydia said, it was brave of her to tell me and I should have been grateful, not lashed out.

I am tired. So tired. It's been twelve hours since I found Ajit gone. And he is *still* missing.

TWENTY-NINE

DAY 1

12:30 p.m.

'Jo,' Yash says, as soon as we are alone in the bedroom where the inspector had questioned me before. 'You need to calm down. I know it's hard, but... You're scaring the kids.'

Although I agree with Yash, his sensible tone makes me lash out again. 'I don't need you to tell me how to behave.'

'Jo, love, please. The inspector... he was asking all these questions...'

'What questions?'

'Well...' Yash is hesitant.

'What questions, Yash?' I ask again, an edge to my voice.

'Paul told the inspector about you taking the kids AWOL yesterday and not answering our calls,' Yash says, all in a rush. 'And the girls told Rachel and Bella some crazy tale about Ajit being mowed down by a rickshaw and kidnapped by a madwoman...'

Oh God, that's all I need.

I haven't told Yash about what happened at the market. I couldn't, after I overheard his conversation with Lydia, the graves that I'm sure I saw, and the text that I'm positive I received. I was feeling ganged up on, my husband and best friend didn't believe me, and I did not want that reinforced. This was also why I had gone along with my husband and friends to the beach shack that evening, even though I would rather have stayed with the kids and caught up on sleep; I didn't want to give them more ammunition, the chance to discuss me unhindered, decide that what I had seen was more evidence that I was losing it, and stage an intervention. It was also why I had drunk so much, trying to put all that had happened, the nightmare day I'd had, behind me. Ha! The joke was on me. While I sat stewing my sorrows in alcohol, the nightmare was just beginning...

'Yash, this inspector... why hasn't he found Ajit yet? It's been over twelve hours.' *Twelve hours.* My stomach cramps and head pounds with the effort of trying not to imagine what might have happened, be happening, to my beloved boy even as my arms ache to hold him. The anger, the impotence, the frustration, I need an outlet... 'I don't know whether to trust this inspector to find Ajit. I've read that Indian police take bribes and they might—'

'That's enough, Jo.' Yash bites through gritted teeth. 'The inspector appears to be working hard to find our son. Let's give him the benefit of the doubt.'

I flinch from the venom in his voice. Although I'm sure Yash doesn't mean to sound quite so sharp, I feel berated. We are both stressed and upset, and a part of me understands that Yash, like me, is taking out his anguish on those closest to him. But it *hurts*, and I understand, remorse and guilt heaping on top of my angst, how Paul and Lydia and Rachel must have felt when I snapped at them just now.

'I'm thinking of Ajit...' I begin.

'I know, love. I am too.' He is gentle now, but that annoys me too. I am not a child to be managed.

What is happening to me? My emotions are so close to the surface, like a pot at boiling point, and they spill over into anger one minute and irritation the next at the smallest provocation.

'Please let the police do their job,' Yash is saying and I hear the desperation in his voice, the desperation I myself am feeling. 'They are liaising with Interpol, so they will be doing everything by the book.'

'The inspector is already wasting time by suspecting *me* because Paul told tales...' *Did you also?* I want to ask.

'Well, you don't remember going for a drunken amble around the cottage,' Yash says. 'You were upset with me, accusing me and Lydia of not believing you about the text messages. You were threatening to take the kids and run again like you did that morning.'

My brain feels fuzzy as I try to remember the drunken evening – was it just yesterday? – which I would do anything to go back to and relive and this time I would stay with my children, not let them out of my sight. I had woken from my alcohol-induced slump with my throat feeling hoarse, as if I had shouted at somebody... Yash. I'd been railing at Yash. But I can't recall it. Much of the night after the third glass of wine, including the part Yash is referring to, is a sluggish blank.

A knock at the door. Hope flares, even as my hand goes to my heart. *Please.*

It's the inspector, followed by Lydia and Paul, all looking grave. The bedroom feels too small suddenly, claustrophobic despite the window being open and the briny sea air, humid and moist and sun-baked, drifting in.

The small burn of hope dies just as quickly as it ignited, replaced by raw, naked fear at the expression on the inspector's face. 'What's happened?'

Is it something to do with what I shared with him, who I thought I saw at the market? Has he found JT? Does JT have Ajit? I don't care if it all comes out – I just want my son.

'We are still looking for Ajit,' the inspector says.

He hasn't been found. But it isn't anything worse.

He's alive. He's safe, I tell myself. They *will* find him.

'Your children are in the living room. One of my men is keeping an eye on them,' the inspector explains, looking at me, somehow knowing that I needed that reassurance.

'Why are you here, Inspector?' I ask.

'We've been liaising with Interpol and the British Consulate and...' He pauses. 'Some information has come to light that I've questioned Mr King about and feel it would be fair for him to let you know.'

'What information?' Yash barks.

Paul goes red, a myriad of expressions fleeting across his face. Embarrassment, defensiveness, guilt, shame, finally settling on anger. *Guilt? Shame?*

Why?

Beside him, Lydia squeezes his hand.

'Hang on,' I say, my voice shrill. 'Inspector, are you saying Paul, *our* Paul, had dealings with the police?' I turn to Yash. 'Did you know about this?'

But Yash is alert, outraged, looking at Paul with murder in his eyes. 'Paul, what's all this?'

Yash doesn't know either.

'It was baseless,' Paul explodes. 'It was when I was coaching Kids Club football. An anonymous call to the police.'

'Saying what?' Yash asks, belligerent.

Paul pulls at the neck of his T-shirt as if it's choking him. 'I... I was accused of touching a child.'

'Wait. *What?*' Yash cries while I'm speechless.

I cannot comprehend Paul's words. They make absolutely zero sense. *Our* Paul? Touching a ... No. No. It can't be. It cannot, I tell myself even as I frantically try to count the sheer number of times I've left my three with Paul.

I feel sick. Why didn't I know about this?

The children... My precious, beautiful, innocent children. Has he...?

No. *No.*

My mouth is dry, my voice raspy as if I've been screaming endlessly, unleashing my befuddled terror. 'Lydia, you knew?'

My best friend looks at me with wild eyes, pleading for understanding. 'There was an investigation, but the police found *nothing.*'

My friend has lied to me. She's allowed me to put my children in danger. I cover my mouth with my hand, trying to stem the fresh bout of nausea.

'Lydia you *knew* and yet you stayed with him, and not only that, but allowed this man... this predator near your children. Mine.' A whisper is all I can manage.

'I'm no predator,' Paul storms, face florid, eyes incensed.

I shudder, thinking of him with my children. God, he's even taken them swimming! Has he...?

No, not *Paul.* Gentle giant, we call him fondly.

Oh God. My children. How to ask them if Paul has...

No – please, no.

'Paul,' Yash is saying, 'look at me. Look at me and tell me it isn't true.'

'It isn't, I swear. You know me, Yash, mate. I'm not that sort,' Paul says emphatically.

Lydia believes him. And it is *Paul.* I cannot believe he'd do this. I am desperate, *desperate* to accept Paul's innocence. For the alternative is too horrible to comprehend.

And Lydia... Lydia knew. She's known all along.

My mouth tastes bitter, nausea swirling in my stomach. I'm angry, raging, fuming, recoiling from the sheer horror of it. 'You should have told me, Lydia.' My voice is a keen. 'You should have let me decide whether I believed Paul or not, if I wanted my children anywhere near him.'

I shiver, once again thinking of all those times I've left my children with Paul. I'll have a chat with the kids about whether they've ever felt uncomfortable with Paul. I will book a counsellor when we get home... Home... Ajit. For a moment there, in all of this, I actually forgot that Ajit was missing... How can we go home if Ajit...?

No, he *will* be found. And soon. Today. In the next hour. Please.

'I wanted to, Jo, but...' Lydia is saying, 'you worry, Jo, so much, especially about the kids and whether you're doing right by them.'

'You know why I do,' I say, thinking back to the terrible times when I failed my children. Each time, I had promised myself that I wouldn't do so again, that I would be the best mother I was capable of being. But I haven't kept that promise – I've failed them, over and over, and now, this, losing one of my children.

'I know,' Lydia is saying, 'and I've told you often enough that I think you're overly hard on yourself. But coming back to Paul... Even though he was found not guilty, you'd agonise. You would stop seeing us, bringing the kids round. We wouldn't be friends any more.' She looks at me, eyes wide with anguish and plea. 'I acted selfishly, I agree. But you... our friendship, it's special to me.'

And despite everything that's going on, my heart warms a little at this. I've always believed our friendship to be one-sided, with me needing Lydia more than she does me, but now she's telling me that she needs me too. It doesn't make what she did, keeping this from me, right, not by a long way. But still... I understand why she did it.

'And I love your kids like my own,' she's saying.

This I know without a doubt. And while she loves my girls, she has a special spot for Ajit. Him going missing must be hell for her too, I realise suddenly. It should be self-evident, but I haven't been thinking straight since I found Ajit gone. Lydia always wanted a boy herself. 'But it was not to be,' she'd said, shrugging, eyes shimmering. 'And in any case, I've Ajit.'

'Believe me,' she is saying now, 'if there was even a suggestion, the smallest hint, that our children – yours, mine – were in danger, I would have left him immediately. But, Jo, I promise – and you know this too – Paul is a good man.'

'It was still my... Yash's and my...' I look at my husband. Following his initial bluster, he is now shell-shocked, traumatised, as he tries to come to terms with what's been revealed. Yash's face is drawn and grey; he appears beaten. This ordeal has aged my husband, who usually looks younger than his years. I turn to Lydia, finish what I was saying, '... decision to make, to decide on what was best for our children.'

'Yes,' she agrees, eyes shining with tears. 'I'm so sorry, Jo.'

My head is a swarm of thoughts. There's something nudging, poking. Something from the night Ajit went missing. Was it only yesterday? It feels like forever ago since I've held my boy in my arms. My memory is fuzzy, but the detail that is angling for my attention finally comes to the surface.

'Paul, you went to get another bottle of wine for us just after Lydia came back from checking on the kids. This was around an hour before I went to check on them and discovered Ajit gone. I remember looking up at the bar, but you weren't there.' My voice is frenzied with accusation. Raw. Coarse. Not quite mine.

'What're you implying, Jo?' Lydia asks, and now her voice is sharp. 'That Paul had something to do with it? Haven't you been listening to a word I've been saying?' She laughs, a mirthless, harsh bark. 'Why would he, Jo? Even if, like you've assumed, as if you don't know Paul, haven't called him your friend for the last decade and a half, he's... what you think he is...' Her voice breaks. 'Even if so, why would he take Ajit when he had access to him right here?'

I shudder at the thought.

Lydia notices and cries hoarsely, 'Think, for God's sake.

Where would he take him? And why would he scare you, all of us, like this?'

The inspector clears his throat and we startle. In all of this, we've forgotten him. And he has been standing here, watching us blame each other, turn on each other. Does he suspect us? Of course he does. I read somewhere that the first people suspicion falls on when a child goes missing are the parents. And in our case, I suppose their friends too, as we are all staying together. It dawns on me that this is why he wanted to be here when Paul told us about this, so he could record our reactions, and try to gauge our guilt or innocence, move us up or down his list of suspects, as it were.

Would he do the same with what I've confided in him about who I thought I saw at the market? I have no doubt he will bring it up in front of everyone when the moment is right, if he thinks it will help his investigation. And in a strange way, this thought strengthens my shaky trust in the inspector. He's willing to do all he can, stopping at nothing, like Yash said, to find our son.

'Look,' I say to the inspector, and my voice is despairing. I don't recognise it. This ordeal is changing me just as much as Yash, wringing me inside out, turning me into the very rawest version of myself, a mother desperate for her child.

I think of that harsh bent to Lydia's voice just now that I've not heard before, Paul's eyes wild, his face incensed... It is changing not only us but our friends too, making them into strangers.

'Yes, Mrs Kumar?'

'I know you're looking into us and that's fine.' I was upset that he was asking my friends and husband about me. But now I get it. There are secrets even between us, and they need to come out so we get to the bottom of this. Find Ajit. My husband will likely find out what I've been keeping from him. He will be hurt and that will hurt me, heap guilt on top of what I already feel for what I did, but in the grand scheme of things, if it helps to find Ajit, then that's all that matters. Yash is keeping something from me too, he all but told me... And who knows what else will be unearthed, but if there's even the smallest chance that it might be connected with Ajit's disappearance and lead us to finding my son, then I'm all for it. 'I understand it's your job, but please, don't just concentrate on us...' My voice breaks.

'Mrs Kumar, please be assured that my men and I are doing everything in our power to find your son. We are leaving... what's that expression you use... no stone unturned.'

I nod, but our conversation is interrupted by my husband, who's been quiet until now, processing everything, his face haggard, gaze tormented, now crying, 'How could you keep this from me, Lydia?'

'Paul didn't do anything wrong,' Lydia snaps, clearly at the end of her tether.

'How do you know?' Yash challenges.

'What do you mean, how do I know? I'm his wife, in case you hadn't noticed, Yash,' Lydia says, emitting a joyless chuckle.

'Husbands and wives keep secrets from each other,' Yash says and there's something there. Some pointed implication that causes me to look at my husband keenly. But he's looking at Lydia, eyebrows raised in question. It makes me wonder if he knows something Lydia is keeping from Paul. Perhaps Lydia is not only sharing *my* secrets with him but her own too.

'You work with Paul, spend more time with him than I do.' Lydia laughs harshly. 'You know he wouldn't do this.'

'I'm standing right here,' Paul blusters. 'I've already said, mate, and I'll say it again: I didn't do it. I'm not that sort.'

But Yash ignores Paul, he's focused on Lydia. 'I deserved to know when you found out,' Yash cries, voice breaking. He fists his left hand and punches his right palm in frustration. 'For Chrissake, he is bringing up my daughter.'

What is he talking about?

Lydia has turned red.

Paul is staring from her to Yash. '*What?* What did you just say?'

Yash has dropped his head into his hands.

'What did you mean, Yash?' My voice is a cowering mouse, squeaky soft, even as Paul, quicker to get there, bites, his voice dangerously quiet. 'Which daughter?'

THIRTY

DAY 1

1:15 p.m.

'This isn't true. Yash, tell me it isn't true,' I whisper, gripped by an entirely different fear to what I've been experiencing since Ajit went missing.

'Aargh, I'm such a fool.' My husband, this man I've known and loved for fifteen years, is looking at me with pain-filled hollows for eyes. 'I'm so sorry, Jo. I didn't mean to...'

'You didn't mean to... what? Disclose your dirty secret? Sleep with my wife? Pass off your daughter as mine?' Paul booms. 'Which daughter?' he asks, again.

'I...' Yash rubs a weary hand across his brow, the gesture resigned, defeated. 'It's... um... Rachel... She is mine.'

I cannot process it. I cannot. Yash and Lydia. The image of the two of them, my husband and my friend, entwined, seared behind my eyelids, the wretchedness of the betrayal tasting of bile and vomit in my mouth.

No. No, no, no.

I think of the ring on Lydia's finger that I was sure was

mine. Which I last recall putting in the safe. The safe to which the only other person who has access is Yash.

Lydia's bikini among Yash's things.

Lydia and Yash in our bedroom, yesterday, with the door closed, whispering, while Lydia's husband slept next door and I snoozed on the veranda. *Only* whispering?

'The text messages...' I murmur. 'They were right.'

'No, they were not, Jo. I've not had an affair, I'm not... It was just the once fifteen years ago when I started dating you.' He is defeated, his voice despairing. Remorseful.

But what's the point of remorse now? 'So you were with me when...'

'I... I'm sorry. It was just the once.'

As if that excuses it. And how can I believe him, this man I thought I knew inside out? What else is he keeping from me? How many lies? How many secrets? How many children?

'Is Bella...?'

'No! It. Was. Just. The. Once.' He emphasises every word, jaw clenched.

Why is he getting so angry? So defensive? Once is one too many. Why? Why did he do it? How can I trust him after this?

I know I was thinking just minutes ago that everything needs to come out so the inspector can do his job, sort the relevant from the inconsequential, but this... It hurts, oh how it *hurts*. Even now, even with the terrible wound of Ajit missing, this hurts too, bruises my already abused heart. I will never again be able to look at Rachel and not be forever searching for bits of Yash. I can never unlearn this.

I have to rethink everything I have believed. The foundation of my life with Yash is rooted in lies. My husband has been lying to me for as long as I've known him and so has my best friend. I thought, when I didn't know Lydia smoked, that it was because I was too self-absorbed, too lost in my own problems to ask her about hers, find out more about her. Now I see it in a different light. She has been deliberately keeping things from me.

'Lydia, how could you?' I look at my best friend. Her familiar features rendered strange by what I have learned. 'I thought you and Yash were just friends.'

She looks at me with sadness in her eyes. 'I wanted to tell you so many times.'

'Why didn't you?'

'How could I?'

'You slept together when Yash was with me.'

'Just the once.' Lydia repeating Yash's words.

It shouldn't need saying but I say it anyway, to my supposed best friend, 'That doesn't make it right.'

Paul bunches his hand into a fist and brings it down hard on the bedside table. We all jump back, startled.

'Now, Mr King,' the inspector cautions.

And once again I am shocked, disorientated, to see the inspector here, observing everything, taking note.

The skin on Paul's hand is flaring red, but he ignores it, saying, through gritted teeth, 'I cannot believe it. How could you, Lydia?'

'It was one indiscretion.' Lydia sounds upset, sad.

And again, I think, what's the point of sadness, upset, regret after the fact?

'But you've been lying to me all our married life,' Paul states and his voice is a river of pain. 'Rachel,' he cries and it is a lament. 'My little girl.'

I am conflicted about Paul, but right at this moment, I feel for him, reciprocal tears stinging my eyes.

'Paul, I was convinced she was yours. It was only recently that I found out...' Lydia reaches for him and he recoils, stepping back, bumping against the bed.

'I cannot do this,' he says and storms out, the inspector moving aside to let him out the door.

We hear a bang and we all flinch.

The inspector nips outside to check.

Lydia comes to me, takes my hands in hers. I pull them away, roughly.

'Jo, look at me, please.'

The tears in her voice, the sheer anguish, a tone I haven't heard before from Lydia, make me do as she asks. She is my best friend and despite it all I love her.

'It happened before we were friends. When Yash had only just met you,' she says. 'Paul and I were going through a rough phase.'

'Why didn't you and Yash get together then?' I challenge, but my voice is hoarse, it comes out a whisper.

'You were the one for me, Jo,' Yash says. 'I was blown away by the strength of my feelings for you from the first time we met. They scared me, and I was worried you wouldn't feel the same. I slept with Lydia in a bid to stop me feeling this much for you, but it only made it clear to me that it was you I wanted.'

It makes a weird kind of sense. Yash has always been this way. When he feels too much, he retreats, steps away. When our children were born, he buried himself in work. He cannot deal with too much emotion, especially in himself. It scares him and he runs away from it. Yet, this doesn't excuse what he did, sleeping with Lydia because he cared too much for me and worried I didn't feel the same.

Lydia has tears in her eyes. She says, 'I have felt so terribly guilty ever since.' She sniffs. 'Especially once I got to know you. I... I have tried to tell you several times, but I didn't want our friendship to end. You are so loving and loyal but also insecure...'

'Oh, so now you're blaming me...'

'No, not blaming, just saying that it's why I didn't, I couldn't tell you. I... I knew things would never be the same between us once I came clean and... I didn't want that. I love you. I love your children like my own, especially Ajit...'

Ajit. It hits me afresh, the ache to hold him, the worry, the fear about what might have happened to him...

A knock at the door.

Again my heart rises in hope. Again it falls when I see it's the inspector, who gently shakes his head at me, noting my hopeful gaze, his eyes kind.

I don't want his kindness. I want him to find my boy.

'The noise was Paul going to a bedroom and slamming the door shut,' he explains. 'And I checked on the children. They're fine.'

I nod.

'Jo?' Lydia says. 'Let's call a truce, for Ajit's sake?'

I know Lydia means it – she is not using Ajit as a pawn to brush over what she did. She loves my boy like her own and his disappearance must be taking nearly as much of a toll on her as it is on me. Lydia once confided in me that she had wanted Bella to be a boy so badly. 'Of course I wouldn't change her for the world, but perhaps that's why I've such a soft spot for Ajit,' she'd said. Lydia adores my son. In fact, she was the first to hold him after Yash and me, and my girls. She had looked after the girls while I was in labour and brought them to the hospital to see their baby brother. She had held him in her arms, rocked him gently, tears running down her cheeks. 'Happy tears,' she'd said. 'He's so lovely.'

But I knew that in part she was imagining holding her own little boy.

She had always wanted three children, she told me, but she suffered a miscarriage after Bella and the doctor told her it was too risky to try again. I was upset that she hadn't felt able to confide in me but she said that I was going through my own hell back then, and I understood. I had been in no shape during that time to help anyone; I couldn't even help myself. But it didn't stop me wishing I'd been there for her like she had for me through all of my ups and downs. I look at her now. Lydia, who has listened to my problems and my impulsive and often rash actions without judgement, offered solutions and help, cared for me and looked after my children during that terrible time, and kept my secrets. Now I know why she always insisted our friendship was two-way. I thought I was burdening her with my problems, but she took it as her due after what she had done, what she was keeping from me: the accusation against her husband; the indiscretion with *my* husband.

I clear my throat. My voice, when I find it, is wet and wobbly. 'I need some time.'

'I understand. I love you, Jo, and I'm truly sorry.'

She means it, I can see. But how can I believe her when the very foundation of our friendship is based on the lie that she and Yash were *just* friends?

'I'll go talk to Paul,' she says, sniffing.

'I must be going too, checking on my team. I'll be back soon with updates,' the inspector says. His face is impassive, this man who has just watched us fall apart, been party to our darkest secrets, our worst emotions. What must he be thinking? I find that I do not have the energy to care. All I want is for him to find Ajit.

'Come back with my boy,' I say.

'I'll try my best, Mrs Kumar.'

Once we're alone, Yash looks at me. 'I'm so sorry.'

I'm sorry too. For what you've done. What you've kept from me all these years. For what I'm keeping from you. The hurt that's going to be caused when it comes out. The fallout from all of this. For our mistakes, our failings. 'What else are you keeping from me, Yash? The text messages...'

'Are lies. It was just the once.'

Do I believe him? Why would he lie about that if he's being

honest about Rachel being his? Why do I even care when our son is missing?

But I care. Yash is *my* husband.

You *are lying to him*, my conscience chides. *Keeping secrets from him.*

'Please, Jo. We need to come together for Ajit, not splinter apart. I love you, Jo. I married *you*.'

But I can't dismiss it that easily. 'Why sleep with her?'

'Because I was scared. The strength of my feelings for you shocked me and I... I ran into Lydia's arms.'

'But she was with Paul.'

'They were going through a phase. You know I told you, and I'm sure Lydia has too, how she and Paul were on again, off again during their first years together...'

'She also told me that they only settled down when Rachel came along.'

Yash looks guilty. 'She was sure Rachel was Paul's. It was only when Rachel had to go into hospital that time she fell off the trampoline; Paul was away at that IT conference...'

'You went with Rachel and Lydia while I looked after Bella and our kids,' I say, remembering.

'When the doctor revealed Rachel's blood type... we realised she was mine.'

I taste betrayal, bitter on my lips. Lydia and Yash playing happy families while I looked after our kids at home.

'If you had known about Rachel earlier, would you have...?' *Left me for her*, I want to say, but I cannot finish the sentence because of the brine flooding my mouth.

But Yash divines it anyway. 'No, Jo. It's always been you for me since the first time I saw you.'

'But you slept with Lydia anyway.'

'I'm sorry. So very sorry.'

'Why did you keep Lydia close after what happened?'

'She's family,' he says simply. 'You know how strict and uncompromising my parents were – Lydia was my confidante, more my family than anyone else, even my parents.'

He's told me this before. And I had accepted it. Have I been a fool to do so?

'Wasn't it awkward, when she and I became friends, and you both were keeping this secret from me?'

'It was horrible, Jo. But I... I didn't... couldn't bear to lose Lydia.'

'You should have thought of that before you slept with her,' I snap. I am angry. I feel betrayed. Devastated and wrung out by what I've learned.

'It was a mistake. One mistake which we've both regretted since. As I said, we didn't find out about Rachel till later. I'm so sorry for what I did. *You* are the love of my life.'

Do I believe him? Would he believe that I love him, that he's the love of my life, when – if – he found out everything I've been keeping from him?

In the end, it comes down to this: I love Yash. I love Lydia. They are the family I have chosen. They are all I have now when I face the worst crisis of my life. And right now all that matters is Ajit.

'Let's go see our girls,' I say wearily, thinking, even as I say it that 'our girls', for him, also includes Rachel.

Does Rachel look like Yash? She is the image of Lydia but dark where her mother is fair.

Dark. Both Paul and Lydia are fair.

Stop this.

Then a thought occurs to me.

Ajit has always been closer to Rachel than Bella. Even, I sometimes think, closer to her than to his sisters. They have a special bond. Because on some level they recognise they are siblings?

I am so weary. I thought I knew everything about Yash and nearly all there was to know about my friends. But I'm learning that you can know someone for ages and yet not really know them at all.

THIRTY-ONE

DAY 1

2:00 p.m.

I am sitting on the sofa in the living room with Mia and Zoe on either side of me, my arms around them.

Everyone is here. Lydia, Paul and their girls are seated at the dining table. I cannot look at Rachel, this girl I've known all her life, and unsee Yash; I feel that her every feature, every expression mirrors Yash's in some way.

Yash is next to Zoe on the sofa.

We are all being perfectly civil, pretending in the way of adults that we are still the best of friends, that long-buried secrets have not detonated in our faces, rupturing our bond, opening up cracks that might well never be repaired.

My phone beeps with an incoming text. I *must* check who it's from and what it says, although I don't want to. The inspector has warned that if Ajit was taken – *no, please* – we might get a demand for ransom.

'But we're not rich,' I'd stupidly said aloud, the first thing that came into my head.

'By the standards of ordinary folk in India, you are. In any case, they equate foreigners with wealth, you see.' The inspector was gentle.

I swipe my phone with trembling fingers. The text is not a ransom demand, but it's damning all the same. My whole body shakes as I read it.

You are not the good mother you pretend to be, Jo Kumar. This is not the first time you've carelessly abandoned your son, is it?

How does this anonymous sender know so much about me? How did they find out about *this*, what they are referring to, one of my worst failures as a mother? I am pretty sure only two people in the world know about it – Lydia and myself. I haven't even told Yash.

I look up at Lydia. She's reading to Bella, softly, two blonde heads bent together over the page. Paul, also blonde, is opposite Bella, with Rachel next to him, both on their phones. Rachel's is the only dark head among three blonde ones. Why didn't I notice this before? I am sure Lydia has not shared my secret with anyone – she's loyal, steady, honest. But is that true of her now that I know she's been keeping two huge secrets from me throughout our friendship?

As if aware of my scrutiny, she looks up, meets my gaze. 'Are you all right, Jo?'

No, I'm not all right. Only you and I know of the incident the text is referring to and I didn't tell anyone. How did they find out?

'Can I talk to you for a second?'

Yash looks at me quizzically, but I hold up a hand.

'I just need a moment.'

'What is it, Jo?' Lydia asks when we are alone in one of the bedrooms.

'Did you tell anyone about that time I...' I scrunch up my

face, close my eyes. I don't want to think about it. But I must...
'left Ajit in the car?'

'Of course not,' she says at once.

'But I got a text...'

'Let me see it.'

I give her my phone.

But once again, as with the text about the graves, it's gone. How is that possible? I didn't delete it. I'm sure I didn't... did I?

'It was there, I swear.' But my voice lacks conviction.

'It's all right, Jo,' she says, but there's a hint of pity in her voice.

It angers me. 'Don't patronise me, Lydia,' I hiss. 'I know you don't believe me, that you think I'm imagining these text messages.'

She sighs tiredly. 'Where is the message then?'

'I... I don't know. It's disappeared.'

She shrugs. Turns to go, but before she leaves, she squeezes my hand.

I yank it away.

'I did not tell anyone. Your secrets are safe with me,' she calls over her shoulder.

Why do I get the feeling she's mocking me? This is Lydia, my best friend. As was.

I don't think our friendship is ever going to be the same. How can I trust her again? I seem to question her every action, her every word.

I look at the phone in my hand. No accusatory text. Did I receive it or was it my mind playing games?

Never mind trusting Lydia, can I trust myself?

THIRTY-TWO

DAY 1

3:00 p.m.

'I can't take much more of this,' I cry, my voice trembling.

Mia and Zoe are once again seeking refuge from trauma in sleep. Bella and Rachel are in one of the other bedrooms. Lydia, Paul, Yash and I are in the living room, waiting for news, the policeman in the corner, but there's a palpable tension among us, the silence seething with hurt, anger and resentment.

Yash puts his arm around me. My instinct is to pull away. My husband is not my favourite person right now, but I am at my wit's end with worry and pain. And so I take the comfort he's offering, rest my head on his shoulder.

'I need a drink,' Lydia says and leaves the room. Paul takes it as his cue to leave too, following his wife wordlessly. Have they talked? I wonder. I have noticed a distance between them since the showdown a couple of hours ago. A restraint. Will their marriage weather this ordeal and the revelations in its wake? For that matter, will ours? Even if it does this time round, will it when – if – what I'm keeping from Yash comes to light?

'I will go and check on the girls in a minute,' I say. 'Just to make sure Paul is not—'

Yash sits up, removing his arm from my shoulder to look at me. 'Surely you don't believe—'

'I'm not taking any chances.' Previously I would have refused to believe that Paul had been questioned by the police with regards to a horrific accusation, and I would have laughed away the suggestion that Yash and Lydia were anything other than friends of long standing. But not any more... I'm questioning everything and everyone now.

'Jo, you do realise this is too little too late?'

I shudder.

My husband puts his arm around me again, kisses my head, says softly, 'Jo, love, this is Paul, our mate. He loves our kids but not in that way. I believe him when he says it was a baseless accusation.'

'I want to as well, because the alternative...' I shiver again. 'I've been such a bad mother,' I whisper. 'I've failed in my foremost duty, to protect my child.'

'You're a good mother, Jo,' Yash says softly.

A good mother wouldn't leave her five-year-old son in the care of a fourteen-year-old in a strange new place and lounge intoxicated on the beach.

And I haven't been a good mother to my girls either, I think, remembering.

THIRTY-THREE
EIGHT YEARS PREVIOUSLY

All my life, I'd always wanted children, a family of my own, and when I found out I was pregnant, I was over the moon. Then I had a miscarriage. That sent me into a deep depression that only shifted when I got pregnant again a year later. Mia arrived and, ten months later, Zoe.

Having two babies in quick succession was harder than I'd imagined. Yash and Paul's business was in its early stages and Yash was hardly home. I found no time to get anything done as both Mia and Zoe were poor sleepers. As soon as I got one into bed, the other would wake. I felt like I was feeding, changing, burping, soothing all the time. I stopped washing, stopped caring for myself. What was the point? I would get vomited or urinated on as soon as I washed – the babies seemed to have a sensor: 'Ah, Mummy is clean, let's get her dirty again.' I smelled of sour milk and looked a fright.

I had no time for Yash. He would come home buzzing with news of big deals and new clients, while I rushed around him, putting away toys, sterilising bottles, asking him to shush as the babies were finally asleep for the fifteen minutes they allowed me each day. I barely listened to him – nothing stayed in my mind for longer than a minute anyway; I was operating on no sleep and autopilot. I envied Yash his work; it seemed easy in comparison to what I had to do and sounded so glamorous when contrasted with changing nappies and burping babies. I resented that he got to leave, to stay away all day and swan home smelling of the adult world: smoke and crisp air and cologne. He would open a bottle of wine, peek in the fridge, look at the empty stove and sigh, then settle down in front of the telly with a packet of crisps and say, hopefully, 'Join me, Jo?'

'In a minute,' I'd snap. 'Can't you hear Zoe crying? It's time for her feed.'

And then, somehow, I got pregnant again, this baby conceived during one of those increasingly rare weekend mornings when both Mia and Zoe had been asleep for half an hour at a stretch.

Yash wasn't thrilled. 'It isn't the right time. The business is just taking off. And as it is you're having a hard time with two.'

'We'll manage,' I said. Serene. Glowing. Happy, despite being sleep-deprived. Pleased, despite knowing Yash had a point. I had always wanted three children. And now, our family would be complete.

Ten weeks on, I suffered a miscarriage.

'All your fault,' I screeched at Yash, raining blows on his chest as he tried to comfort me. 'You did not want it and now it's gone.'

'It's all right,' he murmured, gently. 'It's OK, Jo.'

'It's not OK,' I yelled, turning away from him. 'Nothing is.'

I sank into depression then. Even the girls couldn't rouse me from my melancholy – in fact, they made it worse. It went on for several weeks and when I couldn't even summon the energy to get out of bed, Yash called the doctor.

4:00 p.m.

Beside me, my husband sighs, dropping his head into his hands, jolting me from my rumination. 'What is this doing to us, eh?'

My thoughts exactly.

Despite all that's going on between me and Yash, the secrets we've been keeping from each other, our lies, the hurt we've knowingly and unknowingly inflicted on each other, I need him. There is no one else in the world who understands what I'm going through. Here we are, two anguished, desperate parents in the worst possible situation.

'Have you checked your phone?' Yash asks after a moment's silence. 'The inspector said that if Ajit's been taken, the kidnappers might contact us...' Yash's voice falters.

I throw my arms around myself, shivering although it's warm. 'I haven't received anything,' I lie.

'I... I haven't told anyone at home yet. I keep waiting for him to be found,' Yash remarks.

There are no grandparents on either side to tell. Yash is the only child of parents who both succumbed to cancer, his father when he was at uni and his mother a few years ago. She met me, but died before the kids came along. My own mother is not in the picture – she left when I was a child and hasn't kept in touch. My father drank himself to an early grave. I am estranged from my sister, Lori. She was gone from my life long before Yash and I met. I tried so hard to create a family as different to my own messed-up one as possible. I failed.

Lori.

Just the thought of my sister makes me shudder. I have no doubt she is capable of taking Ajit just to torment me. She holds grudges like nobody's business, but, at last count, it was *she* who wronged me.

And yet my mind circles back to my sister, whom I've not spoken to since I was a teenager. Even if it *was* her, why *now*?

THIRTY-FIVE

DAY 1

9:00 p.m.

'Mr and Mrs Kumar, please may I have a word?' Inspector Sharma says, his knock on the front door jolting us. We are sitting at the table and we are praying. Yes, *praying*. Lydia's idea.

We are back at our cottage, from where Ajit went missing, the police having completed their investigations. Some of Inspector Sharma's men escorted us here after the last lingering reporters packed up and called it a night. We hadn't seen Inspector Sharma since he took leave of us this afternoon after being party to the explosive revelations that shook the foundations of our marriages and friendships; he was hopefully finding Ajit. But now, here he is, without my son.

The kids are in bed. I bathed my girls – they submitted meekly to my ministrations, although they can both bathe themselves. I scrubbed behind their ears, washed their bodies and pretended the tears streaming down my face was water from the shower. Last night at around this time, or perhaps a little earlier, I was washing my son. I had wrapped him in his SpongeBob towel and held him close, warm and wriggly and fragrant, smelling of lime from the soap and the sweetness that was uniquely him.

Tonight I tucked my girls into bed, kissing them goodnight. Both of them wanted me to stay until they fell asleep. Even if Mia and Zoe hadn't needed me, I would have stayed. I promised them that once they were asleep, I would be in the living room, like Rachel had been the previous night. They nodded trustingly, their eyes heavy with impending slumber.

When I came into the living room, Yash, Lydia and Paul were congregated around the table. They looked as haggard as I felt. The policeman who has been keeping an eye on us was sitting unobtrusively in a chair in the corner.

Yash pulled out the chair next to him. 'Come, sit,' he said. Our marriage was facing its worst challenge yet, indiscretions and secrets revealed in the wake of Ajit's disappearance. Would it weather this trial or fold under its weight?

Lydia leaned forward, placed her hand on top of mine. 'Jo,' she said. 'I regret suggesting we go down to the bar last night. You don't know how many times I've berated myself since all this...'

I nodded once, then retrieved my hand from under hers, but not before I noticed that she was wearing that ring. *My* ring?

I couldn't trust Lydia any more. I looked at her and thought, *What else are you keeping from me?* I wondered if she'd told anyone about my leaving Ajit in the car. She said she didn't, but how could I believe her when she broke my confidence and told my husband that I hadn't been taking my pills? When she had slept with my husband, when one of her daughters was my husband's, when she had lied to us, Paul and myself, for all these years? Perhaps she told Paul about my abandoning of infant Ajit in the car and *he* was the one sending me those texts? Perhaps *Paul* had taken Ajit and was keeping him somewhere? Perhaps he was arranging it when he went to get a bottle of wine but was gone for at least ten minutes and wasn't at the bar when I looked? I thought Paul was a gentle giant, that he wouldn't harm a hair on my children's heads. Now, I wasn't so sure...

After a bit, 'Shall we... shall we pray?' Lydia offered.

'Pray?' Yash asked. He looked washed out, weary, old. I no doubt looked the same.

'Do you have any other suggestions?' Lydia asked.

'Let's pray.' Yash sighed.

And that is what we are doing, hands joined, heads bowed, when Inspector Sharma interrupts us.

Yash and I walk onto the veranda with the inspector.

I try to read the inspector's face, my heart beating a staccato rhythm in my chest: *Why is he here?*

It is quiet. The sand now shrouded in darkness, the waves, inky swells, roaring gently, a background sound I have become accustomed to hearing. Policemen murmur softly on the beach. The bar shack we were lounging beside the previous night is shut – early considering it was open until after midnight last night.

I wonder if someone came up these very steps, walked past sleeping Rachel, picked up my son and climbed with him out the window, or perhaps handed him to an accomplice on the other side. Just last night. So much can change in twenty-four hours. A world can be overturned. A world can be lost.

Inspector Sharma clears his throat and my heart dips. It doesn't sound like good news.

My feet give way and I lower myself onto one of the chairs on the veranda.

Why didn't we sit on the veranda yesterday? Why did we have to go to the bar? I think it was the heady belief that we were in paradise – the ordinary rules governing our everyday lives had been relaxed, and nothing could touch us. We had earned this holiday – our once-in-a-lifetime getaway – and the right to let go, unwind. We could stop being parents for a couple of hours, surely? But being a parent never stops – how could I have believed I could be free of it, even briefly? How could I have been so lax with the most precious gifts I have had the privilege of being blessed with – my children?

'I have to tell you that we are now operating on the possibility that Ajit was taken. We have no evidence to suggest that Ajit came to harm in this cottage,' the inspector says.

'Came to harm here? In this cottage?' Yash echoes, his voice strident.

'Mr Kumar, what I'm trying to tell you is that, from the evidence we've gathered, it appears that your son left this cottage unharmed sometime last night, most likely through the window.'

This is not new information. At least not to me, for I've been thinking along these lines all this time. Why does the inspector only now seem to be confirming this, seemingly having placed the focus on something happening to Ajit in the cottage, at *our* hands? Once again, I'm starting to question the competence of this man to whom I've entrusted my son's fate.

Before I can say anything, Yash asks, 'And you know this how?'

'We can't say for certain, of course, but Ajit was awake and talked to Rachel just after Mrs King checked on the children at eleven p.m. We haven't found traces of blood in the cottage or any evidence to suggest a violent attack.'

I shut my eyes tight hoping that by doing so I will be able to push away all the images that arrive, grisly and terrifying, in my head.

'And what, you expect us to be pleased about this? Give you a pat on the back?' Anguish and fear magnifies Yash's voice.

Policemen stop their reconnaissance of the cottage surrounds to look at us, silently offering their super their support.

'We have scoured the beach and searched the surrounding areas – the neighbouring cottages, shacks, huts, wells, everywhere we can,' the inspector continues evenly, apparently unfazed by Yash's tantrum. 'No trace of Ajit. Given he is only five, in the small window of time between him going missing and us arriving on the scene, he couldn't have got far. Unless...'

Yash swallows and his voice is very soft when he says, 'Unless someone took him, or he walked into the sea.'

I hug my stomach to stop the scream that's inside me from escaping, for Yash has just given voice to my worst nightmares. Has the sea swallowed him within its undulating depths, my beloved boy gone forever? Or, perhaps worse – this is what I'm reduced to, weighing unimaginable outcomes – is he even now with the wrong person, one harbouring malicious, lustful intent...?

No. *No, no, no...*

'We're not ruling out either possibility.' Inspector Sharma's voice is gentle. 'And we are widening the area of search and also going over the area we've already covered just in case we missed something the first time round. Also' – he clears his throat again. I am beginning to hate that sound – 'in the course of our enquiries, we discovered that there has been a spate of burglaries in the area.'

'Oh.'

'Thieves have been targeting tourist villas and cottages. They scope the property before the tourists arrive and... You see, the cottages in this area are similar – they all have a window at the end of the corridor. The thieves very cleverly wedge the window so it can't be shut properly. Mr Kumar, it was you who shut the windows last night?'

'Yes.' Yash's voice is subdued.

'And were you able to close that window fully?'

'I've been mulling over that all day, but I cannot remember.' Yash sounds frustrated, angry with himself.

'I think – if the precedent from other cottages is anything to go by – that the thieves got to this cottage too and that you were able to pull the window closed but not lock it.'

'So you reckon it was a burglary?' Yash asks, his voice unsteady.

Instead of answering Yash's question, the inspector asks one of his own. 'Mr and Mrs Kumar, have you noticed if anything is missing, any belongings you cannot find?'

'I... I don't know,' I say.

I'm expecting Yash to say the same, but he surprises me with, 'I checked. Paul did too. Nothing was taken... apart from...'

'Apart from the most precious treasure of all.' My voice is sharp, cutting, like hail. I'm furious that Yash thought to check our possessions to make sure nothing was taken when we have lost our son.

You're being unkind. He needed something to do. You know how meticulous he is.

Meticulous or mercenary? How can my husband even *think* of material things when our son is missing?

'That implies that it wasn't a burglary. And if the burglars did tamper with the window, then they were planning the burglary for later and were usurped by what happened. Which is the best explanation, considering that in the other cases, they have attempted the burglary later on in the tourists' stay, on the fourth day or so. And the burglaries have always taken place in the daytime, when the occupants were at the beach.' The inspector pauses, his gaze upon the horizon, where the dark swell of sea converges with the awning of sky. 'It's all conjecture at this point. We *will* find the burglars, but, personally, I don't think it's them. They wouldn't take the risk. And burglars don't suddenly switch to kidnapping.'

I shudder. This is my son the inspector is talking about. My sweet little boy who loves SpongeBob and cuddles and is afraid of the dark. His slippers and the SpongeBob soft toy he sleeps with are missing. If someone took him, why pick up his slippers from beside the bed and his SpongeBob soft toy, especially if they were pressed for time, worried about Rachel waking?

But then again, perhaps Ajit, unable to sleep, in tears after Rachel shouted at him, did climb out the window himself when he found it wasn't locked and came looking for us and encountered someone horrid instead.

I try again to recall my walk around the cottage. Was the window open? But my memory is still a frustrating blank. Why can't I remember?

'In any case, if it is a burglary-cum-kidnapping, I would have thought that there would have been demands for ransom by now,' the inspector says.

'Why else would they take Ajit, if not for ransom?' Even before the question is out of my mouth, I regret asking it.

Inspector Sharma fiddles with the collar of his shirt – the rim of which is stained yellow with sweat, I notice, absently – as if it is strangling him.

Yash closes his eyes and runs his hand across his face.

Of course I know why else they would take Ajit – there's a roaring trade in organs, I've read. Children's organs.

And there's also the oldest trade of all.

No. Please no.

Why my Ajit? Because he was the youngest. The easiest to carry, the most pliable. The closest to the window. On his own in the room.

We made it so easy for the kidnappers.

If he was taken. I am still clinging to the hope that he is hiding somewhere, waiting to be found. Far better than the alternative.

But... it is night again. If he is hiding, lost, then he must be terrified, wanting his mum. I feel helpless, useless, unable to be there for my child who needs me, failing in my duty as a mother. Again. I bite my lower lip, hard, but even when the hot metallic taste of blood floods my mouth the pain is nothing, *nothing* compared to the agony of not being able to comfort my child.

'How come you didn't know of these burglaries before now?' Yash asks, his voice harsh, like gravel scraping skin.

'The local police were investigating the burglaries.'

'Not you?'

'I tackle the more serious crimes.' The inspector has the grace to look embarrassed. 'But now we're on their case.'

'Bit late, isn't it?'

'Mr Kumar, the burglaries are just one possibility. I just... I wanted to keep you informed. We're keeping a police presence around the house. The search for Ajit will continue through the night. All exits out of the state of Goa and all the neighbouring states and big cities are being checked. We've circulated images of Ajit to airports, railway and bus stations, harbours and missing children portals. We are in touch with other states, national and...'

The inspector keeps talking, but I cannot listen any more. I clutch my stomach and bend forward. I want to keen, to scream my agony. I want my baby.

'Now, is there anything you've recalled since we last spoke, anything at all that you think might be relevant to our investigation?' The inspector's words pierce the fug of pain ambushing me, his gaze piercing, even in the dark populated by shadows and grief, his pupils shining bright white in the humid gloaming.

'No.' My throat is dry, tasting bitter, of bile and regret. 'Just... find him for me. Please.'

'We're trying our best, ma'am,' he says, nodding once in our direction.

Then he is gone and Yash and I are left alone with our grief, our agony, our mistakes, our lies.

THIRTY-SIX

DAY 2

12:15 a.m.

I cannot sleep.

Once the inspector had gone, I left our sleeping girls in Yash's care and went searching along the beach and behind the cottage for my son, calling his name gently, ignoring the pitying looks the policemen keeping watch and scouring the area were giving me. I searched until Yash came in search of *me*, gently holding me while I sobbed, exhausted and beaten in his arms. 'Where is he, Yash? Where is our boy?'

Now, I pace the living room, the policeman the inspector has assigned to us nodding off in his seat. I go over our actions repeatedly, what I'd do differently if given the chance to wipe out the previous night, start again. I think of the burglars mentioned by the inspector, targeting cottages in the area. I try very hard to recall if I had noticed the window open when I walked around the cottage. But my memory of yesterday evening is fuzzy at best and I can't recall my drunken amble at *all*.

The image of those three graves with my children's names

shimmers before my sleepless eyes. Did I actually see them or was it my imagination?

Counting down the sluggish hours of night, watching my daughters sleep and wondering where my son is, the horrors of what might be happening to him hounding me, I think of Paul, the man I have known for fifteen years and counted as my friend. Was there some truth to the accusation against him? Even as I recoil from the thought, I wonder where Paul had been during those missing minutes when he was not at the bar, when he took so long to get the wine. Did Lydia share my secrets with him? Is he the one sending the texts? Has he taken Ajit? Was he arranging the kidnapping when he was missing from the bar that fateful evening?

Stop obsessing.

But the hours of night devoid of my son drag and I cannot stop, my thoughts drifting without pause from Paul to Lori.

My sister. My foe.

THIRTY-SEVEN
CHILDHOOD

'Mum, why does Lori always get new stuff and I get cast-offs? Even if she is older it's not fair,' I cry.

I was in my room, finishing off my homework diligently, trying to win Mum's approval as usual, when Lori had swanned in, wearing the dress I'd had my eye on ever since I saw it in the shop window, creamy teal patterned with buttery-yellow daisies.

'Look what Mum got me, swot,' she'd said with a smirk, twirling in the dress I had hoped Mum would gift me for my upcoming birthday – I'd dropped enough hints.

And here was Lori wearing it – the dress I thought of as *mine*.

I couldn't stop the hot tears crowding my eyes from spilling.

Lori spotted them and her eyes gleamed with delight as she sashayed away.

'Well, sweetie.' Mum eyes me critically. 'Life isn't fair. You are pretty enough. But Lori, she is beautiful.' Mum's voice is dreamy with pleasure. 'She will always get everything easily in life, but you... you will have to work for it or make do with cast-offs. I'm only preparing you for life.'

I bunch my hands into fists so my fingernails dig into the soft flesh of my palms. Ironically, the physical pain momentarily takes my mind off the hurt I feel at Mum's words and stops me from weeping – I will not cry in front of Mum too.

'Anyway, that dress is her colour. It wouldn't suit you,' Mum says dismissively. But then she adds, perhaps noting my dismay – I've managed to stop the tears but my lower lip is wobbling dangerously – 'But while she has the beauty, you have the brains. You will learn to get what is yours. Fight for it.'

I decide then and there that that is exactly what I will do.

The next evening, after Lori is asleep – she's worn the dress all day, flaunting it in my face – I wreak my revenge.

When Mum berates Lori for ruining her dress, I keep a straight face.

Lori protests of course, says, 'Jo did it. She's jealous.'

'Even if she did—'

'I didn't,' I protest, a bit too quickly.

'Even if she did,' Mum repeats, unfazed, 'it is *your* dress. You must learn to look after your things. Keep them safe from your sister and others who might wish you harm.'

'I didn't.' And now I cry, hiding from my actions behind messy tears, fooling no one.

Lori looks at me like I am the devil, pinching me under the table, but I can't complain for Mum shoots me an assessing look, eyebrows raised, which says, 'I know exactly what you are doing.'

Growing up, it was always like this, Mum pitting us, her daughters, against each other. We were always competing for her love. She made a sport out of withholding affection, sharing unequally, always comparing us. We were forever trying to win against each other, Mum egging us on, Dad uninterested in anything apart from the lager he consumed by the six-pack.

Then, when I was sixteen and Lori seventeen, Mum left us for her lover without a backward glance. By then we were conditioned to blame one another, each deciding it was the other's fault Mum had left. Dad was drinking more than ever – it wasn't clear if he even noticed Mum had gone.

I fell in with a bad crowd – cutting school, drinking to excess, smoking weed.

I would have ended up in prison if not for Tom.

I met Tom at a party I went to because Lori called it 'lame'. I wanted to prove her wrong.

'No party is lame if I'm there,' I boasted.

She laughed, looking me up and down, eyebrows raised, just like Mum. She did not even need words to put me down, reduce my hard-won confidence to mere bluster; a mocking glance was enough.

It was maddening.

She was effortlessly slim, ethereal, graceful. She looked good in anything she wore, carrying even the dullest outfit off like a model on a catwalk. I was chunky – I had never been thin. I had to work at looking good. But I would show her.

And so I dolled up and went to the party, even knowing that none of my friends, the edgy crowd I hung out with, would be there.

But it changed the course of my life. For I met Tom.

I had been flailing since Mum left, but Tom became my foothold to sanity. He was my rock. We became inseparable. I lost my virginity to him.

I knew better than to introduce him to Lori, although she asked me several times what I was on, why I looked so happy. Too happy, she mocked, her gaze hard and suspicious.

And then I found out I was pregnant.

I was over the moon. A child. Mine and Tom's. A family of

our own. I could move on, away from Lori and Dad, from Mum's horrible legacy.

I decided to tell Tom on our six-month anniversary.

But I never got the chance.

'I'm so sorry to do this to you,' he said. 'But I've met someone. She's the love of my life. We're starting a family together. Yes, she's pregnant. You're a lovely girl and you'll make somebody very happy. Just not me.'

And I knew who it was that had stolen Tom from me even before Lori emerged, tall, stately, elegant, cradling her stomach, throwing her arms around him, looking at me triumphantly even as she kissed him.

I swallowed down my tears, I had had years of practice. I walked away, head held high, heart shattered.

Perhaps it was the heartbreak that did it, but I lost my baby that evening.

The very next day, I left home, never going back, not even for Dad's funeral. I didn't want to cross paths with Lori.

I haven't spoken to her since.

THIRTY-EIGHT

DAY 2

3:15 a.m.

Could Lori have taken Ajit? Could she be sending those texts? Is there a connection between Ajit's disappearance and the texts?

It would be so like Lori to mess up my life and sanity – God, could she hold a grudge! She had used indelible marker on my dresses for months after I ruined the dress I wanted that Mum had bought for her. When she was in Year 9, I had smiled at her then beau and he said I was cute, so she spread rumours about what a slut I was, ruining the rest of my time at secondary school.

But, and I keep coming back to this, if it *is* Lori, why now? When we have been out of each other's lives for years?

I wouldn't put it past her to sleep with Yash and send me texts gloating about my unfaithful husband. But how would she know about me leaving Ajit in the car? How would she know about my family at all, given I haven't spoken to her since we were teenagers?

THIRTY-NINE

Opinion piece appearing in the Commentary section of *The Goan Times*:

Police Investigation Into Missing British Child: Long Way To Go

Posted by Mr Navin Suri, 14 February

The investigation into the whereabouts of Ajit Kumar, five, who went missing from his holiday cottage in Galgibaga Beach, has been labelled 'high profile'. Don't get me wrong, I am all for finding missing children. But therein exactly lies my point. Hundreds of children go missing from the streets of India every day. What is being done to find them? Many of those children do not even merit an investigation, let alone a high profile one. This case, then, of a missing little boy is high profile only because the child in question is of foreign nationality. Does this mean that Ajit's situation is more urgent, his life more precious, more high profile than the thousands of Indian children who are missing just because he holds a British passport? What does this say of this country that we take so much care, spend time and resources, to find missing children who do not even belong here while neglecting thousands of our own?

Now with regards to this high profile investigation being conducted by the police – what exactly is being done to find Ajit? We hear that police are searching the area, that they are questioning the neighbours. But what means are in place to get Ajit back, save him from his fate if he has been taken? Have all exits from Goa been checked? Have the airports been alerted to look out for someone travelling with a child matching Ajit's description?

All the police will tell us is that they are 'keeping all avenues open at this time'. What it means is that the police know nothing – they don't know if the little boy has been kidnapped for ransom, if he has been killed, God forbid, or even if he has run away.

The policeman in charge of this investigation is none other than the (in)famous Inspector Sharma. Yes, the very one who was involved in those corruption charges where top politicians were also implicated. The one who allegedly took bribes in the Hassan murder case. The one who botched the 'high profile' Belinda Fernandes (daughter of supermodel Jessica Fernandes and actor Remo Fernandes) kidnapping case. And yet, he has been put in charge of this investigation. Why? Perhaps the fact that he has friends in high places has much to do with it. Photos of Inspector Sharma socialising with the Home Minister and the Chief Minister were published in this very newspaper after the bribe scandal.

Where is the justice for Hassan, brutally murdered in his own home? His killer(s) are yet to be found. What about Belinda Fernandes who is still missing, twelve months on? Given his track record, is it right that Inspector Sharma be put in charge of another 'high profile' case?

•   •   •

Comments:

Adish, Bicholim 06:10 IST: Dear Mr Suri, Totally appreciate that hundreds of lost Indian children are not given the attention that this case is generating, but that surely doesn't mean that Ajit's kidnapping shouldn't be investigated?

Mr Jude Serrao, Baga 06:15 IST: Mr Adish, with all due respect, Mr Suri was not saying Ajit's kidnapping shouldn't be investigated. He was asking what's being done about the hundreds of Indian children going missing every day.

A Concerned Citizen, Sinquerim 06:50 IST: Mr Suri, correct me if I'm wrong, but I was under the impression that Inspector Sharma refused to take bribes in the Hassan case, which made him unpopular with the politicians. Those pictures with the Chief Minister and Home Minister were taken before the case, and not after, I believe, because since then, I've heard, those higher up have wanted nothing to do with him. He's been put in charge of this case precisely because he will not bow down to corruption, take bribes, rather than the other way round, is what I've been told by friends in the know.

Pinky, Calangute 07:09 IST: Belinda Fernandes's parents have something to do with her disappearance which is why she hasn't been found. And I'm sure this is the case here too. Something very fishy about Ajit's parents and, for that matter, their friends. I despair for that little boy.

Scroll down for more comments.

FORTY

DAY 2

7:15 a.m.

It's finally morning. Another morning without my son. My eyes gritty, my throat lumpy, chest heavy with the scream I'm holding in.

Ajit has spent two nights and one whole day somewhere without us. He has never stayed away from us before now.

'You've spoiled him, Jo. He's too attached to you,' Yash used to complain, when Ajit persisted in coming into our room almost every night. In the beginning, I had carried him back to his room, but when he kept coming back, I just moved up, making space for him. In truth, a part of me enjoyed having my little boy next to me. There would come a time, like it had with the girls, when Ajit would not need his mum so much any longer – I would enjoy it while it lasted.

We sit at the table, making an attempt at breakfast – I know I must eat, keep my strength up for Ajit's sake, for when he gets back, but everything I put in my mouth tastes of guilt, regret. *You don't deserve to eat when you don't know where your son is.*

You don't deserve to be doing ordinary things when he might be suffering.

But the girls are tearful and upset and so I pick at my toast, putting on a calm front for their sakes.

Outside, the beach is once more swarming with reporters, news vans. They reconvened at dawn, the drowsy beach startling awake, bright with their lights, loud with their chatter. The quiet, secluded beach we arrived at mere days ago is now inundated with vehicles and people. Even the roar of the sea struggles to be heard.

Once the girls finish eating, Rachel shepherds them to her room to do a craft activity. She is no doubt heeding a prompt from her mother – she would never have willingly done this before Ajit went missing, spent time away from her phone and with the younger girls. But, like all of us, she has changed in the short time since Ajit went missing, a docile and subdued youngster in place of stroppy teenager. My girls follow meekly in Rachel and Bella's wake – they are confused by the frenetic activity on the beach and by their brother still not found.

Once the door to Rachel's room is shut, Lydia says, her voice tentative, 'A hotel would be better for the kids, perhaps, rather than this cottage with its constant reminders of Ajit's absence and the paparazzi outside, laying siege.' She sweeps a hand around the room.

'I'm not going anywhere. I am waiting right here until Ajit comes back, and he *will* do so.' I cannot control my voice, high-pitched, almost a shriek. Everyone turns to look at me and, pierced by their gazes, my voice flounders. 'I'm staying until he is found.' My voice shrinking, as the brief flare of defiant hope is doused by my fears.

'I don't want to worry you further,' Lydia continues hesitantly, 'but they're saying that Inspector Sharma is incompetent.'

I stare at her. 'Who is?'

'The newspapers and social media.'

I haven't dared read the news or access social media. I can't even bear to look at my phone with its screensaver of our three taken ridiculously early on Christmas morning, in their PJs under the tree, presents on their laps, surrounded by wrapping paper, laughing, Ajit showing the gaps in his mouth where his adult teeth are yet to grow. It hurts to look at it, wonder where my son is, what is being done to him, whether he will ever grin like that, carefree, again; whether I will ever get to see his beloved face, his smile again.

There have been no ransom demands either to me or to Yash – I don't know whether that is a good sign or bad, whether it means Ajit's fate is worse off or better for it. We haven't switched on the TV, having decided, without actually discussing it as such, that the kids are traumatised enough by the uproar outside without subjecting them to more conjecture and rumour via the telly.

Lydia has taken on the role of messenger – reading the news and feeding us snippets she thinks we can stomach. She is saying, in response to my question, 'Apparently, Inspector Sharma bungled up the missing persons case he was in charge of before.'

My stomach swoops, the few bites of toast I managed to swallow threatening a quick exit.

'They say he is not above taking bribes. That he might have been in cahoots with the perpetrators in cases where he was in charge,' Lydia is saying.

'*What?*'

I realise now that I was pinning all my hopes on the inspector. Despite what I had read about the Indian police, I had decided to trust Inspector Sharma, even given his grilling of all of us. Perhaps *because* of it. Inspector Sharma's handling of the investigation, teasing out our secrets while keeping mine for as long as it doesn't hinder the investigation, means I had begun to believe this man was doing all he could to find my son. Now I know I cannot trust *anyone*, not even the policeman in charge of finding my son. Despair overwhelms me.

'Is this true, Yash? Is it?' I cannot stop the hysterical note shrilling my voice.

He rubs a hand through his stubble – he hasn't shaved since we arrived. 'Whatever the newspapers might say, the inspector seems to know what he is doing.' Like me, Yash sounds like he desperately wants to believe this, for the alternative cannot be countenanced. 'In any case, British police are involved via Interpol. They will be liaising with Inspector Sharma, making sure his investigation is thorough. They'll not stand for any slip-ups.' It seems as if he is trying to convince himself as much as anyone. 'I'm sure they're all doing their best to find Ajit.'

Yash tries to sound upbeat, reassuring. But... it's not helping. Nothing is.

FORTY-ONE

DAY 2

8:20 a.m.

'Jo, I'm going mad sitting here twiddling my thumbs waiting for Ajit to be found,' Lydia says. She is pale, despite the tan she cultivated when we were sunbathing by the sea and my son was safe, dancing in the water, content and happy.

Lydia reminds me of Lori, always has done. They both have the same svelte figure, the same effortless beauty and elegance, the same entitled assurance that whatever they want they will get.

But Lydia, unlike Lori, does not make me feel insecure, bring out my competitive edge, the worst in me. Instead, she does just the opposite, making me feel better about myself, bringing out the best in me.

At least she used to.

Now everything is helter-skelter. Nothing is as it was. Now, I think, is Lydia implying that I'm not doing enough to find my son?

'Sorry, Jo,' she says, reading my thoughts. 'That came out wrong.' Her voice breaks. 'You know how much I care for Ajit.'

I nod, tasting salt in my mouth.

'I was thinking I could start a campaign on social media for him? People could get in touch if they'd seen or heard anything?' She roots about in the pocket of her shorts for a tissue and noisily blows her nose.

I am so weary. I cannot think, cannot decide if what she's suggesting is a good idea or not. 'Won't it muddy the waters? Trolls and such coming forward? Can't we just leave it to the police?'

'If you like,' she says. 'But I honestly think it will help.'

'I think so too,' Yash says, coming up behind us.

Lydia flashes him a small smile. I turn away. Despite everything that's going on, I still can't help feeling unsettled by the truths that have been revealed with regards to Lydia and Yash's relationship.

'Jo?' Lydia asks, turning to me.

'OK, but better run it by the inspector first. Incompetent or not, it wouldn't do to step on his toes.'

'Of course,' she says.

Yash comes to sit beside me. 'All right, love?'

I nod, and he puts his arm around me, pulling me close. He smells of sweat, exhaustion and worry.

I happen to glance up and catch Lydia watching us, a speculative look on her face, eyes hard as peach stones. When I meet her gaze, she looks away.

Did I imagine that look? What does it mean? Why am I being suspicious of my best friend, questioning everything she says and does?

That ring on her hand. Is it mine? If so, why, how does she have it?

No. Stop. You need to concentrate on Ajit, not fuel your mind with baseless suspicion.

But is it baseless?

FORTY-TWO

DAY 2

10:30 a.m.

Inspector Sharma comes by with an update. He looks grim, his face set in a scowl as if rebuffing all slurs to his character and his handling of the investigation into my son's disappearance.

Since Lydia raised concerns about the inspector, feeding into and escalating my own fears, I've thought of almost nothing else, wondering if we are making a mistake trusting this man, thinking that perhaps we should start over with someone else. But just the thought of the amount of time it would take to jump through bureaucratic hoops, time better spent finding my son, has stalled me. For now, at least, Inspector Sharma is our best chance at finding Ajit in this country that I don't know.

And, like Yash pointed out, Interpol are keeping an eye on him, and I, like Yash, have to hope they'll pick up on any slip-ups or shady dealings on the inspector's part and pull him up on it.

Nevertheless, I want to make sure the inspector knows that *we* are keeping tabs on him too. 'The newspapers are saying that you botched similar investigations, that you're leading this investigation only because of your connections. You still haven't found that missing girl from your last case and it's been twelve months since she...' My confrontational tone loses steam as I contemplate the horrible scenario of not knowing where Ajit is a *year* from now. But I plough on. 'They said you took bribes from kidnappers in the Belinda Fernandes case.'

Inspector Sharma runs a palm across his face, the action weary. 'The media will say all sorts to sell their papers.'

'So it's not true?'

'No,' he says shortly.

'Then why hasn't she been found?'

'Believe me, my team and I tried our hardest to find her.'

'So is this what we can expect a year...?' I cannot finish this sentence. I will *not* expect this. I won't.

I know the stats – if a child is not found within the first twenty-four hours of going missing, the chances of finding them are drastically reduced. But I cannot afford to think that way. Ajit *will* be found. He *must*, even if it has now been more than twenty-four hours.

I think of other kids missing while on holiday abroad, who still haven't been found. In those cases, blame was directed upon the investigating police and their ineptitude, the media alleging that if the investigation had been more focused and thorough, the child in question would have been found. Is it already too late for Ajit?

No, I will not think that way. If I do, I can't go on. I have to believe he *will* be found.

'Interpol has been in touch?' Yash is asking. His voice jerks me back into the here and now. I have zoned out and missed part of the conversation. I need to focus – I don't want to risk missing anything of importance.

'Yes and we're liaising with them and the British Consulate,' the inspector replies evenly. 'Mr and Mrs Kumar, I understand your concerns, especially when the media is after me. But, rest assured, my team and I are doing all we can to find your son.' He sighs. 'The criticism of the media is part and parcel of being in a public-facing role. The media always focuses on black and white, while the truth is somewhere in between.'

'So what's the truth in your case, Inspector?' I challenge.

'Let's just say they like to target me because I have enemies in high places. I'm not here to make friends and bow down to bribes and corruption, I'm here to find answers. And those in power who thought I could be swayed don't like that, hence they've turned certain factions of the media against me.'

It's the longest speech he's made – until now he's stood back and observed, encouraged *us* to talk – and I am momentarily appeased, for I can see he's sincere.

'Now, Mrs Kumar,' he says, and although he is small and unassuming, pinned by his unblinking glare, I flinch. 'A piece of information has come to my attention about you which changes things.'

'What?' My stomach dips. Is he going to reveal my secret? Is the person I saw at the market – JT? – behind all this?

But the inspector said 'about you'.

Even as I dread the inspector's next words, I am relieved that Lydia and Paul are with their children and my girls, with the policeman keeping watch, in the living room – the inspector having wanted to talk to Yash and myself in private, so we are in our bedroom which hasn't been slept in. Again.

'Mrs Kumar,' the inspector is solemn, 'I received an anonymous text this morning. I wonder if it might be from the same person who has been texting you.'

Anonymous text. The inspector got one too?

See, Yash, I want to say, *the inspector believes me, even if you, Lydia and Paul don't*. But then the implications of what the inspector said hit me...

I look at him. He is watching both myself and Yash, assessing us, waiting for our reactions. He has worded this carefully, for maximum impact. He's doing exactly what he did before, with Paul's revelation. And now, once more, I dread what's coming even as I whisper, 'What did it say?'

'That you once left your son in a hot car and he nearly died.'

The bluntness of the inspector's words feels like a literal punch and I recoil from it, swaying on my feet.

'What?' Yash cries, looking at me in horror. 'You did *what?*'

'I...' I gather saliva in my dry throat, my heart pounding in my chest as I remember that time.

I had severe postnatal depression, even worse than after the girls were born. I was pumped up on pills. I was not thinking, didn't know if I was coming or going. But it doesn't excuse the fact that, after I'd dropped the girls off at nursery and play-group, I forgot about Ajit. My baby. I left him in the car and walked off. I just wanted to get away. If it hadn't been for the window on the other side being ever so slightly open – and I wasn't even the one to do this; I have to thank one of my girls for that – I don't know what would have happened...

'It was a terrible time. I was suffering from postnatal depression, not thinking straight. It doesn't excuse what I did, of course,' I whisper.

'It doesn't,' Yash grinds out, looking at me as if he doesn't know me. Appalled outrage in his eyes. 'You put our son in danger.'

'I know and I'm sorry.'

Yash snorts in disgust and turns away from me.

'You received a text informing you of this from a withheld number?' I ask the inspector.

He nods.

I am winded. 'I received one too.'

Who knows about this other than Lydia and myself? Is Lydia lying when she said she hasn't told anyone? Has she told Paul? Is it him behind this? Or did Lydia tip the inspector off? Is she the one sending me those texts?

'You didn't tell me about this message? Why?' the inspector is asking.

'It was gone when I showed Lydia.' And then I remember that I handed Lydia my phone to show her the message – she could have deleted it then.

And why would she do that? Get a grip, Jo.

Yash snorts again, loudly. 'That happens quite a lot with these messages, doesn't it?'

'Yash, I know you think I'm making them up, but explain how the inspector received one.'

My husband's lip curls and he turns away from me.

When did this happen? When did we become strangers to each other, my husband and I, believing the worst of each other? When did my husband become someone I cannot trust and who obviously doesn't trust me?

This crisis has brought everything to a head, fracturing relationships, exacerbating the cracks occasioned by a long marriage that we had papered over, pretending not to notice them, although we knew they were there.

I turn to the inspector, who is watching both of us intently. 'I... I'm ashamed of what I did, Inspector, leaving Ajit unattended in the car. I will regret it all my life. I love my son. I wouldn't knowingly harm a hair on his head.'

'But you still suffer periods of blackouts, don't you, Mrs Kumar? You don't remember going for an amble around the cottage at about the time your son went missing.'

Who has told him about the blackouts? Did Lydia, or was it Paul, when they mentioned my ill-advised drunken walk around the cottage? Or is it my husband who has? And what exactly is the inspector suggesting? 'I wouldn't take him, why would I? I love him, I love my children. They are my life.' I am yelling now.

Yash is looking at me appraisingly, as if deciding if I'm

telling the truth. My own husband doesn't believe me. He definitely doesn't believe that I am a good mother any more.

Is he right? Did I invent those texts? Only Lydia and I knew of me leaving Ajit in the car. And if Lydia isn't lying about not telling anyone, and if she didn't send the message to the inspector, perhaps I did? The inspector said the text was from a withheld number... I have an app that does that on my phone. Yash and I saw a programme about it. I had downloaded the app and sent him a message from it, just to check, and it had worked, hiding my number, making it seem like Yash had received an anonymous text. We used it for a while to set up dates, and it was fun, romantic. Then life got in the way, he got busy at work, and I forgot about it. But perhaps my subconscious didn't and has been sending messages from that app...

Am I going mad? Has my mind, always fragile, finally become unhinged?

Yash is saying, 'You were threatening to take the children and go away that night. All the others corroborate this. Perhaps you put your threat into action?'

'I did not.' But why can't I remember? And if I can't remember this, then what else have I forgotten? Am I imagining the texts, using them to air my deepest fear – before Ajit going missing when I realised what absolute terror really means – the question I haven't dared ask Yash but have entertained several times in my head: *why are you with me, a woman who is barely functioning, only just keeping her head above water, a passable mother who just about manages to get her children and herself through each day? A woman who keeps making foolish choices she regrets, when she should know better.*

I think back to the day before Ajit went missing, when I took my kids and hailed a taxi to that insanely busy market – another rash, impulsive decision that I regret. Given Ajit's brief but horrifying disappearance, with the fortune teller's ominous prediction preying on my mind, had I imagined the graves and that horrid text message soon after?

And once Ajit went missing, had I aired my guilt, my self-recrimination at being a bad mother who failed her son, not once but twice, by sending a text revealing my failing to the inspector, because I felt I deserved his judgement?

I might have sent that text to the inspector, and conjured up those graves; I might not recall my walk around the cottage the night Ajit went missing, but I do know, with absolute conviction, that I did not take Ajit. 'If I took my son, Inspector, then where is he? Why didn't I take my girls? Why am I still here, going out of my mind with worry?' I flop defeated onto the bed. 'Please, find my son.'

'We are pursuing all avenues.' The inspector is gentler. 'There have been no sightings of Ajit so far. We're still in the process of interviewing your neighbours and hawkers in the area and following up on vehicles and people seen in and around here. Anything comes up, we'll let you know immediately.'

I listen to the inspector and feel desolate. Hopeless.

'Lydia was thinking of running a social media campaign to find Ajit,' Yash says.

'That might be a good thing.' The inspector nods thoughtfully, rubbing his chin. 'We've been sharing on social media, of course, but it's always helpful if you do it too. People – especially those not completely innocent themselves, like pickpockets and petty thieves – who saw or know something will more likely approach a member of the public than the police.'

I should be pleased that Lydia's suggestion was okayed by the inspector and I *am*. Anything that helps with finding Ajit is brilliant – I'm all for it. But I can't help agonising over why *I* didn't think of this, when it is *my* son who is missing. Why, even now, even here when it is a matter of my son's well-being, am I thinking like this and feeling inferior, less? It shouldn't matter. Nothing should except doing everything we can to find Ajit. But that's just it. Again, Lydia is proving herself better, more capable, and it brings to the fore, once more, my failings as a mother.

'I'll tell Lydia to go ahead,' Yash says.

'That's also why I came, actually. We'd like to get the press involved. Are you both up to doing an appeal? You see, we've established that there were a couple of unsavoury characters hanging about that day on the beach.'

I'm finding the inspector's words hard to process. Unsavoury characters... what does he mean by that? Unsavoury, as in, like Paul...? No, not Paul, he wouldn't... He isn't...

'Other than the burglars?' Yash is asking.

'Yes.' The inspector nods.

'Where?'

'During questioning of the neighbouring cottages, we found out that there were some local boys known to us operating in the area. You get these sorts hanging about the tourists. They beg for money or pick pockets, that kind of thing. Most likely they're not involved, but we want to rule nothing out.'

I nod my agreement while inside I'm thinking, *And we thought this beach was safe. How could we?*

'We're still looking for that beggar you had an altercation with. He couldn't walk, so wouldn't have been able to take Ajit, but nevertheless, we want to question him, confirm that he didn't ask his friends to take Ajit. We've yet to question the taxi drivers. However, we've located their whereabouts that night – they were on other jobs and nowhere near this beach.'

'But they too might have asked one of their friends to grab Ajit if they truly wanted to,' Yash says.

'We're looking into that. We've talked to the families holidaying in the cottages nearby and the ones you met on the beach. We've talked to the proprietor of Parradis Cafe, and are in the process of locating all the customers who dined there around the same time as you did, in a bid to determine if anyone took a special interest in Ajit. We've also questioned the builders on the site a few paces across the road from here. No solid leads have emerged yet, but someone may have seen something and if they have, perhaps the press conference will jolt their memory.'

I close my eyes trying to shut out the knowledge of how easy it would have been to take my son. There we were sitting on the beach smug in the knowledge that we could see Rachel. But someone could have parked their car by the road, in the shade of the coconut trees, and walked a couple of paces to the window, climbed inside, grabbed my son and driven away. All in a matter of minutes.

It has taken this tragedy for me to see how vulnerable my children really are – they were never safe; there's danger all around, even, especially, from those closest to them. Even myself.

I shiver, try to focus on the inspector's words.

'If we appeal, if they see you, it might nudge people who've been reluctant to come forward so far, for whatever reason, into doing the right thing,' the inspector is saying.

I look at Yash.

'We'd like to do it,' I say at the same time as Yash says, 'Yes.'

'All right then, we'll schedule the press conference for this afternoon. It's best if we have it here, on the veranda of the cottage. It might jog memories, seeing you, the grieving parents at the scene of the crime, so to speak, and prompt witnesses to come forward.'

At last. Something constructive to do.

I stand, fired up. I will look into the camera and appeal to the person who has my child, plead with him or her to give Ajit back.

If Ajit has been taken, that is.

Of all the horrible scenarios, I would far rather a ransom demand. Money being the motive for snatching my son, nothing more. But there have been no demands so far.

'At the very least, it will provide context, make people aware of how vulnerable little Ajit is, with the sea in front of us and the road behind us,' the inspector is saying.

I shiver, hugging myself with both arms, wishing I was hugging Ajit, holding him in the fortress of my embrace, protecting him from the world.

When I find you, son, I promise, I will not let you down again.

FORTY-THREE

DAY 2

Noon

The crowd of journalists that has been loitering outside appears to have swelled to ten times its size since the inspector announced the press conference. Cars and vans have been arriving non-stop, cameramen unloading equipment, news presenters applying make-up, the beach reverberating with loud shouts, raised voices, car horns and beeps from the long line of vehicles jostling for space, the road behind the cottage grid-locked with them.

There are photographers, journalists, newscasters and busy-bodies, reporters with microphones broadcasting from outside the cottage. The barman has been supplying drinks constantly, his daughter nimbly circulating with a tray, and his wife has not stopped cooking, the smell of spiced grilled meat wafting on the brine-soaked air. The bar shack inadvertently benefitting from our loss. A missing child is good business for the barman and his family and for the reporters and journalists; our misfortune is their gain.

There's national and international media. I picture news about our missing boy broadcast all over the UK. I have read similar headlines over my morning coffee and toast, shivering with empathy, feeling blessed that it wasn't my child. Except that this time, it *is*.

As we wait for the press conference to begin, I look at my phone, which has been beeping constantly. There are no ransom demands. I take a deep breath and go on social media, thinking that, if nothing else, it will prepare me for what I will no doubt face from the gaggle outside very soon. My social media is awash with a mix of kind concern and shocked sympathy, alongside nasty messages, blaming me and Yash. I am inundated with texts, but thankfully nothing from the anonymous sender.

I skim through them, deleting as I go. I know that they are judging me, every single one of them, even the sympathetic ones, like I have done in that blessed time before this nightmare when I was just a voyeur into the pain of other parents with missing children.

There's one message on Snapchat, which I'd installed to see what the fuss was about, which gives me pause. It is from 'A Well-Wisher', personal and judgemental, albeit different in tone from the anonymous messages I've been receiving with their insinuations and intimate knowledge of my family's secrets:

Jo, I forgive you for what you've done.

The message makes me uneasy. I think, *Who are you to impart forgiveness?*

I scroll through the other messages on Snapchat – there are several from this sender. All in a similar vein.

Jo, I am sending love even though you don't deserve it.

Jo, I care for you despite you being so careless with your children.

I want to show the inspector, but this being Snapchat, the messages self-destruct as soon as I read them.

Could it be my sister sending them? But I can't recall us ever saying 'I care for you' or 'I am sending love' to each other, or for that matter to our parents, or hearing it from them. We were never that sort of family. Which is why I've tried to be different with my kids, never missing an opportunity to tell them how much I love them. And yet, I've failed them repeatedly. My actions proving me wrong, rendering my words empty. And now, here we are.

These texts, could they be from... JT? Whose profile I thought I saw at the market when Ajit disappeared briefly. About whom I've told the inspector (who's looking into it, he assures me), but not my husband. I keep waiting for the inspector to bring JT up in front of my husband and friends and I know that he will; he's waiting for the right moment that will have the maximum impact, shake more secrets free.

I asked him, privately, whether he and his men had made any progress in finding JT.

'We are on the case, Mrs Kumar. It is taking a while to pinpoint his whereabouts since he left the UK six years ago, but we *will* find him. And if he has anything to do with your son going missing, we will make him pay. Rest assured, our first priority is to make sure Ajit is found safe and sound.'

Perhaps the inspector hasn't brought JT up yet because he isn't relevant to the investigation, although I could swear it was him I saw that fraught day at the market. But can I really trust myself, when my judgement has been so flawed lately?

JT. Who would tell me he loved me, over and over...

I don't deserve either love or forgiveness, I think, furiously. *I cannot forgive myself for leaving my children unattended that night.*

FORTY-FOUR

DAY 2

2:00 p.m.

Inspector Sharma arrives to escort us to the veranda for the press conference. He has changed into a uniform which is crisp and neat, ironing creases still visible. No yellow perspiration stains along the collar.

Yash is sweating in the smart shirt and black trousers he brought along on holiday in case we went out for the evening. He has shaved, but his eyes are bloodshot and he looks as weary and drained as I feel. He and I have arrived at a truce, presenting a united front for the sake of the girls, who are with us, and Ajit, who is not, deciding for the time being to ignore the chasm splintering our relationship, growing every hour that our boy is missing.

I am wearing the only dress I packed – an incongruous, too bright, summery affair, green with yellow flowers. I had concentrated on packing for the children and when it came to myself, I seem to have only brought shorts and T-shirts and this one dress. I cannot even borrow trousers from Lydia as hers are too small for me. She has looked after herself after having kids while I've let myself go. I've washed my face and even put on some make-up to rid it of its grim pallor.

'Mummy, you look lovely,' Mia said, throwing her arms around me when I came into the living room after changing. She has reverted to calling me 'Mummy', something she grew out of ages ago.

I managed a smile for her benefit, my cheeks aching from the effort it took to keep the smile fixed on my face, to look at my daughter and not at the hubbub outside, which Yash and I would wade into in a few minutes.

'Ready?' Inspector Sharma asks, pushing his shoulders back and looking firm, resolute.

Yash puts his arms around me. I lean into his embrace, wishing we were anywhere but here. We step onto the veranda and into a palisade of noise, questions flung at us like weapons. Cameras stutter, a constellation of flashes. Yash pulls me closer to him and his presence, the smell of his sweat and his fear – the fear that I feel too – is a comfort.

A Babel of voices raining on us, a cornucopia of accents.

'Do you believe Ajit has been kidnapped?'

I try to rein in my rising panic, bunching my hands into fists, attempting to gather courage from somewhere.

'Can Ajit swim? Do you think he went into the sea?'

I feel claustrophobic. I want to run away from these reporters and their incessant bombardment.

'Have you received a ransom note?'

Cameras clicking, the flashing lights disorientating, making me flinch, cower, shy away like a startled horse.

'Inspector Sharma, is it true that you're taking bribes from the kidnappers?'

It feels like a siege. *Stop*, I want to cry. *How is this helping find my son?*

'Why are you focusing on only Indian suspects, are white people above you? Couldn't one of the tourists have taken Ajit?'

Inspector Sharma warned us before we stepped into this mob that some of the questions would be deliberately provocative. Even so, I can't help wincing now.

'Inspector, will you botch this investigation too? Will Ajit be missing a year from now, like Belinda?'

I look at the inspector. He is poker-faced, seemingly unaffected by the accusations lobbed at him.

'Inspector Sharma, what about all the Indian children going missing every day? What is being done to find them?'

'Inspector, are you focusing closer to home, on the parents, their friends, other tourists? If it was someone else, why would they go to the trouble of breaking into a tourist resort when they can take a child from the street?'

'Do you think Ajit might have been taken for his organs? There's a thriving trade in children's kidneys, isn't there?'

'Or perhaps he was taken because he's mixed race, very fair, with European colouring and Indian features, a much sought-after combination in certain circles, commanding very high prices?'

I want to cover my ears, shut them against what I'm hearing. Don't these people have a heart? Don't they realise this is a child they're talking about, within his parents' hearing? Or are they too jaded to care?

Inspector Sharma raises his hand and the press posse slowly quietens down, voices fading to rustling and the occasional whisper. He reads out his statement, appealing to people with any information to please come forward.

Then it is our turn.

Once again, cameras go off, so many flashes, like stars popping in front of my eyes. Yash opens the piece of paper with the plea we prepared earlier, and begins to read – we've agreed that he will read it as I cannot be trusted not to break down.

'Our five-year-old son Ajit disappeared from his bed on the second night of his, of our, holiday, here at Galgibaga Beach. He was reported missing at twelve fifty a.m. on the thirteenth of February. He is wearing pyjamas – a short-sleeved top and matching shorts and slippers, all yellow with the cartoon character SpongeBob's face on each of them – and is carrying a SpongeBob soft toy. We... we...' Yash gulps, chokes on his tears.

I squeeze his hand, but he cannot continue. It is heartbreaking watching my husband, who prides himself on his self-control, fall apart so completely, especially, now, here, in front of everyone. But one of us has to be strong for our boy. And so I hold back the grief threatening to overwhelm me, swallow down the salty lump in my throat with effort, and look up at the cameras. 'Please, if you have him, please bring back our boy. We miss him and love him. If you have seen anything, or think you know something, anything at all, that might be connected to Ajit going missing, please come forward. Ajit, we love you.'

I look at Inspector Sharma, who nods and shepherds both of us – Yash, shoulders shaking with the sobs he cannot contain, me dry-eyed, holding myself together with my everything – from the veranda into the cottage, closing the door behind him on the questions that are being yelled at us from every side. As the door slams shut, one final, emphatic query, thrown at us, ringing in my ears, devastating me all over again: 'Do you believe that Ajit is still alive?'

FORTY-FIVE

Blog post appearing on shobhaspeaksout.in:

Missing Little Boy: Did The Parents Do It?
Posted by Ms Shobha Nair, 15 February

Five-year-old Ajit went missing from his holiday cottage in Galgibaga Beach in the late hours of February the 12th. His whereabouts are still unknown.

The police investigation is led by the notorious Inspector Sharma, who said, at the press conference yesterday afternoon (click here to see the video), that 'the police investigation is ongoing and we are following up on several leads'. Didn't he say the same thing, word for word, when investigating Belinda Fernandes's disappearance (click here for more details)? Belinda Fernandes is *still* missing. Will this also be poor Ajit's fate given Inspector Sharma's track record?

I'm sure those of you who watched the fiasco of a press conference will be thinking what I'm thinking. Did the parents do it?

For me, the parents' appeal reeked of performance. It felt

pat, wooden, as if they were (not very good) actors practising for a show. The father broke down – questionable – but at least something natural in the circumstances. But the mother... cool and collected. Dressed as if for a party, a summer picnic with the queen. She was also wearing make-up. No expression on her face. Absolutely no emotion in her voice.

I am a mother myself and if it was my child missing, well, I'd be in pieces. I definitely would not care what I wore. I would certainly not take the time to beautify myself for the cameras.

What kind of mother are you, Jo? Did you do it? Mistreat your son, make him disappear? Did you plan all this? Choose Goa and orchestrate a disappearance here, having heard that Indian police are notoriously incompetent, knowing that your son not being found could be put down to police negligence? Perhaps you even asked for Inspector Sharma personally – after all, his shocking ineptitude is a matter of public record.

Or perhaps it wasn't planned. Perhaps it was an accident – Ajit the unfortunate casualty. Did something happen to him, Jo, and you panicked, concocted this elaborate plan? If not, where is your angst? Where is your pain? Where is the emotion you must surely be feeling?

Comments:
Aadya, Margao 05:42 IST: #TheMotherDidIt
Jennifer, Panaji 05:48 IST: I'm with you, Aadya. Did you see her face? Not a tear. She is guilty as hell. #TheMotherDidIt
Harish, Aguada 05:53 IST: Stop the blame game. There is no one way to show grief. We all react differently. #FindAjit
Jennifer, Panaji 05:55 IST: Don't let Jo's looks cloud your judgement, Harish. She is guilty as hell. I'm a Catholic and don't swear lightly. #TheMotherDidIt

Scroll down for more comments.

FORTY-SIX

DAY 3

6:30 a.m.

Two and a half days since I've known the whereabouts of my boy. Two and a half days that he has spent away from his family.

All the phones in the cottage have been going non-stop. Last night, when I returned, defeated, after yet another scour of the beach and surrounds for my son, I scrolled through mine just to check for ransom demands. But there was nothing of the sort, although now I think that I would actually welcome it, for then at least I would be close to knowing where my son is and be able to do something to get him back, other than combing the beach and surrounds for miles each night, calling for Ajit, after the reporters have gone home. I was inundated by messages – none from the withheld number that has been goading me since before this holiday, thank God. There were several of the Snapchat messages from 'A Well-Wisher', unsettling, passive-aggressive, persistent. The rest were from strangers who have judged me and found me guilty. No more sympathetic messages. I am being reviled and hated, blamed for Ajit's disappearance.

My friends, my husband, and even Rachel have been giving me surreptitious looks since the press conference, walking on eggshells around me, so I knew I wouldn't have come off well. Yet still, when I checked my phone last night, I couldn't help but recoil from the loathing, the vitriol aimed at me. I knew I was a bad mother, but now the world knows it too. Everyone hates me, even more, it appears, than I hate myself. I feel splayed open, my worst qualities, my abject failings held up for complete strangers to comment upon. I don't mind, I tell myself, as long as Ajit is found. But I am shaken by this utter venom directed at me from all sides. How does the inspector endure this public crucifixion and still do his job anyway? I have new-found respect for him.

That article I read about Indian police before we came on holiday must have been biased. The media is not always right, I'm discovering, more so now their reporting is skewed against me. They are prejudiced, their journalism coloured by their views and politics, however much they may claim to be impartial.

Speaking of which... Here they are, although it's barely dawn, cars pulling up, radios going, chatter.

The kids are asleep, but the four of us adults are awake and in the living room, Yash and Lydia drinking coffee, Paul zoned out on the sofa. Me pacing, unable to sit still.

I've been keeping a beady eye on my girls, making sure they're never alone with Paul, watching for any signs they're uncomfortable with him. To be honest, I haven't seen any evidence of it since I began keeping tabs. And deep down I do think I agree with Yash – this is *Paul*, for Christ's sake. But, nevertheless, I'm not taking any chances when it comes to my kids' well-being.

Too little too late, my conscience mocks. *What about Ajit's well-being, eh?*

I shudder, throwing my arms around myself, but it is scant comfort.

The doors are shut – well, as far as the sticky front door will shut, the mesh screen locked and yet, the reporters' cries worm their way indoors and one comment pulls me up short.

'Jo, did you do it? Your sister definitely believes so.'

My sister.

Lori.

My phone has been beeping non-stop, but I haven't had the stomach to look at it since last night, telling myself that the demand for ransom will arrive on Yash's phone too. And wouldn't the kidnappers call rather than message us?

Now I check my phone.

Breaking news.

Not what I've been hoping for, that Ajit is found, no. Instead, Lori's photogenic face, her supermodel figure, tall and willowy, hogging the headlines.

She's posted on Facebook and it's gone viral, so much so that all the news channels are reporting it.

On Facebook, Lori, Jo Kumar's sister, has made wild accusations about Mrs Kumar, missing five-year-old Ajit Kumar's mother: 'My sister is no saint. She might have hurt Ajit, accidentally or otherwise, and made him disappear to hide her crime. As to where – the sea is at their doorstep, isn't it?'

Lori hasn't changed at all, in fact, she looks better now, age adding grace and elegance, accentuating her features, rendering them more defined. And she hasn't changed in nature either, always quick to undermine, criticise, find fault with me.

'Jo is an attention seeker, always has been. She will do anything for notoriety, even kidnap her child. I'm absolutely convinced of it. After all, she has form. She was caught stealing as a teenager, issued a caution by the police. Look no further than Jo. She is to blame. She drove our mother away, our father to drink. He drank himself to an early grave and she didn't even attend his funeral. When we were children she would...'

Her words, trending on social media, blur before my eyes.

And, of course, there are pages and pages of comments on all the news sites, in the same vein, united in crucifying me: *No smoke without fire! #TheMotherDidIt*

My secret vice, when I get a minute from the children, is to watch reality shows – I am gripped by other people's dramas laid bare for the world to see, the more messed-up the better, cringing from them even as I hungrily devour them and wonder why I am so addicted to them. It is, I see now, because it makes my own messed-up childhood seem tame in comparison.

Now, *my* worst nightmare is the reality show the world is obsessed with. I am the maligned woman whom her sister, her own blood, has damned, declared guilty, capable of kidnapping her son for attention.

And yet still I read on, and one sentence catches my eye:

Lori was not available for comment as she is out of the country, on holiday with her family.

Lori is out of the country. Is she... here? Is she the one who has taken my son? I absolutely wouldn't put it past her. Another way to get back at me, and the publicity, her comments making front page news, well that would be the icing on the cake.

I shut my eyes, sway on my feet.

'Here, this will help,' says Lydia, putting one arm around

me, with the other offering me a cup of tea, her rings in my eyeline.

She leads me to the sofa, sits me down.

I fixate on the ring to take my mind off my sister's lies, her skewed version of our childhood out there for the world to judge and comment upon. My worry that she might have something to do with Ajit's disappearance.

'Your ring, that one on your pinky...' My voice is hoarse, as if out of practice.

'Yes?' Lydia says.

'I think it's mine.'

Lydia sucks in her teeth, her face pinched. She takes a deep breath. 'Jo, love, I know you've had a shock, but that doesn't mean—'

'Mine was chipped in exactly the same place. And the woman I bought it from assured me it was one of a kind.'

Lydia's gaze is incredulous. 'Goodness, Jo, are you saying I *stole* your ring?'

'Or someone gave it to you. My husband, the only other person with access to the safe.'

'Can you hear yourself, Jo?' Yash cries. 'Please stop this, it's not helping.'

'It's my ring,' I say stubbornly. The thought has been festering in my head since I saw the ring on Lydia's finger and I want to air it. Now's as good a time as any.

Lydia says, 'Honestly, Jo, why would I take *your* ring when I have several of my own?'

'Why would you take *my* husband when you have one of your own?'

Lydia winces as if she's been slapped.

'Jo, that's enough,' Yash snaps in the same tone he uses on the kids when they're being contrary.

A part of me knows I've behaved badly, lashing out just like

I used to as a child when pushed into a corner, which is how I've felt since the backlash from the press conference, Yash getting away lightly but me coming in the firing line, vigilantes screaming for my blood. Other mothers damning me. I feel swamped, judged, bullied. I feel pierced by a thousand eyes, like that fortune teller's necklace. It is as if the judging – discerning? – public is able to see through the front I project to who I really am, the person I shy away from in the mirror. What I've been hiding, even from myself, exposed alongside my missing son. Now, the world knows too – that I'm a liar, a cheat. They can see that I've not been the best mother to my children, that I've failed them again and again.

But if there is one thing I have learned, it is that you cannot undo the past. You have to move on, accept whatever hell you devise for yourself because of your reprehensible mistakes.

I am so angry, at myself most of all. My skin feels constricted, too tight for my body. It is as if ants are crawling under it. I feel impotent, furious, frustrated. I am raging, at myself for losing my son, at Lori for what she said, at the world for believing her, finding me guilty. I feel blamed, and so I want to blame someone else, push the onus on them. Surely I don't deserve my childhood, as seen through my sister's lying eyes, made public?

That was the last straw. When I saw my sister on the screen of my phone, I reverted to childhood, wanting to hurt, retaliate, and Lydia was right there, flaunting that ring.

I don't want to believe my friend took it, or that Yash gave it to her. But... there is that small persistent niggle in my head, crying: *That ring is mine. How does she have it?*

It's petty, I know, to bring it up, but it's an outlet for my simmering rage and upset.

I don't know why I'm so disturbed by it – I think because it implies, along with Lydia's bikini among Yash's things, their whispering together before Ajit went missing, that they're *still* lying to me.

You are still *lying to your husband too*, my conscience points out.

Those texts I received implying Yash was having an affair... I don't want it to be true. But I feel lied to, cheated on. Hurt.

You've lied, cheated, hurt too, my conscience chides.

'Maybe you should talk to your counsellor over the phone – it might help,' Yash is saying. 'Perhaps your meds...'

'They make me groggy,' I say.

'They might stop you forgetting things,' Paul interjects. 'Do you remember anything more about that walk you took around the cottage the night Ajit went missing?'

Is he deliberately goading me? Is this his revenge because I called him a predator?

'They might also stop you imagining things,' he goes on. 'You imagined seeing the graves.'

I shudder at the image of those three child-sized graves bearing the names of my children. So very real.

But Paul can only know about my seeing them if Yash told him. My husband has been discussing me not only with Lydia but with Paul too.

I turn to Yash. But he will not meet my gaze. The traitor. When did I, his wife, become other; why has he been discussing me with Lydia and Paul?

'Perhaps they will also stop you accusing your friend of stealing, of all things, a twopenny ring,' Paul is saying.

He *is* riling me. 'How dare you?' I hiss. I might have sensed a distance between Lydia and Paul since the revelation about Rachel, but when push comes to shove, Paul comes to his wife's defence – turning on me. I am going through all kinds of hell, with my son missing and my sister dissing me to the world, and it hurts that Yash is not doing the same for me, standing up for me, defending me. Instead, he gangs up on me alongside Lydia and Paul.

'Bear in mind, Lydia is not the one who has form,' Paul says.

I am winded by his words, as if I have received a physical blow, my outrage replaced by pain. He's read Lori's post and believes my sister's lies – and if this man who's known me for fifteen years does so, then what hope do I have with anyone else? In the court of public opinion, I'm damned.

But then, by the same token, I realise that I've believed some stranger's accusation over Paul's insistence that he's innocent. I've labelled him guilty even though every instinct and years' worth of friendship is telling me otherwise.

I deserve this. But I don't know how much more I can take.

'You've been talking about a stalker, you think they've followed you here, to India, from England...' Paul continues. 'Some determined stalker,' he scoffs.

Now I erupt. 'My son is missing. Picking on me won't bring him back.'

Yash blanches. Rubs his face. 'We're not picking on you, Jo. We're concerned. The meds might help. You should call the counsellor, tell her the pills make you groggy. She would—'

'I'm *not* imagining the stalker,' I cut Yash off. 'Have you considered that it might be them who's behind this?' Could it be Lori? She is on holiday abroad. Is she here? Is she doing this? And then, my mind flits to JT, whom I thought I saw at the market. Could it really be him and has he taken Ajit? The inspector has promised me he is doing all he can to find him. But it's taking too long. The waiting is the worst. How do parents whose children have been missing a year or more endure it? *Please, let Ajit be found and soon.*

Yash sighs. 'Jo, love, there's no evidence—'

'Would you rather it was one of us then?' I snap, pushed to breaking point. I am angry with Yash for siding with Paul and

Lydia against me, although he calls it concern, for discrediting my worries, thinking I am making things up.

Yash pales. 'Why would one of us steal Ajit?'

'Honestly, if it's anyone, it would be you, just to create more drama,' I think I hear Lydia hiss.

I rear back, shocked.

And that is when I notice the policeman sitting quietly in the corner watching us, silently taking it all in, hearing my husband and supposed friends damn me, accuse me.

8:00 a.m.

The kids are having breakfast at the table in the living room and Yash and I are pretending to do the same, when there is a knock at the door. We cannot go out onto the veranda as the beach in front of the cottage is once again busy with reporters.

'Did you do it, Jo?' they shout as I open the door to Inspector Sharma and they get a glimpse of my face. 'Was it an accident and have you buried Ajit in the sea, like your sister claims?'

I recoil from their words, which they toss so carelessly, as if they aren't pointed barbs wounding, drawing blood.

'Mr and Mrs Kumar, a word?'

I try to read the inspector's face. He looks even more impassive than usual, his moustache polished, his eyes grave.

'We can talk in the bedroom,' Yash says, voice clipped.

The bedroom, repository of our luggage, which includes one SpongeBob suitcase with Ajit's clothes. The bedroom opposite the room from which our son disappeared.

'Mummy, I want you here with me,' Mia cries. She has

regressed at least three years in the last three days. She had stopped calling me Mummy and chewing her thumb when she started school, and now she's back to doing both.

While Mia is becoming clingier, Zoe has withdrawn into herself, her eyes huge and wet with worry. Both have stopped asking when Ajit is coming back – resigned to the fact that their brother has disappeared and that their cottage is awash with policemen and that they can't go outside without questions being shouted at them. They no longer ask to go to the beach. They sit in the cottage and they wait, wide-eyed, for their brother and normalcy to return.

I kneel next to Mia. 'I'll be back in a few minutes, sweetie, I promise. Now eat your toast, there's a good girl.'

Yash opens the window in the bedroom slightly and cool air, carrying a hint of morning, a whiff of the sea, freshness and salt, seaweed and sunshine, wafts in, bringing with it noise from the crowd outside.

Inspector Sharma clears his throat.

I sit down on the bed, beside my son's suitcase, as I wait to hear the inspector's news. This whole ordeal seems to be a lesson in different kinds of torture. Just when I think I can't take any more, new information and with it more heart-stopping moments of worry, anxiety, all-consuming dread.

'We've searched every bit of the beach for miles around and no sign of Ajit has been found,' the inspector says.

No sign.

'We located that beggar who cursed you, questioned him. He's harmless. Yes, he was angry, but we've reached the conclusion he had nothing to do with it. He said he would never harm a child and I believe him.'

Surely someone, somewhere knows *something*?

'The taxi drivers, likewise, have been interrogated, and again, we don't think they've got anything to do with it. They're family men, no previous convictions, no history of violence, no gang connections. Just ordinary, hard-working men. They were quite affronted to be considered capable of kidnap just because you didn't pay them a tip.' The inspector takes a yellowing handkerchief out of his pocket and wipes his face with it. Is it just the heat or is this case getting to him? And if so, what does this bode for my boy?

'The preliminary results of lab tests taken from samples in the room, in the cottage, Ajit's bed have come back,' the inspector says. 'Unfortunately, they show nothing out of the ordinary. If Ajit was abducted, the kidnapper has been very careful and conscientious so as to leave no trace.'

Despair settles heavily in the pit of my stomach.

'We talked to the vendors who were circulating on your stretch of beach that day, the ice cream seller, the peanut and bhel hawkers, the coconut vendor – none of them saw anything suspicious.'

'Do you think they themselves might have been involved?' Yash asks.

'We checked and we've found nothing on them.'

'The burglars?'

'We're on the lookout for them. As soon as we find out more, I'll let you know.'

How much longer? The wait feels endless.

'We've interviewed and looked into the restaurant owner and also the man who runs the shack and his family – nothing.'

Yash and I nod, defeated.

'We interviewed the German family whom you met and talked to on the beach. They've been allowed to leave now, return home. We've questioned the other families on the beach that day, the Italian family with the boy Ajit played with, and others, and the builders on the site up the road and none of them saw or heard anything.' Inspector Sharma pauses to take a breath. 'I've questioned your friend, Mr Kumar, the one who recommended this cottage to you. He too seems above board.'

'He is,' Yash says. 'I've known him for years.'

'However...'

Both Yash and I look up at the inspector.

'We found a few prints on the windowsill which do not belong to any of you – they might match those of the burglars. We will be checking that once the burglars are caught – and rest assured we *will* catch them.' A pause, then: 'Also, there are three as yet unidentified vehicles which were seen loitering by the beach the day you arrived – two cars and an auto-rickshaw. All others have now been accounted for.' The inspector rubs a hand across his jaw. 'We've been trying to find them, to no avail. One of the cars was a grey Maruti Esteem, another a battered cream Ambassador that had seen better days. The rickshaw has a picture of Goddess Kali hanging from the mirror in front of the driver's seat. We're appealing to the public to come forward with information about them; we've released descriptions to the press.'

'What about the press conference?' Yash asks.

I know we have to ask this and I want to hear what the inspector has to say but even so, I can't help but feel uncomfortable, knowing the inspector won't have failed to see the backlash against me. I would rather he focus on finding Ajit than believe the public and waste time concentrating his investigation on me.

'Ah, I was coming to that. The press conference yielded several leads and we are in the process of following up on them. There are reports of sightings, most of them unusable. But...' Here the inspector pauses, looking from one to the other of us.

'But?' Yash asks.

'There have also been a couple of sightings of a boy matching Ajit's description on his own.'

'Why didn't the people who saw him do something?' I cry.

'There are lots of children on their own, wandering the streets of India,' the inspector says.

I think of the car journey on our way here, how, when we were stopped in traffic, a ragged little girl barely older than Ajit had tapped the glass of the window, hungry eyes, dirty face, begging bowl. Ajit was asleep, but my girls had been shocked, upset. The car had started up and they had said, 'Why was she moving between the traffic, Mum? Wasn't she worried about getting run over? Why were her clothes torn? Why was she sad? What was she asking us?'

'There have also been sightings of a boy matching Ajit's description by the water,' the inspector goes on. 'One lady in particular was going for an early-morning walk on the morning of Ajit's disappearance and thinks she saw a little figure weaving by the water in the distance. She ran up to the figure, but by the time she reached the water, whoever it was had gone.'

'Where was this?'

'A mile or two along the beach from here.'

I hug my stomach to try to keep the keening grief inside. My baby was on his own, lost, possibly looking for us and I could not help him, be there for him. Where did he go? Into the sea?

No. *No, no, no...*

The inspector clears his throat. I look up and read, in his gaze, that something significant is coming.

Please let my boy be unharmed.

'A couple of people have come forward – separately – to say they've seen a boy matching Ajit's description with a man, tall, over six feet and bespectacled. They are working with a police artist to create a likeness of the man.'

Ajit with a man. So he *was* taken. By a man who matches JT's description.

Could it be JT? JT whom I thought I saw briefly at the market?

I cover my mouth with my palm. I don't know which is worse. My son wandering the streets alone. My son weaving by the sea and disappearing, sucked into the hypnotic swell and drag of the ocean. My son with a strange man… or not a stranger at all but someone known to me?

And as if the inspector has followed the direction of my thoughts, 'This is our strongest viable lead and it might very possibly be connected with something you've shared with me, Mrs Kumar. I'm giving you the opportunity to tell your husband before I do.'

He raises an eyebrow at me, gaze impassive. I sense this is another instance of putting us on the spot, that tactic the inspector is so good at, but this time at my expense. But I don't care if the secret that I was guarding from Yash is out, that he is hurt – I don't mind anything at all as long as my son is found, hale and whole. *Please.*

'Jo, what's this?' Yash cries. 'This man who has Ajit is something to do with *you*?'

'I need to go,' the inspector says, 'but I will be sending the police artist round, Mrs Kumar, for you to give a description of the man you think you saw at the market who is connected with your past. If you have any pictures—'

'I don't. I told you that already.'

'Yes, but I was just checking in case you'd found any since we last talked.'

'Jo?' Yash says again.

I ignore him, tell the inspector, my heart wailing in my chest, 'No, I haven't.' I have trawled through my social media accounts, and all of my photos, but I don't have any pictures of JT. We were very careful during our affair; the clandestine nature of it was part of the thrill, I see now.

If JT has Ajit, and it seems a very real possibility that it *is* him, then I will never forgive myself. For it is the mistakes of my past that my precious child is paying dearly for…

The moment the inspector leaves, Yash turns to me. 'Jo, who is this man who has our boy? How is he connected with you?'

My husband is no fool. But I've made him one by coming clean to the inspector about JT but keeping it from him. I take a deep breath, preparing myself for the revelation...

'Mummy,' Mia calls from the living room.

'We'll talk about this later, Yash,' I say, standing up, tiredly, and leaving the room with the gait of a much older woman to embrace my daughter who has regressed to a much younger child. I gather her in my arms, while my second daughter watches me with huge, wary eyes that seem to have lost their innocence – that look like the eyes of that little girl who had knocked on the window of our car as it stopped in traffic on the way here. That same air of despair that is too old for young eyes.

FORTY-EIGHT

DAY 3

12:30 p.m.

I have been avoiding being properly alone with Yash since the inspector left.

It hasn't been too difficult. There are the children, who are being needy; Lydia, who's mothering us all; Rachel, who's taken to following me around since her confession, as if by attending to me, it will negate the guilt she obviously feels; the ever-present, ever-watchful policeman in his chair in the living room; and Paul, who appears not to know what to do with himself, standing up one minute, sitting down the next, driving me absolutely crazy with his barely contained restlessness.

I have avoided being alone with my husband for I know there's a conversation we must have – in fact, there are several different conversations we need to have. But I don't have the energy. I am exhausted, drained. I cannot cope with anything else, anything more.

With Inspector Sharma gone, a gloom has descended on both of us. We have done the press conference, done our bit. I have worked with the police artist, who arrived, to a great buzz of interest from the press, half an hour after the inspector, to create a likeness of the JT I knew six years ago and thought I glimpsed at the market. Yash asked me, once again, about this person of interest from my past, and I promised him I would come clean but right then the girls, who were, understandably, clingy, needed him, while I liaised with the police artist.

Now we wait. More interminable waiting.

The children drift off to sleep in my arms – their routine is all over the place. They eat when they're hungry, sleep when they feel like it. Yash carries our girls, one by one, into their bedroom, tucks them in bed.

Paul is pacing the length of the living room, up and down, up and down. Just as I'm about to snap at him to stop, he says, 'I'm taking Bella out for a walk. Most of the reporters seem to have dispersed for lunch. I'll bring back something to eat.'

'I'll come too,' Lydia says. 'Rach, why don't you come as well, darling? Stretch your legs a bit?'

Rachel nods passively. A few days ago, she wouldn't have liked her mum calling her 'darling', she'd have had something to say about it. And she wouldn't have wanted to be seen anywhere near her family. But now she is a different girl, ironed out by tragedy. A pale facsimile.

'Can we paddle in the sea?' Bella asks and I close my eyes as I recall Ajit tugging at my hand when we had stepped out of the taxi, saying, 'Mum, please can we go to the sea, please, please?'

Lydia shoots me a guilty look before saying to Bella, 'OK then, change into your swimsuit.'

I think of Ajit's SpongeBob swimming trunks drying on the windowsill of our bedroom – I haven't had the heart to take them down and they must be bone-dry by now.

Don't go, I think as they all gather by the front door. *Don't leave me alone with Yash, with our grief, our secrets, our hurt, our mistakes and no buffer.*

But they open the door, and I hear the few reporters who have stayed behind shout their interminable questions: 'Where are you going?' 'Lydia, Paul, why did you leave the children with a fourteen-year-old? How do you feel about this, Rachel?' 'Are Jo and Yash coming too?' 'Who do you think did it?' 'Was it Jo? Is that why she's hiding?' 'Do you know what happened to Ajit?'

Then the door closes behind them and we are alone, my husband and I, except for the policeman dozing in the corner. I suspect the dozing is just an act – he misses nothing, I'm sure. But by now I'm past caring. I just want my boy back.

Yash is sitting at the table, his head in his hands. I am on the sofa, staring at the ceiling. For a long moment, neither of us speaks.

A lizard scuttles in the beams of the ceiling. I wish I had its life, nothing to worry about except searching for prey.

Prey. Is my son someone's prey?

I shudder.

Yash looks at me, but before he can ask about JT, I say, 'Listen, I think Paul is hiding something.'

That grabs his attention. 'What?'

I have been mulling this over and I want to get Yash's take before we move on to JT. 'He was supposed to get the wine, but he was gone for nearly fifteen minutes. It might be connected with Ajit...'

'Think about what you're saying, Jo,' Yash cries.

The policeman jolts upright, blinking at us. We both ignore him, focused only on each other.

After fifteen years together, I can read my husband's non-verbal cues very well indeed. And right now, I know why Yash is being so tetchy, why he is frustrated with me. He wants to know about the tall man with the boy who might be connected to me. And sure enough...

'Tell me what *you* are hiding from me, that the inspector

knows about, that might be connected with our boy going missing,' Yash says. 'I assume that's also the reason the police artist was here?'

I nod and take a deep breath, bolstering myself. And then I tell him.

FORTY-NINE

SIX YEARS PREVIOUSLY

Over several weeks, after my breakdown following the miscarriage, with regular counselling sessions and the pills the doctor prescribed, I started getting better. I started dressing up for when Yash was due to come home, and cooked meals for him – something I had not had the energy to do when I was in the throes of depression.

But Yash was coming home later and later – more clients meant more work, he said – and I ended up throwing the food I had so painstakingly prepared in the bin more than once and getting my good clothes dirty soothing the girls while waiting for him to arrive. Mia and Zoe seemed to wake as soon as I lay them down in their beds, so I had taken to sitting with them asleep on my lap and picking them up when they started crying and one woke the other.

I think it was during one of those long evenings that it struck me something was not right. The children had just fallen asleep and I was watching an inane programme on television as I waited for Yash to come home. I must have dozed off because I jerked awake to wailing. Both of my kids were fast asleep beside me, Mia on her side, sucking her thumb, Zoe on her back, her hands lifted up in abandon on either side of her. I squinted blearily at the clock. Ten minutes to eleven. Yash was still not home.

On the telly, one of the characters was crying her heart out – this was the sobbing that must have woken me – because her husband was having an affair. 'He's never home,' she was saying, her face wet with tears. Uneasiness curled around my stomach then, as, like the woman on the screen, I wondered where exactly my husband was.

I had promised myself that when I got married, I would make it last. My children would have two parents, unlike my own fractured childhood. But now I questioned if our happy family was a myth, a fantasy I had concocted because I wanted so much for it to be true.

I began observing Yash, certain that he was having an affair. I went through his clothes, checked his phone. I convinced myself that the odd receipt in his pocket for a meal out, which he told me was with clients, was actually with his mistress. I imagined I could detect a woman's perfume on his clothes – not mine. I wondered why he smelled so fresh at night when he had been at the office all day – he said he'd been to the gym on the way home, showered there, but I took it as further proof of his cheating.

I followed him. I took the girls with me, put them in the car in their seats and tailed him. It took an accident in which we all nearly died, me and my girls, because I was too busy following Yash to concentrate on the road, for me to wake up to the reality of the situation. For Yash to find out, to his utter chagrin and distress, that I was convinced he was having an affair and had been obsessively tailing him to the point that I had put our girls in danger. For him and Lydia to stage an intervention, get me the help I needed. I had a spell in hospital, while Lydia looked after my girls as well as hers.

I returned home determined to be a good wife to Yash and a

good mother to the girls. But once more, the mundane, non-stop reality of caring for the girls, while Yash worked long hours, threatened to get me down. Lydia was there, offering support, a helping hand. She was being kind, wonderful, but it only made me feel more inadequate. I couldn't seem to manage to get through a single day without feeling out of my depth. Even the simplest of tasks overwhelmed me.

And it was then, at my lowest point, that I met JT.

I meet JT at one of the parties I have to attend as Yash's wife.

It's still early days after my accident and hospitalisation and I'm really not in the mood. But, for Yash's sake, I make an effort. I wear a sequinned silver sheath dress that shows off my body, now back to its pre-pregnancy sleekness. I may not be slim, but I am curvy in all the right places. I apply make-up carefully, and when I am done, I know without a doubt that I will turn heads.

'Wow,' Yash says when I come downstairs after having tucked the girls in their beds and double-checked that the babysitter knows about the night terrors Mia has been experiencing recently, and he kisses me with a passion he has not displayed since before we had Mia and Zoe.

Sometime during the evening, while Yash is hobnobbing with clients, I sneak away, onto the terrace, breathing in the cool air fragranced with apples and wood smoke, glad to be rid of the scent of money and competition, one-upmanship and expensive perfume. I am much better than I was, but nevertheless feeling a little vulnerable after my ordeal, and coming here, being among this crowd has taken a lot out of me. I feel out of place and although the combination of pills and counselling is helping keep my paranoia with regards to Yash straying at bay, I can't quite relax completely – I still have the odd doubt about Yash although now I'm skilled at pushing it away rather than giving in to it.

'You look like you could do with a smoke.' A voice behind me.

I haven't smoked since I was a teen, but right now I desperately crave a cigarette. 'Would love one,' I say. And although I am intrigued by the accent and the velvet voice that wields it, I do not turn around.

A masculine hand with long, elegant fingers extends a packet of cigarettes towards me and I pick one, put it in my mouth.

When he bends forward to light it, and I meet his gaze, I suck in a breath. The look in this stranger's toffee-caramel eyes reminds me of the way Yash used to look at me when we first met. It feels like a gift, as if, for a brief while, basking in this clearly appreciative stranger's appraisal, I can pretend I am still that woman – girl, really – who Yash fell for.

We stand smoking side by side in the shadowy dark and I am aware of the attraction fizzing between us.

'You're hiding too?' His eyes sparkle with mischief even as his lips rise in a conspiratorial smile that makes my heart skip a beat.

With effort, I pull my gaze away from his mesmerising one, taking a deep, comforting drag of my cigarette. Possessed by an urge to stoke this stranger's regard, that flame in his eyes as he looks at me, I say, dryly, 'I *never* hide.'

He laughs and it is a wonderful sound, masculine and addictive. 'I absolutely believe that.' His voice is admiring and I can feel his warm gaze on me.

A shiver of desire tickles my spine. When was the last time I felt like this? I cannot remember.

I suppress an urge to giggle, even as I muse that this man has well and truly reduced me to my girly self. And it is she who asks, archly, 'Who are *you* hiding from?'

'Oh, everyone really,' he says, blowing a perfect smoke ring, navy mist in the secretive dark. 'I hate these things.' A beat, then, 'Excluding present company, of course.'

I laugh, then cough as I inhale smoke.

'Are you OK?'

'I'm fine.' I wave his concern away. 'So why are you at the party then?'

'I'm sorry?' His eyebrow arches in question, his eyes the glazed gold of burnt sugar. He really is beautiful. I wonder, briefly, how his lips would taste. The thought, which comes out of nowhere, startles me. A little harmless flirting is all well and good, but... Why on earth am I, a married woman and mother, thinking like this?

'You said you hate these things,' I manage in a steady voice.

'I had to be here. I'm representing my company. It's one of the IT vendors doing business with Yash and Paul.'

The familiarity with which he mentions Yash's name incites a moment of uncertainty over how well he knows my husband. I take a breath to compose myself, push the unease away – I am feeling flustered by this man's attention, focused on me. I am not used to it. 'They couldn't send anybody else?' I say archly.

'No.' And again that impish sparkle in his eyes. 'I said "company" to impress you. There's just me.'

'Oh.' I laugh, feeling warmed. 'I *am* impressed by the fact that you run your own company.'

It is his turn to laugh. Celebratory and unrestrained, like champagne bubbles popping. 'I'm JT by the way. And you are?'

'Jo.'

'Jo,' he repeats.

Nobody, not even Yash, not even when we first met, has said my name quite that way, like it is a treat to be savoured.

'I've been watching you, Jo.'

I'm taken aback but also very flattered. 'Do you make a habit of watching strange women at parties?'

His voice is soft, intimate as a caress, as he says, 'Not any other woman. Only you.'

Perhaps it is the intensity of his words, the way his eyes never leave mine, but I believe him.

'I was going to say hello to Yash and Paul and leave, but then I saw you...' He pauses, looking at me in such a way as to electrify me with another bolt of thrilling desire. 'You're welcome to tell me where to get off.'

'No, please go on.' My voice is low, breathless.

'I noted a certain vulnerability in you, which you tried to mask behind a fierce grace. I couldn't leave after that. I was hoping to talk to you – I stepped out here for a smoke to gather my courage to approach you and, well, here you are! Nothing has ever come easy for me in life, so I guess the universe owed me this. You.'

I blink back tears, completely bowled over by this man's speech. He's only known me a few minutes, but he's noticed the vulnerability I have been trying to hide. However, unlike Yash it doesn't worry or scare him. Instead, he sees beyond it, to strength I didn't know I possessed. I like the version of myself I see reflected in his gaze – not the struggling mother and failing wife but a beautiful, complex, *desirable* woman.

The band starts up indoors, a rousing jig.

JT stubs his cigarette, holds out his arm, golden eyes twinkling at me. 'May I have this dance, please, ma'am?'

There's something about this man that inspires confidence, makes me feel secure and at ease, at the same time as sexy, as if he is an old flame still igniting sparks. So I loop my arm in his and allow him to lead me indoors.

'Yash does not realise how lucky he is.' JT's richly accented voice sends shivers of desire down my spine as we dance, his lips so tantalisingly close to mine, his hand searing the small of my back. My husband is still busy with clients – he hasn't missed me, or spared a glance in our direction. 'To be married to the most beautiful woman I've ever seen.'

I laugh, even as I glow. 'You exaggerate.'

'I've never been more serious in my life,' he declares.

JT holds me too close and I revel in it and the way his gaze never leaves mine. He whispers compliments and endearments and I blush, my body tingling as his lips brush my ear, even as I bask in his adoration.

At the end of the evening, JT asks for my number and I give it to him, heady and sated by his regard, ignoring the strident voice in my head that asks: *What the hell are you doing?*

He calls the very next morning. 'You are a drug I do not want to get out of my system.' He utters those words, exhilarating, over-exaggerated, in his mellifluous voice, like he means them.

'I'm a mother of two children.' I sigh, my body liquid.

'You're a beautiful, sexy woman,' he whispers down the phone. 'I want to see you and I cannot wait. Are you free for lunch?'

And I find myself saying yes.

It doesn't take JT long to break through my defences – feeble where he is concerned – and kiss me. He kisses like I have never been kissed before, with his everything, demanding the same from me. If I wasn't lost before, I am then. And even as I pull away, using my children, my status as a married woman as an excuse, my body angles towards him, wanting everything he is promising with his lips, his tongue.

He professes his love for me on the six-month anniversary of our meeting. JT likes to commemorate every occasion, in this way making even the most ordinary day feel special – he takes me to Kew Gardens to celebrate. And on the treetop walkway, the fecund, beautiful and exotic world spread out below us, the organic, fertile scent of vegetation, tree branches brushing against us, whispering ripe-green, dew-speckled secrets, the deliciously clandestine taste of forbidden desire, he says, 'I've never been in love before. But I know now what it is like. I cannot get you out of my system. I don't want to.'

I am taken aback, even as my heart thrills. I know he means every word. 'I'm married. I—'

But he leans forward, his lips claiming mine, and my excuses disappear as he kisses me atop the bridge, between earth and sky, green foliage swaying below and around us.

During those charmed months with JT, I am short and annoyed with my children, who learn not to come up to me when they need something, to gauge my moods and to be wary of me and to try to please me. I do not notice as they withdraw into themselves, barely acknowledging them.

Later I will be sorry, adding this shameful neglect of my children to my long list of regrets. But not then. Then, all that matters is JT.

FIFTY-ONE

DAY 3

1:15 p.m.

'Jo, how could you?' Yash's voice is a hollow reed of pain. 'You suspected me of having an affair when all the while you—'

'I'm sorry.' It's all I can say. It's not enough.

'I... My God... I can't...' My husband bunches his hands into fists, his eyes shining with hurt. And again he asks, 'How could you?'

And, as always, when pushed into a corner, I retaliate. 'How could *you?*' I ask. 'You slept with Lydia, have stayed friends with her and gone into business with her partner, knowing that the child he's bringing up is actually yours.'

Again, I think, will our marriage survive the repeated battering it has received in the course of this terrible ordeal?

As if he's thinking the same thing, Yash slumps on the sofa, his head in his hands. 'What are we doing to each other, Jo? What have we done?' His eyes bruises, voice a wound, bleeding hurt. He blows his nose noisily. I've never known him to be this broken before. This is why I didn't tell him sooner.

No, you didn't tell him because you are a coward.

'Have you been in touch with JT?' Yash says.

'No. But...'

The profile I saw at the market. So scarily familiar...

'But?' Yash prompts.

'When the children and I went to the market, I thought I saw him.'

Being with JT restores my self-worth absolutely

After being abandoned by my mother for her new love, my father for alcohol, my sister for Tom and vice versa, my husband for his business, or so it feels, JT's singular devotion is heady and addictive and I bask in it, revelling in every moment, throwing caution and marriage vows to the wind. I cannot wait, every day, to drop my children off to the childminder Yash has arranged to give me some time to do my chores so they don't overwhelm me. But I ignore the chores, I ignore my children, I am lost in JT.

In bed, after making love, we talk, taking pleasure in unearthing everything there is to know about each other. JT, short for Jithusan, was born in Sri Lanka in the midst of civil war between the Hindu Tamils, of which he was one, and the Buddhist Sinhalese majority. When JT was a teenager, his father became a casualty of the war. With the conflict showing no signs of stopping and the violence escalating, JT and his mother joined the scores of people fleeing in ships bound for Europe. But the harrowing journey proved too much for JT's mother. JT made it finally to the UK alone – the dream country his mother was aiming for: 'You can be anything you want there, son. People with nothing have gone on to make a success of their lives, as will you.'

He was taken into care, and at school and into adulthood worked extremely hard to realise his mother's dream for him, starting his own IT business, putting down a mortgage on a flat. But he was lonely, yearning for someone to complete him and he found that, he said, finally, in me.

'All I ever dreamed about was having someone to see me, love me, complete me,' JT tells me. 'And now, with you, that dream has come true.'

Every once in a while JT's intensity, the way he is so focused on me, scares me a tiny bit. But I understand it. He has been alone and unloved for much of his life. He has not had a home, a country, anyone or anything to call his own. It is why, I realise, he likes to commemorate every small milestone: the monthly anniversaries of our first meeting, our first kiss, the first time we slept together. He is creating memories, just in case. Being a child of war, he does not have the innate trust most of us do that things will turn out well; life having taught him otherwise.

It is thrilling to be so thoroughly and singularly adored and so I push the unease I sometimes experience firmly away. And the thrum of danger I sense only adds another layer of excitement to our clandestine affair.

JT kisses every one of my stretch marks. He loves my curves. With JT, I feel like the woman I was meant to be before I became the depressed mother and tired wife. Loving him, I understand what my mother must have felt, what propelled her to abandon her family for her lover without a backward glance, and I wonder if perhaps I am more like the mother I despise than I have acknowledged.

A memory surfaces, hidden in the recesses of my mind for years. A day out with my mother. We were shopping for clothes

– both Lori and I had had a growth spurt; I was curvier than Lori now and couldn't wear her cast-offs. Mum had been in a pensive mood. It was the Sunday before she would leave us. We were at the food court and when Lori went to the loo, my mother had clasped my hand – her fingers digging into my flesh, leaving marks – her gaze so intense it scared me a little.

'You're like me, Jo. We're led by the heart, not the mind. Choose someone who loves you more than you love him. Never stay with someone whom you love more than he loves you, promise me.' Her mouth close to mine, her hot breath flavoured with the burger she'd just had, her hand sweaty in mine, her eyes huge and insistent.

I nodded, said, 'I promise,' savouring her words, hugging them close. I would treasure them. All my life so far I had competed for her affection, upset when my sister won again and again, and now here was proof that she loved me the most.

Even after she left – *especially* after she left – I cherished her words, 'You're like me, Jo', although a part of me questioned if she had ever loved us at all. If she had, then how could she leave us so easily, without a backward glance? And although I still don't understand her decision to leave, I have finally connected with the meaning of her words of being led by the heart. Before JT, I could never envisage a way in which I would undermine my marriage, comprehend and accept my mother's betrayal, but now I see that I am just like my mother, and that scares me, even as that forever-seeking-Mum's-approval part of me thrills to it.

I push open the curtains one morning and there is JT, in the copse of trees opposite the house I share with Yash, staring at the window as if knowing that it would be me drawing the curtains, smiling when our eyes meet, giving me a little wave.

My heart jumps with fear and love. He looks dishevelled,

stubble blooming on his cheeks. It is apparent he followed me home after our rendezvous the previous evening and has not left, keeping vigil outside my home, watching my every move. JT has never experienced family life. So he is spying on mine – the life he wants with the woman he loves.

'Tell me your routine,' he's asked when we meet. He wants to know everything I do when we are apart; he never tires of hearing me recount what for me has been boring drudgery, revelling in even the most mundane details of my day. Seen through his eyes, my ordinary life is interesting, what I take for granted is for him magical, something he has always aspired to, ached for, dreamed about.

He has confided how he would, as an orphan in care, roam the streets, familiarising himself with this new strange country his mother had talked about with starry eyes, in which he found himself all alone. He would walk for miles, along residential streets, spying on families going about their day: children sitting at tables doing homework, helping their parents set the table, sprawled on sofas watching TV, sitting down to dinner – and wish himself inside, instead of always on the outside looking in.

JT's deepest wish is to have a family with the one he loves, to recreate the happiness he had only ever experienced as a child too briefly before war tore his parents from him. 'Come to me,' he pleads. 'I will make sure you and your children are always loved. You will never want for anything.'

His dream is so simple – me, him, my girls, the family he's always wanted. I know I have to tell JT that his dream for us to be together may never come true. I won't leave Yash, disrupt our family, upset our girls, do what my mother did to me, Lori and our dad. But I can't bear the thought of losing JT, even though I know it is cruel to string him along when I cannot give him what he wants most in the world.

Each time I meet him, I go with the intention of breaking up with him. But his love is a balm. It is a drug I can't get enough of and I come back without having done so. *Just one more day*, I think.

I am being selfish. He deserves someone else, someone free with whom to have the family he so desires, the life he yearns for. But even knowing this, I am loath to give him up because he offers something so refreshing, so remote from the banalities of my life, where Yash is still absent and my children still demanding.

While JT's passion, his single-minded pursuit is thrilling, it also terrifies me more than a little that morning, when I see him outside the house. My recounting details of my daily life is no longer enough, it seems – he wants to see it for himself. And that is when I come to my senses.

I run outside on slippered feet, pulling the door closed quietly behind me, so as not to wake Yash or the kids.

JT beams when he sees me.

But not for long. Making sure we are tucked within the embrace of trees, I hiss, 'Do you want me to be found out?' All the while keeping an eye on my house and its neighbours to make sure there's no sign of movement, that Yash and the children are still asleep and none of the neighbours are watching.

'Yes,' JT retorts, eyes flashing. 'You won't leave that husband of yours who doesn't realise how precious you are. I love you like you deserve to be loved. If you were married to me, you wouldn't need to look elsewhere for love. Yes, I want him to find out.'

Now, fear drumming a tattoo on my chest, I realise that this has gone too far. It has to stop. I need to bring this to an end. 'It's over, JT. This cannot continue. I will not leave the father of my girls and come away with you. I will not repeat my mother's mistake.'

'You won't be like your mother. Bring your girls. We will be a family. I will be the best father to them. Please.'

For a moment, I am tempted. I barely see Yash. He is never

home. He has been absent since he started the company and even more so since the girls were born. Some father he is proving to be.

JT senses me wavering. He pulls me to him, kisses me. He smells of sweat and desire and the outdoors.

Even though I want to meld into his embrace, I pull away. 'I will not be my mother,' I say again.

'It will not be like that.' He is desperate now.

'Please, JT, just go.'

'I love you, Jo. Please come with me.'

I turn away from him, go home, shut the door on him.

But JT is resolute. In the days that follow, he is there when I open the curtains in the mornings and when I shut them at night.

I'm afraid Yash will find out. I'm afraid the neighbours will notice. I'm afraid Lydia will, when she drops by with her girls. I tell Lydia everything, but I haven't been able to tell her about this because I'm ashamed of my actions. Not only have I been a bad mother and wife, but now I'm an adulteress as well, accusing Yash of a non-existent affair while I conduct a real one.

My girls do notice, asking about the man who smiles and waves at them when they look out the window. I'm afraid for them. I feel unsettled, panicked about my two worlds colliding. I do not like it that my girls are exposed to JT, who was and, I am determined, must remain my secret. I worry that they'll tell their dad about him. I'm afraid to leave the house. I'm afraid of what my thoughtless, impulsive actions have spawned. I start to spiral into depression again, the high of being with JT gone.

'Please leave,' I beg, again and again. 'I'm not coming back to you.'

'I'm not going anywhere until you do,' he snarls, his face contorted into something I do not recognise.

And now, I am afraid of him, this man who can be so loving, but has morphed into a possessive and dangerous stalker.

'Then I'm calling the police,' I say with a bravado I do not feel.

JT has confided in me that he has been cautioned for stalking before – his standing outside houses and spying on families hadn't gone unnoticed and a couple of them had complained to the police. I had blithely overlooked this at the time, even seeing it as endearing, that he just wanted to be loved, belong, like everyone, but now I am waking up to the threat I have brought to my own door.

'You won't,' he says, but I can see the fear behind the defiance in his eyes.

'I will. I am right now. Look...'

And in his eyes, betrayal and hurt as I press the number. I know that it is, finally, over. The feeling of being cleaved in two, I tell myself, is exactly what I deserve.

FIFTY-THREE

DAY 3

1:40 p.m.

'He was stalking our house?' Yash is outraged. 'Waving to our girls?' And, softly, pain oozing from every word, again he asks, 'How could you, Jo?'

'JT is in my past and he has stayed there,' I say with more conviction than I feel. For now, I am beginning to wonder. Has he really stayed in the past?

'That doesn't make it right.'

Exactly the words I had used when he told me about his indiscretion.

'No, it doesn't,' I whisper.

'Has he tried to contact you since...?'

'No. But the stalker...' The texts, the feeling of someone following me that I can't quite shake, always putting me on edge...

'Jo...' Yash runs his hand through his hair. 'That might feel real to you, but you know the counsellor said—'

'Stop patronising me. It could be JT.'

'But why *here*?'

'I heard through a friend of a friend that he left the country, went to Sri Lanka as the war there had finally ended.'

'That still doesn't explain it.'

'I have been posting countdowns to the holiday on social media.'

'And you think he might have seen... Is he your friend on Facebook?'

'He could be. I accept any friend requests I get.'

'Even if you don't know them?'

I colour. I get a window of five minutes or so each day in between looking after the children to go on social media. I don't have time to vet everyone. Easier just to press accept. But now I see how foolish I've been. How utterly careless. I have been blasé about my privacy settings too – I keep meaning to update them and then forgetting. After all, I think, what do I have that anyone might want?

My children, I see now. My precious, precious treasures.

'But why would JT surface now?' Yash is asking. 'After all this time?'

'I... Some of the parents of Ajit's friends invited to his fifth birthday party wanted photos, so I uploaded pictures onto Facebook.'

Yash is looking at me in incomprehension.

'JT... He might have seen Ajit's picture, his birth date, and thought—'

'What? What are you saying, Jo?' His face blanches, and he appears even more wan than before. He is staring at me, utterly shocked, mouth open, eyes stark.

'He's yours. Ajit is yours. I'm sure of it.'

'No. No, I can't take this.' Yash stands up, starts pacing, a fist in his mouth to stop his hurt from escaping, I imagine.

'I'm so sorry, Yash.'

He brings his hand down hard upon the table. I jump. The policeman stands up, comes to Yash, pats his back.

Yash shrugs the policeman's hand away, looks at me, gaze raw and stripped back of everything but pain, wild and tormented. 'What else are you keeping from me, Jo? What more will I find out? What about the girls? Are they—?'

'What about you? What else are *you* keeping from me? I had the affair because something was missing from our marriage. You. You weren't there when I needed you the most...'

'That's right, blame me for your cheating, why don't you?'

'Why not, when you've blamed your feelings for me for sleeping with Lydia?'

Yash throws himself down on the sofa, runs his hand down his face. It is haggard, done in.

I feel the same. Winded. Spent. I don't think we can come back from this.

I did not want our family to splinter like my own had done. But it is doing so right now – the revelation of my secret, coming on top of what Yash was keeping from me, has sounded the death knell upon our marriage.

'You're like me, Jo. We're led by the heart and not the mind,' my mother had said and I had treasured her words, cherished them.

'You're like me, Jo.' *I am, Mum, and look where it's got me.*

The policeman is back in his chair, looking tired himself, worn out from all of our dramas.

The silence in the room is thick with recriminations, remorse, guilt, taut with revelations and exposed secrets, swirling with wisps of a disintegrating marriage, two people who have lied, cheated and hurt each other while claiming to love the other.

And the children, our beautiful, innocent children are the casualties in all of this.

'The sighting of the man with the boy, you think he's JT?' Yash asks, not looking at me.

'He was tall and bespectacled, like JT.'

'God,' Yash cries, cradling his head in his hands.

'I just... I'd rather Ajit was taken by someone we know...' But not Lori, please no. Not my sister. 'If it was JT, he wouldn't do anything to Ajit, hurt him, harm him. That's why, I believe, he took Ajit's slippers and his SpongeBob soft toy along.'

He won't abuse Ajit.

I can't say it out loud. But I think it.

I can't believe it's come to this. Weighing evils and hoping for the lesser one...

'Mum, Dad, why were you shouting?'

We both whip around. Zoe is standing near the table, her lower lip wobbling, her eyes swelling with tears.

Yash and I have forgotten to be quiet. How long has Zoe been awake? What has she heard?

I gather her in my arms.

'Are you angry with Dad?' Zoe asks, gaze wide and anxious. 'Will he leave too, like Ajit?'

'No, sweetheart. Nobody is going anywhere,' I whisper into her hair.

'But Ajit is gone, Mum. It's been days and he hasn't come back. When is he going to return?' She's trying hard to be brave, my Zoe, but her lower lip trembles with the effort of holding back the tears that glitter in her eyes. It breaks my heart to see what all of this is doing to my girls.

'The police are looking for him, sweetheart. They'll bring him home soon,' Yash says, coming over and sitting down next to me, patting Zoe's head.

'I saw Mia asleep in her bed when I woke up, but where are the others? Have they gone away too? Will the police bring them back too?'

'They've just gone for a walk and should be back soon, my love.'

Yash's eyes meet mine over our child's head and a truce is declared.

For now.

FIFTY-FOUR

DAY 3

10:00 p.m.

'Jo, hun, you really need to eat something,' Lydia says.

I want to swat her away. My emotions are all over the place, anger quick to ignite. I am raging at myself for leaving my children alone that night, for betraying Yash, for all of my mistakes. I am distressed and worried that Ajit has still not been found, and while I will never give up hope, I am despairing as to why there's still no news. No leads. Nothing.

The children are in bed. The reporters have given up and gone home. Yash and Paul have taken advantage of the lull and slipped out. Yash has gone for a walk along the beach to 'clear his head', and, no doubt, conduct his own search for Ajit, like I have been doing each night. Paul is getting the groceries, although this late at night, I think it is just an excuse to get away from this nightmare he's inadvertently finding himself involved in. Or is he to blame? Is he slipping out to keep an eye on Ajit, wherever he's hiding him? Do I really believe this? I don't know what to believe, but I make a note to mention my suspicion with regards to Paul to the inspector again – I did tell him about Paul going missing from the bar shack and my conjecture as to what he was actually doing, and the inspector had not laughed it off, just made a note with his trademark impassive expression which gave nothing away. It only made my conviction that the inspector was keeping tabs on all of us, that we were all suspects, stronger and I wondered what the others had told him about me...

Now, with Yash and Paul gone, it is Lydia, myself, the quiet, all-seeing-and-hearing policeman, and a house full of sleeping children – all of hers accounted for and two of mine.

Where are you, Ajit?

My arms ache to hold him, smell him, ruffle his hair, kiss his cheek, see his face light up in a smile.

'Here, have this.' Lydia thrusts a plate of cut mango in front of my nose. The fruity, sweet smell makes me want to gag.

'I don't feel like it, Lydia.'

'You need to keep up your strength, Jo.'

I have had enough. 'You're not my mother, Lydia,' I snap.

She pauses in the act of putting a piece of mango in her mouth. She is brown from the sun, tanned and lithe.

I can't recall the last time I washed – I think it was before the press conference yesterday. I am sweaty and rank with grief, my hair unkempt, my face salty with dried tears.

This is not a competition.

Since my sister Lori turned up uninvited in my life, damning me to the world, I've regressed to my childhood self, it seems, comparing myself to everyone else, lashing out at them, even when they're being kind.

Lydia sets the plate of fruit down carefully and turns to me, saying tightly, 'You know, Jo, I get that you're hurting. But I am too. We all are. And we're getting a little tired of you using us as your human punchbags. At this rate, you'll be left with nobody on your side.'

I think of my marriage, ripped apart by our betrayals. But

I'm damned if I'll admit this to Lydia. When did this happen? I used to share everything with her, once.

'I don't mind,' I retort defiantly. But my mouth is heavy and bitter with the lie. I miss the uncomplicated friendship I shared with Lydia, back when I did not know she was lying to me throughout our acquaintance. 'As long as I find Ajit.'

'And if you don't?' But even as she says it, she claps her hand over her mouth, knowing she's gone too far, eyes shining with tears. 'I'm sorry, Jo. I didn't mean that. I want nothing more than for Ajit to be found.'

She sits down beside me, pushing back her hair wearily. She smells of sweat and fruit. And for the first time since I've known her, she looks her age.

'Jo?' She holds out her hand, a peace offering.

I turn away from her, unwilling to take it. How dare she, my supposed friend, suggest that Ajit will not be found?

I hear her sniff, dig out a tissue from her pocket, blow her nose.

What is happening to us? My marriage is breaking down and my friendship too. All it takes is one ill-considered decision, one devastating mishap, for all the years of love, of closeness to rupture, for I am discovering that the bonds are fragile, built upon lies and untruths and betrayals and secrets.

Lydia has apologised, yet still I want to punish her for her ill-considered comment. 'Did you take Ajit?' I ask, thinking, even as I do so, that this ordeal has turned me into my worst self, the child I was, mean-spirited and vengeful, always trying to get back at my sister for one slight or another.

Lydia gasps, moving away from me. 'Do you hear yourself, Jo? What's happened to you? I don't recognise you any more.'

I've started this and so I plough on, regardless. The longer Ajit remains missing, the more doubts circulate in my head, multiplying every minute, whispering suspicions, turning me against those closest to me. 'You were the last to check on him before I discovered that he was missing.'

'How do you explain Rachel seeing and talking to him afterwards, then?' She flings at me, and then mutters, almost to herself, 'I cannot believe I'm even engaging in a discussion with you about this... this preposterous notion.'

'You could have asked her to lie for you.'

'How dare you suggest that I'd ask my child to—?'

She is interrupted by a small voice. 'Mummy?'

Mia stands at the doorway leading to the corridor, clutching her Lamby and sucking her thumb.

'Mia, sweetie, what're you doing up? It's late. You should be in bed.'

'I remembered something, Mummy.'

'What, sweetie?'

'I woke up that night and I came to find Rachel as I was scared.'

'Which night, sweetheart?'

'The night there was the noise and Ajit went away.'

I kneel in front of her, my heart thudding.

'Was there a noise, sweetie?'

'A loud noise, like a big bang.'

I exchange looks with Lydia and the policeman, who is leaning forward in his chair, as I gather Mia up and settle down on the sofa with her on my lap.

'Did anybody else hear it?'

'I don't think so. Zoe and Bella were fast asleep.'

'So what did you do?'

'I was very scared. So, I waited for a while with my eyes shut tight.'

Salt flooding my mouth as I remonstrate myself, once more. How could I have left my precious gifts of children unattended, without proper adult supervision, in this cottage that night? Out loud, I prompt Mia gently, 'What happened then, love?'

'Then I called to Zoe in a whisper voice, although I knew she would say I was a scaredy-cat.' Mia takes a breath. 'But she didn't wake up.'

'What did you do next?'

'I thought of waking Bella. But then I remembered Rachel. So I came here. But Rachel wasn't there.'

'What?' Both Lydia and I say in unison.

Mia looks scared. Her lower lip starts to wobble as she hugs Lamby close.

'It's OK, sweetie. Sorry we startled you. So then what did you do?'

'I looked for her, Mummy.'

'Where did you look for her, sweetie?'

'In her bedroom. It was dark and I was scared. But she wasn't there. I thought she may have gone out the window.'

'The window?' Again, Lydia and I exchange looks, our earlier skirmish forgotten. For now.

I don't think we can go back to how we were, not after our heated exchange before Mia interrupted us. I feel a pang of sadness skewer me. Even if I find Ajit, I will have lost so much in the process, just like Lydia warned, everyone I love and hold dear. But I will accept that price, if I get my boy back. *Please.*

The policeman is almost falling off his chair, he's leaning forward so much in order to catch Mia's every word.

'It was open and banging. That was the noise I heard I think, Mummy, because it did it again as I came out of Rachel's bedroom. So I went to bed and I shut my eyes tight and I held Lamby to me, like this.' She hugs Lamby close.

I push away the tears that stab at my eyes as I contemplate my daughter, lying there scared as her brother was being taken. Oh dear God, why on earth didn't I stay with them that night, my beautiful children, holding them close, revelling in the sheer beautiful miracle of them? I swallow past the lump in my throat, prompt, 'And then?'

'And then I slept again. And I woke when I heard Daddy shouting for Ajit. But now I want you to come and tuck me in, Mummy.'

'Come on then, sweetie.'

I lead Mia back to her room, tuck her into bed. I pull the blanket tight around my daughter as I mull over what she has said, knowing that in the living room, Lydia and the officer will be thinking over what my daughter has revealed too.

'Please, Mummy, can you lie down beside me?' she whispers.

I climb into bed beside her, drawing comfort from her soft warmth, and wait until her breathing is steady, and she is fast asleep. I lie there, watching my girls sleeping – one in my arms, the other in the bed opposite – and I wonder what happened two nights ago.

Why was the window open? Who opened it?

Why can't I recall if it was open or shut, why can't I remember walking around the cottage as the others insist I did that night?

Where was Rachel when she was supposed to be minding the kids? What was the sound that Mia heard which woke her up?

I shudder as, once again, it strikes me how vulnerable my children really were. The window was open. Rachel wasn't there. Mia – someone could have taken her too...

It is too horrible to contemplate.

I plant a kiss on my daughter's soft cheek and imagine I am holding Ajit, cuddling my boy.

And then, for the first time since this nightmare began, my eyes close and I give in to the tiredness weighing my eyelids down.

FIFTY-FIVE

Opinion piece appearing in the Commentary section of *The Goan Times*:

All The Missing Children
Posted by Mr Navin Suri, 16 February

The disappearance of British tourist Ajit Kumar from his holiday cottage in Galgibaga Beach has been making regional, national and international headlines.

Inspector Sharma, in charge of the investigation into Ajit's disappearance, says that the police force is 'pursuing many leads'. And yet, the boy is still missing. Where the inspector is concerned, these 'leads' seem to involve appearing on television looking self-important and appealing for information from the general public.

Here's what I think, and I echo the sentiments of hundreds of our readers who've come forward since Ajit went missing. Why is the entire police force of the state of Goa involved in the search for this one missing boy when most of the 180 plus Indian children who go missing every day do not even merit a search, or, if they do, it is cursory at best? This is because their parents are poor, from the slums more often than not, and do not have the means or the resources to raise a hue and cry about the police force's failings. Does this seem fair? Is not every child, whether rich or poor, equal in the eyes of the law? Apparently not – some being more equal than others.

Much of the time it is the police officers themselves – the very ones who are supposed to protect the children – who are either involved in the abductions or paid to turn a blind eye. The fate of these kidnapped children is dire – there is a thriving business in the sale of children's organs. And there's child prostitution, of course.

It goes without saying that I would like Ajit to be found. With the number of police assigned to his case – this paper has reported on the police presence at the cottage from where Ajit went missing and the beach surrounding it and the regular updates given to his parents by Inspector Sharma himself – I'm sure Ajit's chance of being safely returned to his parents is very high. And therein exactly lies my point.

Why is there no interest shown by our police in other, poorer missing children whose parents are just as desperate and line up at police stations for hours every day asking about progress, only to be turned away? Isn't it an absolute travesty that one foreign child's life is worth more than that of the hundreds of children who disappear from Indian streets simply because he is someone whose parents can hold the police and politicians to account? It is appalling that this is the case even in this day and age. It makes me deeply ashamed to call myself Indian.

Comments:
Adish, Bicholim 07:08 IST: Dear Mr Suri, you make a very passionate case for missing Indian children. I get what you're

saying. But Sir, I think every missing child, whether white or brown or any other colour or nationality, deserves someone on their case.

Benny, Panaji 07:18 IST: I agree with you absolutely, Mr Suri. This case is getting disproportionate and frankly unfair attention at the cost of several other missing Indian children and no one is doing anything to find them.

Anonymous, Anywheretown 07:21 IST: At the moment there's talk of organ harvesting being a motive for Ajit's disappearance, but I wondered why the culprits would go to the trouble of breaking into a tourist resort and drawing such attention to themselves when they can take a child from the street and no one cares?

Mr Raj Rao, Margao 07:28 IST: You're right to put Inspector Sharma on the spot, Mr Suri. Why is the inspector only focusing on Indians as suspects? He's let the other – white – tourists go. And what's more, they've barely been questioned. Inspector Sharma is an Anglophile. He's letting our country and its people down.

Scroll down for more comments.

FIFTY-SIX

DAY 4

7:30 a.m.

'*Mum,' Ajit calls, 'look at what I found!'*

'*What is it, son?'*

'*Come and look. Come with me, Mum. I need you. Please, Mum... Mum?'*

I open my eyes and for a few precious seconds, everything is all right with my world. Golden sunlight slants in from somewhere and sets the room alight, dappling it in glorious cream and yellow. My back aches, my body is cramped, and yet I feel rested. Invigorated. I need to go to my boy; he called to me.

And then the knowledge is there, a weight on my chest, crushing me. My boy isn't here. He's missing. I want to close my eyes and sleep away the distress ambushing me. I want to be back in my dream again where Ajit was with me, speaking to me, holding my hand, leading me somewhere, urgently...

'Mum?'

It is Zoe, looking at me with that wide, slightly lost look she has been sporting the last few days.

'Yes, princess?'

'Why're you sleeping in Mia's bed?'

'Am I?' It is only then that I take in the bunks, see where I am. The girls' bedroom.

Mia. My heart gallops in terror. 'Where is Mia?' My voice tinged navy with panic.

'She's having breakfast.'

My heart settles. I open my arms and Zoe surprises me by walking into them. I gather my fiercely independent middle child, who is the least cuddly of my three kids, into my embrace. She smells of toast and honey.

'I just came here to check on you,' she whispers. 'They told me not to wake you up.'

'You didn't.'

'I did, Mum. I'm sorry.' She looks close to tears.

'It's time I woke, sweetie, if it's already breakfast time. Thank you for coming to check on me.'

I don't want to leave this room, face another day without Ajit. I want to lie here for as long as I can, with my daughter in my arms, my face in her sweet-smelling hair.

'Mum?'

'Hmm?'

'Do you think a monster took Ajit?'

The question shocks me even as I understand that Zoe is just parroting one of the reporters she must have inadvertently heard when the door opened briefly to let someone in or out, although, of course, Zoe's idea of a monster is very different to what they were implying.

I turn my daughter to face me. 'No, my precious,' I say firmly, and her solemn little face settles, the crease between her eyebrows relaxing.

'Then where is he?'

'We don't know, my sweet. Remember when Mia's Lamby gets lost and we all have to look for him? It's like that. Ajit is lost and the police are trying to find him.'

'I hope they find him soon.' Her voice trembles.

'Me too, my darling.' It takes all my willpower to keep my voice steady.

'Nothing is the same without him, Mum. Mia has become like a baby again and she cries all the time. You and Dad are fighting and angry and—'

'Zoe, we... your dad and I...'

She looks up at me, lower lip wobbling.

'Sometimes, when adults are worried, they shout at each other. That doesn't mean they hate each other, my love. You and Mia argue sometimes, don't you?'

'Yes,' her voice is very small.

'But you still love your sister, don't you?'

'Yes.'

'And she loves you too.'

A nod.

'It's the same with Dad and me. We argue but we love each other really.'

Perhaps. But is it enough?

'When Ajit comes back...' she starts.

'Yes?'

'I'll never fight with him again. I'll even share my favourite rainbow pen, the one he likes but I've never allowed him to use.' She takes a shuddering breath. 'I miss him so much.'

I hold her while she sobs, my beautiful, imaginative, fierce little Zoe. My eyes are wet and I surreptitiously wipe them when she is not looking.

FIFTY-SEVEN

DAY 4

8:30 a.m.

After I have – finally – washed and changed, I corner Rachel in her bedroom.

I knock on her door, which is ajar. She is face down on her bed, legs bent at the knees, feet in the air, headphones in her ears, her fingers flying over the keys of her phone. Does she look like Yash?

Stop it.

'I don't think I can type half as fast,' I say.

She hasn't heard me.

I knock again, louder. 'Rachel?'

She looks up, face flushing, and puts her phone and head-phones hastily away. 'Oh, hi, Jo. Is there any news...?' Her voice fades when she sees my face.

'Not as yet.' I can't help the sigh which escapes. 'I just... Can I come in for a bit?'

She looks surprised, but sits up on her bed, pushing away the clothes that are strewn everywhere, which she was lying on top of, making space for me.

'What is it?' she asks, her tongue flicking over her lower lip. She is pale, looks scared. Why is she so apprehensive? What was she doing when she was supposed to look after the kids?

'Rachel, Mia said something yesterday and I just wanted to check with you...'

'I know,' she says. 'Mum already asked me.'

'She did?' Lydia didn't tell me she had already talked to Rachel about this but I'm not surprised. She's decidedly chilly towards me this morning, just about managing to keep a civil front because of the kids. Before Ajit went missing, falling out with Lydia would have upset me. Now, all I want is for Ajit to be found safe and sound. Nothing else matters. Or so I tell myself.

'You want to know where I was when Mia came looking for me?'

'Yes. Rachel, you're not to blame in any way for what happened,' I reassure. 'It was very brave of you to tell me that you shouted at Ajit and fell asleep after. I... I should have been looking after the kids that day – we shouldn't have left you in charge.'

'But I shouldn't have had that drink – it was irresponsible of me.'

I nod. I know I should absolve her, say, 'It's not your fault,' or some such thing. But I can't bring myself to. 'Where were you when Mia came looking?' I ask.

'I think it was when I woke up and went to the loo. She must have come for me then?' She pauses, pondering. 'That's the last time I was away from the sofa. Or wait... perhaps it was earlier, when I was in the kitchen maybe, getting the drink.'

'When was this?'

'Just after Mum came to check on us.'

'Did you see the open window on your way to the kitchen?'

'No. The window must have been shut then – I think I would have noticed if it was wide open and swinging.'

'If Mia heard the sound of the window banging and then woke and came looking for you... That must have been when you were in the loo *after* you woke up. So Ajit had already been taken or had climbed out the window then.'

'Yes, that makes sense. When I woke from my snooze, I went to the loo. That must have been when Mia came... Jo, I haven't... I... When I woke up... I...' She looks sheepish suddenly.

'What is it?'

'I do vaguely recall hearing a sound, a thud, which is possibly what woke me up. But... I was groggy, my stomach was iffy and I desperately needed the loo and...' She looks at me with anxious eyes. 'It's just this vague impression I have, almost dreamlike, of footsteps.'

'Footsteps?'

'Jo, what I'm trying to tell you, why I didn't tell you before is...'

She is almost in tears. The sensible side of me warns, *Don't push*. But the grieving mother wants desperately to hear everything this girl knows.

'I don't know if I dreamed them, the footsteps, or really heard them. I'm not sure if my mind is making them up after the fact because I'm trying so hard to remember what happened... This is why I didn't tell you or the police. I told you about the drinking, but I couldn't tell you about this as I wasn't sure if it was real – I'm *still* not sure. I have this impression of footsteps, then sound. A rattle and a thud. But I was all over the place...' She fiddles with her hair, tears spilling from her eyes. 'Then Mum said Mia also heard a sound and I thought, what if it wasn't my mind making things up? What if I actually heard something?' She drags the back of her wrist across her cheeks, spreading the tears all over her face, a wet sheen. 'Perhaps that sound was what woke me...' Her voice tapers off.

'You're sure you didn't leave the sofa for anything else?'
I ask.

'No. I have thought and thought, but I really didn't, Jo,
except to go to the kitchen and the loo.'

I nod. 'Thank you for being honest with me, Rachel. Will
you tell the police what you just told me? Even if it was only a
dream.'

She nods. 'I'm really sorry, Jo.' Her eyes spill. 'I miss Ajit.
He is such a lovely boy.'

He is your half-brother.

I leave Rachel's room, my mind churning. So... Rachel may
or may not have heard footsteps. Mia and possibly Rachel heard
a noise that woke them up – a rattle and a thud, Rachel said.
This confirms what the inspector suspects, that someone – JT?
– boldly grabbed Ajit from his room and left with him out the
window while Rachel was asleep on the sofa and we were
sitting on the beach just a few paces away.

FIFTY-EIGHT

DAY 4

9:00 a.m.

I stand at the living-room window, hidden behind the curtains, and watch the sea, glimpses of blue beyond the mob of paparazzi. I imagine it growls and roars as it bashes against the rocks. It is wild and raging, yet it has a surreal, hypnotic beauty, unlike the reporters, who hurl questions and accusations at us, relentlessly. 'Is it true that there's a suspect?' 'A man?' 'Is Jo Kumar in cahoots with him?' 'Is that why the police artist was here?'

Inside this prison of a cottage, the atmosphere is no better, rife with suspicion and tension, anger and doubt and mistrust among us adults, although we are trying to keep it civil for the kids' sake.

The rabble outside gets louder, noisier. 'Inspector, what steps are you taking to find this man who was seen with Ajit?' 'Does Jo know him?' 'Is he one of her lovers?'

How do they know so much?

A knock at the door.

The inspector is here. What has he found? My heart jumps

with hope even as it seizes with anxiety: *Please let it not be bad news.*

In the bedroom once again, the inspector says, 'JT's sketch is being circulated across the police service, CID, Interpol and other enforcement agencies, alongside the custody image UK police had on record. CCTV is being checked at all the major airports, ports, train and bus stations against the photofit to determine when and if he came into the country. Rest assured, we are hard at work to find him.'

He clears his throat. Whatever he's about to impart is not good news, I can tell.

'We have his passport details, but that passport has not been used since he left the UK. There's a record of Jithusan Chandrakantan arriving in Sri Lanka six years ago, but nothing at all after that. If it is JT you saw at the market, and in the sightings reported, then he is most likely travelling under a new name on a new passport.'

'Fake?' I whisper, divining what the inspector is not saying.

'We are trying to determine that. We will find him, but it's taking longer because of this.'

He clears his throat again. More bad news.

'We showed the sketch to the people who reported the sightings of a boy matching Ajit's description with a man, along with JT's custody image...'

'And?'

'They said they couldn't be sure. We compared the sketches the police artist made based on the descriptions they gave to the one of JT and it *could* be him.' He takes a breath. 'One said the man she saw had a beard. The artist added a beard to your sketch, but even so the woman was unsure. She said she didn't look at the man properly, only at the boy.'

'What about the number I had for JT?' I ask.

'It's out of service.'

JT and I weren't friends on social media during our affair, again being careful, but I have been desperately mining my social media and the web for any trace of him. I have accepted friend requests from anyone who's asked and I've been going through each of them to check if one of them might be JT. But so far, I've had no luck. If I have accepted a friend request from JT, he is being very careful not to give himself away. I've gone through the photos of the party where I first met him, but he was very good at shying away from the limelight for there's not a single picture of him, not even a profile or back view. Yash has been trying to contact business associates who might have known JT and has given the inspector their details as well as that of JT's company...

'Were you able to find anything on JT through his company?' I ask.

'No. He closed it down six years ago when he left the country.' He answers my next question before I've asked it, 'We've got in touch with his business associates and none of them have been in touch with him since.'

I feel desperation claw at my throat.

'When I return to the station, we're going to circulate JT's sketch, along with the ones the artist produced based on the descriptions given by the people who think they saw a man with a boy matching Ajit's description, to reporters and media, appealing to the public for information.' He hands me a couple of photos. 'Do any of these look familiar?'

They are of cars I've never set eyes on before. 'No,' I say. 'What is their relevance?'

'We obtained photos of cars which closely match the unidentified cars hanging about the area that day.'

I stare at them, racking my mind, but nothing stands out. 'Sorry,' I say.

The inspector nods as if that's what he was expecting. He

looks tired. Dark circles under his eyes. The press is back to pillorying him. He got a brief respite when, after the press conference, I was public enemy number one. Now he is up there again, right beside me.

I wrap my arms around myself, wishing it was Ajit I was holding safe in the protection of my arms. But would he be safe with me – I who cannot even remember what I was doing that night when someone was taking him?

FIFTY-NINE

DAY 4

11:30 a.m.

It is hot, sweltering. Lydia and Rachel are in their rooms, and I am sitting on the sofa, my eyes fixed on the beach, where my girls build a sandcastle alongside Bella under Paul's supervision, while Yash walks up and down the beach, searching, one more time, for our boy, hoping, like I am doing, that this time, we will find him.

The kids were getting antsy and Paul and Yash decided to brave the reporters and take the children for a paddle in the sea. As soon as they stepped out, they were ambushed and I saw Mia and Zoe flinch and hide behind Yash. Paul was the one who told the mob, firmly, 'This is a difficult time for all of us, especially the children. I'm asking you to please allow them an hour on the beach to forget their ordeal and just be children, eh? Thank you.'

The reporters did back off and have convened at the bar shack waiting for updates, action. I have positioned myself on the sofa, such that I have a clear view of Mia and Zoe playing on the beach, drying off from their swim.

The policeman is nodding off in his corner of this room. It is quiet in here, without the kids. I toy with the telly remote before setting it back down – nobody has dared turn the telly on since that eventful night, not wanting to brave what the reporters and the media are saying about us, although, of course, we get it all on our phones anyway – the vitriol and the hate, of which, of all of us, I am the main target. And now, it's even worse; they're talking about Ajit in the past tense. When I saw that, along with some sites declaring my beautiful son most likely dead, I threw my phone down so vehemently that the others looked up, startled from whatever they were doing. I have tried not to think about it, but it is there, hovering, lancing, drawing blood and tears, the unfathomable, horrible outcome that the press and public have decided the most likely, that Ajit is dead. No. No, I will *not* accept it. I cannot.

Mia and Bella take turns running to the water with the plastic pails that I had packed and that haven't been used until now. Zoe is digging what looks like a moat. Paul stands beside her, offering suggestions which she ignores, I imagine. Yash is but a dot in the distance, searching, searching for our son. The kids are all wearing hats. Ajit's lies unused in his SpongeBob suitcase.

I swallow down a lump of salt-edged grief. The last time my children were on the beach, Ajit was with them, playing and dancing and gambolling in the water, his face alight.

I want to lift my face up to the sun, to luxuriate in its glory if only for a moment. But even that feels like indulgence.

My gaze frantically tracks my children around the beach. For I know now that anything can happen in a moment. Dreams can morph into nightmares. Children can disappear.

And although I am almost convinced there was no substance to the accusation against Paul, I'm still not taking any chances.

A couple walk past, hand in hand, and I wonder how long

they've been together, whether they are happy or just staying together out of habit, or because of something more sinister, what secrets they are keeping from the world and from each other, who is holding whose hand, who needs the other more.

I blink, reining my wandering imagination in, as, outside, the reporters jump to action, questions and cameras following the inspector as he enters the cottage.

Hope rises in my belly, only to fall again as I catch a glimpse of his tired, perspiring face.

'May I?' He indicates the chair beside the sofa.

I nod, my gaze not leaving my girls.

He sits himself down. He smells of sweat and hard work and spices. He must have just eaten, something his wife packed for him, perhaps.

I suddenly remember Yash telling me how his mother would pack rice and dhal in a stainless-steel tiffin box for his father every day. His father would take it, even though he got ribbed for it. He had to eat in a corner away from all the other men at the factory where he worked because they said his food smelled.

'Our love will rival theirs,' Yash had said to me, his eyes sparkling.

This was in the early days, when our starry-eyed dreams had not yet been tarnished by the paintbrush of reality.

On the beach, Mia laughs at something one of the others has said, clapping her hands. Zoe stands up, puts her hands on her hips and says something to Bella. A small skirmish ensues and Paul and Yash, who is back with the girls now, intervene. It all appears so ordinary, a snapshot of family and friends on holiday.

The inspector sits companionably beside me, watching the kids too. I know I should ask him why he's here, but I want to postpone whatever it is – lack of progress, bad news? – for a little while longer. If it was good news, he'd have told me by now.

'You didn't want to go to the beach, join the kids?' he asks, after a beat.

I wanted to feel the hot sand shift under my feet. I wanted to swim in the water, which I knew would be warm and velvety. But that's precisely why I didn't. Why should I do what I want to when my son cannot? When he would have loved to play on the sand with his sisters and his friends and he is missing out? Missing.

'No,' I reply shortly.

'They don't seem to feel the heat, do they?'

I can't stand it any longer. I know this man is not here to make small talk. 'Inspector, why are you procrastinating? What is it you don't want to tell me?'

His voice is gentle when he says, 'We found the burglars. They admitted to tampering with the window in preparation for breaking into your cottage, but they didn't get the chance, what with everything that happened. We've found no evidence to connect them to Ajit's disappearance. They're just petty burglars, not kidnappers.'

'The fingerprints on the windowsill?' I ask.

The inspector nods. 'Two of the unidentified fingerprints matched those of the burglars. But there's still one print for which we haven't been able to find a match.'

'You think that might be...'

'The kidnapper's, yes. We are almost certain he left with Ajit through the window.'

He clears his throat. There's more non-news.

'And the photos I showed you this morning?' He looks at me.

'Yes?'

'One of them was an unregistered taxi being used illegally, and the other belonged to one of the holidaying families down the beach – they had rented it for the day. We've ruled them out.'

'Oh.'

'We're still following up on leads. Please don't give up hope.'

'I will *never* give up hope,' I say fiercely. I don't care if the media has given up on Ajit being found alive, I haven't. I would know, wouldn't I, if my son was gone? I would experience a hollowness, an emptiness in my heart in that space reserved for my son, that right now throbs with a missing, longing ache for him. Wouldn't I?

'Have you made any progress in locating who sent me those Snapchat messages?' I ask the inspector. I've stopped opening the messages that make me uneasy, knowing they will self-destruct when I do so. Those messages, all in a similar vein: *Jo, I forgive you for what you've done* and *Jo, I am sending love even though you don't deserve it*. They feel personal and intrusive, and I am sure they are from JT.

'Whoever's sending these to you has switched on ghost mode, which means we cannot access their location. We have requested information from Snapchat.' The inspector pauses. Then, 'We've been in touch with Sri Lankan police to deter-mine if JT is in Sri Lanka and just did not use his passport since landing there. But if it is JT who you saw at the market and JT in the sightings with a boy matching Ajit's description, then that means he's changed his name and we are trying to determine what he's going by now.'

'If he changed his name when he arrived in Sri Lanka, isn't that suspicious?'

The inspector shrugs. 'Perhaps he just wanted a fresh start.'

I blush, nod. I feel guilty even though the inspector likely meant nothing by his comment. I strung JT along, played with his feelings, hurt him so badly that he left the country his mother had had such high hopes for.

'What's suspicious,' the inspector is saying, 'is if he did change his name and didn't officially register it. We are looking into that as it means he's travelling under a fake passport.' The inspector sighs. 'Rest assured we'll find him, but it's taking longer than we hoped.'

He stands, wincing a little as he does so. Bad knees perhaps. Or even just tiredness. He looks like Yash does, that same weary droop around the eyes, which are baggy, indicating he's not been sleeping since all this began.

'I'll let you know if there's any news,' he says, wiping his face, once again, with his soaking handkerchief, spreading the sweat all over.

How many times have I heard this litany over the last few days?

Nevertheless, I say, 'Thank you.'

Then he is gone, and I go back to looking at the beach, where my girls play. And all I see is what is not there, the child who should be with them but is missing.

SIXTY

DAY 4

1:00 p.m.

I clasp a cup of tea in my hand and watch the sea. The sun is a fiery ball. The sky a white expanse of glaring, liquid heat. Searing. Branding. The sea shimmers in the distance, golden light sparkling on hazy blue. I feel as if I am in a dream, an endless dream of waiting, marooned in a strange country that brands with heat and demands sweaty liquid recompense.

The children had come back from the beach beaming and tanned – despite the suntan lotion I had smothered them with, their pails full of shells and sea-smoothed pebbles, declaring their sandcastle 'the best in the world', annoyed at the 'naughty waves that nearly washed it away', chattering about the fish and the crabs they encountered, and all I could think of was how much Ajit would have enjoyed it.

The girls wanted me to bathe them and I did so, my mind snagging on a few days before, when I had performed the same action with Ajit. His wriggly warm body, his joyous excited chatter.

The girls were subdued when I washed them, their bodies hot and still. Tired out from the heat. Drowsy and clingy.

'I wish Ajit had been there, Mummy,' Mia said, as, wrapped in a towel, she waited for me to get her clothes.

'Yes, it wasn't the same without him. He would have been so excited about the sandcastle,' Zoe said.

I mused, as I gathered them into my arms, their freshly washed lemon and honey scent, that this was the first time Zoe had agreed with Mia. Normally, if Mia said something, Zoe made sure to say the complete opposite.

They picked at their lunch – chicken sandwiches, with fruit for afters – and now they are pooled on the sofa with Bella watching cartoons on Lydia's iPad.

Lydia is on her phone, looking grave. Working hard on the social media campaign, no doubt.

Rachel is in her room.

The men are silent, each lost in their own thoughts.

I take a sip of the tea. Lukewarm. Looking and tasting like dishwater. I look up and freeze despite the perspiration slick on my body, dripping down sweaty limbs. I blink once and again. Could it be...? Is it...?

There's a little boy standing by the sea, framed by the simmering heat haze. He looks as if he is on fire, encompassed in a glowing halo.

Ajit.

My cup shatters on the floor.

'Jo?' I hear Yash call.

I can't speak, can't answer. I am standing up and then I'm running. Down the veranda steps, onto the sand, ignoring the reporters who descend on me like vultures. 'Jo, Mrs Kumar, where are you going?'

I run all the way to the sea, the sand so hot on the undersides of my feet that they burn at first and then go numb. But it doesn't register. Nothing does except the boy standing there, at the edge of the water. All I know is that I have to reach him. My boy. My beloved Ajit.

I have to touch him, hold him, gather him to me before he disappears. I have been given a chance, one chance to make everything right.

I run through the sand, breathless.

'Mrs Kumar, Jo, what's the matter? Why the hurry?' the reporters call. 'What do you know?'

'Jo, where on earth are you going?' I hear Yash's voice, perplexed, calling for me.

'Mummy!'

I know, rationally, that the sound, that call of 'Mummy' is coming from behind me, from the veranda. But another part of my mind is convinced it is Ajit. The boy who is slowly coming into relief through the haze.

As I get closer to the water, the gritty sand becomes soft and smooth and wet, my bruised, boiling feet stinging as they sink into its cool depths. The roar of the sea is loud here, but not as loud as my heart beating against my chest. *Ajit. Ajit. Ajit.*

He is standing at the verge of the water, dipping his feet in the sea. He is so cautious, quite unlike my Ajit, who would have been jumping and dancing and splashing and lolling, fearless, treating the sea like a long-lost friend.

What happened to you in just four days?

'Ajit,' I call and he turns to me.

I stop, bending over double, heaving, as the breath comes back to me, on a crashing wave of distress.

This boy is taller than Ajit. Older than him. He has curly hair, unlike Ajit's straight and slightly too long locks. He has a long face, as opposed to Ajit's round one. His brown eyes – completely unlike Ajit's tawny, almond-shaped ones – are scrunched up in befuddlement.

He is not Ajit. He is not my boy.

I collapse right there on the hot, wet sand, out of breath, sobs juddering out of me.

The boy's curious gaze morphs into one of alarm. He opens his mouth as if to say something.

I shut my eyes. I cannot look at him. It hurts too much, the disappointment of his features, which are not Ajit's.

'Jo.' Yash's voice is tender. His arms around my shoulders. I lean into him, bury my head in his chest, his smell of musk and sorrow. He holds me as I sob, the harsh sun beating down on us, relentless. Mocking me. *How dare you expect a happy ending after everything you've done?*

Yash gently lifts me up onto my abused feet. When I look up, I see that the boy has been joined by his mother and they are both trying not to gawp at me, unlike the reporters, who are rubbernecking avidly, their senses heightened by this unexpected thrill of fresh news: The Mother Gone Mad.

I send the boy's mother a silent message: *Hold on to him. Don't lose sight of him, like I did my child.*

I look away from the pity in her eyes. I am now a woman to be pitied. With my naked grief on display, making a spectacle of myself in public, running on scorched sand in bare feet and nearly accosting a boy whom I took to be my son.

I was blessed with three beautiful children and I became smug, complacent. I even went so far as to take them for granted and this is the result.

Gently, my husband leads me back to the cottage from which my son disappeared. The reporters, for once, are silent. Perhaps they do have some heart after all.

My girls watch me with anxious eyes.

'What happened, Mummy?' Mia asks as I hobble into the living room and sink into the chair Paul pulls out for me.

'I was being a silly-billy, sweetheart. I thought that little boy on the beach was Ajit.'

Mia squints at the beach, pointing. 'That boy! He looks nothing like Ajit. Oh, that really *is* silly, Mummy.'

My girls climb onto my lap and I hold them, using their warm bodies as a shield from the adults, their judging, pitying gazes.

SIXTY-ONE

DAY 4

2:00 p.m.

I sit on the sofa in the living room, listening to the chatter of my girls and Bella wafting from the kitchen. They are making fruit salad with Lydia and Yash. Paul has begged off, saying he needs to catch up on sleep. Rachel is in her room, on her phone, I bet.

'Not like that, Mia, don't make such big chunks,' Zoe chides bossily. Even though she is the younger child, she has always taken the lead, lording over her older, pliant sister.

The fraught look on Zoe's face has relaxed a teeny bit after her chat with me this morning and the girls' spell on the beach; she seems more herself.

If Ajit was here, he'd be fooling around and the girls would be running to Yash with complaints and when that failed, they'd come to me.

I close my eyes, imagining the salt-stained breeze caressing my face, whispering assurances. The doors and windows are shut against the intrusive barrage of reporters' questions and insinuations and the air in this room is close and rank with worry, pain, trepidation.

A loud giggle. Mia. 'What have you done, Zoe?'

Then Zoe's laughter echoing Mia's and Bella joining in too. A moment of normalcy in the madness. Will it be so from now on, trying to cultivate and hold on to moments like this while the loss of Ajit is a constant, throbbing ache in the background, insinuating itself everywhere, a loud pulsing presence shouting out my son's absence from everyday activities such as these?

'It's nice to hear them laugh, eh?' Paul pulls up a chair beside me.

I nod, but, although I open my eyes, I don't turn to look at him, fixing my gaze instead upon the hypnotic swell of the waves just visible beyond the huddle of reporters.

'Makes us feel insignificant, doesn't it, the sea?' Paul muses.

I watch the boat nodding at the edge of the horizon as I digest Paul's words. And I realise why, despite the possibility that Ajit might have been swallowed up within its depths, I am calmed by looking at the sea. Because it is bigger than all of us. It has been around for so long and it will still be there when we are all gone. It has seen a million tragedies like mine and it will see many more and yet it will still bash against the rocks, still growl and thunder and perform.

'Yes,' I say.

I can't quite trust Paul, although I don't really believe the accusation against him. But I also feel a kinship with him, if only because I am sorry for him. All these years I don't think he's ever once suspected his wife; and he still loves her deeply, I can see, from the way his eyes follow her about.

'Choose someone who loves you more than you love him,' my mother had advised – possibly the only advice she ever gave me. Well, Lydia certainly did.

'Jo?'

'Hmm?'

Paul clears his throat. Apparently, whatever he wants to say is not easy. And instantly my fear is back. I am on edge. There have been so many secrets, so much subterfuge. What is this man hiding? What will I find out?

'Lydia and I... we were thinking that perhaps... what with the kids' schools starting back soon, we'll return home as planned.'

The pain I feel is huge, all-consuming, all the more wretched for being unexpected. They can go back. They can forget all this. They can get on with their lives. For them, this is a story to tell over a few drinks in years to come, a sad story, but a story all the same, not their *life*: 'That time we went on holiday with friends and it turned into a nightmare.'

I have forgotten all about school. Ajit had been so excited to be starting school with his sisters last September. He had looked so proud in his uniform, that big grin bursting from his face. I had taken so many pictures. He had clutched his new lunchbox, school bag on his back, so very excited right up until the moment he realised it was for real and then he turned, his face small and worried, and waved, forlorn. I had stood there long after the other mothers left, that image of my son's face etched in my mind.

I was the first mother at the school gates at collection time. And when I saw him come out, a big grin lighting up his face, that was when my heart settled. He had enjoyed it after all. He chatted about his day on the way home and all that evening, not allowing his sisters a word in edgeways.

And so it had continued all term. There hadn't been the blip I was expecting, like with the girls – they had turned teary after the first two weeks when the novelty wore off. Ajit loved school. He loved his teacher and talked non-stop about her. If we needed him to do anything, we only had to say, 'Your teacher will be so pleased when we tell her you...' and he would get to it before we could even finish the sentence.

Oh God, I think, as a fresh wave of angst hits me. We have to inform the school, the head teacher, Ajit's teacher.

But most likely they already know, thanks to the press.

I picture Ajit's sweet, young teacher in her dressing gown, opening the paper and reading of Ajit's disappearance. She would read about the 'off' mother, the 'distraught' father and she would grieve for Ajit.

I cannot imagine when we might go back and inhabit the life that was once ours. I suppose we will have to, for the sake of the girls, some time. If not next week, then next month...

What if Ajit is not found by then? How can I abandon him here and go back home? How to survive when my son is half a world away?

I will not believe what they are saying on social media. My son is not dead. He *will* be found, alive and safe and unharmed. I have to believe this, otherwise I... I'll lose my will to go on. And I must go on. My girls need me and so does Ajit.

'Of course we'll check with the inspector first,' Paul is saying.

I want to lash out at Paul. *It's all right for you*, I want to yell. *You horrid, smug man.*

But he is not being horrid or smug. If anything, he looks defeated.

'Jo, the inspector...'

'What about him?'

'He asked me where I was during those few minutes when I was not at the bar getting us drinks, like I was supposed to be.'

'It was more than a few minutes.' My voice is strident. All the anger I feel, the hopelessness, I direct at him.

'Yes, you're right.'

I turn, finally, look right at him. 'What were you doing?'

And suddenly, as I ask him the question, I remember walking around the cottage that night – the hazy memory suddenly, absolutely clear. I recall Yash, Paul and Lydia earnestly telling me I needed to start taking my medication again, that I was imagining things, making up texts, seeing graves. I remember feeling fed up, shouting at Yash to stop patronising me, that I *had* received the texts, that I *did* see the graves, that I was an adult and quite capable of deciding whether I wanted to take medication or not. I had threatened to take the kids and leave, right that moment, go away and never return. I remember standing, weaving through the sand towards the cottage, ignoring their calls for me to come back. I was overcome with the need to hold my children, breathe in their pure, perfect innocence. But as I'd approached the cottage, Rachel had lifted her hand up in a wave. I remember thinking that I couldn't stand to talk to her right then – I wasn't in the right frame of mind. And so I had pretended not to see her and had changed direction, going around the cottage instead, rather than inside it.

Oh, if only I had gone indoors, endured the chat with Rachel, gathered my children to me and not let go, Ajit would still be here.

With effort, I push away the pain ambushing me and try to recall if I noticed the window, or any vehicles on the road or beside it, now that I remember my walk around the cottage. But no, lost in rumination and upset, maudlin with drink and angry at Yash and Lydia and Paul, I had not noticed anything at all.

And again, how I wish I could go back and undo my actions that night – all the many, unthinking mistakes...

'Money has been going missing from the business,' Paul is saying.

'I know that,' I say. And, looking at Paul, 'Yash has been looking into it in his own time. He didn't want to worry you until he'd managed to trace it.'

'What?' Paul stares at me. 'And here I was thinking I'd spare him the worry by trying to trace it myself. I found the money was going to a supplier we hadn't authorised. But when it proved difficult to locate this shady supplier, I employed a bloke, one of those young ones who are whizzes at these sorts of things and do freelance work, to look into it. He messaged me to say he had an update and would like to speak with me, that night when we were at the shack. So I said I was going to get drinks and then I went behind the shack and called him. That's what I was doing during those missing few minutes. And before you ask, I've already told the inspector.'

Paul is earnest. I believe him. So he wasn't arranging to kidnap Ajit during those unaccounted for few minutes. Not that I *really* believed he was. 'And?' I ask. 'Who is it who's been stealing money from the business?'

Paul runs a hand down his face. 'He's close to getting the actual details, but he is pretty sure the only person with access would be one of the directors...' He looks pointedly at me.

It takes me a moment but then I get it. 'You think it's Yash...'

'Well, it's certainly not me.'

Our marriage might be on shaky ground, but I do know that Yash wouldn't steal from the company he and Paul created, that he loves almost as much as his children. 'Paul, you've known Yash for years, how could you believe this of him?'

'One thing I've realised since we've come on holiday is that I know *nothing*,' Paul barks. 'I don't know my wife and I don't know my so-called friend.'

'Have you confronted Yash about this?'

'This isn't the time...' Paul says.

A thought occurs to me then. 'You took this call just before Ajit went missing...'

'What are you saying, Jo?' Paul's voice is dangerously low. 'I thought you didn't remember anything from the night.'

I continue as if he hasn't spoken, following my train of thought, 'You thought Yash was stealing from the business into which you've put your everything. Your savings, your life and soul these past ten years.'

'Jo.' Paul puts his hand up, palm outward. 'Stop right there. I would have talked to Yash first.'

'You're a gentle giant, but Lydia has told me that you have a temper. It flares very rarely, but when it does, you go wild, crazy, she's said. This was one reason why she kept breaking up with you in the beginning of your relationship.'

'Jo, whatever it is you're implying...' Paul begins tightly.

I think of all the times Paul has been out by himself, 'getting groceries'. He could easily have been looking in on the child he'd kidnapped. Do I believe what I'm accusing Paul of? A few minutes ago, I'd decided I didn't think Paul could have done it. Now I'm not sure what to think. It might be JT who I think I saw at the market. But what if it's not? What if it is someone closer to home? I swallow, say, 'The business is your baby. Would you have taken our bab—'

'Jo,' Paul bites. 'Read my lips. I did not take Ajit, all right?' He is fierce. He seems earnest.

It might be bravado.

I will park the thought for now, but I must remember to tell the inspector.

Paul looks at me, sighs. 'Jesus, Jo, you don't believe me, do you?'

'If you thought it was Yash stealing from the business—'

And now Paul explodes. 'But why on earth would I take your child whom I also love...' And at the expression on my face, 'Jesus, *not* in that way!'

I stare at the sea until it blurs before my eyes. 'I don't know what to think, what, who to believe any more.'

He sighs, rubs his chin, stares gloomily out the window. 'I can't say it's great being at the receiving end of your suspicions, being interrogated by the inspector, having to relive one of the worst times of my life,' – he lifts his face up to the sun – 'but I do understand. If it was one of mine missing, God forbid, I'd be the same, trusting absolutely no one.'

Surprise renders me speechless. Of all people, I was not expecting *Paul* to be the one who would get it.

'For what it's worth, I didn't take Ajit, even if I thought Yash was stealing from the business,' he says, his voice rising. 'As a parent myself, I wouldn't subject anyone to what you both are going through right now.'

He sounds sincere. I'm inclined to believe him. But... it could all be an act. One thing this ordeal has taught me is that nothing is what it seems and nobody is who they say they are. I don't *know* anyone, not my husband of more than a decade or my supposed friends of as many years. I don't even know or trust myself.

'Jo, I'm so sorry about what has happened. Ajit... I hope he's found soon and safe.'

Is he sincere? He definitely sounds it. 'Thank you, Paul.'

I turn to look at the sea, my mind churning more than the waves, nauseous with worry, suspicion, despair, remorse.

SIXTY-TWO

DAY 4

3:00 p.m.

'But we agreed...' Paul's voice drifts out into the living room from Lydia and Paul's bedroom – they must have forgotten to shut the door.

Although Paul is whispering, it is high-pitched, whiny. He sounds just like Bella when she doesn't get her way.

The kids are in their rooms, and Yash is in our bedroom, having a siesta in the drowsy, stultifying heat of mid-afternoon. I'm on the sofa, my feet bathed in lotion, while my heart is breaking, shattering more every minute my son is unaccounted for. Is Ajit, beloved Ajit, gone for good?

Our policeman guard snoozes in his corner, although I'm convinced the snoozing is just an act and that he misses nothing.

Like me, he too must be hearing the slivers of the argument, Lydia and Paul quarrelling in hushed tones that carry in the seaweed- and coconut-flavoured breeze.

'I never agreed to anything.' Lydia's hissing is very much like how an angered snake would sound, I imagine.

Their argument must have woken Yash for he comes into

the living room and slips onto the chair next to the sofa, where Paul was sitting earlier. There's space on the sofa beside me, but my husband chooses the chair – that says something about what this ordeal and the secrets revealed in its wake have done to our marriage.

'We discussed returning home as planned if the inspector gave us the go-ahead.' Paul's voice is getting angry as well now and is morphing from whisper into shout.

'Shh, quiet. You'll wake the kids. And we didn't *discuss* it, you *told* me we should consider it.'

'Well, have you considered?'

'I'm not going anywhere until Ajit is found.'

'Lydia, I know you care for Ajit. I do too, but it's looking increasingly unlikely that he's—'

Don't say it, I think, at the same time as Lydia barks, 'Don't, Paul.'

'This could drag on, Lydia. The kids, their school...'

'They can miss a few days.'

'But what will they *do* here? We can't even go out without being ambushed. It's like being under house arrest.'

'We're needed here...'

'You mean *you* are needed.'

'Excuse me?'

'This is not about Ajit, is it?'

'What do you mean?'

'Forget I said anything.' Paul's voice is huffy and he is about to lapse into a sulk, I can tell.

'Fine, be like that. But I'm not leaving here as planned, Paul, if Ajit is not found by then.'

Paul doesn't reply.

I turn to Yash. His cheeks are flushed, he looks embarrassed to have been caught eavesdropping on our friends' argument.

I think of the ring. *My* ring, I am sure, on Lydia's finger. I think of Lydia's bikini among Yash's things. I think of the two of them skinny-dipping in the sea that night, the night I would *do* anything to go back to, hold my boy to me and not let go. I think of Lydia and Yash whispering together with the door shut in the bedroom I share with Yash when they thought the rest of us were sleeping. I think of what Paul said just now, in the heat of their marital argument, what he implied.

How far do I trust my husband? My friend? Do I trust them at all?

I think of the text messages, exposing my deepest fears, laying bare my insecurities: *Your husband is having an affair.*

'Are you having an affair with Lydia?' I ask Yash, my mouth swirling with bile.

Four days ago, I would have been appalled at myself for even considering this. My husband and my best friend. Together. I wouldn't even have joked about it. Now I'm serious. I want to know. So much has changed in less than a week. So much broken. Especially trust.

'What are you saying? What's got into you, Jo?' Yash cries. 'I don't know you any more.'

Exactly what Lydia had said when I asked if she took Ajit. They're even parroting each other's words.

'I don't know you either. You slept with Lydia, had a child with her and have kept her close all these years. So, I'll ask again. Are you still carrying on with Lydia?'

He stands up so abruptly he knocks his chair down, startling the policeman in his corner. 'I can't do this. You've gone crazy. She's my childhood friend.'

'Not *just* your childhood friend.'

'I'm not sleeping with Lydia. Jesus, I can't believe I'm saying this.'

I almost believe him. 'But the bikini...'

'I *told* you. I don't know how it got there.'

'Skinny-dipping in the sea...'

'For God's sake, it was *fun* on *holiday*. You are policing me now?'

'I don't know what to think...'

'I don't know how many times I have to say this.' He runs his hand through his hair, the gesture supremely weary. 'I married *you*, not her.'

'Because she was with Paul.' I voice the thought that has been preying on my mind since I found out about Yash and Lydia.

'No. Because I love *you*, not her.'

'Funny way of showing it, sleeping with her because of your intensity of feelings for me...'

'I made a mistake and I'm sorry.' He pauses, looks at me and his eyes are sad and tired. 'I married you because I loved you, Jo. But I don't know any more. I've had just about enough of you throwing suspicions and accusations left, right and centre. Can't you see' – his eyes alight with tears – 'I'm suffering too. I cannot deal with this on top of—'

'Mr and Mrs Kumar...'

We've not heard the inspector arrive, immersed as we are in our own drama. How long has he been standing there?

'Have I caught you at an inconvenient time?' he asks.

Yash laughs, a grating joyless bark. 'You could say so.' Then, 'Do you have any news?'

The hope in his voice splicing my already shredded heart.

'Yes,' the inspector says.

We both stare at him, hope and panic.

He appears grave.

I'm about to beg him to please tell us what he knows when he says, looking at me, 'We've located JT.'

'Oh.' One hand creeping to my heart. For it's not good news, I can tell.

'He goes by Chandra Shan now.'

'OK?' My voice rising in question, hope and fear.

'He arrived in India a week ago.'

'Oh.' I manage at the same time as Yash storms, 'So he *is* here?'

'He was at the market.'

'What?' Yash cries, while I am speechless. A part of me knew it was JT I saw that day and yet I had doubted myself... But I was right. It *was* him. It is no consolation, for my heart contracts in fear. JT is *here*, in Goa, just like I thought. He has been stalking me. Did he take Ajit? *Please let my boy be safe. Please.*

'He rescued Ajit from the rickshaw and gave him to the fortune teller. The fortune teller told us that he paid her to scare you, put the fear of God in you.'

'What?' Yash yells. 'How *dare* he?'

I shiver as I recall that day, the torturous terror that Ajit was under the rickshaw, a precursor to what I've been experiencing since Ajit disappeared, the fortune teller's ranting, feeling harangued by her necklace's thousand painted-on eyes...

'No,' I manage. 'No.' My entire being is wild with fury, the rage I feel reflected in Yash's eyes, his palms bunched into fists. I have no doubt that were JT here now, Yash would punch him, if I didn't get there first. How could he? But wait... 'Inspector, you said he *rescued* Ajit from the rickshaw?'

'Yes.'

'And he paid the fortune teller to scare me?'

'Yes.'

'I don't understand...' I begin. But I do. Suddenly it's clear. He wanted to scare *me*, punish *me*. Has he also taken Ajit with the same intent? But he wouldn't hurt Ajit, surely? Not JT. *Please.* 'Those Snapchat messages – I'm sure they are from him,' I tell the inspector. Judgemental yet personal. Exactly JT's style.

The inspector says, 'We're waiting for Snapchat to release any data they have on the user.'

'Jo,' Yash yells. 'JT has been sending you messages?'

'They're from "a well-wisher" but they sound like him.'

'Mr and Mrs Kumar,' the inspector says, and something in his voice makes us both stop and turn to him. 'JT, or Mr Chandra Shan as he is now, was seen hanging about the beach by the builders up the road the day you arrived here.'

'He was here when we arrived?' Yash booms, while I hug my stomach which churns with nausea. A scream is trapped in my throat which feels choked. JT was stalking us, watching, waiting... 'Inspector, where is he now?' Yash roars, urgency pulsing in his voice. 'Have you found him? Does he have Ajit?'

'He's not been seen since that day at the market.'

'The evening of which Ajit disappeared,' Yash cries.

Oh God, oh God, oh God. JT has my son. *He has my son.*

'We are continuing our enquiries,' the inspector says.

'They're taking too bloody long,' Yash blusters.

'His passport photo is being circulated everywhere. We've put out a nationwide alert for a man and boy matching JT and Ajit's description. He will be found and soon.' The inspector takes a breath. 'I know it is frustrating, Mr Kumar, but we're trying our best.'

'Your best isn't enough for my boy,' Yash yells. 'Why are you here, instead of out there searching for this man and my boy?'

'My men are—'

Yash punches the dining table, hard. The policeman in the corner stands up even as I flinch. Paul and Lydia come rushing. 'What's going on?'

Neither of us reply – we are in our own personal hell. Yash rubs his hand, which is flaring red. The inspector is inscrutable, quietly watching us.

Yash points a shaky finger at me, his face contorted in anger. 'Jo, this is all because of you.' He bites. 'Your JT has taken my son.'

'What?' Lydia and Paul gasp while I double up, clutching

my stomach. What Yash is saying is true. Oh God. What have I done? I can't breathe, the consequences of one impulsive action beating in my throat like a trapped fly.

'I'm puzzled as to why he didn't take Ajit that day at the market,' the inspector says.

And now I can breathe again. I look up at the inspector. Yes, what he's saying makes sense.

'Why did he ask the fortune teller to threaten Jo?' Yash yells. 'Perhaps taking my boy is a game to him.'

Lydia and Paul are looking from one of us to the other, gazes wide and shocked as they try to make sense of what's going on.

Yash turns to me, eyes wild. 'You go about accusing everyone, Jo. But have you had a good look at yourself? You... *you* are responsible for this. You had the affair with JT.'

'Jo, you had an affair?' Lydia cries.

But Yash interrupts, staring daggers at me, despair and rage. 'It is because of you our boy is gone.'

And hearing my husband, the man I have loved and lived with for fifteen years, judge me, blame me, damn me, is my breaking point.

I run to the loo, make it just in time, am sick over and over. I retch until there's nothing left, not even bile, but it's not enough. It's not enough.

You caused this.

My son is suffering, lost, because of me. I deserve to be punished.

A lizard in the corner of the cracked ceiling watches me with unblinking bulbous eyes.

I throw water on my face and, wanting to avoid Yash, Paul and Lydia who are grouped in the living room, hobble, on blistered feet, to our bedroom – Yash's and mine – where we haven't slept since the first night of our holiday when Ajit was safe in the room across from us.

I lean against the window and look out, beyond the huddle

of reporters and across the expanse of sand to the sea, serene and imperturbable, glittering turquoise gold.

Someone clears their throat behind me.

The inspector. 'Are you all right, Mrs Kumar?'

'No, I am not all right. I'm a bad mother – the worst. I've lost my son, and even before that, I wasn't a good mother to him, to my children. You see, Inspector, I've been accusing everyone because I want them to be guilty so it will absolve me of *my* guilt, this guilt that is killing me. I failed in my foremost duty, to protect my children, keep them from harm. And I hope that if it is someone close to us, they won't hurt my boy. If JT has him, he won't hurt him, will he? He saved him from the rickshaw accident...' Everything I've been thinking comes out of me in an unstoppable gush.

The inspector listens quietly to my lament, face expressionless. Once I've stopped, he says, gently, 'Mrs Kumar, there's no point in beating yourself up. We all make errors in judgement. Parenting is a very difficult job, the most challenging, in my opinion. Compared to it, policing is... How do you say it?... a piece of cake. You ask any parent, your friends, myself, my wife and we will all say that we feel guilty about something we did in the course of our parenting that we regret.' He pauses, takes a breath.

The sand shimmers, divine gold, and beyond, the sea gambols playfully, growling as it surges and ebbs, teasing the rocks with salt-sprinkled spray.

'You've had the worst happen to you. It could have happened to any of us. You are unfortunate, that's all. It doesn't make you a bad parent.'

'Thank you, Inspector, for saying that,' I say through a mouthful of brine – it feels as if I have swallowed the sea.

Everyone has turned against me and yet this man who knows all my worst secrets is not judging me. He's not damning me even though I've lost my boy. It steadies me. The earth had shifted under my feet, but now I am able to set them down again.

My phone beeps. A new text.

An eye for an eye.

A tooth for a tooth.

A child for a child.

Keep searching. Keep looking.

Good luck with that.

He's gone.

I gasp.

'What is it?' the inspector asks.

'A text from that withheld number that's been messaging me about Yash's affair and leaving Ajit in the car,' I whisper. 'Here.' I thrust the phone at him, unable to look at the words again. But they're there, in my mind: *He's gone.*

No, no, no.

Who is doing this? Is it Lori? This text, so vengeful, just like my sister. That post that went viral and was picked up by the media – it was on Facebook, which she could have accessed from anywhere. One of the newspapers reported that she was out of the country on holiday. Could she be here? If JT is, then why not Lori? Could she have taken Ajit?

I shudder. Please, no. Lori is ruthless. I wouldn't put it past the sister I grew up with to take my son and then publicly point the finger at me.

But... She was pregnant with Tom's child when we parted

ways. She is a mother too. Even if she has Ajit, she wouldn't hurt him, would she?

Hope flickers. *Please let Ajit be alive...*

But then I think of Lori pushing me down the stairs because Mum praised me over her – for what I cannot recall now. She'd smiled as she'd stepped over me lying crumpled and in pain at the bottom of the stairs and walked out of the house. Dad found me eventually. I suffered two broken ribs and a fractured ankle. The doctor said that if the stairs hadn't been carpeted it could have been a lot worse...

The brief flare of hope dies.

But if it is Lori, what does she mean, *a child for a child?*

'What are you showing me, Mrs Kumar?' the inspector is asking.

'I...' I look at my phone. This message too, like the others, is gone. I clear my throat which feels as if it is clogged with sand. 'There *was* a message.' My voice trembles like a raindrop clinging to the underside of a leaf.

'Yes, I heard the beep of an incoming text on your phone,' the inspector says.

He is not instantly dismissive like Yash, Lydia and Paul. This gives me the courage to say, 'I saw it, but when I showed you, it was gone.'

'Ah.' The inspector, instead of discrediting me like my friends and husband had done, rubs his chin thoughtfully. 'I will check with my IT team, but it is possible that someone has hacked into your phone messaging service and is sending you messages and then deleting them after you've read them.'

'What?' I am flustered, even as the words from that text ring in my head: *He's gone.* No. Please, no.

'We came across this when investigating another case. You said these messages started arriving around three weeks ago?'

'Yes.' I jump on his words, nearly not letting him finish. I cannot believe it – someone is finally taking me seriously. And not just anyone but the inspector himself. And he appears to have a plausible explanation for what's been happening.

'Do you recall leaving your phone unattended in the week or so before the first message arriving on your phone?'

I think of how busy I was in the lead-up to this holiday, with the school runs, the packed lunches and after-school clubs, running around after three kids and their myriad activities while Yash worked all hours. I'd left my phone at Ajit's swimming lesson more than once, his instructor dropping it off on his way home. I'd also once accidentally posted it in Mia's PE bag along with her kit. Then there was the time I left it behind after the PTA meeting...

The inspector clears his throat.

'I leave it unattended all the time,' I say.

'Is it password protected?'

'It locks, and I draw an L to unlock it. But, to be honest, everyone who knows me knows how to unlock it, the children included.'

'And even if not, it's easy enough for anyone looking over your shoulder or even following the movement of your fingers to pick up on.'

'Yes,' I whisper, unsure what this all means in terms of who has been messaging, who has taken Ajit. Frustration and upset heaps on top of more guilt that I couldn't even get this right.

'Mrs Kumar, it's more than likely that whoever is sending you these messages has Ajit. Is it all right to get your phone looked at by our IT team, please? I will get it back to you soonest.'

'Here. Find my son, please.' I hand the inspector my phone. 'So I'm not going mad? I *did* get the messages.'

'You did. Now, Mrs Kumar, what exactly did the message you just received say?'

SIXTY-THREE

DAY 4

3:30 p.m.

The inspector leaves and I come into the living room, ready now, to face the others.

I am not mad. I was not imagining either the stalker or the text messages. Both are real.

But that's scary too.

'Jo.' Lydia turns to me. 'Yash told us that it's almost certain this man you had an affair with has Ajit. When was this affair?' These last few days have ravaged Lydia too. Fine lines sprout from the corners of her eyes, dragging her lips down. 'You didn't tell me about it.'

'I... I was ashamed, Lydia.'

'And now, look what you've done,' Yash mutters. 'Posting pictures on Facebook, making your unhinged boyfriend think Ajit was his.'

'What?' Lydia asks, shocked. 'He isn't yours, Yash?'

'She says he is, but how can I believe her?'

Lydia is staring at me, appalled. A shadow marring her gaze, a flush creeping up her neck.

A phone rings, shrill and loud, and we all startle.

I scrabble about for my phone, panicked for a moment or two before realising it's with the inspector.

It's Paul's phone that's ringing. He stares at it. Is he blushing?

'Go ahead and answer it, mate, before you wake the kids,' Yash snaps.

The tension is getting to him. Like me, he too is at breaking point.

Please, let Ajit be found soon, safe and well. My refrain, chant, prayer. But it is getting harder to believe the longer he is gone. No, I will not give up hope. But the text message: *He's gone.*

'I'll take it later,' Paul mumbles.

'Who is it, Paul?' Lydia asks sharply.

'Just some bloke...' Paul is acting very shifty. I'm immediately alert. What's he hiding?

Lydia must think the same for she says, voice cutting, 'Which bloke?'

'I...' Paul looks at Yash, rubs his face. Guilty. He looks guilty. What has he done? 'Now's not the time...'

'Now is exactly the time,' I say. 'What are you hiding?'

'You know about it, Jo. It's the bloke I hired to look into the money going missing from the business.'

'Paul thinks it was you,' I tell Yash, filled with a pressing need for everything to be out in the open. There have been too many secrets. Perhaps if the air is cleared, everything will be clearer and Ajit found?

'What?' Yash is shocked. 'Mate, how could you even...?'

I tune him out, for I've just seen Lydia's face. She is ashen, her skin tinged green. Is she going to be sick?

'Paul,' she says faintly, 'you hired someone to...' She stops, apparently unable to continue. Despite all that's going on, all I've found out, despite the fact that our friendship is definitely over, I feel a pang for her. Ajit going missing has taken its toll on all of us.

Paul's phone rings again. 'He's persistent, I'll give him that. I might as well take it, see what he has to say.'

'Wait, Paul,' Lydia cries. 'There are other more urgent—'

But Paul has already activated the call. 'Hello, mate? What have you got for me?'

We all watch Paul, an uneasy silence in the room, punctuated by Paul saying, every so often, 'What?' 'Are you sure?' 'All right, cheers.'

Paul cuts the call and looks at Yash, his gaze uncomprehending, puzzled.

Why is he looking at Yash that way? Has Yash been stealing from the business despite his vehement denial? I find it hard to believe but not impossible. *Nothing* seems impossible any more. My son is missing. My best friend slept with my husband. My best friend's husband was accused of touching a child. The man I loved once, briefly, headily, intensely might have kidnapped my child...

Nothing is sacred. Everything tainted by our secrets, our lies – my child likely caught in the fallout from it all. But not dead. Please God, not dead. Although as regards this too, my hope dwindles with every passing hour, although I try and hold on fiercely to the belief that my son is alive and well. *Please...*

'What's the matter?' Yash asks Paul.

Lydia is twisting a tissue to shreds, wispy twirls dropping like confetti onto the floor, which I note is dirty, littered, in addition to the snowy tissue curls, with cornflake and toast crumbs. None of us have bothered with housekeeping.

'He said...' Paul shakes his head. 'The bloke said... He swears there's no mistake... He is convinced, he said he'd send me the proof...'

'Paul,' Yash says, 'mate, you're not making any sense.'

'The bloke... He found the account the money was going

into. The guy was very clever, he said. IT savvy. Used all the hacks to make sure the money wouldn't be traced...'

'But your guy traced him?' Yash asks.

'Yes. But here's where it doesn't make sense. He said the money is going into an account that's registered to me. But that's impossible. I did not create that account.'

'It might be a hack to make it appear as though you're legitimately moving the money.'

'That's what I said. But the bloke says he checked and it's genuine. The money *is* apparently going into an account, registered to me, that I know nothing about.'

'What?'

'But trust me, mate, trust me on this, I *haven't* been taking it. I didn't know about this. If I did, why would I hire someone to look into it?'

'But if it isn't you, then how...?' Yash leaves the sentence hanging.

'I'm sure there's some mistake. There *must* be, although this bloke claims there isn't. He checked and double-checked, he said.'

Lydia's face is blanched white as the moon peeking through a glower of clouds.

'Lydia, is it you?' I ask.

Lydia's eyes flash as she turns to me. She opens her mouth, but before she can speak, Yash explodes.

'I don't care about the money. I don't care about the business. I just want my son.'

And now Yash folds, his anger gone, distraught despair in its place. He buries his head in his hands and he breaks down, right there, in front of us all.

I should help soothe his grief. But I am rooted to the spot.

Paul mutters something about checking on Bella and leaves the room, looking embarrassed on Yash's behalf.

Yash keens and it is Lydia who goes to him, puts her arms

around him. He rests his head on her shoulder and he sobs his agony and she holds him, his tears soaking her neck.

And I think, what a beautiful couple they make, and I chide myself for the thought, but it is there. It is there.

They are right together. They always were. It is Yash and I who are wrong. Yash and I who broke each other during our fifteen years together, our marriage buckling from the strain of maintaining fronts, acting as normal when the poison of our lies and the secrets we were keeping from each other was slowly but surely infecting us, and now, our innocent, precious children are suffering from the fallout. How did I think any of us could get away unscathed?

But now, it is over. We are over. Losing our son is the fatal hurdle that has tripped up our marriage.

I am assaulted by memories: Yash smiling at me across the crowded room the first time we met. Yash's eyes looking at me with such pride and love the day we got married. Yash holding Mia in his arms, unable to speak, his face shining with awe as he gazed upon the miracle we had produced together. Yash's overcome gaze meeting mine over our daughters' tender heads as they cooed over the infant brother they were meeting for the first time... Will they, will we, be reunited with Ajit again?

SIXTY-FOUR

DAY 4

4:00 p.m.

In the corner, the policeman's phone rings. He is usually so quiet and unobtrusive that we startle.

He answers, and from the pulsing urgency in his voice as he conducts his one-sided conversation, we can tell something has happened.

'What...?' I'm not able to complete my query, my heart jumping with hope and fear.

Yash and Lydia both look up, Lydia's arm around Yash. My husband's face tear-stained, swollen eyes wide with the same mix of panic and hope I am feeling.

The policeman looks at Yash and me in turn, and there's a heaviness to his expression, a sombre gravity mingling with... worry. And that scares me more than his words: 'The police... um... searching for your son... they...'

'Yes?' Yash and I cry in unison.

'They find his slippers.'

My heart soars. This is good news. So why does the policeman look so grave?

'But not Ajit?' Yash asks.

The policeman shakes his head, no. I knew that, of course. If Ajit had been there, he'd have told us so first.

'Where?' Yash asks, his voice bright with hope. He hasn't clocked the expression on the policeman's face, the 'but...' that I'm sure is coming, that is making my heart catch.

'In cottage in city near... how you say... where someone saw man with boy after press conference. The cottage empty – owners, old couple, living far away and visiting only in holiday. They no kids. But neighbour hear child crying...'

'A child crying?' Yash turns to me, beaming, his excitement and hope mirrored, I am sure, in my eyes as I cry, 'He is *alive*. Our son is alive.'

I read the policeman wrong. Thank God. Thank you, God.

'Come, let's go.' Yash jumps up, shrugging Lydia's hand off, bouncing on the soles of his feet. 'Take us to him.'

Like me, Yash can't stop smiling.

The policeman, however, is sombre. 'I not finish.'

We look at each other, Yash and I, our highs coming crashing down, hearts taut with fear again. Here's the but...

It is Lydia who asks the officer the question we cannot. 'What do you mean?'

'Child cry two days ago. After that, nothing. The neighbour call police today. They check cottage...' He pauses, takes a breath.

'And?' Yash barks.

'What is it?' I ask softly, dreading what this man is hesitant to share.

He looks at me. 'They find blood.'

My legs give way and I crumple right there at the police-man's feet.

'No,' Yash says fiercely. 'I will not believe my boy is... that he...' His voice stumbles.

But no body, I think through my pain. No body. So there's hope.

The policeman helps me up to the sofa beside Lydia, who moves away as if she can't stand to be beside me.

But I don't care. I don't care about anything except Ajit... Ajit...

Please God.

'He gets nosebleeds when he's upset,' I say, looking at Yash, who nods vigorously, both of us clinging to this nugget of hope, an explanation for the blood, as if it is precious gold.

I don't want Ajit to have been so distressed and inconsolable that he suffered a nosebleed, but the alternative is so much worse...

'Take us there, mate. I want to see it for myself,' Yash cries.

'Inspector say you stay here. They checking cottage, taking samples...'

'I want to see where my son—' Yash booms.

'Please,' I beg.

The policeman looks conflicted. 'Inspector say stay here. Press know somehow. They coming...'

Before he finishes his sentence, all the phones go off at once and even more news vans congregate at the beach, flinging questions at us: 'Is it true that Ajit's slippers have been found along with his blood at a cottage in town?' 'Is Ajit dead?' 'Why is there no body?' 'Did you bury him in the sea, Jo?'

Both Yash and I flinch, helpless and desperate, our son, who loves SpongeBob and the sea, who is scared of spiders and creepy-crawlies but loves frogs and is fascinated by snails, squatting on his haunches to watch them, missing, and in his place, the detritus of our ruined relationships, our desperate trust that wanes and surges much like the sea.

SIXTY-FIVE

DAY 4

7:00 p.m.

We wait for news, frustrating though it is. We'd rather be out there searching, doing, Yash suffering from the inaction more than I am.

I try to exist, with the stone in my heart, the knowledge weighing me down that my marriage is broken and my son is gone. I try to recall how Ajit felt in my arms, his voice, his scent, his laughter.

If JT has him, then this is my fault. The fallout from my unthinking, selfish actions.

I sit on the sofa watching the sea arch towards the horizon. Mia and Zoe climb onto my lap after their dinner. I have to maintain a semblance of normality for my daughters. They need me to be their mum. I have to go on even if I feel like I am dying inside. It is a privilege, holding them, something I took for granted. Will I get to hold Ajit again? When I kissed him good-night that evening, was it for the last time? Enough, stop. He is alive, I tell myself. He is well. I must believe this. I must.

Together, my daughters and I watch the sun set in a kaleidoscope of colours, the sky a multihued panorama. There is beauty even in the midst of madness.

'So beautiful, Mummy,' Mia says, echoing my thoughts.

'Yes, isn't it?'

'I hope Ajit is watching it,' Zoe pipes up.

The pain shatters me. 'I hope so too,' I manage, breathing in my children's smell of honey and soap and sweetness and innocence. An innocence all the more precious for knowing that it will be lost very soon, alongside their guileless conviction in happy-ever-afters, when they have to deal with their parents' break-up on top of everything else. Even though Yash and I haven't spoken about it explicitly, it is a foregone conclusion, whatever happens with Ajit – we cannot stay together after everything that's happened, all that's been revealed, after hurting each other with our lies and secrets and evasions.

I breathe my daughters in and picture Ajit, his tawny eyes the colour of glowing embers, his red-gold hair, his myriad expressions. Who took him to that cottage? And the blood... my son's blood. What have they done to him?

'Mum, why are you tearing that paper?' Zoe asks. My perceptive child, looking at me with worried eyes.

'Oh, no reason, love, just thinking.'

I look at the paper confetti beside and around me. I don't want to dwell on what a hash I have made of my life, putting my children in harm's way, and yet that is all I can see.

'Do you think Ajit misses us, Mummy, just as much as we're missing him?' Mia asks, hugging Lamby to her, her eyes huge, her thumb momentarily removed from her mouth. Her expression – the way she cocks her head, so very much like her younger brother. A gift, warming my desolate heart even as it fires up a futile ache to see Ajit, smell him, hold him.

I compare everything my girls do and say, every little one of their mannerisms, with the picture of Ajit I have in my head. In their smiles, rainbows after a summer shower, I see Ajit. And in some small way, it comforts me.

'Mummy?' Mia tugs at my arm, Lamby brushing against my face. Lamby smells sour and is sandy. Normally, I would have coaxed Mia into handing him over; I would have washed him. But these are not normal times.

'I'm sure he does,' I agree.

We watch the sun dip into the sea.

'Look, Mum, the sea has eaten the sun,' Zoe says.

'Yes, it has.' I smile, my cheeks aching from the effort.

Slowly, black creeps from the edges of pink and orange sky and wipes away the colourful streaks. Shadows dance in the twilight. The sea roars goodbye to the sun. Mosquitoes hover around my little girls, having somehow got in despite the mosquito mesh screen.

'Time for bed.' I gently nudge them off my lap and lead them into their bedroom, I tuck them in and watch them sleep. And I wonder if I will get the simple, precious privilege of tucking my son into bed, kissing him goodnight, watching him sleep, something I took smugly for granted, again.

SIXTY-SIX

DAY 5

5:00 a.m.

Light spills over the horizon heralding a new day, another one without my boy.

I watch the pink smile of dawn wipe out any lingering darkness and the sun emerge majestically in a rainbow of colours, creamy rose and saffron brushstrokes chasing away the shadows cast by night, the sea sparkling fresh and lovely like a woman decked up for a party.

I walked up and down the beach looking for Ajit when the press posse decamped for the night, the air settling from humid to cool, carrying the flavour of darkness and secrets. I searched, even knowing it was futile, the beach having been scoured several times already. I walked around the cottage, even looked in the coconut grove, calling my son's name. The policemen stationed around the beach nodded to me, their gazes shying away from the desperation in mine. They understood that I couldn't sit still. A grieving mother, the bitter taste of roiling salt in my mouth.

When my legs threatened to give way, I collapsed onto one

of the chairs on the veranda, and watched the waves ripple and swell in the darkness, under a navy canopy spattered with stars. I wondered if JT had boldly climbed up these steps a few days ago, when we were on the beach by the shack, putting on an act of being happy and carefree while tensions bubbled underneath. Had he walked past Rachel, passed out on the sofa? Had he lingered in each room or just walked straight into the last one, picked up Ajit, and then climbed out the window, not risking coming back out through the front door in case Rachel woke up or we saw him? Had he taken him to that cottage? If so, why did they leave? And where was Ajit now?

The questions as to my beloved boy's whereabouts festered while the hours of night dragged, cool air caressing my face, the blisters on my feet throbbing, the whispering darkness, the sea a swelling giant stretching to infinity. If JT had taken Ajit, I had caused this and I would never forgive myself for it. As a mother, my duty was to protect my children. But in having an affair with JT, I had brought danger into my innocent children's lives. I suppose I have my mother's streak of moving on and not looking back, and her selfishness too. I used JT, revelled in his adoration because it made me feel better about myself, despite being aware that he desperately wanted a family, something I wouldn't, couldn't, give him as I was not about to leave Yash.

As a new morning washes the horizon the startling maroon of a fresh bruise, I acknowledge that perhaps despite the inspector's assurances I don't deserve my children, my husband, the life I have secured for myself upon the tragedies of others. I deserve this hell I am living now. But my son does not deserve whatever is happening to him. Please, let him not be hurt. Let him be safe. Please.

SIXTY-SEVEN

Blog post appearing on shobhaspeaksout.in:

Is Missing Ajit a Pawn in a Sinister Game?
Posted by Ms Shobha Nair, 17 February

The disappearance of five-year-old Ajit Kumar from his holiday cottage in Galgibaga shocked Goa. And there is still no sign of the little boy.

The man in charge of the investigation into Ajit's disappearance, Inspector Sharma, is notorious for being in the news for all the wrong reasons. And this is looking to be another botched investigation to add to the inspector's 'Bungled Cases', of which there are many.

Ajit's disappearance and subsequent investigation have, so far, for me, and for the readers of my blog who have taken the time to comment over the past few days, spawned more questions than answers. Are the Kumars paying the corrupt Inspector Sharma to hide their involvement in the disappearance of their son? The inspector appears to be extremely pally with them. And it is no secret that the inspector was involved in a high-profile case where it is alleged that he took bribes to cover the identity of the real murderer. Is that what is happening again? This supposed 'suspect' could be a stooge, the boy's slippers at a cottage in town planted there. All these so-called witnesses who've heard children crying in empty cottages and reported sightings of the suspect with a boy matching Ajit's description, could have been arranged by the inspector. Perhaps he is angling for a British visa, a new life in the UK, putting his colourful, infamous past behind him.

For, if not, why have they not managed to catch this man, who is only now emerging as a suspect, based on evidence that is flimsy at best and easily discredited, despite an ongoing police investigation that seemingly involves the entire police force of the state of Goa?

Comments:

Anoop, Mumbai 07:12 IST: Good post, Shobha. I agree with most of what you are saying. Personally, I think the father, Yash, is innocent and that Inspector Sharma is covering something up for Jo Kumar. Did you see how he looked at her during the press conference? There is something going on between those two, mark my words.

Jaya, Anjuna 07:15 IST: Stuff and nonsense, Anoop from Mumbai. You should be ashamed of yourself for feeding off the parents' misery and creating rumours. You too, Shobha Nair, indulging in gossip and hearsay. I am unfollowing this blog immediately, and with some regret as I have really enjoyed some of your posts, especially your heartfelt coverage of Belinda Fernandes's disappearance. But this seems to be a witch hunt now, with you and your followers intent on crucifying the mother just because she is trying to put on a brave face in public. After all, the British are known for their stiff upper lip.

Not all women wail in public and display emotions like some of us Indian ladies.

Latha, Cavorim 07:39 IST: I agree with Jaya. Also, it appears you have a personal vendetta against Inspector Sharma, Shobha. Inspector Sharma has been involved in cases where he has delivered results, secured justice for grieving families. Surely that should count for something? Also isn't Inspector Sharma famous for being seemingly incorruptible, which is why politicians and a certain faction of the media have taken against him, and not the other way round?

Scroll down for more comments.

SIXTY-EIGHT

DAY 5

8:00 a.m.

My girls wake and come looking for me. They smell of sleep and dreams. I love them so much.

'Have you been here all this time, Mummy?' Mia asks, taking her thumb out of her mouth.

Coconut trees wave in the gentle breeze. A man walks briskly down the beach, arms swinging, nodding hello to the patrolling policemen.

'Yes,' I reply. 'I watched the sunrise.'

'Come and have breakfast, girls,' Lydia calls and they obediently tumble off my lap to run indoors.

As she climbs off, Zoe tugs at my hand. 'You come too, Mum.'

Zoe is not clingy and yet, now, she needs me and this warms my heart.

After the girls have had breakfast and are settled in the living room with the Lego, I come out onto the veranda again.

Yash follows me, sinking into the chair next to mine. We've not talked since the inspector left the previous evening.

I look at the performing waves and wonder what's happening. Where the inspector is. Whether he knows where my son is and with whom. I do not think of the blood they found in that cottage alongside my son's slippers. I have to believe my son is alive. It is the only way I can go on.

We sit side by side, as we wait to hear the fate of our son, myself and this man with whom I am bringing up three children. I *was* bringing up three children. But now... I shudder, drawing my arms around myself. This man who is the only other person going through the same pain that I am.

'This waiting. It's killing me,' he says softly.

I flinch at his choice of verb.

He blanches as he realises what he's said. 'I'm sorry.'

'Do you still hold out hope that our son will be found alive?' I want to ask. 'Do you think, like I do, even if I try my hardest to keep the thought at bay, in the moments of utter despair that are now triumphing over hope, that we are indulging in wishful thinking, that he's long gone, our little boy?'

'The inspector... I wonder what's going on,' Yash is musing when the inspector's Jeep pulls up alongside the first of the news vans arriving on the beach.

And I wonder what today will bring. Whether this will be the day my son is found and returned to me. Or...

SIXTY-NINE

DAY 5

8:30 a.m.

'We'll wait inside for the inspector,' Yash says as he ushers me indoors and shuts the living room door as reporters spill out of vans and onto the beach, firing staccato bullets of questions, shattering the uneasy calm with shouts, noise.

The refrain going around and around in my head is: *Please let Ajit be alive.*

Paul looks up from where he is sitting on the floor with the kids and helping them with their Lego. Rachel is in her room. Lydia's drawn face watches Yash, her gaze never leaving his. And looking at her looking at my husband I acknowledge something that has been glaring at me but that I've only opened my eyes to since Ajit went missing. For this tragedy has stripped us back to our basic selves. We've not bothered to put on our faces, to hide behind artifice or niceties, especially when we've thought no one is looking.

But *I* have been looking when Lydia thought I wasn't and now I understand the truth. It is something which I think, deep down, I have inherently known but refused to recognise or accept. Now, with nothing left to lose, I see it. I see *her*. My supposed best friend.

Lydia loves Yash, intensely, absolutely. It is not a recent occurrence either. She has always loved him thus. Perhaps she got together with Paul to make Yash jealous, try to spur him into fighting for her. But Yash met me, and when Lydia realised he was serious about me, she must have slept with him, even if it meant risking their friendship, muddying it, which is why she hadn't done so until then. I've wondered, since I found out, why Yash slept with Lydia just when he was getting serious about me – I believe him when he says that he was scared of the strength of his feelings for me, but knowing Yash, he wouldn't have slept with Lydia, his lifelong friend, if she hadn't made some sort of move first, timed perfectly for when he was feeling most nervous and insecure that his feelings for me weren't reciprocated. Perhaps he confided in Lydia and she 'comforted' him.

It is all conjecture on my part, but I can bet this is what happened. Knowing Yash and Lydia like I do, this is the only explanation that makes sense.

When, after she slept with him, Yash still chose me, Lydia went back to Paul, and married him when she found out she was pregnant, convinced that she was carrying Paul's child. In any case, by then, Yash and I were engaged.

For Yash, Lydia was family, and he wanted her in his life, and so he relegated the one-night stand to the back of his mind, compartmentalised it, like he is so good at doing – although it must have become near to impossible when he discovered Rachel was his. As for Lydia, although she couldn't have him, she couldn't let Yash go, and so, she accepted being near him, on the sidelines, her life interconnected with his, setting out to make his wife her best friend, loving his children like her own. This is why she was there for me, through my breakdowns, providing a listening ear, helping with the children as this would ease Yash's life, take the strain from him.

It hurts like all truths that cut too close to the bone – she was my friend for Yash's sake.

Her love for Yash was also why she convinced Paul into starting a business with Yash, willing to settle for a piece of him. This is why Lydia has been insisting to Paul that she will not return home as planned, despite Paul wanting them to go back and get on with their lives. She does not want to abandon her love at one of the worst moments of his life, even if it means subjecting her children to the stress and pain we are experiencing, even if it means they miss school, even at the cost of her marriage. This is why she has been mothering us all – it is her way of looking after and looking out for Yash. This is why for the first time since I have known her, she looks her age, her face gaunt and drawn – she feels for her love and she cannot comfort him, so she aches alongside him. Lydia loves Yash like JT loved me. Completely, unconditionally, unwaveringly.

They grew up together, Lydia and Yash.

'He was the skinny little Indian boy who moved in next door,' she had told me once, when we were exchanging drunken confidences. 'I was peeking out of my window when they moved in and when I saw Yash get out of the car, I wasn't impressed. And then, he looked up and smiled at me. A beaming star of a smile that involved his whole body and I knew then,' Lydia said, her slightly slurred voice soft with reminiscence.

'What?'

'Huh?' She had a goofy grin on her face.

'What did you know?'

'That we were going to be friends. But damned if I was going to make the first move.' She smiled, nursing her glass, her eyes far away. 'His parents asked mine if he could walk with me – he had enrolled at the same school. I walked two paces ahead and he tagged behind, trying and failing to catch up, as every time he sped up, I did too. I was much taller than him at the time, you see, him with his spindly legs.' She grinned fondly at the memory. 'I didn't answer any of his questions, I completely ignored him – I wanted to establish right from the beginning who was boss. But then, in school, I saw him being picked on and I fought for him, earning a bloody nose. My parents were called in. Yash came to the office and said it was his fault – the new boy, knocking timidly on the headmaster's door and taking the blame; that must have taken some courage and I was impressed. After that, we were inseparable.'

And she made sure they stayed that way, even when Yash and I fell in love.

Now I see that she must have slept with Yash, just after he met me, even if it meant putting their lifelong friendship in jeopardy, to convince him that he was meant to be with her, not me. When that didn't work, and he chose me, and she understood that if she wanted Yash, she had no choice but to put up with me, she decided to make me her friend, in this way keeping me onside.

When I met Lydia for the first time, it was like meeting my sister. Lydia reminded me of Lori so much. The same casual elegance, the effortless beauty, the conviction that the world would bend to their every whim. I was wary, but Lydia won me over. She listened to me, cared for me, or so I thought.

I imagined that my friendship with Lydia was very different from my relationship with my sister. But I see now that I have always felt second best around her. Insecure. Inadequate. Dazzled that she chose me to be her friend despite my many shortcomings, which I understand now are only so when held up against her perfection.

When I fell in love with Yash, he made it clear that Lydia would be in our lives. 'Our bond goes back a long way, Jo. She is part of my life. She has shaped me, in her way.'

I had him and yet he would never be fully mine. A part of him would always belong to Lydia. I didn't realise just how big a part, until I found out about his indiscretion, and Rachel.

I championed so hard for the family I created with Yash to be different to my own dysfunctional one. But the core of it was rotten from the start, with two of us competing for my husband's love, his attention.

A knock on the door jolts me from my thoughts. The inspector enters, looking grim, rocking on his heels, an urgency to him, a palpable intensity that hasn't been there before.

My mind has been settling on Lydia as a buffer against what is to come. Now, as I look at the inspector, my stomach swoops and I feel nauseous.

It is a testament to how used the children are to the inspector and this state of events that they barely pause in their playing.

But Yash looks at Paul and something unsaid passes between them.

Paul stands, stretches and says, 'Right then, kids, time to pack up the Lego. Let's go into the kitchen and make smoothies, shall we?'

I have watched my girls with Paul since I learned about the accusation against him and I believe that my gut instinct with regards to Paul is right – that the accusation against him was baseless, that he is not of that sort. In any case, I tell myself, even if there was a small chance that Paul was that way inclined, he wouldn't try anything, not with us and the inspector in the living room...

Mia claps happily. 'That's a great idea, don't you think, Bella?'

Bella says nothing, looking first at her father and then at us. I can tell she wants to stay in this room, find out what's going on.

'Come on, pack up the Lego, chop chop,' Paul says.

'Can we make a mango and pineapple smoothie, Paul?' Zoe asks.

'Anything you want, sweetheart,' Paul says gently.

My emotions are helter-skelter. I don't want to think about what the inspector has to tell us and so I focus on Paul. I feel for him. This man who agreed to go into business with Yash at Lydia's urging. This man who has been fooled so much more than any of us, myself included.

I speculate on this because it is easier than wondering why there is, for the first time, a fissure in the inspector's impassive facade.

Let Ajit be alive. Please.

SEVENTY

DAY 5

8:45 a.m.

The children and Paul finally decamp to the kitchen.

'I'll just shut this door here, you know how much noise the blender makes,' Paul says, and then we don't hear anything else as the door to the corridor leading to the kitchen and bedrooms is shut.

'What is it?' I ask, unable to keep my voice from shivering. I want to ask, 'Has Ajit been found?' But I know the inspector would have told us, immediately, if he had.

Lydia is still looking only at Yash. I wish she wasn't here, listening in, watching my husband as if he is her everything. Why didn't she go with Paul and the kids?

The inspector says, 'We found the man who took Ajit.'

'JT?' Yash asks, while my hand goes to my throat, which is choked up.

'No,' the inspector says.

'What?' Lydia and I cry in unison, while Yash looks confused. '*Not* JT?'

'It was not JT who took Ajit,' the inspector says. 'But JT was responsible.'

'What?' Lydia and I cry, again, while Yash blusters, 'Inspector, you're not making sense.'

'JT paid a taxi driver to take Ajit, and we have that man in custody,' the inspector says. 'He is the driver of the car that ploughed into the rickshaw at the market. He said JT paid him to do that – apparently JT wanted to hurt you, Jo.'

I feel fury, red hot, burning. If JT was in front of me now, I'd kill him with my bare hands. 'Hurt me by trying to kill my son?'

'Apparently the driver didn't see the rickshaw. It was just meant to give you a scare, not maim Ajit,' the inspector says.

As if that makes it any better. I recall the horror of that day, the dread, a precursor to what was to come...

'The man says JT also then paid him to wait by the road behind the cottage in his car after dark and snatch Ajit when the coast was clear.'

'But how did he know we'd be at the beach?' I ask.

'JT was keeping watch,' the inspector explains.

This is why I was feeling stalked. But that doesn't matter now. What does is... 'If you have the man who kidnapped Ajit...' My voice stumbles on the word *kidnapped* before my son's name.

'... Where is Ajit?' Yash finishes for me.

'The man doesn't know. He dropped Ajit to the cottage...'

'Where the blood was found,' I whisper, shivering, my mind shying away from the image of my son's blood. My son hurting, wounded...

'And Ajit's slippers, yes,' the inspector confirms.

'But where is my son?' Yash's voice is a howl of pain and desperation.

'There's an alert out for JT and Ajit. They will be found, and soon.' The inspector takes a breath.

'But, Inspector,' I whisper, 'JT's already changed his identity once.'

The inspector nods, acknowledging my comment. 'We will find him, Mrs Kumar, before he disappears again.'

I shudder. 'Please,' I whisper.

The inspector nods. 'Right, I need to get back...'

'I'm going mad here waiting for news,' Yash says. 'I'm coming with you, Inspector.'

'Sir, you'd be better placed...' the inspector begins.

'Please. I'm going crazy imagining the worst. Let me help.'

'You will stick with me, sir, and—'

Yash does not let the inspector finish. 'Yes, anything. I just need to do something constructive.'

The inspector nods.

I can't believe it. He's letting Yash go with him. Why didn't I take the initiative, like Yash has done? Because I was convinced the inspector would refuse. But I should have tried. Now I can't ask to go too as one of us needs to be here for the kids. I am frustrated, so angry at myself. Once again, I am trapped here in this cottage my son was taken from, waiting, always just waiting while Yash actually looks for Ajit.

And then they're gone, braving the reporters who throw questions at them: 'Where are you going, Mr Kumar? Are you under arrest? Are you helping the police with their inquiries? What about the suspect whose photo is still being circulated? And we heard you've arrested someone, Inspector? Did he tell you the parents are behind this? Why haven't you arrested Jo as well? You're arresting people and branding others as suspects, Inspector, but there's still no sign of the missing child, is there?'

Once the sound of the inspector's Jeep fades, along with the clamour from the reporters, Lydia says, not looking at me, 'Right, I'll see what the children and Paul are up to.'

She can't bear to be in the same room as me, even for a minute. But right now I don't care about anything except holding my boy in my arms. If JT has him, he wouldn't harm him, surely?

But something niggles in my head. Something doesn't add up.

And if there's one thing I've learned from this ordeal, it is that I must trust my instincts more. They weren't wrong. I *did* have a stalker – JT. It *was* him I saw in the market. I *was* getting messages that disappeared...

Ah, I forgot to ask the inspector about my phone, if there has been any progress in finding who was sending me messages and if they had hacked into my phone...

I collapse onto the sofa and go over everything that's happened, to find the source of the niggle.

And then I get it. 'It doesn't add up,' I say out loud.

The policeman looks up from his corner. 'Ma'am, you say something?'

'It doesn't add up,' I repeat and he looks puzzled. 'I just don't believe JT took Ajit.' Why hire a taxi to mow down my child only to save him and return him to me via the fortune teller? Why chance paying that same taxi driver to steal Ajit from the holiday cottage, go to all that trouble, when JT could have taken him at the market?

The policeman takes out his phone. 'You want call Inspector?'

'Not just yet,' I say. For there's something else nudging me, something that wants to come to the surface, something obvious, but I just cannot access it.

I stand and start to pace the room, which is suddenly too small and claustrophobic.

One of the Lego pieces that the children forgot to tidy away pierces the blister on my bare foot and I wince.

Slippers. Blood. Ajit. Does this mean that his kidnapper – JT? – bought him shoes or that he doesn't need shoes any more? *No, please.*

I close my eyes and rock on my feet as outside the reporters lob questions at the closed door of our cottage. From the kitchen comes the faint whirring sound of the blender and the children's chatter and from my head and my heart comes the loudest sound of all, a plaintive wail.

Those Snapchat messages which I'm convinced are from JT: 'I am sending love…' 'I care for you…' If he cares for me, and thinks Ajit is his son, why would he do this? It doesn't make sense that he didn't take Ajit when he rescued him from the rickshaw, like the inspector pointed out. But if it wasn't him, then who took my boy? Where is he?

My head aches. There's something, quite apart from JT, angling for my attention.

Sunshine slants into the room, its harsh glare seeking out secrets, washing away pretence, bringing hidden shadows to light. Dust motes swirl, glinting seductively.

Text messages.

That last text from the withheld number that has been goading me since before this holiday.

An eye for an eye.

A child for a child.

Who sent it? And the other texts, insinuating that my husband was having an affair, playing on my insecurities.

I'd thought only one person hated me enough to do so. My sister.

But now…

Now I can think of someone else whom I'd never have considered before. My mind whirring as everything finally makes sense even as I pray, *Please, let it not be too late.*

Am I right in thinking what I'm thinking?

If so, then I know exactly who has Ajit.

And I know why.

But the question is, what are they capable of?

I have to be very careful. The life of my son – if he is alive, please God – hangs in the balance.

9:10 a.m.

I check that Lydia, Paul and the kids are in the kitchen.

They are, with the door shut. I can hear them chatting away.

Rachel must be in her room. Her door is shut.

I walk, bold as anything, into Lydia and Paul's room. Shut the door behind me. None of the bedroom doors have locks. If anyone comes, I'll say I was looking for something. Like Lydia said she came looking for sunscreen in our bedroom and left her bikini behind among Yash's things.

The room is neat. No clutter, suitcases open and spilling stuff like in our bedroom next door. Lydia's stuff on her side. Paul's on his.

I check again that the door is closed. Then I begin searching.

I don't know what I'm looking for, just that I want proof that my conjecture is correct.

As I root about among the clothes neatly arranged in the

wardrobe, making sure not to disturb them, give myself away, I second-guess myself, wondering if I've gone quite mad.

But no... I'm right. I *know* I am. It all makes sense.

The money from the business going into an account registered to Paul.

Those texts, insinuating about Yash having an affair, goading me about my worst transgression as a mother before now, leaving Ajit in the car. And the most recent message: *a child for a child.*

I don't have much time, maybe a few more minutes, before one of the others comes looking for me. I can't be here then.

I feel desperation swirl in my mouth, clamp my throat. There is nothing incriminating here. What was I thinking? That there would be proof lying around?

I'm just about to give up and leave, running my palms under the mattress as a last resort. I'm not expecting anything, so it's an absolute surprise when my fingers close around a hard rectangular shape.

I pull it out. A phone. Not one I recognise. This is neither Lydia's nor Paul's nor Rachel's. Bella doesn't own one – not for lack of trying, Lydia jokes, wryly.

I didn't expect the hiding place to be so obvious. I expected better from the devious mind that has fooled us for so long. The phone is locked, requiring a six-digit code.

I try Rachel's birthdate. Doesn't work.

Bella's. No.

Paul's. No.

Lydia's. No.

Yash's. It pings.

My fingers shake with nervous tension as I scroll through the phone. Ah, the app that I had downloaded on my phone, from which I would send anonymous messages to Yash, is installed. I open it.

And there it is. Sent yesterday at 3:15 p.m. to my number: *An eye for an eye...*

'What are you doing?'

I turn. My hand closing around the phone. Proof.

'It was you,' I whisper.

And Lydia smiles, shakes her head. 'You've gone completely bonkers.'

'Where is he, Lydia? Please.' My voice is breaking. 'Please tell me, where's my son?'

9:30 a.m.

'What are you talking about, Jo? Didn't you hear the inspector? It's JT who has Ajit,' she says easily, the merest flicker of calculation in the slight narrowing of her gaze. Now that I know what I'm looking for, it is so obvious.

I think of Paul looking puzzled when the person he'd hired to investigate found out that the money missing from the business was going into an account in his name. Lydia was so clever. She must have paid a hacker to siphon the money with the caveat that if anyone did manage to look into and trace it, to make it out to Paul, so it would appear as if one of the directors had use for the money. They must have also shown her how to hack into my phone and remotely control my messages, delete them once I'd read them.

I swallow, gathering strength. I need to keep my wits about me. She has my son and I want to know where he is and that he is unharmed. *Please.* She loves him, doesn't she? Or was that too an act?

'JT was convenient for you, wasn't he?' I say. 'You didn't

know about him, but when you found out, he became the scapegoat.'

She sighs, shakes her head. 'Jo, you really must think about starting your medication again.'

She lies so glibly. She is so completely at ease while I'm sweating. The phone, proof of what's been going on, fisted in my nervous, perspiration-slick palm, hidden from her, I hope. I'm terrified, knowing my son's life is at stake – if he isn't already...

No. I will not believe it. He is alive and I will find out where she's keeping him if it's the last thing I do.

'You were the last to check on Ajit before I discovered he was missing,' I say, trying, like her, for calm. But my voice is shrill, laced with panic and urgency. She's always made me feel like this, I see now, like I am not good enough. But she will not win this time. I will not allow her to. She's taken so much from me already. My husband. My trust. My secrets. My confidence as a mother and person. My sanity – for she was the one who gently urged me to stop the pills, insinuating that I was careless with my children while on them; and sending those texts, then deleting them and making me question myself, to mess with my mind.

God, I've been so gullible. But no longer. She can't have my son. She *cannot.*

'Think about what you're saying, Jo, for God's sake,' Lydia warns, one eyebrow raised.

I should be careful. The life of my son is at play. But she wouldn't do anything to him, would she?

She took him. She's put you through hell.

I think of the blood found at the cottage. I shiver.

Lydia is capable of *anything*. She fooled me completely, fooled us all.

I open my mouth, tasting salt and fear, find my voice. 'Where is Ajit, Lydia?' I ask, again, gently.

'Have you gone completely mad? Why would I take Ajit?' Her eyes glitter dangerously.

'To punish me. Because you think I don't deserve him. That I don't deserve Yash. To break up our marriage.'

She smiles. And now that the scales have dropped from my eyes, I see her face for what it is: that of a calculating stranger, a person whose schemes have worked. 'You've managed it quite well yourself, breaking up your marriage.'

'I should have guessed it was you when you had the presence of mind to take colouring pens and drawing pads when we were rushed out of the cottage in the middle of the night so the police could investigate Ajit's disappearance. It's always niggled. Who would think to pack something to occupy the kids? That showed that you knew it would all take a while. That Ajit wasn't just hiding and would be found in a few minutes. And you'd only know that if—'

'You've finally, completely lost it,' she snaps.

'Please, Lydia,' I beg. 'Please tell me Ajit is all right.'

She doesn't reply. But she glances, swiftly, at the door. And I see now that not only has she shut it, but, in the absence of a lock, she's dragged a chair against it so it's harder for somebody from outside to push open.

I didn't notice because I was busy spying on her things while she crept up on me. Does she know I've found the phone? I feel fear slither up my spine. She's trapped me in here. What is she planning? Whatever it is, I'm not giving in until I know my son's whereabouts.

'Where is my son?' I ask again.

She looks at me and now I see her. I see her.

'You took money from the business. You've been planning this, or something like this, not going as far as kidnapping one of our kids, perhaps, but definitely giving me a scare to show me up, for some time.'

Again she doesn't say anything.

'Perhaps you took the money thinking you'd start a new life with Yash once he and I separated...'

She raises an eyebrow but remains silent.

'You sent me those texts about Yash having an affair. You wanted to wrong-foot me before the holiday. You also most likely took my ring – you are the only one apart from Yash and myself with access to the house, you have our spare key – and kept waving your hand in front of my face, waiting for me to notice it.'

A small smirk playing on Lydia's lips.

It is the smirk that gets to me: *Look at me, how clever I am.* Lori used to sport the exact same look. I broke ties with one psychopath, only to cross paths with another. And I didn't see it. I absolutely didn't.

Until now.

My mouth tastes of desperation. I want to get her to tell me where my son is.

Please let him be all right.

'You also put your bikini top among Yash's things to create mischief, make me even more paranoid, knowing I wasn't taking my pills. In fact, you were the one who prompted me to stop them, telling me with fake concern that I wasn't myself when on them, that I ignored the children.'

Lydia's lip curls. I know what she's thinking: *There you go again, Jo, blaming everyone else for your foolish decisions.*

I continue, focused on goading her into acknowledging that she has Ajit and telling me where he is. 'After finding the bikini, I told you I was going for a walk, but you must have seen me heading to the taxi rank behind the cottage. You messaged your taxi driver contact – you had got his number somehow, dark web is my guess.'

She raises an eyebrow.

'Yash has told me all about it. He likes to talk about every-thing that's going on in IT endlessly, as you know.'

She nods, smiling wistfully.

How can she smile at a time like this? The knot of terror weighing down my chest grows heavier, nearly robbing me of breath. But no... I cannot give up, not now. I have to find out where she's keeping Ajit.

I take a breath, find my voice. '*You* paid the man to follow me and plough into me at the market. You hadn't reckoned with the rickshaw. You didn't want to hurt Ajit. It was me you wanted to hurt.'

And now, finally, she speaks.

'You are very creative, Jo. And here I was thinking I knew everything about you,' she sneers. 'But, sweetie, keep up. The taxi driver has been caught and is claiming JT paid him.' She is grinning merrily, eyes twinkling, enjoying this.

I push on. 'You were relieved when JT rescued Ajit at the market, although you didn't know about JT then, of course. But he's been convenient, hasn't he, someone to blame?'

A knock at the door. Then someone trying to push it open. 'Lydia, you there? What have you done to the door?' Paul.

Lydia looks at me. Slaps a finger to her lips.

I raise an eyebrow as if to ask, 'Why should I do as you say?' Even as my conscience cautions: *This woman is dangerous. She has your son.*

'Give me a minute, Paul,' Lydia calls, even as she comes towards me, so close I can smell the mangoes she's been cutting with the kids, and her floral scent. I try not to flinch away from her, stand my ground.

'Hide in the wardrobe,' she whispers in my ear. 'And afterwards I'll tell you all you want to know.'

And there it is. An admission of sorts.

Do I do as she says? Do I trust her again? I've already been fooled one too many times. But she has my son.

'Stop dithering,' she hisses. Eyes glittering dangerously. Those familiar features rearranged to form a snarling monster.

And then I feel it, the point of a knife at my neck. I shy away, startled.

Lydia grins. 'I'm always prepared.'

The knife pricks my neck and I can feel blood oozing from the scratch, smell its coppery scent. Oh God, oh God, oh God. *Who* is this woman? Is this what she's done to Aji...

No, no.

Lydia smiles. 'Now will you go in the wardrobe or should I make you?'

The force of Paul's knocking shifts the chair slightly. Lydia turns. I pounce on her, try to grab the knife from her with the hand not holding the phone, but she's quick to pull it away. It cuts my palm and I recoil, blood gushing.

SEVENTY-THREE

DAY 5

9:45 a.m.

Lydia roughly pushes me into the wardrobe and shuts the door. I cower in the sudden darkness, shivering. *Please let her not have hurt Ajit.* But it is getting harder and harder to believe.

I hear her outside, opening the door. I am sorely tempted to shout out to Paul, cry for help, warn him about his wife, alert him to who she is, that she most likely has Ajit. But will he believe me? *I* wouldn't have believed me even a few hours ago. And if Lydia has Ajit and I go against her, what will she do to him, if she hasn't already? I'm terrified for my girls too. What if, in anger, she turns on them? The woman I just glimpsed, who held a knife to my throat, is capable of *anything.*

'About time. What were you *doing* in there?' Paul asks.

'Isn't a girl allowed some privacy?' Lydia, coquettish. How can she switch guises so easily? What has she done with the knife?

'God's sake, Lydia, we've been married years.' Paul is having none of it. Does he see through her too? 'Have you seen Jo?'

'No.'

'Strange, the policeman thinks she came down here.'

'Don't tell me she's disappeared as well.'

Even as I panic and agonise as to my son's fate, I marvel at my former friend's ability to dissemble so expertly, to change personas depending on the people she's with: caring wife, loving mother, loyal friend, maintain the facades expected of her.

'Not a joking matter, Lydia,' Paul hisses. 'The children are asking after her and Yash.'

The children. I bite my tongue to stop my pain from escaping. Although every instinct urges me to jump out of this wardrobe and go to my girls, I need to find out where my son is and for this, I need Lydia onside.

'She must have climbed out the window and gone for a walk. Or to search for Ajit. That's what she was doing last night, the policeman said,' Lydia is saying. 'Now that's an idea. Why don't you take the kids for a walk along the beach? Ask Rachel as well, she's been cooped up indoors long enough. You might bump into Jo.'

I realise, suddenly, that I'm still holding the phone. Quickly, with shaking fingers, I unlock it, not caring that it's getting bloodied from my injured palm.

'What about you? Don't you want to come?' Paul is asking.

My fingers are shaking almost too much to cooperate, so it takes nearly three tries to open up the app and start typing a message to my phone – my number is saved on there – and Yash's as well – his is the only one I know by heart – for good measure...

'I've a terrible headache, which is why I'd shut the door, to get some rest, and the sun will only make it worse,' Lydia is saying.

'I'm sorry.' Paul sighs. 'You should have said.'

'I did, but you were busy with the kids.'

'This is getting to all of us.' Paul sighs again. 'All right, the walk is a good idea. See you later, babe.'

I've got up to *This is Jo. I am messaging from Lydia's* when the wardrobe door is flung open.

'What are you doing? Give me that.' Lydia makes a grab for the phone, but I am quicker, flinging it behind me, into the mess I have made of the neatly arranged clothes.

Did I press send?

'You bitch.' Lydia tries to push me aside, scrabbling for the phone.

But I stay put, even as she hits at me, eyes wild. The real Lydia.

A knock at the door. 'Mum, are you OK? What's that sound?'

Rachel.

'Go for a walk with the others, Rach,' Lydia calls over her shoulder.

'Aren't you coming?'

'I've a headache,' Lydia says. 'Please tell the policeman on your way out that I'm resting.'

'Will do.'

'Come on, Rach. Bye, Lydia,' Paul calls.

'Bye, Mum.' Bella.

'Bye, Lydia.' My girls. My heart jumping at their sweet voices. How I want to hold them to me and not let go. But not until I know where this madwoman is keeping my son.

Then the sound of the front door closing.

'And now, we are alone,' Lydia leers. And in her grin, those eyes, I see the lunacy that's gone undetected by all of us this whole time. How? It's so terrifyingly obvious to me now.

'Not quite,' I say, unable to keep the tremor from my voice. 'The policeman...'

'Who's been told I'm resting.' She grins widely again. Then, her voice dangerous, 'Give me the phone.'

I reach behind me, find it, try to check surreptitiously

whether I've sent the message. But before I can, she snatches it from me, grimacing at the blood splashed across it.

'You always were messy, Jo, and grubby with it. I don't for the life of me know what Yash sees in you.'

'Please, Lydia. You can have Yash. Just tell me where's my son.'

But she's looking at the phone. 'This isn't yours.'

'No, it's yours. The secret one from which you were sending me those messages.'

She smiles. 'Oh what fun that was. You are so easily spooked.'

And here she is, unmasked at last. But, I wonder, fresh fear staking my chest in a stranglehold, why is she admitting it now?

She's going to kill me, like she has my son.

Enough. Don't think this way. You need to be strong for Ajit. You're the only one who knows Lydia is responsible for taking Ajit. Only you can save him. He's alive, please God.

I gather saliva in my dry mouth. 'You sent the texts. Did you also ask someone to dig the graves?'

'That wasn't me,' she snarls, baring her teeth. A monster in place of the Lydia I thought I knew. 'That's your own messed-up mind,' she mocks harshly. 'You were – you are – so easy to manipulate. A few well-chosen words, a few text messages, and you start to question yourself. Bring up your sister and you second-guess yourself.'

Even though I am wise to her now, I still do a double take at the scorn and derision in her voice. This woman I thought was my best friend. I thought she was perfection itself. Held up against her, all my many imperfections jarred and stabbed like stones in rice. Why didn't I think or consider that nobody is that flawless, that she was hiding something, that she was not who she said she was? But I was dazzled by her friendship. So very grateful for it, making me blind to her scheming, her manip-ulation.

Compared to Lydia's master trickery, Lori's childish games pale to insignificance. At least Lori was direct – I always knew when she was messing with me. Not so Lydia. I never once saw through her.

Until now.

Perhaps Yash saw through her, subconsciously, which is why he chose me over her. Or perhaps I'm giving him too much credit, my insecurities once again refusing to let me believe that I am worthy of love just as I am.

I swallow, decide to change tack. She has not responded when I've asked where Ajit is. So I'll approach this sideways. 'Why take Ajit?' I ask.

The smirk is replaced by a flame of rage, flaring bright. Anger so violent that I recoil.

Please, *please*, let Ajit be unharmed.

But my heart dips, especially when Lydia says, 'If Yash hadn't chosen you over me, none of this would have happened.'

I shiver. What a fool I've been! All that worry about dangers that might befall my children and the monsters were with me all along, fuelling my anxiety. No wonder I was paranoid. 'I thought of you and Paul as my family. I love... loved you. After what Lori did, I thought of you as my real sister,' I say softly.

'More fool you.' Lydia laughs.

I fear for Ajit, my heart palpitating with terror. Will I put him to bed again, hold him, see him smile again? I *must* find out where my son is.

'You didn't plan to take Ajit,' I say, thinking out loud, 'but when you saw my reaction to the bikini, my storming off to the market, and the cracks in my marriage widening, you suggested we spend the evening by the shack. Perhaps you decided then, or maybe when I had the argument with Yash and threatened to take the kids and run. Perhaps that is when you finalised your plan. You would take Ajit. That same man, the taxi driver whom you'd paid to scare me at the market, could take him.'

I can see in the way her eyes shine that this is what happened. And so I continue.

'When you came in to check on the kids, you left the window open. You were the one who convinced us that the kids were fine, who dissuaded us from checking, distracting Yash when he was insistent he'd look in on them, giving the man time to slip in, grab Ajit and leave. I think you asked him to take Ajit and not one of the girls because he was on his own in the room and nearest the window too. You knew I would go crazy, so Yash would finally see me for who I was. Anxious, hysterical, incapable.'

Lydia is nodding now.

'Stealing Ajit was your last-ditch attempt to cause problems in our marriage, show Yash how unhinged I am, that he is better off with you.' From her expression, I know I'm right. 'You questioned Inspector Sharma's competence, not because he wasn't capable but because he *was*. You worried that he was good. That he'd see through you.' I recall Lydia's insistence that Inspector Sharma was not right for the job, that she'd read that he was taking bribes, that he had botched similar cases. 'When it was evident that he was staying in charge of the investigation, you suggested the social media campaign to get in Inspector Sharma's good books, to take the suspicion off yourself.'

'How did you guess it was me?' Lydia sneers. 'Or was it just a case of narrowing down the culprits until you came to me? But it couldn't have been that because you've accused me once or twice before, but you didn't really believe it. Now you do.'

'The text,' I say. '*Eye for an eye. Child for a child.* I connected the dots with your miscarriage. That and finding out about the money from the business going into an account in Paul's name that he knew nothing about.'

Lydia scoffs, shaking her head. 'I couldn't resist sending that. How was it fair that you had the son I'd always wanted, three healthy children despite your neglect of them, while I couldn't have any more? You leave Ajit, an innocent babe, in the car at the height of summer and forget about him and yet still he is fine and you get away scot-free.'

'You sent the texts to me and the inspector about my abandoning Ajit in the car. You also must have been the one leaking updates to the press, the "anonymous source" vilifying me, so the media and public would hound me. Inspector Sharma wondered more than once how the press was getting hold of all this information so quickly. Lori's Facebook post going viral was an added bonus...'

She nods. 'You deserved it and more.'

'Why?' I ask. 'What have I done to you that's so bad?'

'You had what I wanted.'

'Yash,' I breathe.

'Yes, and his son.'

And now, what she just said hits me. *Had.* You *had* what I wanted. Does this mean...?

No. No, I will not believe it.

I take a breath. Another. 'But you have his daughter,' I manage.

'He stayed with you because of his son. He might have rebelled against his parents and their culture, but when it comes right down to it, he shares his father's antiquated beliefs about the son continuing the family name.' Lydia's voice is bitter.

And I suddenly recall us having the mother of all fights when Ajit was born and Yash said, 'At last, a son to carry on the family name.'

'What's wrong with the girls?' I'd asked.

'Nothing. But a son...' Yash's eyes going misty.

I hadn't talked to him for a week.

'I lost Yash's son while you got to keep his boy. How is that fair?' Lydia's words jolt me back.

'*Yash's* son?' I am taken aback.

She laughs cruelly. 'Yes.'

'It wasn't just the once?'

'No. Keep up.'

'He lied?'

'He's been lying to you all your married life. I tried telling you via those texts.' A harsh bark of a chuckle. Then, 'That time when your girls were little, when you suspected he was having an affair...'

'And he told me he wasn't...' I whisper.

'He was. With me.'

What else will I learn? How much more can my heart take? Even though we're over, Yash and I, this betrayal hurts. Oh how it hurts.

'The affair we convinced you was in your mind. We blamed it on your postnatal depression.' Malice in her voice as she laughs bitterly, mockingly at me.

'You and Yash made me think I was mad when I was right all along.' That was why I felt so depressed. Because, deep down, I knew Yash was cheating. Perhaps this was why I turned to JT... 'When I followed him in the car and had the accident...' I whisper, still processing everything in my head.

'He was coming to see me,' Lydia supplies. 'Which is why we arrived at the hospital together. You should have died in the accident. That would have been best all round.'

I gasp, but nothing she says really shocks me any more. I'm past that now. 'But *why* did he do it?' I cry. 'Marry me, keep you close, sleep with us both.'

'He says it's because he loves us both in different ways. He's insecure, that's his excuse. Always looking for love and valida- tion, because his parents' love was conditional. When he feels you withdrawing, he sleeps with me. When he worries I've had enough of his dithering, he sleeps with me,' Lydia spits.

'Why do you put up with it, Lydia?'

And now, in the shadow of pain that crosses her face, I finally recognise the woman I have loved all these years as a friend. 'Because I love him. I have always loved him. I know he is using me, but I don't care. I want him. And he... he can't choose between us, he says,' she says bitingly, eyes spitting orange sparks.

'You seem to have accepted it all these years. So why send me texts, scare me, take Ajit, *now*?'

'Because I've had enough,' she barks. 'I've just had *enough*.' She takes a breath. 'I gave him an ultimatum. I told him to choose.' Another breath. 'I was convinced he'd leave you – he complains about you enough.'

It should hurt but after everything, it doesn't. Not really. I just want to find out where she's keeping my boy.

'I was sure he would choose me, which is why I found this hacker on the dark web who helped me siphon money from the business, for our future together,' Lydia is saying. 'It wasn't actually stealing. Yash had invested savings in the business. I was taking them for our life together. But Yash, he strung me along and when I finally put my foot down, he chose you, because of the kids, he said. What about Rachel, then? I asked. He had no answer. And I knew he chose you because of Ajit. His son.' Her voice is a raging fire.

'And you started sending me those texts.' Yash accused *me* of causing Ajit's disappearance, because of my affair with JT, but it is my unfaithful husband who has caused all this.

'I wanted to show him how unhinged you were,' Lydia is saying. 'That I was the better mother and wife.'

But it is Lydia who is unhinged, sending me the texts, stealing money from the business her lover and her husband had built together for a future she was determined she would have with her supposed best friend's husband, by hook or by crook.

I think of the afternoon before Ajit went missing, waking up on the veranda to hushed whispers: Lydia and Yash holed up in the bedroom I shared with Yash. Lydia perhaps trying to convince Yash one last time to leave me, and when he refused, coming up with her plan...

'Where is he, Lydia?' I cry. 'Where is my son?'

'You don't deserve him.'

'Please, Lydia...' I beg of this woman whom I considered my best friend, my soul sister, whom, until a few hours ago, I trusted with my life, and my children, whom I love more than life.

'It was only meant to be until Yash realised that you were crazy and left you,' she says. 'When I went to check on the kids, I made a production of taking the cashew liquor from the suitcase and putting it in the fridge, laughing with Rachel about how I had forgotten to do it earlier. I also dropped my smokes right by where she was lounging, knowing she wouldn't be able to resist trying both the contraband items. And just to make sure, I ground one of my sleeping pills into powder in the kitchen and dropped some into her water glass, just a touch so she would be sure to fall asleep.' I gasp and she snarls, 'No need to be so shocked. I recall you exclaiming in wonder that your kids slept so well on my watch.'

'You drugged them?' I whisper.

'As I said, just a touch. No harm done.' She shrugs.

And I let this woman babysit my children countless times. I resolve to get them checked by a paediatrician the moment we can, but first, Ajit... I shiver with horror, dreading Ajit's fate.

Please.

'That is why your babies always slept so well. I thought I was a bad mother as mine never slept. I blamed myself and you fed into it,' I say.

Lydia laughs. 'Get over it.'

'Where is Ajit, Lydia?' I ask again.

'The man I hired knew of a cottage in town where he could keep Ajit undetected.' And now, Lydia's voice is sharp: 'But he wanted more money than we'd agreed on and when I refused, he threatened to hurt Ajit and it all got out of hand...'

My heart seizes at her words. The blood at the cottage. Ajit's blood...

I find my voice, a choke of pain. 'Please Lydia, did the man hurt...?' I cannot finish the sentence, my voice frightened into hiding in my terror-clogged throat.

'I loved Ajit like my own,' Lydia throws at me.

Loved. Is he...?

Is my boy...?

And that is when there's banging at the door, which Lydia has barricaded again, with both the chairs in the room this time.

SEVENTY-FOUR

DAY 5

10:05 a.m.

'Mrs King, Mrs Kumar, open the door.' The inspector.

Lydia is on me suddenly, knife pressed to my stomach. I can feel it pushing through my T-shirt, poking tender skin. She pushes me against the wall, inching me next to the door.

I can hear my heart pounding above the banging on the door. I can smell her, madness and rage, see the crazed whites of her eyes.

'The IT guys came back. Mrs Kumar, your phone was hacked. It's linked to a number that's been traced here, to this room. Mrs King, please open the door.'

Once again, like when Paul knocked, Lydia raises a finger to her lips. 'I will kill you, if you so much as say a word,' she whispers, her breath hot and sour. The knife nicks my skin, to prove her point, and I wince.

She smiles, even as Yash cries, 'Lyddie, open please. The policeman said you're in here...'

And the policeman, 'They say she's resting.'

'Is Jo with you?' Yash.

'Shh...' she says, grinning crazily. She's mad, clever, dangerous, desperate. But I am even more so.

'Please, Lydia, I'll help you escape. I'll not tell them a thing we've shared in here if you only reveal where my son is. Please.'

The inspector, Yash and the policeman are beating down the door.

'Please tell me where he is,' I beg, biting my tongue in anguish, tasting hot iron. 'Lydia, please, we are friends.'

She laughs soundlessly.

The chairs barricading the door fall with an almighty clatter. Instead of moving away, she inches us closer to the door, so we are flat against the wall beside it.

'Please don't hurt her,' I shout. 'She knows where my son is.'

The door bursts open.

I feel the plunge of the knife. Hear her – my former best friend, my nemesis, this woman who has my son – whisper in my ear, 'Good luck finding him.' And then she pushes me, hard so I land smack bang onto the floor, right as the inspector, Yash and the policeman who sits vigil in the living room charge in. They rush to my side, and as they do, Lydia sneaks out the door behind them.

I feel faint, but even so I manage to scream, 'She's escaped,' holding my stomach where the knife thrust in, in a vain attempt to stem the blood.

Just before I lose consciousness, through the wide-open door, I see her climb out the window through which Ajit was taken and disappear into the shimmering haze of sun and sand...

SEVENTY-FIVE

DAY 5

3:45 p.m.

I rush into Madgaon Railway Station in Yash's wake, anticipation, dread and hope warring in my heart. The station is crowded, heaving. Rickshaws dropping people off, edging taxis out of the way. Bicycles and motorbikes, even a cow placidly chewing cud. Harassed families, crying babies. Porters juggling suitcases while hefting multiple bags on their heads. A bustling mob at the ticket counters, shouting, frustration, chaos.

Body odour and tired frustration coming off people in waves as we push past them, mingling with the smell of tea and coffee, steamy sweet, and spices frying, onions and dough, cardamom and burnt sugar. Children sit on luggage, hollow-eyed with tiredness, some sleep on the floor among the milling masses. I look at each one, searching for the beloved features of my boy. Hope rising as a profile or an eyebrow or the curve of a nose looks familiar, then falling when it belongs to someone else. *Please*, the refrain going round and round in my head, a chant, a prayer. *Please let him be alive.*

The taxi driver Lydia had paid to kidnap Ajit came clean

when told about Lydia. He said she'd asked him to say JT had paid him to kidnap Ajit, if he was arrested. She promised to transfer a substantial sum of money to his family if he did so. On the other hand, if he told the police the truth, that it was she who had paid him to kidnap Ajit, Lydia threatened the taxi driver's family with grievous harm. He believed her, for he had first-hand experience of what she was capable of. He insists he doesn't know Ajit's fate since leaving him at the cottage at Lydia's say-so. Inspector Sharma is convinced he's telling the truth. 'Believe me, if he knew, he would have told us by now.' The inspector's impassive facade had slipped briefly, his eyes glinting dangerous onyx sparks.

A battalion of police, plain-clothed, so as not to alarm the public, are discreetly but thoroughly, I hope, searching the station and have been since the inspector received a tip about a boy matching Ajit's description spotted here. The woman who called it in said she'd seen him briefly as their train left the station and that the child looked familiar. She only made the connection to Ajit when the train was out of the state of Goa. She couldn't say which platform she'd seen him on and couldn't pinpoint where exactly he'd been either. It was, sadly, just an impression of a familiar face.

When the inspector relayed all this, I clung to hope. If Ajit was seen, that means he's alive and well, isn't he? But the police haven't found Ajit yet. Does this mean the sighting was just a case of mistaken identity? The inspector did warn us that the tip might be a hoax. But... he sounded cautiously optimistic that it wasn't.

Please let it be Ajit the woman saw, safe and sound. But... why hasn't the army of police searching this place found him?

I insisted on coming along although everyone – the doctor who tended to my injury, Yash, the inspector – advised against it. The knife, thankfully, had just grazed my stomach. I am bandaged heavily, and apart from feeling weak, more from still not knowing the fate of my son than the blood loss, I reckon, I'm fine. I *had* to come. The girls are with Paul and the policeman who's become a permanent fixture at the cottage. Several other police officers are positioned all around our cottage, providing an additional layer of security, which is why I was able to leave my girls.

We told them that Mum and Dad had to go out for a short while, but that we *would* be back and soon.

'With Ajit?' Mia asked, hopefully, while Zoe was solemn, regarding us with a grave gaze too old for her years.

'Hopefully so, my love,' I whispered, keeping my fingers crossed behind my back. *Please.*

'And Lydia?' Mia again, and this time both Bella and Zoe pincered us with grave gazes, even as Paul turned away, roughly swiping at his eyes with the back of his hand. Rachel was in her room, door shut, music loud, her way of signalling *keep out.* Angry and upset, understanding more than the younger ones and trying to come to terms with it in her own way.

'I will talk to her later,' Paul had said, sighing grimly. He looked haggard, wiped out, and enraged as he too tried, and failed, to understand what had happened.

'Perhaps,' I said, taking the cheat's way out in reply to Mia's question about Lydia. There would be time enough for explanations later.

Now, I think, like I have done a hundred thousand times since Lydia climbed out that same window Ajit was taken from: Lydia would know exactly where Ajit is. I should have tried harder to get it out of her. Have I failed my son irrevocably? Is it too late?

I shiver, hugging myself, my stomach hurting.

Platform One is overcrowded and stinks of urine. People bite into ball-shaped bright yellow snacks, raining crumbs. They sip tea from tiny stainless-steel tumblers and, as a train pulls in, whistle screeching, brakes grating, rush to it in a great big scrum, grabbing their bags and yelling at the top of their voices as they scramble to find a seat.

Where is my boy?

Yash and I run up and down the platform, desperately scanning the press of people for our little boy, hope and fear intermingling. We run inside the overcrowded waiting rooms, the stinking, smeared toilets, the kiosks. We turn over sleeping commuters bundled in blankets to check their faces, even as they shake their fists and shout expletives interspersed by yawns. We search inside the train waiting at Platform One, walking down each compartment, looking inside and under every berth, ignoring the scandalised looks from the women-only compartments at Yash's presence.

We even look on the train tracks. We are unmindful of the rubbish and faeces, of the rats and the stray dogs and cats that scurry out of our way, of the shouts and calls of shocked onlookers, as Yash and I jump onto the tracks and turn over every bundle in despairing fear that it is too late, warring with desperate hope that it is Ajit, that we've found him just in time to save him.

But we find no sign of Ajit.

I'm beginning to think that the sighting was a hoax after all, despite the inspector's cautious optimism.

Lydia, what have you done? Where is my boy?

From the bridge, I scan Platform Two and then my heart skips, it sings, it glows, for I see him.

I see him.

My little boy, precious, vulnerable, perfect, seemingly unharmed.

Am I dreaming?

No. No, thank God, I'm not. For in my excitement, I grabbed Yash's hand and his gaze followed mine and now he's staring at our boy, like I am, avidly, with amazement and exhilaration writ large upon his features.

He is crouched behind a coffee kiosk. He is hiding, but I see him from my vantage spot on the bridge. He hugs his tatty SpongeBob to his chest as he squats on his haunches. He is wearing clothes I do not recognise. He is tanned from the sun.

He peers from behind his hiding place, watches the people around him, scanning the crowds, searching like he does at the school gates, his eyes darting this way and that, trying to find a familiar face. He wears the same expression, his lips down-turned, his face worried.

I will never ever take the sight of him for granted again.

My heart overflows with love and happiness as Yash and I elbow people around us, as we rush down the steps of the bridge and onto the platform and barge through the crowds, irrationally worried that he'll disappear by the time we get to him.

'Ajit,' we yell. 'Ajit!'

He looks up, turns around and, when he sees us, his whole being lights up in that smile I have missed so very much, that I thought I would never see again.

'Mum! Dad!' He rushes towards us, his little legs working and then he is running and I am running and he launches himself into my arms and I hold him and kiss him all over, Yash throwing his arms around us. I bury my head in my son's hair, the feel of him, precious, perfect. He smells different, of sandal-wood and spices and dust, and yet, also, uniquely of himself. 'Mum, Dad,' he says, 'why are you both crying?'

And it is only then that I realise that we are, tears running unchecked down our faces, united in the miracle of our son.

'We missed you, Ajit,' I say, 'and we're so happy you're back. They're happy tears.'

'I missed you both too,' he says, 'especially at night. But the first man was fun. He sang songs and he told me stories. Then he left and I was alone. I was scared. I had a nosebleed. Then after a long, long time, another man came. He said we were playing hide-and-seek. I had to hide here and Lydia would come to find me.'

Yash and I exchange glances. When Lydia heard that the man she'd employed to kidnap Ajit was apprehended, she must have arranged for another man to bring Ajit here.

'I waited and waited, but Lydia didn't come. You did instead.' Ajit beams.

Yash's phone rings. 'Yes, Inspector.' Yash's voice is celebratory. 'We found Ajit, just now. By the kiosk...'

I tune out, delighting in the precious gift of my son, safe and sound and whole, revelling in holding him, savouring his little arms around my neck, the rightness of it. He is safe, he is unharmed, he is here.

My phone, which the inspector returned to me at the cottage, beeps with a text.

An eye for an eye. A child for a child.

I shiver.

Once she climbed out the window, Lydia had run into the coconut grove. Police patrolling the beach and road behind the cottage were alerted, but she managed to dodge them. She was spotted running into the sea, but by the time police got to her, it was too late. A full-scale search was launched almost immediately and is still ongoing, as they haven't found her body.

The hair at the back of my neck stands to attention.

I look around. The station is busy, packed. She could be anywhere, watching, waiting. Planning her revenge.

Yash cuts the call, and squats down to gather Ajit in his arms.

I want to show him the text, share the fear that is branding tattoos into my chest, as he drops kisses on our son's tousled, beloved head.

But, of course, like Lydia herself, it has disappeared.

SEVENTY-SIX

Blog post appearing on shobhaspeaksout.in:

Missing Little Boy Found
Posted by Ms Shobha Nair, 17 February

Missing British boy Ajit Kumar, who disappeared from his holiday cottage in Galgibaga Beach in the late hours of Monday, 12 February, has been found and returned safely to his parents.

The person involved in the kidnapping has been, to all intents and purposes, caught, with Inspector Sharma the hero of the hour. But, my instincts, honed from years of reporting and commenting on the news as it breaks (you can check my credentials here), tell me that there's something shady going on. Mark my words, there's more to all of this than meets the eye. Case in point: why did Lydia King, mother of two, Yash and Jo Kumar's friend, run into the sea at around the same time Ajit was spotted in Madgaon Station? She is yet to be found. And what about the 'person of interest', Chandra Shan, whose photo was circulated to the press, and for whom a nationwide alert was issued? Where is he? Why hasn't he been arrested?

I think as always where Inspector Sharma is concerned that there is foul play involved; bribes exchanging hands. I wouldn't put it past the man to have engineered the kidnapping in order to raise his profile internationally, and to have a closed case to add to his records. And although Ajit has been found, a wife and mother's life has almost definitely been lost, so I wouldn't class this as a win for the inspector.

I stand by my opinion, which I put forward in my previous post and which caused much discussion and controversy, with many people unfollowing my blog (sorry to see you go), and just as many more following it (welcome, you will be party to lively debates), that Inspector Sharma was in cahoots with the family. It is my understanding that neither the parents nor their friends are completely innocent – rumours have emerged (of affairs between the couples, criminal offences kept under wraps, questions regarding the parentage of the children) worthy of a Bollywood blockbuster. Looks to me like they've all got their hands dirty. So much so that it compelled one of them to take her own life? As you can see, this case has raised more controversy than answers, despite the 'happy'(ish) ending.

Whatever the truth, the only silver lining in all of this is that the child has been found safe and sound and reunited with his parents – although I understand that there is some doubt whether the couple actually *are* his parents. Nevertheless, now that the drama involving foreign nationals is resolved, let's hope things get back to normal and our police concentrate on tackling local crimes (or pretending to, as is most often the case). Inspector Sharma, you better watch out; we are keeping our vigilant eye on you.

Comments disabled.

It's happened.

They are divorced.

Yash is free from her clutches. Finally, he will be mine alone. Like he was before she came along.

Apart from that one text message when Jo and Yash were reunited with Ajit, I have been careful. Quiet. Watching. Waiting.

It was easy enough to escape the police. I was a triathlete through school and uni, and have kept the training up. I am a competition runner and very strong swimmer. I can hold my breath underwater longer than most. I swam to the next town and there met my contact – yet another contact found on the dark web, the money I had squirrelled away from the company coming in useful. The first thing I did once I swam ashore was take the phone from which I had been sending Jo messages from my pocket – I had tucked it into a waterproof bag and it was intact – and send her that message. Later, when I read the news coverage, I realised that I had sent the message at almost exactly the moment that Jo was reunited with Ajit. I took that as a sign.

I have been biding my time ever since. And now, I am ready.

I want my children, my family, my love, my life back.

Yash and I will be a blended family, seeing our kids when it's our turn to have them, and catching up on all the time we have been denied together when on our own. Yash has missed me, I know. I've watched him grieve for me, for what we had together. It required all of my willpower not to go to him, comfort him. But I wanted to do this right. And so, I've waited. Been patient. *Not much longer now, Yash.*

It's all Jo's fault I've had to wait this long. Stay away from Yash and my children. I must admit I underestimated her. I thought she too, like the others, would fall for my misdirection and assume it was JT who had taken Ajit. Like she accused, JT was a convenient scapegoat, but she was wrong in thinking that I didn't know about him. I found out about JT from Jo's girls around the time I issued Yash the ultimatum and he chose Jo. They'd come round to play with Bella and one of them, I think Mia, mentioned the creepy man, their mum's friend, who would hang about outside their house for hours on end.

'When was this?' I asked.

'Ages ago,' they said. 'Before Ajit was even born.'

I was intrigued, especially as Jo, who would tell me *every* little thing, yawn – seriously that woman had no stop button – had not mentioned this. So, I did some digging and found out about JT and Jo's affair.

After that, hurting from Yash's rejection and thinking I could use JT as ammunition to show him that the woman he had chosen over me was not as perfect as he assumed, I set about trying to find JT. He had covered his tracks reasonably well, once he left the country after his break-up with Jo, but I wasn't giving up. With help from my contacts on the dark web, I traced JT to Sri Lanka. I had started sending Jo anonymous texts by then and given how rattled she was by them, I thought it would be great fun to summon JT to India, spring him on Jo in front of Yash, light the match and stand well back to watch the fire burn.

I sent JT an unsigned letter with details of our holiday. I assumed, rightly, that he would think it was from Jo, and I knew also that given his obsessive personality he wouldn't be able to resist taking the bait and coming to see her.

He proved the perfect stooge to shoulder the blame for Ajit's kidnap. Until Jo foiled it. Just like she stole Yash from me.

I pick up my phone. Type out the text.

An eye for an eye. A child for a child.

She is framed in the window, having just said goodbye to her children. Yash is having them this weekend. And very soon I will be with him, with them too. I savour the feeling, hugging it close.

I watch as her phone beeps, as she reads the text, as she drops the phone as if it has scalded her, as she looks out of the window, her gaze haunted, one hand upon her throat as if it is choking her, as she shuts the curtains.

No matter. I have seen enough.

I am coming for you, Jo.

* * *

Jo,

I loved you completely and wholly from the first time I set eyes on you.

I wanted a family with you. But I was too late. Yash got there first.

As you know, I was prepared to love your girls like my

own. You came with a family, and that was all the better for me.

But I understood the reasons why you chose to stay with Yash although I didn't agree with you stringing me along, making me believe I was in with a chance. I couldn't cope without you. So, when my father's sister in Sri Lanka contacted me, asked me to visit, I went. But I think being in Sri Lanka made it worse. Memories of the war came flooding back. Losing my father. My mother's desperation. Her dreams of a better life for me. I hadn't really got over losing my parents. I had internalised my hurt and pain, the trauma I'd experienced growing up a child of war, the displacement I suffered arriving in England an orphan, the bullying and cruelty in the children's home. Losing you... I had a breakdown.

My aunt convinced me to seek help. I was in hospital for a long time. When I felt well enough, my aunt set me up with a girl from my hometown. But when I looked at her, all I could see was she was not you. I knew then that I'd not be able to move on unless I exorcised you from my heart completely. I thought, foolishly, that if I looked you up, saw how happy you were, how you had moved on, it would allow me to do the same.

In the event, after years of trying to forget you, finding you was so easy. Your privacy settings on social media are non-existent, and I could see all your posts. Far from getting rid of my obsession, looking you up made me realise how much I loved you. For a short while, you were mine and I had never known happiness like it. I wanted that again. I wanted *you* again.

Perhaps this was why all those doctors had warned me never to look back.

And then I found a photo of your children. I knew your two girls, of course, Jo. But I didn't know the little boy grinning from the photograph, a chocolate smear on his left cheek. I read the caption on the photograph: 'My beautiful Ajit is five years old today.' I did the maths and my life turned upside down once more. This boy, born almost exactly nine months after I lost you. And his name: Ajit. JT with two extra vowels. I knew then that he was mine.

How could you keep my son from me? When you know how much family means to me, how I have yearned for it. It is all I've ever wanted.

Don't you remember me telling you, Jo, how, as a young boy in care, I would peer into houses, getting glimpses of the family life I longed for but was not part of, wishing myself inside rather than an outsider, never belonging?

I should have been a part of my child's life. You took that away from me – in fact, you didn't even offer me the choice. Why did Yash get to play dad when *I* was? You had given up *our* love for the family you had with Yash. But now, we had our own family. Once I found out, I *needed* Ajit and you in my life.

And it was then, as if serendipitously, that I received the letter. I knew, instantly, although there was no forwarding address or contact details, that it was from you. I did wonder how you had found me, when I had changed my name and stayed under the radar – but not for long. You are very determined when you need to be, and I was flattered that you had applied that determination to find me. It didn't surprise me at all that your letter came exactly when I was ready and poised to meet you and my son. As you know, I believe in destiny. It seemed *meant*.

The letter was brief, to the point. But then that had always been the case when we were conducting our relation-ship. You had insisted on discretion, tried so hard to keep me apart from your family. And at first, I had complied...

'We are coming on holiday to India and I'd like to meet

with you, catch up. I hope you can make it.' That was all your letter said. But... you had enclosed the flyer advertising the holiday cottages and circled the one you'd be staying at.

I must admit I bristled a little at the imperiousness of your summons. Your assumption that I would jump to do your bidding after all this time and distance, all that had gone before. But... You were coming to India, so close, only weeks after I had found you again and discovered my son. I *had* to come and see you.

I booked into one of the cottages near where you were staying. I saw you arrive. I waited for my chance to speak to you.

I saw that woman, your so-called friend, mess with your mind. Make a play for your husband.

You once asked me, 'Why did you choose me? Why not Lydia, who was also at the party, the first time you saw me?' I said, 'What, that skinny chick who looks like she could do with a good meal?' And you laughed.

You were so happy and grateful for her friendship. You thought she could do no wrong. But I saw through her, even back then.

You were always insecure. With good reason, for she was playing with you, planting ideas in your mind. On some level, you sensed it, especially when you were in such close quarters on holiday. You needed a break and so, impulsively, you hailed a taxi and went to that crowded market. I followed you, thinking that this would be our chance to talk face to face like you had promised in your letter. Yes, it *was* me you saw that day.

I saved my son from being killed, thanks to your careless-ness. I do understand that your so-called friend drove you to question yourself, but as a mother, your primary duty is to your children. How could you take your children to that noisy, busy market? It was a reckless thing to do. If not for me, that day, I shudder to think of our son's fate.

I was so angry with you. Which is why I paid that fortune teller to frighten you and which is also why, when I saw you stumble blindly into the coconut grove that afternoon, I dug those graves. A warning as to what would happen if you did not take better care of your children. It hurt me to dig a grave with Ajit's name on it, but in a strange way, it was also cathartic. Like when you dream of your family and loved ones dying, when you picture the worst and wake to find out that it hasn't actually happened.

And, just to make sure, I also sent you a warning text. Which I watched you delete by mistake – yes, I was watching you then too – reinforcing your husband and friends' opinion of your paranoia, making you question yourself even more. Believe me, Jo, that wasn't my intention. All I'd wanted was to warn you, scare you into taking better care of your children. I failed in that, didn't I? You went out that evening, just as far as the beach, but even so, leaving your children behind. How could you? And then, if that wasn't enough, you lost my son.

I would have saved him, like I had done at the market, if I'd been there, watching. But, sadly, I was ill that night. I was in my cottage, hovering over the toilet bowl all night. By the time I was well enough, my son was gone.

I blame you for that. You should have taken better care of him. You should have been watching. You should have protected him with your life, not left him unattended and sat on the beach, drinking your woes away. I cannot excuse your neglect. I think that was when my love for you died, when I realised I would take much better care of my son, that he was better off without you in his life.

Jo, you broke up with me because you didn't want your family to break; you didn't want to be like your mother, choosing love over duty, selfish carnal desire over your children. I understood.

But now... Now you and Yash are divorced. Your children are products of a broken home, dividing their time between the two of you. I don't want that for my son. I want for him what I would glimpse through the windows when I would look in on families when I escaped from my children's home. A secure family home with two parents who love him and want the best for him. You cannot provide that any more. But I can.

I have found a nice girl. I have married her. She is pregnant. My Ajit will have a sibling soon.

I loved you, Jo, with my all. But when I saw how you neglected your children, how you did not protect them, how like your own mother you were... well... that love eroded like sand in the wake of a tsunami.

Now I am ready to make my move. I am coming for what's mine.

Ajit.

My firstborn son.

A LETTER FROM RENITA

Dear reader,

I want to say a huge thank you for choosing to read *Two Perfect Couples*. If you did enjoy it, and want to keep up to date with all my latest releases, just sign up at the following link. Your email address will never be shared and you can unsubscribe at any time.

www.bookouture.com/renita-dsilva

I hope you loved *Two Perfect Couples* and if you did, I would be very grateful if you could write a review. I'd love to hear what you think and it makes such a difference helping new readers to discover one of my books for the first time.

I love hearing from my readers – you can get in touch through social media or my website.

Thanks,

Renita

facebook.com/RenitaDSilvaBooks
x.com/RenitaDSilva
instagram.com/RenitaDSilva

ACKNOWLEDGEMENTS

I would like to thank all at Bookouture, especially Maisie Lawrence – you are beyond amazing and I feel incredibly lucky and *so* privileged to have you as my editor. You went above and beyond with this book and I am SO grateful. Thank you for your advice, kindness, patience and insight. You are the absolute best.

Thank you, Ruth Tross and Nina Winters, for your invaluable help in guiding this book to publication.

Huge thanks to Jenny Hutton, editor extraordinaire. I am so grateful to you for homing in on the story I want to tell. I cannot thank you enough.

Thank you, Jade Craddock, for the wonderfully thorough line edit. I'm so very grateful and lucky – you are amazing.

Thank you, Jane Eastgate, for your eagle eye and wonderful suggestions during copyedits for this book. Thank you, Emily Boyce, for proofreading this book.

Thank you, Mandy Kullar, for your help in guiding this book to publication.

A million thanks to Lorella Belli for your help with this book – I am so very grateful.

Thank you Amit Rao, Prajwal Augustine, Levin D'Souza, Maheshwari, Elizabeth Hensman, Cathy Mendes, Peter McKay, Mike Adams, Bhavna Pais for your time and generosity in answering technical questions I had while writing this book.

Thank you to my lovely fellow Bookouture authors, especially Angie Marsons, Sharon Maas, Debbie Rix, June Considine (aka Laura Elliot), whose friendship I am grateful for and lucky to have.

A huge thank you to my mother, Perdita Hilda D'Silva, who reads every word I write; who is encouraging and supportive and fun; who answers any questions I might have on any topic – finding out the answer, if she doesn't know it, in record time; who listens patiently to my doubts and who reminds me, gently, when I cry that I will never finish the book: 'I've heard this same refrain several times before.'

I am immensely grateful to my long-suffering family for willingly sharing me with characters who live only in my head. Love always.

And last, but not least, thank you, reader, for choosing this book.

PUBLISHING TEAM

Turning a manuscript into a book requires the efforts of many people. The publishing team at Bookouture would like to acknowledge everyone who contributed to this publication.

Commercial
Lauren Morrissette
Hannah Richmond
Imogen Allport

Cover design
The Brewster Project

Data and analysis
Mark Alder
Mohamed Bussuri

Editorial
Nina Winters
Sinead O'Connor

Copyeditor
Jane Eastgate

Proofreader
Emily Boyce

Marketing

Alex Crow
Melanie Price
Occy Carr
Cíara Rosney
Martyna Młynarska

Operations and distribution

Marina Valles
Stephanie Straub
Joe Morris

Production

Hannah Snetsinger
Mandy Kullar
Jen Shannon
Ria Clare

Publicity

Kim Nash
Noelle Holten
Jess Readett
Sarah Hardy

Rights and contracts

Peta Nightingale
Richard King
Saidah Graham